Guns for Rebellion

By F. Van Wyck Mason

GUNS FOR REBELLION

F. VAN WYCK MASON

DOUBLEDAY & COMPANY, INC.

GARDEN CITY, NEW YORK

1977

With the exception of actual historical personages, the characters are entirely the product of the author's imagination and have no relation to any person in real life.

Library of Congress Cataloging in Publication Data
Mason, Francis van Wyck, 1901–
Guns for rebellion.
1. United States—History—Revolution, 1775–1783—
Fiction. I. Title.
PZ3.M3855Gu   [PS3525.A822]   813'.5'2
ISBN: 0-385-01330-2
Library of Congress Catalog Card Number 76–42373

This is for "Wink"
otherwise
Franklin R. Foster
Splendid Sportsman
and a true friend
in all kinds of weather

PART I
Ticonderoga

CHAPTER I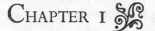

CATAMOUNT TAVERN

BECAUSE SHE'D BEEN forest bred, half Mohawk and half French-Canadian, Nellie Noisy Bluejay squeaked only softly when Jake Razors' palm smacked against the smoothness of her pale-brown buttocks. He then rolled her over and briefly hugged her soft warmth on that sweet-smelling spruce-tip couch he'd constructed across the far end of a rough shack thrown together for use during summer months when he wouldn't be away in the forest clearing farmland, fishing or meat-hunting or scouting for surveyors who generally would pay reasonably well for his skill in such directions. Right now an increasing number of such knowledgeable people were busy running border lines across territories acrimoniously disputed between Connecticut and New York.

"God, Nellie, y'know ye're a damn' sight more pleasin' now than in the dark?" Grinning, Jake heaved up on one elbow, threw back their only covering, a worn woolen trade blanket. "All the same, go cook breakfast."

Yawning, the sinewy young woman slipped over her head a faded blue cotton shift patched and ragged around its hem. Next she flipped twin braids of greasy, blue-black hair over slim

3

shoulders before seeking her cooking place skillfully fashioned of glacier-smoothed stones. After selecting a fresh green lug pole she raked apart a heap of gray ashes in the heart of which a few oak embers still should be aglow. A handful of dead fir twigs dropped on them would kindle a small and nearly smokeless blaze.

Luxuriously, Jake worked fingers to disturb lice in his shoulder-length dark-yellow hair then sat up once more to admire the attractive demi-lunes of Nellie's pale-brown bottom. Yep. He'd sure played in luck last year to come across her lazy, shiftless father, a nearly toothless mother and a gaggle of black-eyed brothers and sisters (most of the young ones went about stark naked when mosquitoes and black flies weren't too abundant) occupying an abandoned trapper's cabin less than a mile away.

Yep. 'Twas mighty dandy that Noisy Bluejay's eldest daughter —maybe all of sixteen—had proved so eager and able to accommodate a timber beast's needs in all ways. While this half-breed wench couldn't really be called pretty she wasn't ugly, not by a long shot. Besides, Nellie not only had proved to be a hard worker but also owned an inviting shy half-smile he was coming to appreciate more and more.

Just now the sun commenced to show through forests topping the Green Mountains, began to cast golden lances across the clearing in which air still smelt unusually fresh and fragrant perhaps because spring had been unusually delayed this year of 1775.

Jake lay, long and sinewy body jay-naked, with narrow jet eyes fixed unseeingly on rough pine slabs he'd pegged to form a roof. Only subconsciously he noticed the faint *honk-honking* of a skein of wild geese belatedly migrating to long-established nesting grounds among innumerable lakes and boundless tundras near the Arctic Circle.

Yawning loudly, Jake flexed arms before slipping into a dirty blue dowlas shirt, the frayed tails of which dangled to a level with his knees. Like most frontiersmen the young trapper didn't fancy under-britches; such, too often, were given to chafing and binding a fellow's parts. Besides, if he needed "to go" in a big hurry 'twould save time simply to flip up shirt-tails.

Absently, he watched Nellie draw a wooden bucket of water from the spring he'd picked for convenience close to the site of his shack. The young half-breed commenced to sing softly a song in a *patois* of Indian, French and English words. In no great hurry Nellie then set about preparing a breakfast of trout, bacon and bannock bread baked on a flat stone. This all was so easy, comfortable and home-like Jake again found himself debating whether he oughtn't to settle down but at the same time guessed that, at twenty-three, he still really wasn't set to become a family man.

No, sir, reckoned he'd best wait awhile. Why should a fella in his right mind keep a cow when milk came so free and easy?

Besides, when he got ready to be hitched, proper-like, he'd want to marry a female owning a certain amount of property. But would a father of substance accept for a son-in-law a man who didn't rightly know who he was? The only reason he had been given the name "Razors" was because a trio of *coureurs de bois*, fur traders, had chanced upon the smoldering ruins of his family's cabin right after a war party of Mohawks had struck. Quietly they had completed looting, then quickly had moved on leaving behind only the scalped and gory remains of his mother, father, sister, and him—a bewildered three-year-old who'd been hunting frogs along a nearby creek when the Indians had struck. Being frontier-trained, he'd remained frozen like a hiding rabbit when the Indians approached. Later, when found, he could only mumble a few words which the *coureurs* might or might not have taken to be English.

In any event, the only possible clue to his identity had been in the form of a leather case containing three razors overlooked by the Mohawks. Since their blades were etched as having been forged in Sheffield, England, he guessed maybe he was of English extraction.

Luckily when he'd been discovered the *coureurs* had been returning to a base camp after running trap lines. A squaw belonging to one of the trappers had taken pity on him. By the way she talked, Jake later reckoned she might have been a Seneca. Sometime later a hard-bitten white named Skelley and his harridan of a wife who were clearing a land for a homestead had taken the savage boy in for a few years, had taught him English and white

5

ways—not always admirable—but they'd worked him so hard and beaten him so regularly he'd run away to live on the outskirts of Rutland till he'd grown big enough to trap and hunt on his own.

Yep. It sure was fine to enjoy warm weather after this unusually long and severe winter. Over duroy pants he tugged on a pair of fringed and fairly new deerskin leggings because today he reckoned to shoulder the last of his winter pelts, sashay down to Bennington and stay sober long enough to turn a pretty penny since his catch consisted only of prime beaver and lynx pelts plus a dozen extra-thick and glossy mink and marten skins.

Once haggling was done Jake reckoned he'd get a little plastered, shoot at marks, pitch horseshoes and generally fool around. And after that who knew? Maybe there'd be some likely new gals in town. There ought to be since more and more people, mostly from Massachusetts and the Hampshire Grants, were establishing land claims close by Bennington on a township newly chartered to Major Ephraim Doolittle, Nahum and Ahab Houghton and other friends.

Instantly Jake stiffened when, amid a patch of bushes, squirrels commenced to bark. The lightning speed with which the young fellow grabbed up and cocked Jenny, a well-worn but still accurate Deacon Bennett rifle, still half in and half out of his pants, and took up a stance just inside his shack's doorframe, was something to wonder over.

Nor had Nellie been taken in by the squirrels' sudden and slightly spurious chatter. Lithe as a doe she'd raced into the shack carrying the hatchet she'd been using to split wood, snatched a steel-headed French spear resting on pegs let into the wall and poised it ready for use.

What seemed like an eternity passed before the gobbling cry of a turkey cock, subdued and nearer at hand, caused Jake to relax his grip of the curly maple stock of his long-barreled rifle. Pursing hard brown lips, he answered softly with the melodious whistling of a thrush.

While stuffing shirt-tails into his waistband he remarked more to himself than to Nellie, "That'll be Paul Thebaud."

She put down the spear and smiled. It always was nice to have a friend drop by—it broke the monotony.

Silently as a shadow a short, dark figure wearing a lynx-skin cap boasting a long night-heron's feather tucked into it halted on the edge of that little glade where Jake's shack stood beneath a canopy of towering maples already budding out. Yes, trouble must be brewing else why should Paul be so noticeably edgy?

"Howdy, folks. Everythin' all right with you?"

"Fine. Come on in, Paul. What's on yer mind?" Already Jake had sensed something in his friend's bearing that was neither familiar nor reassuring. Why would Paul, who lived 'way down near by Bennington, show up sweating and breathing so hard? Something serious must have roused him before dawn to start him running five miles.

"New Injun outbreak?" Jake hazarded. "Hear tell the British and Tories are startin' to stir 'em up."

"Nope. 'Tain't come to that—yet."

The squat trapper sidled forward, dark braids secured by beaded bands swaying to either side of long, red-brown features. In the crook of his arm he was carrying a brass-mounted fusil, favored because of its lightness and its short barrel. Manufactured in Maubeuge—Paul pronounced it "Mobooge"—this French officer's weapon weighed under nine pounds against a Tower musket's fourteen and for a smoothbore was remarkably accurate.

The caller was wearing a rusty-brown wamus or short hunting shirt of well-tanned buckskin. Purely out of habit, while approaching, he raised his right hand in the peace signal.

Jake waited, the Deacon Bennett rifle still held handy-like, "My Gawd, what is it ails ye, Paul?"

Thebaud, whose small but penetrating very dark-blue eyes kept ranging about the clearing, wheezed, "Big news reached Bennin'ton and the Catamount come sundown. There's been a reg'lar big battle 'twixt the Lobsterbacks and a passel of Massachusetts milishy fit up near Boston."

"Where at?"

"Dunno. Dispatch rider claimed the fight began at places called Lexin'ton and Concord—must lie pretty hard by Boston Town."

7

"What chanced?"

Potential dangers having evaporated, Nellie took a final quick look about then, firm young breasts bobbing, returned to squat over the cook fire.

"From what that rider reported," Thebaud continued while setting down his fusil within easy reach, "a considerable war party of Britishers marched out o' Boston to capture cannons, muskets and ammunition the Massachusetters had collected at Concord. They'd likely have seized 'em only some locals at Lexin'ton called 'minutemen' got wind of what was up, got armed fast and stood ready to meet 'em."

Jake stared. "They didn't win?"

"Naw. Some o' them farmers got shot down before they scattered and the Lobsterbacks kept on towards Concord."

Jake experienced a queer breathlessness as his jet eyes narrowed. "Then what?"

Thebaud, after easing throat thongs to his wamus, went over to the spring and, using a birch-bark dipper, swallowed several deep draughts.

"You mayn't believe it, Jake, but them Britishers got driven back 'thout carryin' anythin' away—least of all the cannons they'd mainly come for. Our folks fought 'em, Injun style, from behind trees, stumps and stone walls—really mowed 'em down. Gave the Redcoats such a bad beatin' they backtracked but still keepin' good order."

Jake squirmed broad bare feet into his sturdiest shoepacs, drawled, "So at last it's come to bloodshed." He took down his box of flints, examined each one with care, also a screw ramrod that could be used to extract defective bullets.

"Tell me somethin', Paul. What's all this got to do with us Green Mountain Boys? We ain't neither Massachusetters nor Connecticuters, let alone Noo Yorkers."

Before replying the bearded ranger sank onto his heels, Indian-style, frowning. "Ethan Allen and other bigwigs down to Bennington allow this ruckus soon is goin' grow into our fight too. They say a real big war is brewin'. Cap'n Allen—he wants you, me and the rest of the Green Mountain Boys to collect war gear and hightail fast as we can for Bennin'ton where we kin git mustered in at the Catamount Tavern." He grinned. "Nacherally, Allen would have his headquarters there."

Jake looked hopefully at Nellie's trout, now turning golden-brown. Despite frying noises the girl peered over a half-exposed shoulder, red dotted by insect bites, heard her man grunt, "You sure there's goin' to be a gre't big war, like the one we had 'gainst the Frenchies?"

"'Pears like it. Ethan Allen, Doctor John Crigo, Sam Beman, Amos Callender and his son and Major Beach all think so. A lot of other plain folks think so too, even unedicated timber beasts like you and I." Neither man could read or write. "Anyhow," Thebaud went on, "I judge from what that loud-mouthed Ethan Allen claims—you know how he delights to orate given any excuse at all—there's bound to come a gen'ral 'risin' 'gainst the Crown."

While hefting a shapeless war bag of beaded leather containing an assortment of odd but useful supplies Jake hopefully considered his friend. "This mean we're free to tackle them thievin' boundary-jumpin' Yorkers again?"

"Naw. Not lest they side with the Redcoats. But by most accounts the Yorkers this time are with us."

"What about Connecticuters?"

"Them, too. Heard tell their Committee of Safety is enrollin' their milishy into companies and gettin' set to march, which may or mayn't be so. You know what champion liars most Connect-icuters are."

Once breakfast had been consumed Nellie, watched by a striped, bright-eyed chipmunk perched on a nearby bough, silently set about packing Jake's "possibles bag." In this small knapsack made of deerskin she stowed a kerchief, a pair of socks and his only spare shirt along with a hunk of bacon, a bladder of pemmican, some strips of smoked venison and a few pieces of jaw-breaking, iron-hard firecake.

Meanwhile, Jake secured stout ankle-high shoepacs—elkskin moccasins to which soles of tough but pliant and well-tanned moosehide had been stitched with rawhide sinews.

No noise was made except by chattering chipmunks until Jake Razors slung on his cow's-horn powder flask then belted about his wiry waist a heavy, hard-bladed skinning knife in a fringed sheath—its handle had grown smooth and shiny through use—and a tomahawk. Nellie then helped fasten on a flap-protected leather cartouche box containing a bar of lead for his bullet mould, flints and a length of wood drilled to accommodate a dozen measured and paper-wrapped powder charges on his wide belt's opposite side.

Finally he clapped on a rusty-black, wide-brimmed felt hat set off by a band of red squirrel fur. Jake strapped his best go-to-town gray frieze jacket onto the top of his "possibles bag"—on a lovely warm morning such a garment would be much too hot to wear.

Jake slung his rifle over his shoulder and strode over to deliver a playful farewell slap on Nellie's rear. What he really wanted to do was to take her into his arms, knead her breasts a bit and buss her resoundingly but, before an outsider, a fellow really shouldn't display such signs of affection for a half-breed.

"Keep an eye on the place, lass, and keep the bed warm too," he told her softly. "Likely I'll be back inside of a day or so."

Right now there could be no telling how greatly mistaken he was about this.

On the sixth of May, 1775, the chartered township of Bennington, due to its favorable location on rich soil among only moderately high hills, was expanding rapidly into quite a town. Well over a hundred cabins, houses, barns, warehouses and offices of varied descriptions lay in the immediate vicinity. Moreover, numerous clearings for farms, cabins and dwellings of more elaborate descriptions constantly were being hewed out of the wilderness in various directions and rough bridges and roads had commenced to appear cross-country.

A red-brick church was nearing completion on one side of a spacious and level well-mowed area which inhabitants now had commenced to designate as "the Common." Across from it stood a graceless and small-windowed stone edifice of brown granite known as the "Meeting House"; originally, this sturdy building had been constructed as a "strong house" to withstand Indian raids so was topped by a stone watchtower equipped with the alarm bell which only just now having ceased to peal, allowed a squealing of fifes and the heart-stirring rattling of drums to be heard.

Also facing the Common stood the Catamount Tavern, a new, well-designed two-storey wooden structure of clapboards painted white. Around this tavern milled the largest crowd of people Jake Razors had ever seen in Bennington.

On top of a pole and crouched above a swing board bearing the tavern's name had been secured the poorly stuffed and badly weathered skin of a Canadian lynx—locally termed a catamount. In all weathers this shaggy effigy glared glassy defiance in the direction of the distant Hudson River and the Province of New York lying beyond it.

For years now that vaguely defined area, the vast and beautiful Green Mountain District comprising the southeastern section of the Hampshire Grants, had existed in a state of perpetual unrest, stubbornly calling itself the "Province of Vermont." This conflict was due to the fact that Connecticut claimed ownership of all lands extending east of the Hudson River while New York just as angrily insisted that the legal border dividing the two colonies was defined by the Connecticut River's course.

Today, this normally placid little backwoods village lay in dusty ferment. Dozens of wains, oxcarts, shays and wagons pulled by rough-coated draft animals overflowed the Common but only a few clean-limbed riding horses switched flies before well-gnawed hitching racks.

By the dozens, dogs, children and poultry ran about, girls and bonneted women clutching market baskets clustered in groups waving hands and chattering "sixty to the minute."

Present also were plenty of bearded and dusty farmers, drovers and laborers, mostly these lugging a miscellany of long-barreled muskets and wearing leather jerkins over shapeless homespun garments. Jake noticed one sleeveless coat cut from the hide of a brown-and-white calf. Among such rural types circulated a lesser number of soberly clad officials, clerks, merchants and artisans of all descriptions. Here and there parts of long-obsolete military uniforms could be recognized but nobody wore full regimentals of any description.

In front of the Catamount Tavern's entrance a group of men were clustering and gesticulating about a plain board table supported upon a pair of sawhorses. Behind it Harry Belcher, a nearly bald schoolteacher, sat round-shouldered, his goose-quill pen scribbling down names of volunteers who shuffled up to sign or to have their marks witnessed on a wrinkled muster roll.

For a brief space Jake and his companion lingered around the edges of the crowd just looking and listening until the town crier appeared and clanged a brass hand bell till comparative silence spread over the Common.

"Hear ye! Hear ye! Since, as you've already heard, a trial-at-arms against the Royal Tyrant's Ministerial Government has took place at Concord and Lexington and patriotic blood has been spilled, our leader, Ethan Allen, and other men of substance from these parts allow we must, and right away, join in the defense of our lives, liberty and homes. Any of you feelin' like-minded right now can step up and enroll in a troop the Green Mountain Boys are aimin' to raise."

Through cupped hands somebody yelled, "That's fine, but how long do us fellers hev to be away soljerin'? They's still a lot of land clearin' and spring plantin' to be done."

Ethan Allen, a towering, barrel-chested figure with strong, broad and permanently flushed features, yelled in a booming voice. "That's for the Lord God Jehovah to decide. Most likely you won't be away for more than a few days, maybe a month at the most."

He jumped up onto an oxcart, waved arms and glared about. "Now let's get this straight right now. I don't want any maca-ronis, nice-Nancies, half-hearts or men who ain't handy with weapons to sign up."

Possibly applejack had had something to do with it but some-what to his surprise Jake shoved his way towards the table and found himself with a quill pen clumsily gripped between cal-loused but long and well-formed fingers. He blinked, looked unhappily at the schoolmaster.

"Harry, you know I can't—"

"Sure, Jake, I know you can't write much, so draw your two crossed-arrows mark—like always." He raised a furry brow. "Can you draw a letter 'R'? That'd help make it look more legal."

Jake complied although the loop he sketched was turned backwards. Alongside it was scratched: Jacob Razors of Pawlet, private soldier.

Paul Thebaud had just finished making his mark when came a sound of drumming hoofs. Onto the Common clattered a lanky, bareheaded individual astride a sweating, rawboned gray horse.

"News!" he panted. "Good news! A passel of Massachusetts milishymen are on their way to join us! Oughter show up sometime before dark!"

"How many?" barked Major Doolittle.

"Round three dozen I'd hazard. Well armed, too!"

The galloper's estimate proved nearly correct for, towards sundown, about forty rough-clad militiamen wearing bits of uniforms appeared on the rough cart road leading northward. They were followed by a tall, big-nosed and whimsical-looking captain named Phelps who, as someone remarked, looked fit to wrestle a bear and win. Apparently this new arrival was well and favorably known to Ethan Allen who just now was deciding that, in view of growing responsibilities, he'd better insist on being addressed as "Colonel." Nobody objected, nor were questions raised as to just who had signed such a commission or under what Colonial government's authority.

Never in its brief history had the township of Bennington witnessed such activity as when more and more men tramped in from the back country. Some were accompanied by relatives but a majority appeared alone carrying a firearm, a powder horn and a rolled blanket plus a bag of "possibles." Very few volunteers appeared on horseback; amid such a wild and mountainous terrain most men discovered that only big-boned, heavy-footed draft animals could earn their keep.

Jake Razors and Paul Thebaud as founding members of what snide townsfolk termed "the Bennington Mob" cheerfully greeted fellow woodsmen and welcomed the Massachusetts detachment, sharing kegs of pungent spruce beer plus a demi-john or two of powerful hard cider locally and accurately described as "pop-skull."

One gap-toothed backwoodsman commented the craziest sort of rumors were circulating in Bennington, "Thicker'n turds round a schoolhouse."

William Reynolds, a sharp-faced and narrow-chinned fellow

who lived near Skenesboro and built gundelows, or sailing scows, and bateaux and did some freighting on Lake George, commented, "Fellers, if we aim to accomplish anythin' 'gainst those Redcoats at Ti' we'd best get humpin' our asses."

"What's all this rush for?" demanded a burly fellow wearing a blacksmith's leather apron.

Reynolds waited for people to shut up and listen to what he had to tell them. "Right now a big lot of Lobsterback Reg'lars hev been reported marchin' from Fort George to reinforce Fort Ti'."

Thebaud spat then bit off a fresh chew of tobacco. He didn't like Reynolds much—hadn't ever since the boatbuilder had bilked him on a deal for some prime beaver skins. "Where d'you hear that?"

"Got it straight from old Beaver Teeth, a Injun fisherman I know full well. Stopped by as I was readyin' to leave for this muster and he swore he'd spied with his own eyes a column of Redcoats marchin' north along the Narrows yesterday mornin'."

"How many?" demanded a sharp-eyed man wearing a Connecticut militiaman's well-worn dark-blue jacket.

"Hell, Jonas, you know as well as me Injuns can't count higher'n the number of his fingers and toes. All the same he said there must ha' been a hundred of the King's troops marchin' to military music, flags and all."

When dusk deepened groups of men, usually from the same neighborhood, got together and bivouacked in the woods, produced victuals of sorts along with iron kettles and frying pans and ramrods to roast fowls and squirrels on. Others, lacking local connections, accepted the gruff hospitality of townsfolk who diffidently offered a bait of food and warm milk and told these "outlanders" to make themselves comfortable in woodsheds or barns.

Meantime, a serious dispute and shouting match was raging in the Catamount Tavern's low-ceilinged taproom, made it resound like an Indian signaling log drum. Broad-shouldered Ethan Allen, having shed and placed before him a weathered brass-studded sword belt along with a pair of stout pocket pistols, towered, spraddle-legged and beet-red of face at the head of the inn's long and food-stained table board. Employing a rare degree of self-control, he was devoting full attention to a detailed account being rendered by a lean, steel-spectacled and bookish-looking young lawyer by the name of John Brown who hailed from Pittsfield, Massachusetts, and was a member of the Committee of Safety up there. Since Brown just had returned from Montreal where he'd been sent to sound out how people up there felt about joining in a rebellion, everybody listened to what the lawyer had to say, especially Doctor Jared Weems whose practice covered a considerable area. Right now, to the best of his ability, he silently was passing on candidates for Allen's force.

Leather-featured and angular Major Beach, a taciturn surveyor who had run many of those boundaries at present under dispute between Connecticut and New York, also paid close attention with a hand cupped close around a hairy ear. Several other local leaders of unquestioned patriotism and integrity such as Sam Woolcott, Paul Moore and Doctor John Crigo stood about. At the table next to Allen stood plump and moon-faced Major Ephraim Doolittle, one of the biggest local landowners who also was deemed important because he'd seen considerable action under General Amherst during the last of the French and Indian Wars.

Addressing himself principally to Ethan Allen, Lawyer Brown was saying, "Now if any of us fellows fancy we're going to get real aid or encouragement from French-Canadians—or *habitants* as they're called up there—we're barking up the wrong tree. While Canucks don't admire the British at all they prefer the Redcoats to us."

William Reynolds momentarily ceased to pick at a hairy nostril. "Why so, John? That don't make sense to me."

Under a snuff-colored and long-skirted serge jacket the lawyer shrugged. "'Tis all on account of the so-called 'Québec Act' by which the Crown last year not only guaranteed French-speaking Canadians religious and political freedom but also the right to observe local customs and to handle their private affairs pretty much as they please. This is most unlucky for us since the 'Québec Act' is about the only really sensible law Parliament and the King's Ministers have enacted with regard to American Colonies in a damn' long time."

The Massachusetter Captain Phelps peered over the blackened bowl of a short clay pipe. "Why d'you say that?"

In practiced deliberation Brown surveyed the room strongly redolent of unwashed garments, liquor and blue with tobacco smoke. "Well, gentlemen, it's like this: the *habitants* feel confident the British Government really will enforce those rights and privileges I've just mentioned. While, not without some reason, they're apprehensive of religious persecution and political oppression by Protestant rebels." He grimaced. "Especially those coming from Massachusetts.

"On my way hither," he continued speaking clearly, "I heard more than once that your neighbor, Major Philip Skene, is busy trying to recruit a band of Tories to reinforce the garrison at Fort Ticonderoga."

Ethan Allen's lumpy, freckled hand crashed onto the table so hard it made a leaden inkwell jump. "We'll soon put a stop to that, by Jesus!" He gripped bearded and buck-toothed Captain Willis, unofficial second-in-command of the Green Mountain Boys, by the arm. "Hervey, I want you and Amos Callender should go out right now and spread the word, quiet-like, mind you, that we march for Castleton come first daylight—though I am minded to wait just a little while for those damn' Connecticuters to show up."

He turned to the Constable. "Come over, 'Lijah, I want you to pick out maybe half a dozen extra-able men and go put a spoke in the wheel of that Tory bastard Skene."

"Under whose authority will they act?" Lawyer John Brown wanted to know.

Allen frowned, hesitated momentarily. "Hell, that don't matter. We'll act on our own because as I've said before, I'll not stand tamely by and allow Tories beef up the garrison over in Ti'."

Phelps, the Massachusetts men's leader, demanded slowly, "Just what *is* the situation yonder?"

Doctor Weems tested a large and purplish mole on his jaw. "Aye. We'd best get a late report and find out what we're like to be up against."

Absently Allen rumpled a mane of greasy light-brown hair. "I've heard all sorts of conflicting reports about the garrison's strength but I know of someone who's been inside the fort not a week ago."

Over a shoulder he called, "Willis, suppose you and some others go and bring in a ranger calling himself 'Jake Razors.' Last winter he did considerable hunting for the garrison; kept the officers' mess in smoked fish, fresh game and the like."

Moments later Jake, boisterous and flushed by the unaccustomed amount of applejack he'd been consuming, shoved his way indoors. He was by no means drunk or silly.

"How was it over there?" demanded the dominating figure at the table's end.

"Fort's in poor shape, 'bout the same as usual, Cunnel. Parapets along on the nor'east side are half-rotted through and some outbuildin's too. Thanks to the tough winter we've just had some of the stone facin's along ramparts facin' west and south have slipped a lot and even split."

Captain Phelps's hard blue eyes considered Jake with care. "How much of a garrison do the enemy regularly keep on duty over yonder? Please be exact, this is most important."

Jake scratched his shaggy head, briefly pursed lips in thought. "Why, sir, only two commissioned officers are quartered there reg'lar. Cap'n Delaplace and Lootenant Feltham with their families. Then there's a master gunner and a quartermaster serjeant and nigh on forty or fifty of other ranks *all* Reg'lars of the 28th Foot. Last week Cap'n Delaplace told me to hunt extry hard on account of he was expectin' considerable reinforcements to show up any day. Also he told me he'd sent agents runnin' to various Injun chiefs to stir 'em up, same as durin' the French War."

Billy Reynolds, the shipbuilder, spoke right up. "Hear that, Ethan? Didn't I report Redcoats had been seen advancing along the Lake George road?"

"Maybe your Injun friend weren't mistooken after all."

Ethan Allen looked solemn, fingered a box-like jaw and finally nodded. "Bill, you ain't always been too accurate in some of your talk, but this time I reckon you're right, so I'll not take a chance and let grass grow in our tracks." He turned to his second-in-command. "Tell me, Hervey, where d'you think would be the likeliest spot for us to cross Champlain for our assault?"

17

Captain Willis' reply was prompt. "I'd say we ought to shove off from Hand's Cove which lies less than two miles above the fort, but, first we'll have to rustle up sufficient gundelows and big canoes to ferry us across; we'll have to take care. Although the lake's very narrow thereabouts should a wind blow up hard we'd have a Hell of a time gettin' over, this time of year current runs mighty powerful and we could get swamped by cross-seas and lose a lot of people."

"That's true," Seth Warner agreed seriously. "It's up to some of us to right away start looking for craft stout enough to serve our purpose. Major Skene has some—or had a short while back."

"Then you're not sure his boats will be there?"

"No," Warner said. "He may be off rounding up fellow Tories. Heard there are a few Durham boats at Crown Point—don't know how good their condition is, though."

So it came about that at first daylight Captain Hervey Willis and a dozen leathery Green Mountain men set out for Skenesboro.

"Colonel" Allen took a long pull of rum and water then said briskly, "Now listen, everybody. I want every fit man to turn out before dawn armed and carrying food for two days. You know as well as me it's a long march to Castleton over high hills and trails and roads that're nothing to brag over."

Major Doolittle held up a hand. "Now hold on, Ethan, let's not go off at half-cock. Hadn't we better wait for those Connecticut men to join us? If that rider was telling the truth they would more than double our force; remember, right now we don't count but eighty-odd men all told."

Ethan Allen flared right up, roared, "No by God! We march at dawn if I've only a corporal's guard to lead. All right, fellows, go circulate 'mongst your men; tell 'em what's been decided. Anybody who don't turn out ready to move at daybreak will find himself in a heap of trouble."

Since it still was too early in the season for no-see-ums, mosquitoes and black flies to prove a real plague men clustered around cook fires, smoked, drank, gammed and really enjoyed themselves. Yessiree, to socialize with so many strangers from all over and to anticipate who knew what sort of dangers and excitement came as a welcome break from the humdrum, hardscrabble of everyday life.

For a moment Jake deliberated whether he possibly might make it out to his shack for a final tumble with Nellie and get back by daybreak. He might have taken a chance had there been a moon but tonight sure was blacker than Satan's heart and besides, "Colonel" Allen had 'llowed he wanted him, Paul Thebaud and Noah Phipps, a knowledgeable local youth, to scout ahead and along both flanks once the command left camp.

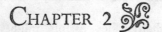

CHAPTER 2

COLONEL BENEDICT ARNOLD

DUE TO THE fact that almost without exception "Colonel" Ethan Allen's Green Mountain Boys for the most part were tough and woods-wise but utterly undisciplined, the little column made good time and by mid-afternoon arrived at Richard Bentley's farm, mostly stump-lots, lying just outside of Castleton. Only a few volunteers appeared tired or footsore, mostly townsmen who'd overloaded themselves with gear or had been sufficiently vain to show off new shoes or boots.

The expedition barely had fallen out of formation and scattered to squat in the shade and delve into haversacks for eatables than a half-breed Indian runner ran in reporting that a party of maybe sixty militia of the 6th Connecticut Regiment were advancing so fast they might show up before dark.

Drawled Paul Thebaud, "Most Connecticuters don't amount to a pinch of coon shit but any time they're wuth a damn' sight more than any snot-nosed Yorkers."

When, as dusk was deepening, the Connecticut militia tramped into Castleton. They numbered about fifty rangy individuals. Some were wearing odd items of uniform but most were clad in an assortment of well-worn civilian garments of leather, duroy, canvas or homespun cloth.

Captain Edward Mott whose face reminded Jake of a nutcracker was commanding the new arrivals and had an indefinable but convincing air of authority about him. Without preamble he informed Ethan Allen that he and his men had been ordered by the Hartford Committee of Safety to go and back up the Green Mountain Boys because by all accounts the Vermonters were getting ready to try to capture an important store of cannon, mortars, howitzers and other vital munitions reportedly stored in Fort Ticonderoga. Such supplies were critically needed by that growing but seriously ill-equipped army now forming around Cambridge, Massachusetts.

Sharp-tongued Edward Mott, when questioned, produced a commission issued by the Connecticut Assembly, dated 28 April 1775, appointing him a captain in the 6th Connecticut Regiment, but to most Vermonters its worth seemed nearly as empty as Ethan Allen's self-bestowed rank. This bothered no one save that thin-faced lawyer John Brown. More than once he'd warned Ethan Allen that, although his lack of a duly executed commission might appear trivial to him and to most of his raucous followers, under time-honored laws of war, armed forces, conducting hostilities against a legal government, meant that, if taken bearing arms would be considered no better than bandits and outlaws who could, and probably would, be executed without benefit of trial or court-martial.

Billy Reynolds quit gnawing at a cold chicken leg long enough to mumble, "So if the Bloodybacks capture any of us we're like to get our necks stretched? I agree with Mister Brown; 'twould be smart for us to 'bide on this shore till Ethan's commission, and mebbe more reinforcements, reach us."

Since nobody took this suggestion seriously the less liquored-up volunteers continued to settle down and bivouac around cook fires about Richard Bentley's comfortable farmhouse and spacious hay barn.

Jake, Paul Thebaud and some trapper friends gulped swigs of watered rum before seeking a nearby stream. After cutting supple alder branches, which made first-class rods, they got out fishhooks without which no real woodsman ever went, and baited them with strips of bacon fat. Happily, they concentrated on catching a mess of plump brook trout. This early in the season the fish proved so ravenous it wasn't long before the party returned, bragging and swinging long strips of alder shoots loaded with handsome and still feebly squirming prizes.

After supper "Colonel" Ethan Allen, Captain Mott of the 6th Connecticut Militia Regiment, Jake Razors, Paul Thebaud, Nathan Beman and half-a-dozen other woodsmen sought Bentley's house for a "nightcap." Of course they lingered there. Men, too excited to sleep, sang patriotic songs, added scurrilous stanzas of their own invention.

Especially popular was a new and catchy tune called "Yankee Doodle."

Some remained quiet only half-convinced an advance to Hand's Cove might not come off entirely undisputed; quite a few suspected Tories were known to be living in the vicinity and their leader, Major Skene, admittedly was rich, resourceful and energetic. Also it was entirely possible for the British, as in the past, to stir up nearby Indian tribes who, more and more, were resenting the relentless encroachment of Colonial farmlands no matter how legally obtained. Nowadays game was growing so scarce many Redmen were going hungry.

Naturally it wasn't reasonable so soon to hear from the party that had been sent to not only capture Philip Skene but also his big schooner, and to seize enough bateaux and gundelows to transport the expedition across Lake Champlain in a single body.

Allen and the other leaders were draining their second round of watered rum when from the direction of the Rutland road excited yells swelled as a sound of furiously drumming hoofs abruptly died away outside Dick Bentley's white-painted farmhouse and barn.

"Who in Hell can be in such an all-fired hurry?" demanded Allen, rising a trifle unsteadily.

His question was answered when to a jingling of large brass spurs a swarthy and short but powerfully built individual marched rather than walked into the Bentley's kitchen. He was wearing a cockaded tricorn hat and a smartly cut but dusty brass-buttoned blue uniform jacket the lapels of which were turned back in dark-red, Massachusetts colors as a rule. Of all things this tight-jawed newcomer was wearing a handsome dress sword. Swaggering indoors he kept a hand on its ornate hilt.

John Brown called out, "B'God it's Colonel Benedict Arnold!"

"How d'you know?" snapped nearly toothless Seth Warner, a veteran of the French War.

"Met him in Hartford not long ago at a meeting of the Governor's Council."

Captain Mike Phelps also recognized Benedict Arnold at first sight by his swarthy complexion, long, thick and very straight nose and by the heaviness of chin now aggressively outthrust. His large and vitreous hazel eyes were deep-set and wide apart. Deliberately Arnold waited for confusion attendant upon his arrival to subside, as, fleshy lips pursed, he surveyed the gathering like the expert politician he was, awaiting proper attention.

Finally he demanded in a condescending yet somehow impressive tone of voice, "Which one of you yokels, er, gentlemen, names himself Ethan Allen?"

Jake picked up his rifle Jenny and started edging towards the kitchen door; years ago he'd learned to select a quick and easy line of retreat when trouble threatened to break out and it sure looked like that now.

Scarlet of face, Ethan Allen surged to his feet. Crumbs from his lap tumbled onto the floor as he swung over to tower over this intruder wearing a Massachusetts officer's travel-marked uniform. Men who knew Allen braced themselves when they saw their leader's eyes narrow and his body tense.

"I am, goddammit, and for Christ's sake what the Hell d'you mean, you damn' tailor's dummy, busting into my headquarters like a rutting bull moose after a cow!"

The dark-complexioned intruder made no immediate reply, only ignored the speaker and continued to survey this smelly, roughly clad gathering.

At length he announced in a suddenly rich and courteous voice, "Sir, as my friend, John Brown, already has informed you, I am Colonel Benedict Arnold." He paused, as if expecting this announcement to impress listeners.

"So what of that?" growled Ethan Allen. "You come to announce the Second Coming of Christ?"

Arnold, still breathing hard from his ride, replied coldly,

"Don't blaspheme. Unnecessary cursing only lowers a fellow in the esteem of educated people and impresses no one except those of his own ilk."

"Farts to you! I'll say what I please," growled Allen, muscles on his powerful and long-unshaven jaws working. "By that pretty uniform I take it you hail from Massachusetts?"

Arnold dropped some of his overbearing manner. "That is correct. I will have you know that I carry a colonel's commission, properly signed and sealed by the Massachusetts Committee of Safety."

A curious silence pervaded the room.

"Well, what of that?" demanded Captain Mott. "There are more than enough such papers being passed around nowadays."

Benedict Arnold half-smiled and deliberately flicked dust from the cuff of a pair of elegant buckskin gauntlets. "For your information I have received orders to take command of an expedition designed to capture Fort Ticonderoga."

"*What!*" roared Allen. "By Satan's smoking prong, you must be clean out of your frigging wits! Do you actually expect to take command of *my* men?"

"Exactly so."

"'Exactly so,'" Allen mimicked. "Well, my fine peacock, how many men have *you* fetched along?"

For the first time the uniformed officer hesitated. "Only because I have ridden so far and so fast to lead you I am, for the moment, accompanied by a single orderly."

"What!" voices rang from all sides. "You've brought *no* reinforcements at all?"

"I command four hundred well-armed Connecticut militia."

For a moment Doctor Weems and others feared Ethan Allen might be taken with a strangury his broad brown face had turned so purple. "The Hell you say! Where are they?"

"Only a day or so's march from here, I'd say."

"'Only a day or so' don't mean much at a time like this." He shouted, "Now, by the Great Jehovah, I *have* heard everything! Who the Hell do you think you are? Your tin sword and regimentals don't impress me one bit so don't try to tell me and my men how to act in our own territory. We don't recognize Massa-

24

chusetts authority in these parts. Us Vermonters would liefer lose our balls than take orders from the likes of you."

Separated by less than a yard the two glowered at each other until all at once a change came over Benedict Arnold. He collected himself, fell back a step, drew a deep breath then wiped the scowl from his olive-hued visage. "Please, sir, forgive my impetuosity. It is most undignified for senior officers to carry on like this, especially in the presence of subordinates, so it would be wise to moderate our language. Believe me, sir, this matter of who holds top command is of first importance to all concerned."

At this point Lawyer John Brown shoved through the angry gathering saying, "A word with you, Ethan. What the Colonel says is true."

Arnold began in lowered tones, "It is, and if Mister Allen—"

"'Colonel' Allen to you, damn you!" the taller man broke in.

Arnold continued to retain self-control and only stared down his powerful nose. "Gladly I will do so once you show me your commission." He held out a sinewy hand. "Please allow me to examine it."

Flushing redder than ever the leader of the Green Mountain Boys roared so loud that spittle flew from his lips. "I hold my commission from the Lord God Jehovah, so it rates a damn' sight higher than any sheepskin scrawled by some goddam Committee of Safety. You can clear out!"

Growing ever more self-contained, Benedict Arnold didn't budge, only negligently rested a hand on the gilded hilt of his sword. "With all due respect to Jehovah, I will not depart until you produce written and legal authority for you to command this expedition."

Shaking with rage Allen, who stood easily a head taller, balled a fist and shook it under the other's nose. "Mister, I'm warnin' you to haul your behind out of here afore I kick it up level to your shoulders!"

John Brown clutched Allen's arm tighter, said so urgently that everyone could hear him, "Take it easy, Ethan! Whether we like it or not Colonel Arnold has a telling point for consideration."

"Consideration be damned! I ain't about to turn command of

us Green Mountain Patriots over to any fancy-dressed popinjay from Massachusetts." All the same Ethan Allen also commenced to cool down. He turned to John Brown. "What is this 'telling point' you speak of?"

From under thick but gracefully arched black brows Benedict Arnold half-smiled. "Sir, you seem a sensible fellow. Who are you?"

Someone informed, "John Brown is a lawyer from Pittsfield and a sound Patriot—same as me. I read law in Boston till my father went broke during the Tea Tax troubles."

Ostentatiously Arnold unhitched his sword belt then propped the glittering weapon against the nearest chair back. Said he, "I feel sure Mister Brown must already have pointed out the main issue. Should you and your followers, lacking legal authority, launch an attack upon the King's fort and are *captured* you can be hanged as common felons or outlaws. Under military law British authorities would have every legal right to do so."

Ethan Allen's prominent and hairy Adam's apple rose spasmodically once or twice. "That may be so but, by God, we're all of us ready to take our chances on that." His voice leveled a little. "Colonel, had you fetched a sizable number of troops along I—well, I just might feel inclined to reach some sort of an accommodation with you, but since your men won't be showin' up straightaway and will be all tuckered out if and when they do arrive, I won't do that."

Recalling the information Billy Reynolds had supplied concerning reinforcements on the way to Ticonderoga there was an even more increasing danger that, granted time, New York Loyalists, of which there were plenty nearby, might rally to defend the King's fort.

"I'm damned if we'll dally. I figger our only chance is to move fast.

Benedict Arnold nodded. "I agree that we should march at the first practicable moment."

Being the only fully uniformed man present it was especially noticeable when, from a wide sash of dark-red silk, he removed a pair of handsome French pocket pistols. Ostentatiously he placed them on the table, declared with engaging frankness, "Since I am equally devoted to the sacred cause of liberty I, well

—I am prepared to consider any reasonable solution to our problems." Smiling, he then looked about. "Gentlemen, could I have a drink? I've ridden a far piece today."

Captain Phelps offered a brimming mug of beer. "Why, sure, sir. Let this wet your whistle."

Arnold's remarks about the risk of getting hanged as common outlaws had struck deep, most of those present were more or less law-abiding persons and proud of it.

Ethan Allen, still breathing deep, fixed Arnold with a hawk's bright, piercing and unblinking stare. "Since you appear so keen on furthering our common cause I am prepared to be reasonable, er—sir. Consider yourself free to come along of us, an you're so minded." While swallowing a short drink his gaze never shifted from Arnold's darkly handsome features.

"Thank you, sir, but in what capacity will I serve?"

"Well, I'd say as a sort of co-commander, but don't for a moment forget that I am your superior."

Benedict Arnold may have thought otherwise but avoided comment being busy weighing the means of outmaneuvering these rustics. Originally from Norwich, Connecticut, he deemed himself, at the age of thirty-four, a real man of the world.

Hadn't he sailed as a capable sea captain, uncommonly successful in the West Indies trade? Like many prominent New England merchants he also had been a smuggler there being no stigma attached to such activities against the Crown. Furthermore he'd demonstrated himself an outstandingly able officer in the Governor of Connecticut's Foot Guards and was on intimate terms with many extremely influential Rebel leaders.

Benedict Arnold stood very straight while continuing in affable tones, "Since we all are serving the cause of liberty I will accept your proposal for the time being. However, I insist that I am the *legal* Commander-in-Chief of these forces but, no matter what happens during the attack, you may count on my full and unswerving co-operation, 'Colonel' Allen." Only a trace of mockery was evident in Arnold's use of the military title.

CHAPTER 3 🙰

FIRST REBEL OFFENSIVE

THE NINTH DAY OF MAY, 1775, proved so fair and warm that spring appeared to advance almost visibly. Bearing out his reputation as an officer of real experience, Benedict Arnold, once the Provincials had assembled on a level pasture near Bentley's farmhouse, divided the Provincials into squads of ten each even while new men were coming in. Singly or by twos or threes roughly dressed and generally silent men appeared from the mountainous backcountry. Walking softly and loose-kneed these fetched along firearms ranging from fairly new Tower muskets to fowling pieces, also antique firelocks, some of whose barrels had been reinforced with bands of brass or copper wire.

Quite a few volunteers were armed only with Indian tomahawks and bows and arrows; a few carried short, steel-headed French pikes or a pitchfork, or a woodsman's broadaxe. About the only thing these rugged individuals had in common was a noisy eagerness to get in some resounding whacks at the Lobsterbacks before returning home as fast as they could leg it.

Although runners had been dispatched to learn what success Captain Willis and his handful of followers had had during their raid at Skenesboro, nothing whatsoever could be learned. The budding hills and forest seemed to have swallowed them up causing definite uneasiness in some quarters. Nor did information arrive concerning the whereabouts of those four hundred Connecticut militiamen Colonel Arnold had so loudly insisted were on the way. All the same, the disorderly throng encamped around town now numbered around two hundred and fifty volunteers of all sorts and descriptions most of whom had fetched along sufficient victuals to last them a day or two. These supplies were amplified through the surprising generosity of local inhabitants rumored to be "near," even for New Englanders.

By now relations between "Colonel" Ethan Allen and Colonel Benedict Arnold had simmered down to something like armed neutrality during conferences, yet their mutual arrogance, envy and mistrust of one another remained so evident everybody felt relieved when word went out that at daybreak tomorrow the expedition, win, lose or draw, would set out from Hand's Cove lying a scant two miles on the eastern shore of Lake Champlain above Ticonderoga that strategically vital fort originally long ago designed by King Louis XIV of France's most famous military engineer, the Marquis de Vauban.

Among officers sometimes fully clothed and lying three in a row across a few sturdy beds only Captain Edward Mott of the 6th Connecticut remained awake despite rattling snores and somnolent mutterings rising in all directions. The principal reason keeping that lanky individual awake was realization that in a saddlebag reeking of horse sweat and at present serving him as a pillow lay an envelope containing a carefully folded sheet of stiff foolscap. Only he was aware that this document was a pompously worded commission signed, sealed and duly executed by a group of sober citizens elected to serve on Hartford's Committee of Safety.

This undated commission bore neither the name nor the rank to be bestowed; said omissions were to be filled in bearing the name of anyone deemed worthy by Captain Edward Mott.

Drowsily, Mott wondered whether after that stormy exchange in the farmhouse he shouldn't then and there have filled in Ethan Allen's name and rank. Yet somehow it hadn't seemed advisable, especially since Ethan Allen had won his way thus far without it. Later on, if the attack on Ticonderoga failed, this document would grant legal status of sorts and would validate Allen's position. Again, Benedict Arnold's commission, issued by the Massachusetts Committee of Safety, possibly held greater validity. Suppose a swarm of Connecticut militia arrived strong enough to depose Allen as Commander-in-Chief and place his force under Colonel Arnold's command?

On the other hand, if the assault proved a success Mott foresaw inevitable, acrimonious disputes over divisions of booty, he then would produce Allen's commission to support the Green Mountain Boys' claims. It seemed wise to delay and see what might happen.

Having so decided, Mott yawned cavernously and immediately joined his companions in malodorous slumber.

CHAPTER 4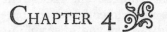

DAWN'S EARLY LIGHT

Because cold and steady rain had set in during the night the expedition setting out at daybreak for Hubbardtown made poor time for the track, following the countryside's line of least resistance, was steep, unusually muddy and meandered across hills and mountains just as it had when first traced ages ago by countless herds of deer, elk and forest buffaloes.

Fortunately rain ceased to fall shortly before "Colonel" Ethan Allen's little command reached a shingle beach lining Hand's Cove, a pretty little inlet well concealed and invisible from Lake Champlain's western shore. Late in the afternoon of the day before "Colonel" Ethan Allen had flown into a fine fury on discovering not a single craft of any description waiting at the landing place's ramshackle dock, Captain Hervey Willis's raid on Skenesboro had proved utterly unproductive.

Worse still, a succession of hard squalls had lashed the lead-blue lake into such a white fury no word concerning the progress of those British reinforcements reported by Billy Reynolds, or anything else of importance, could possibly come over from the New York shore.

Towards sundown trappers and forest rangers and men often exposed to such conditions started to make themselves as comfortable as possible; some even helped farmers and townsfolk to do the same.

At morning muster it had proved odd to Jake and other frontiersmen to notice that quite a few officers including Ethan Allen now turned up wearing swords—probably only because Benedict Arnold was making such a parade of his handsome weapon it lent him an air of specious authority. Most such local swords were heavy-bladed business-like brass-hilted affairs and in several cases resembled Navy cutlasses. Probably they'd first been carried against the French a generation ago.

"Damned show-offs!" commented Jake and other real frontiersmen who knew that a sword in the wilderness was far less useful than a long knife, a spear or a tomahawk.

Until darkness had fallen search parties of woods-wise men led by Jake, Thebaud and others of their ilk probed the lake's tangled rocky shore in opposite directions but the only useful boats they came across were a pair of small gundelows or clumsy freighting boats half-full of water and tied up at a ramshackle dock owned by a farmer named Storer.

At a glance it was obvious that, at most, neither craft could accommodate more than twenty-odd men plus gear and not even that many should the weather continue foul.

To many volunteers it proved instructive to notice how useful, in so many ways, an experienced officer like Colonel Benedict Arnold could render himself. That short and vigorous officer ranged tirelessly about examining doubtful weapons, suggesting the management of packs and offering so many other practical suggestions that, before long, the Green Mountain Boys commenced to forget this energetic officer in muddy Massachusetts regimentals was here only on tolerance.

There was some half-hearted talk about building rafts but everybody knew that, even had suitable materials been readily available, such craft couldn't possibly be completed in time. Furthermore rafts were too slow, too awkward to manage in the face of fire from Ticonderoga's powerful batteries.

Seldom during the course of an active and varied career had "Colonel" Ethan Allen felt so thoroughly disgusted and baffled.

Goddam the luck! Imagine it. Here he was at the head of nearly two hundred tough fighters lying impotent only a couple of miles short of a critically important objective whose garrison might be reinforced at any moment.

Remaining stiffly polite Allen and Benedict Arnold sat up late discussing details of the attack planned for five of the morning. Both recognized the importance of deciding who should cross over first since the gundelows could not safely transport more than a handful of men.

Typically, Colonel Arnold insisted on crossing side-by-side with Ethan Allen. Among others in the lead boat were John Brown, Nat Beman and Jake Razors since these men knew the fort intimately well. The second bateau would be commanded by Major Seth Warner with Captains Phelps and Mott as seconds-in-command. To guide them there was Indian-like Paul Thebaud and Doctor John Crigo, who'd conducted a deal of business with the fort and knew its layout very well indeed, even in the dark.

Aside from the eighty-three men forming the advance party, men left behind cursed their luck and urged the gundelows' crews to break records in coming back for them. All in all, over two hundred men would have to wait for their chance at the Lobsterbacks.

Fortunately the wind dropped during the night but a light mist lingered over Lake Champlain. Jake said he felt pretty certain it would lift before true dawn broke. Around four in the morning the expedition roused, yawning, coughing and spitting, and the first group of men were marched down to the rickety wharf jutting a short distance into Hand's Cove. Despite nearly complete darkness the first detachment managed their weapons without sound having made sure that, despite yesterday's downpour, lock coverings of oiled leather had kept their priming powder dry. They clambered, damp and smelly, into the bateaux which promptly were shoved off then rowed or poled through rapidly thinning mists by men so experienced with handling these ungainly craft that, inside of an hour, Allen and Arnold's party, causing a minimum of noise, commenced scrambling onto Fort Ticonderoga's sagging and splintery supply dock. Since no sentry had been posted there the co-commanders in undertones ordered both bateaux to lose no time in returning for the balance of the men waiting in Hand's Cove.

The last of the mist had dissipated when Allen, having drawn his sword only because Arnold had drawn his, ordered scouts to trot up a winding path through tangles of underbrush towards bastions looming grim and impressive above. Jake Razors, rifle held at the ready, led them along a rutted track leading up to the fort's supply wicket.

Now that the wind had dropped an unearthly stillness prevailed. Never a rooster crowed or a dog barked. Over the soft lap-lapping of waves the eerie ululating cry of an owl sounded somewhere in the forest behind those massive fortifications which several foreign generals had described as the "Gibraltar of the West."

The Provincials in a loose column fell in behind the two colonels marching shoulder to shoulder. As Commanding Officer Ethan Allen took care always to proceed keeping Benedict Arnold to his left.

The sky by now had paled sufficiently to reveal ramparts looming black and ominous above. The Provincials moved as silently as so many stalking catamounts. Jake Razors guided them past circular stone walls protecting that great well which for over half a century had supplied the garrison with plenty of clear cold water which always could be used since it lay within easy range of the parapets.

Still no challenge came from the battlements or from any point along that same curtain wall General Abercrombie's Black Watch had assaulted so valiantly and disastrously back in 1758.

"Damned if I understand this," Allen muttered. "Is their commander setting a trap?"

"Entirely possible if the British have got wind of our coming," Arnold replied softly. "Pity we're so damn' short of bayonets."

Allen motioned Jake Razor's shadowy figure forward, whispered, "Where now?"

"Cunnel, was I you I'd head straight for that wicket gate they use for fetchin' supplies up from the lake, 'Tain't guarded, at least it weren't last few times I brought in game and such-like."

Jake's prediction proved correct. No one challenged even when the Provincials, after breasting a slight slope, arrived before a low, arched entrance built of brick. Its heavy nail-studded portal stood halfway open.

Allen muttered, "Where does this tunnel end?"

"Near to the front of the main storerooms and from there 'tis but a few steps to the parade ground, the magazine, bake ovens and the west barracks."

"Where are the officers' quarters?" Arnold queried in a stage whisper. "Must capture 'em first thing."

"Along the second floor of the west wall."

Side by side, sword blades dully gleaming, both leaders quickened their pace through the short supply tunnel. Incredibly, not even now did anyone challenge until at long last a sentinel below the north parapet spied a dark column of men spreading over onto the parade ground and yelled, "Halt! Who goes there?"

"You'll damn' soon find out!" someone cried whereupon the soldier shouldered his musket. Providentially, the Redcoat's weapon misfired and long knives threatened instant death should he make a sound.

Once the dazed sentry had been gagged and bound and shoved out of sight beneath a bomb proof or ammunition storage space built beneath the parapet, Allen rasped, "Razors, lead me to the Commanding Officer's quarters. You can come along if you like, Colonel Arnold."

He strode off, his sword's blade dimly gleaming in the increasing light, closely followed by Arnold, who, being shorter-legged, was almost running to keep abreast. Jake and other volunteers impatient for a fight to break out trotted after the co-commanders. Meanwhile Captain Mott led soft-stepping attackers to invade the east barracks in which they discovered the garrison—obviously not reinforced judging by their scant numbers—slumbering peacefully until wakened by the sting of knives, tomahawks and spear blades against their throats. Wisely none of the sleep-dazed men made any effort to raise an alarm and, half-dressed, sullenly clambered off their cots to be lined up on the dimly lit parade ground, or *place d'armes*, as the French originally had called it.

The only activity the invaders encountered came when a soldier guarding a short flight of steps leading up to the officers' quarters in the western barracks bellowed a challenge. Allen and Arnold moved in so quickly that instead of firing his musket the soldier foolishly used his bayonet on an overeager fellow from Shoreham named Amos Callender wounding him in the thigh just an instant before Ethan Allen with a single powerful blow from the flat of his sword beat the sentry to his knees. His musket clattered loudly down the stone steps.

Allen barked, "Which are the Commandant's quarters?"

Dazedly, the Redcoat pointed upwards to the second floor. At once the Green Mountain Boys' leader bounded up the steps two at a time flourishing his sword while Arnold a step or so in his wake did the same. Allen began hammering on the door marked "C.O. Quarters" with the pommel of his sword at the same time bellowing, "Come out, you old rat!" He continued shouting and pounding until a lock clicked and a candle's wavering light revealed the figure of a wigless officer wearing an unbuttoned scarlet jacket over his nightshirt. He was carrying a pair of white breeches in one hand.

Intending that everyone should notice his presence Arnold yelled even louder than Allen, "Give your name and rank!"

The Englishman gaped an instant then fell back at the same time raising a defensive arm. "I am Lieutenant Jocelyn Feltham, second-in-command here," he snapped at the same time eyeing the dull gleam of musket barrels below. "What are you doing—?"

"Damn you, we're taking possession!"

While the Lieutenant struggled into his breeches he demanded, "Why have you attacked us like this?"

Allen, realizing that Lieutenant Feltham was playing for time, shouted to the men on the steps, "Somebody take this fellow below and guard him well. If he causes trouble grant him no quarter!"

At that moment Captain William Delaplace appeared in uniform but also minus breeches. He still was wearing a tasseled nightcap. Holding a sword in one hand, he lifted a lantern with the other. More outraged than frightened he sputtered, "I command here! By whose authority are you villains acting?"

Ethan Allen reputedly then shouted words which still ring in American history: "In the name of the Great Jehovah and the

Continental Congress, I summon you instantly to surrender this fort!"

"But—but, damme, this is outrageous! You've no right—"

"I am an officer fully commissioned by the Colony of Massachusetts. Your sword, sir!" snapped Benedict Arnold. He extended a hand but before his fingers could close over the weapon's guard Ethan Allen snatched it away. For an instant the two glared at each other, then Arnold addressed Captain Delaplace and said in level tones, "You must surrender immediately, sir. Your men already have been overpowered."

It seemed from all directions came Indian warwhoops, scalp yells, eerie screeches and all manner of ear-piercing yowlings were ringing out. Considering their small number the Provincials created quite a racket. A terror-stricken woman screamed, small children squalled and wailed over terrifying noises rising from below.

Acidly Arnold snapped to Allen who was tucking the Englishman's sword under his arm, "I suggest you regain control of your men, Colonel. A counterattack may be made at any moment. Half your following's muskets aren't really fit for use; order such replaced from the garrison's magazine. Bayonets and fresh ammunition must be issued at once."

Little heed was paid to such sensible procedures despite pungent curses from Allen and harsh commands barked by Major Beach and Captains Mott and Phelps and other cool-headed men.

Growing daylight found the raiders, except for a few guarding prisoners, still scattered about Ticonderoga prancing and whooping like lads just released from school but a few did run into the guardhouse and armed themselves with stout "Brown Bessies"— otherwise Tower muskets—bayonets or other equipment likely to prove more useful than the antique oddments they'd fetched along.

About then Jake Razors became aware that since debarking he'd seen neither hide nor hair of the fox-faced boatbuilder called Billy Reynolds so decided on what he'd half-suspected for some time—Billy must be a secret Tory and at this moment might be running or paddling at top speed to alert Redcoat officers at Fort George that Ticonderoga was under attack. Possibly Jake was mistaken, but in any case, Reynolds never again was seen by any of the Green Mountain Boys.

Colonel Arnold managed to collect a handful of former soldiers who more or less unwillingly consented to mount guard over the arsenal, the powder magazine and the guardhouse. Meanwhile the forty-odd enlisted members of the garrison only partially clad were herded into an empty storeroom and locked in cursing Fate and the incompetence of their officers.

Ignoring the shrilling of terrified women Jake and Paul Thebaud gleefully joined other poverty-poor woodsmen in a wild and indiscriminate ransacking of the officers' quarters. Among other plunder Jake selected a bright yellow blouse and a billowing skirt of flaming scarlet silk which ought to set off to advantage Nellie's tawny beauty. Also he grabbed a string of amber beads which, for convenience, he slung about his leathery neck along with a tippet of prime mink skins.

After breaking into the fort's supply room the invaders picked out some of the oddest items; a china dog, a small, gilded French clock, pewter plates and bottles of all sorts—even chamber pots. Some took china plates and tableware, brass candlesticks, bed warming pans, kettles, sheets, towels, fine, soft woolen blankets and armfuls of clothing of all sorts.

Almost as an afterthought the more poorly armed grabbed up English officers' saddle pistols and fusees but only a few bayonets. Jake, however, selected a brand-new one even though he knew it couldn't be affixed to his rifle. Still, it might come in handy if ever ill-fortune forced him to exchange his precious Deacon Bennett for a clumsy, smoothbore Tower musket. Already he'd heard a lot about the deadly effectiveness of bayonets at close quarters; once a muzzle-loader had been fired there was no time to reload; such a weapon could only be useful when clubbed.

Before long a second party of volunteers under command of brawny Major Seth Warner of Connecticut arrived from the Vermont shore and, finding the fort already captured, joyfully joined in an orgy of plundering. Certainly, thought Captain Mott, if only a half-company of British Regulars were to appear at this time—as well they might—the disorganized and often drunken Provincials could have been killed or captured to the last man.

Also, there was an urgent need to dispatch a contingent to seize cannon reported to be rusting amid the charred ruins of a great fort at nearby Crown Point, accidentally burned down last year and then abandoned.

Not until midday did any semblance of order prevail in Fort Ticonderoga largely due to the efforts of coldly furious but ever-efficient Colonel Benedict Arnold and profane commands shouted by a somewhat less exuberant Ethan Allen for, belatedly, the Green Mountain Boys' leader had begun to appreciate a desperate need to re-establish discipline in time to repel possible attack. Surely, the British soon must realize the value of these great guns they'd lost and make vigorous efforts to recapture the same. As a stopgap measure Seth Warner, a serjeant and a detachment of twelve militiamen hurriedly were dispatched to take possession of those imposing ruins up the lake.

Among the victors only Captain Michael Phelps and Major Beach, commanding the Connecticut contingent, which finally had appeared around noon, took time to conduct a hasty survey of the dozens on dozens of dismounted and rust-speckled cannon barrels stacked hit-or-miss, suggestive of pigs sleeping beneath brick arches supporting the fort's sagging gun platforms.

Along with pyramids of cannon balls of varying size Major Beach, who'd had considerable experience with artillery during a brief tour of duty in the British Army, noted the presence of around a dozen massive 22- and 24-pound guns—real siege pieces—also a much more generous supply of lesser cannon ranging in gauge from 1 to 12 pounds—very suitable for field artillery. Also they came across eight heavy brass howitzers and over a dozen ponderous iron mortars.

"By God," Beach whooped. "We've indeed struck it rich!" General Washington and especially portly Colonel Henry Knox, recently placed in temporary command of the Continental Army's train of artillery, certainly would be overjoyed to learn about the capture of so many invaluable cannon.

On the chase, breeches or on top of most tubes had been engraved the Lilies of France or the Castles and Lions of Spain, plus complicated monograms of various English monarchs. Many also recorded the foundry's name.

To the surveyors' surprise they noticed the presence of a few

Dutch and Swedish cannon among these neglected pieces. Alas, cannon balls for such exotic guns most likely would prove in short supply.

Major Beach clapped Phelps on the shoulder. "A truly magnificent capture! Only God knows how desperately our Army needs cannon of all weights—especially siege pieces."

Frowning, Phelps commented, "Ain't you forgetting that well over three hundred miles of wild and thinly settled country separates this place from our forces around Boston? How in God's name is it possible to transport heavy artillery through dense forests, across ravines, steep hills and countless rivers and streams likely infested by British-led savages? So far I ain't noticed so much as a single useful field artillery limber or gun carriage, let alone ammunition or supply wagons."

"Nor have I," admitted Beach, "but I've noticed plenty of roundshot which for use in 8- or 12-pound fieldpieces; along with 3- and 6-pounders. Such would form the backbone for a fine train of field artillery."

On this day of May 10th, 1775, only one fact of major importance remained inescapable to anyone possessing even a bit of foresight. For the first time rebellious Provincials successfully had assumed the offensive. After all, those skirmishes at Lexington and Concord, while unexpectedly successful, had been fought on the defensive.

Once the first flush of victory had faded men in varying degrees of drunkenness commenced to sober up enough to make themselves useful. Even Ethan Allen admitted, although only to himself, that when it came to formal or complicated military matters, Colonel Arnold really was both experienced and tireless in getting things done and in order of importance. In no way did Ethan Allen attempt to hamper his co-commander and on several occasions even soothed heated confrontations when fiercely independent Green Mountain Boys refused to take orders from anyone other than their own elected commander.

Woodsmen, long hunters and trappers like Jake and Thebaud were ordered to range the vicinity for signs of enemy reinforcements. Other pickets, largely townsmen, were posted in a close ring about the fort ready to raise an alarm and stand ready to repel any attempt to recapture the fort be the assailants Redcoats, Tories or Redskins.

Early next morning a swiftly paddled canoe arrived from across Lake Champlain bearing welcome tidings. Better than four hundred Connecticut troops belonging to Colonel Arnold's command at last had arrived at Hand's Cove and were eager to cross as soon as possible.

On hearing this news Captain Edward Mott sought the rifled office of the Post Commissary and grouted about till he came across quill pen and a bottle of ink. Next, he unfolded and smoothed that blank commission issued by the Hartford Committee of Safety and took care to date it the twenty-eighth day of April, 1775; he'd noticed that Benedict Arnold's Massachusetts Provincial Congress commission had been dated on the third of May, so if the question of seniority ever arose, Arnold would be forced to yield precedence. Then, in bold black script Mott wrote "Ethan Allen" and "Colonel" in spaces left blank for a recipient's name and rank.

Now that the fort had been won Mott was damned if he'd stand by and allow his commander who, for want of legal authority, would be forced to truckle before an arrogant, self-important glory-hunter like Benedict Arnold.

When opportunity offered he'd take Ethan aside and advise that if asked why he hadn't previously produced the document the Vermonter was to say he'd intended all along to wait until the Connecticuters arrived and only then explain that, among them, was a dispatch rider bearing his commission who'd been misdirected by some Tory and so had ridden nearly halfway to Rutland before discovering he'd been duped.

Uncomfortable as always amid any large gathering of people, Jake Razors next day asked for and received Colonel Allen's consent that he recross the lake and see about recruiting more Green Mountain Boys. He complied after spending a relaxed two days in Nellie Noisy Bluejay's company. The looted finery suited her to a "T."

PART II
Guns from the Sea

CHAPTER 5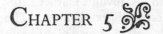

LAST FESTIVITIES

On June 16th, 1775, the weather turned so unseasonably hot, humid and oppressive in Boston that most windows in Major Benjamin Hilton's modest but handsome brick dwelling on Beacon Hill stood opened wide. Through those facing to the north and west Major Hilton and his daughter could obtain a clear view of Copp's Hill, lying lower and closer to the Charles River. Near its base mounds of raw earth, turned up during construction of the so-called "Admiral's Battery," had sketched a series of ugly brown scars along a green pasture where gun emplacements, ordered by Major-General Thomas Gage, had been completed not long ago.

Only some twelve hundred yards of the Charles's slate-gray current separated Boston from the fast-growing but now almost deserted community of Charles Town. Beyond dwellings, warehouses, docks and shipyards on the opposite shore loomed a pair of low and softly rounded hills surrounded by meadows. Having for years been used for pastures the fields yonder were devoid of trees and shrubbery and had been subdivided by many low walls mostly built of small, glacier-smoothed rocks and stones.

Sarah Hilton, acting as hostess due to her invalid mother's further prostration by the heat, explained to Ellen Hunter, "The nearer and lower mound over there is called 'Breed's Hill' and the other one rising farther inland is known as 'Bunker's Hill' though neither is really high enough to be called a hill."

To escape the heat Major Hilton's guests while awaiting summons to partake of "a slight collation" had sought a patch of well-tended lawn edged by flower beds lying back of the house.

Young Lieutenant Gordon Hartley of the Royal Welch Regiment, tall, bony and ruddy of complexion, devoutly wished he dared ease a few buttons on his light-blue waistcoat which in color matched the revers of his scarlet tunic but decided against such an uncouth move. Also present were a pair of youngish Naval officers also suffering under dark-blue jackets of heavy serge, white waistcoats and knee breeches. No. It simply wouldn't do to put on a poor show before representatives of the Senior Service. How greatly Lieutenant Andrew Hunter, Ellen's brother, envied a pair of middle-aged civilian guests who long ago had felt free to undo waistcoats and use lace-edged handkerchiefs to blot faces grown red and shiny with perspiration.

Below, where the Charles narrowed between Boston and Charles Town, four Royal men-of-war lay almost motionless at anchor. Their colors hung limp and lifeless from signal yards just as if they also were suffering from this infernal humid heat. Nevertheless wherries and all sorts of smallboats kept clustering around Rear-Admiral Graves's flagship, H.M.S. *Somerset,* like piglets about a sow. A second-rate ship-of-the-line, the flagship because of her three decks appeared bigger and more impressive than she was. Small by comparison were her consorts H.M.S. *Glasgow* and H.M.S. *Lively,* both trim sloops-of-war mounting 20 guns each. Also close by lay the 18-gun sloop-of-war *Falcon.*

The atmosphere being so sultry and windless familiar sounds such as the creaking of supply-wagon axles, the almost continual roll and rattle of drums and the rhythmic tramping of troops at drill could be heard coming from the direction of the British Army's principal encampment on Boston's Common.

Lieutenant Andrew Hunter, smart in his navy-blue brass-buttoned jacket and white breeches, turned to his sister Ellen who'd brought Betty Oliver, his family's neighbor in Cambridge, over for a brief visit.

Major Hilton's curvaceous golden-blonde daughter agitating a fan inquired brightly, "Please, Andrew, which one is your boat?"

"*Boat*, Ma'am!" Young Hunter flushed. He'd been mighty taken by Sarah Hilton ever since they'd met at a rout some weeks ago. "Oh, I serve in *Lively*—she's the *ship* anchored abreast of the Admiral's Battery. A real beauty, isn't she?"

Sarah clapped hands in gentle enthusiasm. "Oh my, yes! She certainly looks the daintiest of all your boats—ships, I mean. Wish I might watch you conduct a gun drill. Ellen has told me you're very knowledgeable concerning cannons of all sorts."

Ellen Hunter, petite, narrow-chinned and blessed with an abundance of naturally curly reddish-brown hair of practically the same hue as her brother's, turned to Betty Oliver, a girl of about her own age who though round-faced and snub-nosed was none the less a very attractive member of a prominent Tory family living in Cambridge. "Tell me, Betty, was your crossing of Boston Neck impeded in any way? I've heard the garrison is busy throwing up still more defenses there."

"Oh my, yes. The road was dreadfully dusty and crowded by more people and vehicles than I've ever seen it before. You're right. General Gage's troops *are* taking up positions likely to be defended by big guns before long. Surely some important military movements must be afoot."

Ellen Hunter, recalling the British officers present, looked nervously about—lowered her voice. "Don't tell anyone, but Joey, a young cousin of mine, rode in from Blue Hill early this morning and said roads and lanes from the south and west of Cambridge are jam-packed with marching men—independent companies, minutemen and militia of all sorts. Joey said they looked an ill-armed and unsoldierly lot, but that hundreds such are coming in from all over—even from Connecticut and Rhode Island."

She must have spoken louder than she intended for Lieutenant Hartley of the Royal Welch moved nearer to inquire quite casually, "So your cousin claims to have sighted bands of armed Rebels converging on Cambridge?"

Ellen reddened, look aside. "That's what Joey told me. He also noticed that although they marched in disorder those men for the most part looked solemn and purposeful."

Andrew Hunter frowned a little while resetting a once snowy but sweat-sodden neckcloth of fine linen. "Tell me, Ellie, did Joey mention whether our—er, the Rebels were fetching along any artillery?"

"No. He made no mention of seeing any cannons," replied his sister. "He said there were hardly any mounted men among them, either."

Um. So the Rebels *were* short of artillery—which fact greatly interested H.M.S. *Lively*'s Second Lieutenant and Gunnery Officer. Ever since he could remember, artillery of all descriptions had been his ruling passion after, as a callow youth, he'd been permitted to board a first-rate man-of-war lying in Boston for repairs. He'd found indescribably fascinating those sleek and deadly bronze and iron tubes and the power represented by them.

The host beckoned a Negro servant who'd appeared bearing a tray of silver-beaded goblets filled with iced syllabub. "Toby, serve the gentlemen, then fetch lemonade for the ladies."

The bandy-legged Negro dropped his gaze, projected a heavy, purplish lower lip. "Laws, suh, me an' Juno done hunted high an' low a' day fo' lemons, but with de port tight-shut lak it's bin we jest could find none nowheres. De grocers say British commissary officers done bought all whut dey had."

"The Devil you say," grunted Major Hilton, craggy, pinkish-white features hardening. "In that case you'll offer the ladies some of my best and driest sherry."

On the brilliantly sunlit lawn back of the house the groups presented a colorful sight: the three uniformed officers, Major Hilton in bottle-green velvet. Sarah and her female companions wearing full-skirted pink, powder-blue or yellow gowns were hoping perspiration stains wouldn't show though they kept fanning themselves.

Messers Pew and Campbell, garbed in dark-gray and navy-blue coats, afforded a sharp contrast to the officers, especially to Lieutenant Hartley's scarlet-and-white regimentals.

Henry Pew, a cadaverous-faced lawyer, was remarking, "By

the bye, Ben, on my way here I overheard, just as Mistress Hunter's brother reported, rumors of great numbers of Rebels mustering in the vicinity of Cambridge."

Inquired Angus Campbell a formerly prosperous trader with the West Indies, "Why on earth would the Whigs establish headquarters in Cambridge?"

Diffidently, Lieutenant Gregory Lisle of H.M.S. *Glasgow* inquired of Major Hilton, "As a veteran of the Siege of Louisburg what, sir, do you think the Rebels intend?"

Sarah's father replied slowly, "From what I hear fat old General Artemas Ward recently has been appointed the Provincial Commander-in-Chief. Unless he's not become senile I venture he will move to capture those two hills." He nodded in the direction of Charles Town. "From such heights he'd be able to bombard Boston and drive away the men-of-war, but only if he commands some heavy fieldpieces, let alone real siege guns."

Sipping his syllabub then using the back of his hand to wipe away traces of froth Pew commented, "Aye, there's no doubt the Rebel forces are up to something but I don't believe any officer in his right mind would dare to move troops across Charles Town Neck and risk getting 'em cut off."

In silence the Major inclined his neatly wigged white head.

Mister Campbell then commented, "If it's true the Rebels are so short of cannon what good would it do for them to capture Breed's and Bunker's Hills if they lack the means of driving away our men-of-war or bombard Boston?"

Lieutenant Andrew Hunter frowned. "Not much." Once more he carefully considered the Charles Town peninsula tinted blue-bronze by the heat. "Lacking proper artillery only an utter fool would move to occupy those hills."

Commented Lieutenant Hartley slowly twirling a frost-beaded silver goblet, "Even if this armed rabble does succeed in taking yonder hills we'll soon have 'em in the bag, all the same."

Equably his host remarked, "Not soon or easily, young sir. Once they are in position the Provincials won't quit without making a real fight. I know. I served with Massachusetts troops at the Siege of Louisburg back in '45."

"But, sir," Lisle persisted, "all our Regulars have to do is to land on Charles Town Neck and cut off the American Rebels' communications and they'd be forced to surrender or be annihilated."

To the graceful swaying of powder-blue skirts Sarah Hilton approached, tall, golden-blonde and even in Andrew Hunter's opinion handsome rather than beautiful. "Come, come, gentlemen. Haven't you amateur generals dwelt on sober matters long enough? Please join us ladies and let us converse in a happier vein, say about newest dance steps from London, about plays, songs, anything cheerful."

Toby, the Hilton's black, white-haired and enormously self-important butler, had just finished offering the young ladies sherry in long-stemmed glasses luckily imported aboard the last vessel to arrive from abroad before the Boston Port Act had gone into effect and closed the port to commerce, when the front-door bell jangled. Almost at once a maid in a frilly mob cap and apron hurried up to the Major and bobbed a half-curtsy.

"Major, sir, there is a Redcoat soljer at the door; says he's got a urgent message for a Mister Hartley."

"Oh, damn!" snapped the Welch guardee, reluctantly putting down his goblet. "I'm supposed to be off duty today."

Once the scarlet-coated figure and his white-wigged host had disappeared into the house, guests exchanged quizzical glances before making efforts to revive a light and casual conversation.

The Lieutenant reappeared almost immediately, made an awkward leg in Sarah's direction. "I must crave your indulgence, Mistress Hilton." Fixing on her a meaningful look while trying to ignore the fact that his squarish features were bright with increased rivulets of perspiration he explained, "For some reason I've been summoned to Regimental Headquarters. Please believe, Mistress Hilton, I'm infinitely regretful over missing what I know will prove a most delightful repast."

Brightly, Ellen Hunter commented, "How very inconsiderate of your commanding officer but cheer up, Mister Hartley, there are plenty more gay occasions planned for this week. I'll see you're included."

The veteran of the French and Indian Wars added quietly, "Let us pray you're right about that, Ellen, yet at the moment I suffer a curious premonition that this may prove the last joyous occasion most of us shall enjoy for some time." He touched the

Welch guardee's arm, "Young sir, allow me regretfully to see you off."

The supper party proved less astonished when, while they were only halfway through supper, a downy-faced and very young midshipman off H.M.S. *Lively* rang the doorbell to announce that he'd come bearing peremptory orders for Mister Hunter and Mister Lisle to report aboard their respective ships with all speed.

Filled with misgivings as poignant as they were inexplicable, Andrew Hunter murmured to Sarah, "Terribly sorry about this; I'd been planning a serious conversation with you this evening."

Sarah flushed prettily. "I trust we won't have to wait long for such a talk."

From an umbrella rack in the hallway both officers removed handsomely ornamented dress swords. Damnation, thought Hunter casting a distracted look at Sarah Hilton, here's another opportunity to express serious intentions blown to Hell.

Still nervously fanning to hide disappointment the girls watched Hunter and Lisle buckle on their weapons.

"Oh dear, this is awful," Sarah almost wailed. "I'd so been hoping we all were about to enjoy a memorable *soirée*."

Chestnut-haired Ellen Hunter appeared particularly apprehensive when, standing on tiptoes, she pecked her brother's damp brown cheek. In a soft undertone she whispered, "Take care, Andy, run no unnecessary risks. May God bless and protect you."

Once both lieutenants had strode off silver-haired Major Hilton, despite this humid, all-pervading heat ordered his front door locked and barred. Next, he had strong wooden shutters protecting ground-floor windows secured. He made no mention about having recognized the significance of sounds heard increasingly often of late—noises created by angry men in the process of assembling.

Briefly the veteran wondered how well his recent guests might fare on their journey down to the waterfront. Certainly young Hunter and Gregory Lisle, since their tunics were of dark-blue and not too noticeable, were less likely to be harassed than Lieutenant Hartley wearing a scarlet coatee which color to a great majority of Bostonians was as infuriating as the flaunting of a red cloth before an angry bull.

Brow furrowed, the Major returned to his living room, said briskly, "Sarah, pray conduct your lady friends to the withdrawing room; also instruct the maid to make up a bed in the spare room for Mistress Oliver. With things as they are she had better spend the night here rather than risk crossing town to her uncle's residence." He then glanced at Ellen Hunter whose manner now was less ebullient. "Since you've been expected over the week-end your bed is already made up."

Said blonde young Sarah with a feigned brightness—she'd so anticipated a tête-à-tête with Andrew Hunter for whom she felt she was developing a growing degree of attachment, "Very well, Papa, but first I'll look in on Mamma and make sure she's not become unduly alarmed."

Major Hilton walking a bit stiffly because of occasional rheumatics in his joints led Henry Pew and Angus Campbell into his snug library situated to the right of the front door. Most of its wall space from floor to ceiling was lined with books for the most part handsomely bound in calfskin and bearing titles done in gold leaf. He'd been able to make so remarkably fine a collection of the classics largely because, since his retirement from command in the Provincial Militia, he'd owned and still was operating a fashionable bookshop on Cornhill Street in competition with an extremely corpulent but very able and energetic fellow named Henry Knox; an ardent Patriot who, originating in Salem, for a long while had played a prominent part in the activities of the Sons of Liberty.

Precisely, Major Hilton filled three glasses of an especially choice French brandy. "And so, gentlemen, it would appear that another happy occasion has been spoiled, thanks to those purblind idiots in Whitehall. Why in God's name did they ever inflict on us the Coercive Acts—such an unbearable piece of legislation?" Slowly he raised his glass and in metallic tones said, "Nevertheless, gentlemen, here's to His Royal Majesty King George III!"

Angus Campbell puffing shiny, apple-red cheeks cried a trifle loudly, "Aye, the King, God bless him!"

Pale and narrow-faced Henry Pew contented himself by mur-

muring, "Amen to that." Could he safely say less in the home of a man suspected of Tory inclinations because in these uncertain times Benjamin Hilton had continued to entertain British officers?

Of his host Pew demanded, "As an old soldier what is your opinion of our present situation?"

Briefly Major Hilton fingered a box-like jaw. "Well, friend Pew, the Quartering and Quebec Acts were bad enough but, for all I'm a loyal subject of the King, I simply cannot comprehend what has deluded him by allowing his Ministers to order this tyrannical Restraining Act put into effect. Surely, as an overseas trader yourself you can't fail to appreciate what disastrous results this act will have on New England merchants, shipowners, fishermen, even to an unoffending bookseller like myself?"

A swallow-tailed black, grosgrain ribbon securing Henry Pew's queue fluttered to his vigorous nod. "By God, Ben, you are right entirely. Even I, a Loyalist to my finger's tips, question the Ministry's legal right, on top of all the other restrictions, to forbid New Englanders the right to fish on the Grand Banks."

Mister Campbell blinked over his brandy glass. "Unless General Gage and his advisers turn a blind eye many more Colonials will face ruin and will fight before they'll allow themselves to be made paupers."

Stated the host while closely observing his guests, "What really concerns me is that Generals Gage, Clinton, Howe, Burgoyne and other senior officers persist in so contemptuously underestimating the endurances and determination of Provincial troops."

He took a long sip from his goblet and again a frown creased his usually high and shiny forehead. "Wouldn't you think following that painful drubbing the Regulars suffered during their fruitless expedition against Lexington and Concord, the High Commanders would have reassessed opinions on that score? For all it's been a long time since I served at Louisburg. I still recall how thoroughly we raw-necked New Englanders defeated the French King's regulars and Swiss mercenaries." His glance included both guests. "I assume you both are aware that that powerful fortress was taken by us Provincials without the aid of *any* British troops whatsoever! On the other hand, the Royal Navy gave us a deal of invaluable support, possibly made our victory complete."

Campbell grunted, clicked badly fitting false teeth. "Nevertheless, British Regulars have proved themselves invincible all over the world and regularly have licked the best of the French King's white-coated frog-eaters. Benjamin, I'll wager you three-to-one those armed mobs swarming up-river will run like frightened rabbits the moment they sight the King's troops drawn up in line of battle. Any takers?"

Henry Pew hesitated, scratched a long, bluish and not particularly well-shaven jaw. "No. You may very well be right, Angus, since, as I understand it, the Rebels possess no field artillery worthy of mention whereas on the Charles lie four Royal men-of-war which alone mount better than 120 well-manned cannon or so young Mister Hunter informed me recently." The lawyer elevated shaggy brows. "How long do you think those rag-tag and bobtail Provincials will tolerate such overpowering broadsides?"

With absurd precision Major Hilton refilled the brandy glasses. "You may be right, friend Pew, since, as any thoughtful man who has campaigned in America will tell you, our—er—the Provincial way of fighting isn't intended to match European tactics. They'll follow methods they've successfully used against Indians since time out of mind.

"In other words General Gage and his staff envisage a proper battle fought in the European style where the opposing armies are maneuvered till they stand facing one another drawn up in orderly ranks and will advance under fixed bayonets in ruler-straight lines. At the right moment the infantry will halt and point, not sight, their muskets in the general direction of the enemy and hope to mow them down, always provided the other side hasn't fired first. For example, do either of you know what actually happened during the famous Battle of Fontenoy?"

Both guests shook their heads.

"Well, my friends, once the French and our troops got within musket shot of each other the English General commanding lifted his hat, bowed politely then shouted, 'Gentlemen of France, do us the honor of firing first'—whereupon the French commander likewise doffed off his hat and making a leg, replied gallantly, 'No, gentlemen of England—to you I accord that privilegel' So we accepted their courtesy, fired first then charged with the bayonet and won a great victory."

Major Hilton sipped before continuing. "Can you imagine Colonial troops putting up with such showy nonsense? Hell, they'd have been crouched behind every tree, stump or stone in sight and would have begun picking out targets before you could snap your fingers."

CHAPTER 6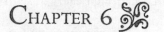

EMBARKATIONS

THAT UNREST IN Boston hourly was growing more intense became evident even before Lieutenants Hunter and Lisle turned into Salem Street on their way down to the waterfront in general and Hancock's Wharf in particular. In almost every alley and narrow street it seemed torches and lanterns danced like demented fireflies about groups of scarlet-clad officers who, unfamiliar with their route, were asking for directions.

When a light infantry captain of the 38th, yellow lapels gleaming, inquired the shortest way to the Long Wharf, Andrew Hunter heard civilians make farting noises. One bowed elaborately. "Why, sir, take the first turn to your right and keep straight on till yer hat floats!"

"Hell, no," yelled another gaunt fellow wearing a drover's smock, "he's funning you! Turn left."

A third ragged individual moved aside only reluctantly, rasping, "If I knew the straightest way to Hell I'd tell you damn' Bloodybacks how to get there, quick as lightning."

Because, as Major Hilton had foreseen, the two Naval lieutenants, wearing dark-blue, remained relatively inconspicuous they made fairly rapid progress while red-coated Army officers now and then were forced to draw and brandish swords and dodge missiles as best they might.

Cobblestones and rotten fruit were flung out of ill-smelling darkness at a platoon from the 10th of Line led by a broad-shouldered lieutenant who nevertheless continued to hold his sword upright and march stiff and straight as though on parade.

From an upstairs window a raddled beldame emptied a slop jar full of excrement on the tall Grenadiers, shrieking, "There's for ye bloody-backed bastards who starve us and our children and ruin our trade!" A cursing Grenadier shouldered his musket and took aim but before he could fire the Lieutenant's blade knocked up his barrel. "None of that! Save your bullets for Rebels under arms. Now close ranks and keep step, damn you, remember we belong to the 10th!"

On noticing two Naval officers sheltering in a doorway he shouted over a rising tumult, "Best fall in with us, gentlemen, else you'll not get far!"

Several times rioters attempted, albeit half-heartedly, to halt the brief column striding steadily on over greasy and manure-strewn cobbles; liberal use of brass-shod musket butts and hard-swung shafts of noncommissioned officers' halberts proved effective. When on Anne Street the 10th's Grenadiers encountered a detachment from the King's Own they joined forces, sent rioters slinking away. Presently other parties of scarlet-clad troops appeared marching steadily down King Street towards the Long Wharf lying at its end.

The 10th's Lieutenant calmly wiping filth from his uniform informed Andrew Hunter, "Now, sir, if like the rest of you Navy people, you are headed for Hancock's Wharf, keep straight on down Fish Street yonder; can't miss it."

"Thank you very much, sir. We'll do that," Hunter said attempting to appear as unshaken as this impressive Army officer. "Hope tomorrow our broadsides will repay this kindness."

The Lieutenant laughed, "Well said, sir. We're counting on your guns to spare us a deal of trouble."

Lisle asked, "How so, sir?"

"Well, we expect that, following our first broadside, those rebellious swine reported to be swarming across Charles Town

Neck will scoot for home and mother." Gradually he returned his sword to its scabbard, "Never yet have heard of an undisciplined mob standing up to a few stout broadsides."

Panted Lisle on sighting clusters of lights weaving on and about Hancock's Wharf, "Well, Andrew, how greatly do you now esteem the chances of your fellow Colonials?"

"A mob, my dear Gregory, is a mob wherever found. They're like a dangerous viper operating without sense or direction." For the hundredth time Andrew wondered why, at the age of fourteen, he'd arrived at an unshakable determination to serve in the Royal Navy despite parental objections. Mechanically he straightened his tricorn, a new one, trimmed in gold lace which had cost him near three months' pay.

Why was it that, right from the start, everyone from the aloof and God-like Captain commanding H.M.S. *Superb*, his first ship, down to the most impudent Cockney powder monkey none made any effort to conceal his contempt for any and all Colonials, especially those wearing His Britannic Majesty's uniform by choice? To be sure, he'd whole-heartedly joined his shipmates in expressing outrage over the so-called "Boston Massacre" although later on he'd discovered this hadn't been a massacre at all; only an attempt by a patrol of the King's troops to protect themselves against a dangerous mob.

Also, he'd openly expressed outrage over American malcontents' burning of H.M.S. *Gaspé* back in '72 and as sincerely had deplored the so-called "Boston Tea Party" raid made in December of the following year.

Only reluctantly did Timothy Hunter's son admit the existence of an invisible barrier rising between himself and the rest of H.M.S. *Lively*'s officers. All the same he got along all right with American-born British subjects impressed from Colonial vessels—despite laws granting them exemption.

Of H.M.S. *Lively*'s complement of 181 men and boys over a dozen seamen bore bitter but well-concealed hatred for the Royal Navy and all its works.

Forcing their way towards the end of Hancock's Wharf, Hunter and his companion continually recognized and were greeted by officers and shore parties returning to the flagship, H.M.S. *Somerset*, and to the sloop *Glasgow*—a sixth rate which, like the *Lively*, mounted 20 carriage guns. Also present were a pair of officers off the sloop-of-war H.M.S. *Falcon*, 18 guns, just returned from patrol duty to prevent Provincial craft of any description from entering or leaving rebellious Boston, so long the principal breeding ground for Colonial unrest.

In all probability the *Falcon* had been recalled because of the Army's humiliating defeat at Lexington and Concord. Since that nineteenth of April the Boston populace had grown so openly truculent British soldiers and seamen on shore leave, no matter how tough, thought twice before venturing about the port after dark unless in gangs of not less than four or five.

Every step Andrew took now further served to confuse his muddled sense of values—not that he entertained any intention of not respecting his oath to the Crown solemnly taken some twelve years ago. Gloomily, he had to admit to himself that a major attack upon the Rebels nearby was in the making. Why else would columns of Regulars in full marching order be converging on the Long Wharf? Once these troops halted even for a short interval they would ground ponderous muskets then ease heavy knapsacks onto cobbles and mop streaming faces.

Ships' smallboats were waiting to receive noisy and sometimes staggering commissioned and petty officers. No ordinary ratings were to be seen, Admiral Graves having ordered that none such were to be granted shore leave.

Already battle lanterns were glowing aboard all four men-of-war. A tall officer from the *Somerset* was especially hot and exasperated. "Damn the bloody luck!" he growled. "Wouldn't this have to happen? Just when I'd started to make a real killing at pharo, our game was forced to break up." Angrily, he gestured in the direction of Charles Town. "What in Hell's all this pother about? Hardly a light's showing over there."

Someone remarked, "Haven't you noticed? Except for a few farmers, Charles Town has been nigh deserted for over two days."

"Such being the case," Andrew Hunter hazarded, "perhaps we're being recalled to attack elsewhere."

"Aye, that might be the answer," agreed an officer off the *Falcon*. "Heard tell serious trouble's been brewing in Marblehead and Salem."

Said the coxswain of the *Lively's* jolly boat knuckling his hat's brim, "Glad ye're safe here, sir. Now by your leave we kin shove off."

H.M.S. *Lively* being only a sloop-of-war, just a handful of men appeared for transportation, so her boat was among one of the first to push off from Hancock's Wharf. Andrew Hunter, awkwardly managing his sword, had dropped onto its stern sheets alongside Second Lieutenant Dubose, commanding this little man-of-war's handful of Marines. He still was cursing Boston and every Rebel in it. His Marine's scarlet jacket showed a torn sleeve and his single epaulette of silver lace was dangling askew. Bareheaded and still breathing hard Dubose dabbed a shallow cut across his chin.

"By God, come tomorrow, damned if we don't make these Provincial swine pay through bloody noses! B'God, you Navy fellows don't know how lucky you are."

"'Lucky'?"

"Yes. Damn' Colonists seldom bother anyone who ain't wearing scarlet." He flicked drops of blood from his neckcloth. "Thought I was done for when what must ha' been a gang of Tory sympathizers drove off my attackers."

Hunter, body yielding to the rhythmic beat of the jolly boat's oars, made out other small craft pulling towards the Charles River's mouth. Turning to the Marine he said, "Can't understand why we've been recalled so suddenly; see no signs of activity along the far shore."

"Nor can I," growled Dubose. "Wish to God these goddam Rebels had armed ships we could engage."

Andrew Hunter jerked a nod. "Aye. Perhaps we could put down this rebellion much quicker. On the other hand maybe it's just as well they've no navy. All along these shores live plenty of tough and capable seafarers who know this coast like their own front yards, even if most of 'em can't tell one end of a cannon from the other."

It came as something of a surprise that while the jolly boat was nearing H.M.S. *Lively's* gangway a dispatch boat was in the act of shoving off. It must have fetched not too reassuring intelligence for, by the time Andrew Hunter having mounted the ladder and saluted quarterdeck, it was to find short, choleric and slightly bowlegged Captain Hugh Purcell and his gaunt First Lieutenant Saxeby, looking outraged.

"Damn and double damn those lop-eared jackasses at Army Headquarters!" The Captain broke off vituperations only long enough indifferently to acknowledge his British-American subordinate's salute. "After calling for 'general quarters' General Gage now sends orders for the squadron not to clear for action after all. Mr. Hunter, you will order the guns run in and battle lanterns extinguished. However," he added crisply, "you will ensure complete readiness to open fire at a moment's notice. All gun crews are to sleep beside their pieces."

Apparently similar orders had been received aboard other units of the squadron but not until eight bells of the night watch had sounded did a noticeable measure of quiet spread over the Charles River's smooth and star-speckled black surface, but it was only after church bells over in Boston had commenced to dispute the exact moment of midnight that Andrew, weary and drenched with sweat, was able to seek his hammock slung by a servant in the officers' wardroom; on a ship of only 600 tons burthen only her captain and his senior lieutenant might enjoy private cabins.

Fingers laced beneath head, Andrew absently listened to the dull, measured tread of Marines on duty outside the Captain's cabin and before the power magazine's entrance.

What a confounded pity he'd been denied opportunity to converse even briefly with Sarah Hilton, or with Sister Ellen concerning family affairs. The Good Lord alone knew how badly he needed to be brought up to date concerning events in Cambridge, especially along what had become known as "Tory Row" where dwelt or had dwelt such outstanding Royalists as the Brattles, the Vassalls, the Sewalls, the Ruggleses and, more especially, the well-hated Thomas Olivers.

Very clearly he could visualize his father's home, a modest but well-proportioned red-brick dwelling completed only twelve years ago at the foot of Spring Street and near enough the Charles to permit ready accessibility to a private dock and a small warehouse.

How agonizing at a time like this to remain ignorant of how far Pa's political sentiments extended and in which direction, for all his business had been well-nigh ruined through passage of the Boston Port Act and subsequent Coercive Acts. Captain Timothy Hunter barely in time had managed to switch from a thriving overseas trade with European countries to commerce with the British West Indies and so avoid bankruptcy which had ruined many a good merchant and shipowner.

When H.M.S. *Lively* first had dropped anchor off Charles Town he had, as soon as possible, hired a skiff to sail him up-river to Cambridge only to learn that Father was away on a cruise down to Barbados, Antigua and other Sugar Islands.

While underway he'd listened to the garrulous skiff owner's complaints about so-called Intolerable Acts for, since the famous "Tea Party" of 1773, Courts, Customs officers and other Royal port authorities, following a long period of neglect, had taken to enforcing laws with ever-increasing severity.

The waterman, spraying tobacco spittle from between gapped yellow teeth, while shoving over his tiller to commence a new tack, rasped, "When the goddam Lobsterbacks closed the port to overseas trade save with Britain we got hoppin' mad, 'specially since now, more than ever, they're enforcin' that damn' Quartering Act. Heard about it?"

"Well, not exactly. What does it mean?"

"Well, sir, it allows the King's officers to quarter troops in *occupied* dwellin's 'stead of only empty ones like before, and on top of that now those great fools over in London have passed another law they called the 'New England Restrainin' Act' which prohibits us Colonials from fishin' the Grand Banks after mid-July! Why, owners of even little coastin' vessels will hev to apply for a permit to clear Boston no matter for what reason."

Viciously, the man again spat over the rail. "'Tis downright outrageous; free-born men like us just won't abide such tyranny. Tell me how you feel about that, young sir." He hesitated. "For all your Navy uniform you don't speak or act like a real Lobster-back."

"Small wonder," Andrew admitted. "I was born over in Dorchester before my father moved to Cambridge a good while ago."

To forestall further conversation on the subject Andrew pointedly directed his attention to the Charles's northern bank, fell to

62

wondering why, apparently, neither the Rebels nor the British had thrown up earthworks. With Father absent and because he was wearing the Royal Navy's uniform he hadn't learned anything of importance.

Shortly before dawn Lieutenant Andrew Hunter, R.N., eased out of his hammock, sought the sloop's dew-drenched deck and felt relieved to note that the ship's state of readiness was normal save for extra rows of shells, carcases and roundshot along with chests of powder charges positioned in exactly the right places and gun crews sprawled like dead men among gun carriages.

To reassure himself he conducted an extra-thorough inspection of the sloop's sixteen 12-pound short cannon and her four long 18-pounders, found them ready for immediate action. Small leaden aprons protecting the gun's touchhole from dampness all were in place and could be detached in a twinkle. Tompions, those ornamented stoppers which kept water out of gun barrels when a ship was at sea, had been neatly stacked in their slots. Tubs filled with sand or water stood between each piece ready to receive linstocks and glowing slow matches.

The night was so sultry that lacking even a trace of wind this hot and humid darkness seemed smothering.

Anxiety gnawed at Andrew Hunter's peace of mind. Having so recently been in company of Sarah Hilton, his ever-vivacious sister Ellen and such a red-hot Tory as Betty Oliver brought realization that should this confrontation end in battle it would become his duty to order the *Lively*'s batteries to fire on, and possibly kill, persons he'd grown up among. Still, there was no point in brooding along such a possibility. Hadn't he solemnly sworn to support the Crown? The Hunter family had prospered for generations possibly because, among their tenets, they weren't given to going back on a solemn pledge freely undertaken.

Successively he roused gun captains and with them checked various loading equipment, ladles, sponges, rammers, wad hooks, fork levers and the like.

Once the *Lively*'s Gunnery Officer had crossed the dew-sprinkled deck he and Lieutenant Dubose, commanding the Marines, sought the starboard rail.

"I say, Hunter, damn bad luck having your shore leave cut so short."

"It was. Everything in order with your command?"

"Aye. Just now I've doubled the guard over the magazine and made sure plenty of cartridges and shot are handy for quick passing." Lieutenant Dubose hesitated. "I've been wondering how American-born Englishmen in our crews will act if and when they're ordered to open fire on their own people."

"Come what may," Andrew said a shade too promptly, "I expect they will carry out their duties."

Presently the Marine cupped a hand over his ear, "Tell me, Hunter, do I suffer delusions or don't I hear noises like those made by a lot of men using axes, picks and spades somewhere back of Charles Town?"

Hunter listened hard at the same time studying the shadowy outlines of that village. "Believe you're right but since no lights are showing yonder whatever the Rebels are up to it can't amount to much, so we'll not make a report. Captain Purcell would raise hob were we to raise a false alarm."

The tide was changing so H.M.S. *Lively,* lying approximately halfway between Boston and apparently lifeless Charles Town, swung gradually about till her bowsprit pointed northward. Riding lights on the *Somerset* and the *Glasgow* lying farther up-river off Lynes Point likewise were shifting.

Automatically, Hunter estimated the range to the river's north bank as about five hundred yards, therefore the squadron's broadsides could be aimed point-blank at Charles Town. Not many volleys would be required to frighten off Rebels lurking in the vicinity, provided this was where Provincials were at work.

In silence Andrew Hunter prayed that lookouts on the other men-of-war would attach little or no significance to muffled trampling of many feet and the sounds of activity somewhere on Breed's Hill. On the Boston shore, however, plenty of lights were glowing in or about the Admiral's Battery at the foot of Copp's Hill.

Presently Lieutenant Saxeby, craggy features waxen and severe by starlight, descended from the quarterdeck and with uncommon condescension remarked, "Surely our generals are unwise to keep our ships out in midstream like this. We could be of far greater use closer to Charles Town Neck." He peered intently at Hunter. "As a native of these parts, are you in agreement?"

"Sir, I know nothing about strategy," Andrew replied stiffly, "or anything beyond the proper service of carriage guns."

A grating laugh escaped Saxeby. "You have rather neatly avoided answering my query. All the same, if the Rebels intend to attack they probably will advance over Boston Neck then establish positions on Dorchester Heights. I have been informed on good authority General Gage is preparing a hot reception for rebellious rabbles."

Andrew drew breath to mention Lexington and Concord but kept quiet.

Chapter 7 🎗

LONG WHARF

AFTER FINDING HIS WAY to the Long Wharf assembly point Lieutenant Gordon Hartley discovered that a good many of the Royal Welch Fusiliers' rank and file already had arrived and were forming into platoons and companies. As second-in-command of the Fusiliers' Light Infantry Company, Hartley felt pleased so many of his men, despite heat, gloom and confusion, promptly had obeyed the summons of drums beating "Assembly." Directed by foul-mouthed N.C.O.'s these were formed into a column of three abreast even while infantrymen belonging to other regiments still were yelling profanities and trying to locate their units.

On Hartley's approach Corporal Edward Barton smartly presented arms. Like the rest of the men he was sweat-soaked and red-faced through carrying the weight of two day's rations plus a fifty-pound pack and a Tower musket weighing twelve pounds, a slung bayonet and three dozen cartridges in a stout wood and leather cartouche box. To Barton as to many others of the Royal Welch's Light Company it came as a relief that, at long last, action of some sort impended, ending the dreary monotony of occupying a hostile town in which civilians either looked aside or sometimes spat in the direction of any red-coated soldier.

Also there was much eagerness to avenge casualties suffered during that tortured, humiliating retreat from Concord and Lexington.

Imagine His Majesty's Regular troops falling back in good order, though continually punished by accurate sniping fire delivered by farmers, country louts and mechanics, cowardly wretches who'd not felt in the least ashamed to scoot about and shoot from behind trees and stone walls instead of standing in ranks like soldiers.

After quitting Major Hilton's *soirée* Hartley had sought his quarters there quickly to exchange his best tunic for a well-worn but clean coatee and had substituted his pretty dress sword for a brass-hilted hanger which he slung to a baldric of white duck slanting across his chest. Next he thrust a brace of hand pistols into his belt then happily exchanged his new tricorn for a Light Infantry cap ornamented in front by a large and shiny brass plate bearing the Royal Welch Fusiliers' insignia. Thank God he wasn't forced to don one of those heavy bearskin-covered and mitre-shaped shakos worn by the Welch Regiment's Grenadier and battalion companies of the line.

Presently stalwart and usually taciturn Captain Farnsworth appeared stating that the Regiment shortly would proceed to the Long Wharf and there await embarkation. Soon afterwards a glittering staff officer clattered up on a prancing mount and, bending low in his saddle, called, "Form column behind the 18th. Keep closed up. Follow their line of march and make as little noise as possible."

In an undertone Corporal Edward Barton, a short, wiry and sharp-faced product of London's East End, muttered to a fellow Cockney, "Gorblimey if it don't look like we're really about to 'ave a go at them bleedin' blighters. Only 'ope them crotch-blistered farmers will stand and put up some sort of a fight afore takin' to their 'eels!"

Dawn remained only a pink presentiment in the sky when the sultry gloom was pierced by the deep-throated *boom-m!* of a heavy cannon fired in the general vicinity of Charles Town. Then more and more Naval guns roared, first on the *Lively* then on the

Somerset and on the *Falcon;* finally the *Glasgow* lying off Lynes Point to the westward of Charles Town joined in the bombardment.

Snapped Captain Farnsworth, "I say, Hartley, what in Hades can the Navy be shooting at?"

"No idea, sir, unless Rebel troops are moving to occupy the heights behind Charles Town."

CHAPTER 8 ❧

"CONTEMPTIBLE LITTLE EARTHWORKS"

As THE SKY brightened watchers in Boston, enjoying observation points of vantage, gradually became aware that, during hours of darkness, an earthwork redoubt appeared to have sprouted, mushroom-like, from the earth. Most British officers were utterly dumbfounded that such so extensive a fortification could have been thrown up so quickly but a few among them who'd served in the American Colonies for any length of time weren't overly astonished.

A major who had fought under General Jeffrey Amherst at Ticonderoga added, "There's hardly a man over yonder who ain't extra-handy with a spade, pick or mattock. Next to axes, such are the principal tools of rural colonists who form a vast majority of the population here in America."

Laughed a spruce young captain, "Yes, sir, they've done something amazing but still it won't take us long to reduce such contemptible little earthworks."

Ears ringing from the first of many broadsides fired by his battery Lieutenant Andrew Hunter clapped a telescope to a clear bright-blue eye and became able to discern that the summit of

Breed's Hill was swarming with dark groups of hurrying men. Um. So the Colonials *had* beaten slothful Major-General Gage in fortifying those two tall hills rising behind Charles Town from which heights even heavy field artillery easily could range not only most of Boston but also tactically important anchorages.

As visibility increased curses broke out aboard the men-of-war once officers and gun captains became aware that broadsides instead of hitting the enemy only were raising brief and harmless geysers of soil on broad and bright-green hayfields sloping gently upwards to those incredible earthworks on the summit of Breed's Hill.

Hunter had been among the first to realize that, firing at point-blank range, his guns couldn't possibly reach the redoubt since the dimensions of gunports on this and many other British-built men-of-war prevented cannon from being sufficiently elevated to cause damage. Furthermore Lieutenant Hunter somehow had neglected to order crews manning the *Lively*'s starboard broadside of 12-pound carriage guns to remove the last quoins—heavy wooden wedges driven beneath a cannon's breech to elevate its tube. Accordingly shot from his battery, as well as from the other warships, could range barely a third of the way to the top of that insignificant hill destined before long to be remembered in American history.

First Lieutenant Saxeby, eyes red and streaming, kept coughing violently amid swirling gray-white fumes of burnt powder. In this windless atmosphere thick layers of smoke were lingering over the ships like a smothering, acrid blanket. Nevertheless, Saxeby noticed a few quoins still in place, rasped, "Goddammit, Hunter. Didn't you hear the order for maximum elevation?"

"No, sir," the New Englander replied and hastily ordered all wooden wedges knocked out. "Sir, I can't range the fort up there till the ship backs off some distance and allows our shot a chance to rise."

"Maybe so," Saxeby growled. "Why didn't you report this to the quarterdeck long ago? See to it you make no more mistakes. I intend keeping an eye on you."

Around eight in the morning even the most optimistic of Navy officers perceived the uselessness of continuing an obviously ineffective bombardment so rejoiced when the flagship hoisted the "cease-fire" signal, barely readable because in this still atmosphere flags hung so limp as to be nearly unreadable. The ensuing silence proved almost deafening after all those thunderous broadsides.

A long wait on the wharf following hurried marching through dark streets, thought Lieutenant Gordon Hartley along with plenty of others, was entirely typical of military procedure. Once again the age-old story "hurry up then wait," "hurry up then wait." Here it was nearly noon and men had been standing on the Long Wharf under a broiling sun still awaiting orders to board barges, wherries and smallboats sent in from the squadron. Thirsty men cursed, incontinent fellows relieved themselves off the wharf sometimes into boats waiting to transport them and evoked sulphurous curses.

Everyone grew increasingly exasperated with Major-General William Howe, who had been appointed to command this expedition, down to insignificant drummer boys, of which there were a surprising number, because at this period, orders in battle were transmitted through a variety of drumbeats rather than by trumpet blasts.

Finally an explanation arrived; no boats were to be loaded and shoved off till flood-tide had set in most landing places fringing Morton's Point were muddy and shelved only gradually towards deep water. Perspiring staff officers estimated probably it would be well after one o'clock before there'd be sufficient water to permit scarlet-clad troops to land on the Charles Town side.

When, at long last, the order to embark did arrive men checked their equipment then did up buttons on scarlet uniforms already dark with sweat before slinging knapsacks. Reluctantly they then donned hot and heavy headgear before scrambling awkwardly down into designated small craft.

"Cor," panted Corporal Barton, "looks like at last we're off on a bleedin' pleasure jaunt. Wish t'God this was the good old Thames 'stead of a damn' murky American river."

Lieutenant Hartley, fingering his hanger's grip, heard a serjeant pant, "God above! Satan himself must be blowing to heat air like this!"

Forming long and roughly parallel lines, boats in increasing numbers commenced to pull away from the Long Wharf. Hartley especially felt sorry for a whaleboat load of Grenadiers belonging to the 38th Line Regiment. While en route those big burly fellows seized the opportunity of casting open heavy woolen tunics and of removing towering, mitre-shaped bearskin headgear. Scarlet-faced, they began easing off knapsacks. All the same these Grenadiers started cursing when they realized that on Morton's Point, their destination, there was no visible sign of enemy troops.

Hell, this business wasn't going to prove more serious than a picnic on grassy green slopes sprinkled with daisies, buttercups and other wild flowers. Most felt confident that once they landed and formed ranks the armed rabble defending that crude earthen redoubt on the hilltop would pull foot before they could be brought to action.

Slowly, dozens upon dozens of boats converged on muddy beaches fringing Morton's Point but never a one was diverted to pull up the Mystic's estuary in the direction of Charles Town. This came as a vast relief to General Artemas Ward who, despite a truly magnificent belly and the fact that he was now in his late fifties, had rendered such fine services during the last of the so-called French and Indian Wars that recently he'd been appointed Acting Commander-in-Chief of the combined Provincial Forces now that small units from Connecticut, New Hampshire and Rhode Island came straggling into the vicinity of Cambridge. Serving under Ward were a few other veterans such as Seth Pomeroy, Israel Putnam, William Heath and Colonel John Stark. The last was in command of New Hampshire contingents manning hastily contrived breastworks of stone and hay rising in irregular directions from the Mystic's beach up the redoubt itself.

To troops aboard landing craft the Charles Town shore now appeared as a narrowing strip of mud flats, then clumps of rusty-green sedge and beyond these open fields of tall green hay grass crisscrossed by low stone fences to form a series of small pastures.

The red-coated regiments successively splashed ashore then with professional speed formed ranks in order of battle. As soon as a boat became emptied, sweating oarsmen started pulling back to the Long Wharf for another load.

After a while, to the troops' no great disappointment, they were ordered to slip off packs, seat themselves on sweet-smelling hay grass and drink from already nearly emptied canteens. A few consumed rations pulled from pipe-clayed haversacks slung to overburdened shoulders.

Remarked young Hartley, resettling the crescent-shaped silver gorget covering his throat, a purely symbolic reminder of a knight's armor, "Serjeant, instruct the men not to use their water so fast; might need it urgently later on." Of course Hartley couldn't possibly foresee how he soon would be right.

Soon it became evident that Major-General Sir William Howe, in over-all command of this attack, had no intention of assaulting that "insignificant little earthwork redoubt" until all his forces had come ashore. From a hillock he and his staff, all a-glitter with gold lace, watched companies from the 10th of the Line scramble ashore, well-polished musket barrels flashing under the torrid sun. They showed orange-yellow facings on their tunics. It was easy to mistake them for men of the 38th since they also wore yellow, but of a lighter hue. The Welch Fusiliers had dark-blue revers while the King's Own showed Lincoln green and the 18th of the Line claret-red.

A battalion of Royal Marines from the squadron at the same time were wading ashore at the extreme left of the British line close by still-quiescent Charles Town; short scarlet coatees, white lapels, black gaiters and low caps rendered them readily identifiable.

Continual disembarkations created a colorful, briefly disorderly scene when infantrymen, jostling and cursing, hurried to fall in with their units. White-wigged officers' swords flashed bravely and serjeants liberally employed spontoons or halbert-like staffs to drive laggards into ranks.

Out in front of those gradually extending lines of scarlet, white crossbelts and bright buttons cocky drummer boys swinging brass-mounted sticks beat "Assembly," sweated as hard as their elders.

Corporal Barton sitting on the hay grass beside a particular friend, long-jawed Serjeant Fletcher, remarked while further unbuttoning his tunic and mopping a low, raw-beef-colored forehead, "Now that we're 'ere, mate, wot in 'ell are we sittin' on our arses for? All we're doin' is to let those perishin' farmers up there finish wot ever mischief they're up to."

Using a grimy forefingernail, the serjeant dislodged a chunk of bully beef from between horse-like teeth. "Aw, let them haymakers enjoy things a while longer, 'tis only the rest o' their lives they're enjoyin' up there. Besides, I can do wit' a breather—here I am, fair tuckered even before we set to work."

By two o'clock some two thousand of His Britannic Majesty's Regular Establishment had landed on Morton's Point.

Conscious of Lieutenant-Colonel Gatsby's steady all-seeing gaze, tall and lanky young Lieutenant Hartley and other junior officers of the Welch Fusiliers' Light Company strode back and forth dressing ranks into flawless alignment, making sure that enormous knapsacks were slung in the prescribed position and, more important, that all bayonets were loose in their scabbards and ready to be locked on. Now and then a man was reprimanded for an unsecured button or that his hat wasn't set squarely on his head.

Whenever opportunity offered, Gordon Hartley squinted up at those raw earthworks on the summit of Breed's Hill not three hundred yards distant. He noticed figures in a variety of drab civilian garments moving about like ants scurrying from a disturbed hill. Also, he counted five or six revetted embrasures built to accommodate field artillery but, as far as he could see, few of these appeared to be occupied, for which he thanked God; nothing else could mangle troops charging in close-packed ranks like a few well-aimed discharges of grape or canister shot.

For the first time he commenced to wonder what it would feel like to get hit. Of course *he* wasn't about to be wounded—just others. He didn't realize that nearly every soldier was thinking exactly the same.

At long last drums beat a signal to fix bayonets and prepare for assault. Not in the least concerned over the quality of the foe they were about to attack the Regulars formed in ranks three deep as precisely as they'd done countless times on parade abroad and at home.

The Fusiliers' commanding officer, portly but utterly fearless

Lieutenant-Colonel George Gatsby, complained to his second-in-command, "How damn' inconsiderate these Yankee yokels are to invite us out into such heat; wouldn't you prefer to be in the cool taproom of some good tavern? Eh, what?"

Dexter, a bandy-legged officer showing a bluish scar across a shiny, beet-red cheek, grated a mirthless laugh, "Don't mention it, sir. I'm fair stifling."

Only Captain Peter Angevine, senior officer of the Royal Welchs' Light Company, looked about uneasily.

"I say, Peterson," he commented to a subaltern, "at least the hayshakers have got somebody up there who's got a grain of tactical sense. See what the Rebels are up to?"

Advancing from the direction of Bunker's Hill had appeared a sizable body of un-uniformed men in deplorable array who began trotting, weapons held any which way, towards the Mystic's bank to reinforce men already positioned behind a series of rail, stone and hay-covered breastworks. These defenses extended from the redoubt all the way down to the Mystic's high-water mark and could prevent the redoubt from being outflanked from the left. Long since the men-of-war had quit firing having discovered that neither their broadside guns nor even heavier pieces could range the redoubt. With the exception of apparently deserted Charles Town there was nothing else to shoot at.

From assault lines formed on Morton's Point brief cheers arose when gold-laced senior line officers marched stiffly out to take position before their troops. Swords glimmering silver-bright, looked deceptively cool under the pitiless sun. Drummer boys ran to fall in on either flank of their unit. Jauntily, the latter flourished brass-mounted sticks over varicolored drums bearing scrolls inscribed with battle honors won by the Regiment during many hard-fought campaigns.

The attacking troops now stood drawn up, regiment by regiment, in ruler-straight lines. The Light Infantry and Grenadier companies then trampled off towards the Mystic River to a rhythmic beating of drums.

Drawn up in parade formation were battalion companies belonging to the 52nd, the 43rd and the 38th Regiments. On a slightly curving uphill slope had been posted the 5th and the

47th while a battalion of Royal Marines occupied the British extreme left.

Major-General Sir William Howe was pleased to note that all his officers and men had their hair dressed, powdered or wore wigs secured into pigtails by broad black ribbons; soldiers who'd used flour for whitening looked ridiculous because soft dough created by perspiration was commencing to draw pale streaks down tanned foreheads and cheeks.

Corporal Barton was feeling resentful when the order to advance was given out. Wot a bleedin' shyme it wasn't a French, German, Spanish or some other organized army they were about to attack. Crikey! It was beginning to look as if this overgrown skirmish wouldn't add fresh battle honors to any regiment.

At a measured parade-ground step with bayonets and muskets held rigidly upright the scarlet-and-white Light Infantry companies moved out along the Mystic's gray and often ankle-deep muddy beach. At the same time the Grenadiers advanced farther inland. Battalion troops of the line commenced to ascend gentle, grass-grown eastward slopes leading to that raw little redoubt crowning Breed's Hill.

Now and then some soldier would stumble over a boulder nearly concealed beneath tall, uncut grass to be roundly cursed by his fellows for even momentarily disturbing alignment. Everyone knew this colorful parade of disciplined power was calculated to strike terror to the hearts of disorganized militia crouching behind low stone breastworks and in the redoubt itself.

Soon it became apparent that the Commander-in-Chief, Major-General Sir William Howe, no doubt to set a good example and to demonstrate contempt for the enemy, personally led his right wing in attacking a pair of flèches—arrowhead-shaped shallow entrenchments hastily dug below the redoubt and to its left.

Major-General Sir Robert Pigot meantime would lead the main assault composed of line companies from all regiments in a parade up Breed's Hill and sweep defenders off its summit.

Following the display of a bright blue banner on a hillock General Howe used for a command post the general advance got underway. Immediately all four men-of-war, in addition to the Admiral's Battery, plus a pair of floating batteries poled into a shallow bay west of Charles Town opened a bombardment as thunderous as it was continuous.

Drummers in near-perfect unison continued to beat the quick-step while the red-and-white lines inclined forward and commenced to breast the slope only breaking alignment long enough to permit scrambling over a succession of low pasture fences made of small smooth stones.

In the fort and along the breastworks persisted an inexplicable silence even when inflexible red-coated ranks, in step and ramrod straight, kept on advancing shoulder to shoulder beneath rows of twinkling bayonet points.

Marching a pace or two behind Captain Peter Angevine, Lieutenant Gordon Hartley, sword held rigidly upright, experienced a strange sense of apprehension. Dammit! Why *wouldn't* those damned farmers open fire?

General Pigot's advance slowed once the gradient became steeper and the enormous weight of his troops' equipment commenced to tell.

When here and there men fainted from sunstroke, panting comrades merely stepped over them as they lay among buttercups, yellow wild mustard blossoms and clumps of daisies.

Meantime the Grenadiers and Light Companies now formed into columns made much better time along the Mystic's shore thanks to wide expanses of gray clay and sand still exposed above the rising tide. By the time the stone breastworks showed less than a hundred yards ahead everyone expected a fusillade to crackle but not a shot was fired. Left-right, left-right, behind the rattling drums. Why in Hell wouldn't the Rebels fire?

No one among the attackers was aware that Colonel Stark had warned his crouching men, "Aim at the pretty waistcoats worn by officers, or at private soldiers' crossbelts but don't anyone shoot till I give word."

CHAPTER 9 ❧

MAJOR HILTON'S BACK PORCH

WHEN, JUST AFTER DAWN, H.M.S. *Lively*'s guns fired for the first time Ellen Hunter sat bolt upright and automatically switched over her shoulders twin red-brown braids she used at bedtime. She realized Sarah Hilton also had roused. Across the bedroom she was blinking like a drowsy kitten half awake. From Betty Oliver, sleeping in the best guest room across the hallway, came no evidence she had wakened.

"What could that noise have been?" Ellen yawned.

Before Sarah found time to reply a series of deep reverberating rumblings suggestive of distant summer thunder beat through windows facing the Charles.

"Why, silly, those are cannon firing," Ellen snapped swinging almost too slim legs out of a small four-poster. "Oh dear, what can be the meaning of this?"

Sarah stretched with the unconscious grace of a feline. "Don't start getting upset; with so many bigwigs coming and going all the time I expect what we hear likely are only salutes fired in honor of some very important person or persons."

"Hope you're right but I'll wager those aren't salutes we're hearing at this ungodly hour but still it's possible they are firing on some unauthorized vessel attempting to enter or leave port."

Sleep-dampened night rails asway above bare feet both young women hurried to lean out of windows overlooking the gray-black river. Already it had grown sufficiently bright to reveal the slender masts and the dark hulls of warships anchored in the center of that narrow channel separating Boston from Charles Town.

For varying reasons both fixed attention on H.M.S. *Lively* over which hung a cloud of smoke dense enough to obscure her hull. Both flinched when Admiral Graves's huge flagship, H.M.S. *Somerset,* spurted yellow-red pencils of fire all along her port side; an instant later sounded a series of heavy, booming reports.

To her left H.M.S. *Falcon,* sloop-of-war, 18 guns, was a bit slower about opening fire but only because her captain had sent out boats to drop sheet anchors in order that, at such a totally windless time, she might more efficiently bring her broadside to bear.

Last to join in what now was becoming a thunderous cannonade was H.M.S. *Glasgow,* 20 guns, lying off Lynes Point at the southern tip of a deep crescent formed by warships hemming in the opposite shore from Charles Town around to Morton's Point and the Mystic.

"Oh, Ellen, let us pray your brother will be spared from harm." Sarah kept her attention on H.M.S. *Lively.* Recently she'd come to realize that Andrew Hunter was becoming more than just uncommon attractive.

Was it imagination, or didn't his strong, bronzed features, normally grave and composed, light up whenever he looked at her while nobody was paying attention? Aside from his overwhelming obsession concerning artillery and ammunition of all types, makes and weights Andrew could converse when he chose pleasantly and knowledgeably upon an amazing variety of subjects. Nor could Ellen's brother be called any part of a prude or a stuffed shirt. Fellow officers on occasion had confided that Andy had a quick and discerning eye for an especially neat-turned ankle and a well-fitted bodice in addition to just admiring a pretty face. Besides, as his friends wryly admitted, Andrew Hunter was almost suspiciously adept at gambling.

Because there still was not even a breath of wind, thickening strata of dirty, gray-yellow smoke soon hung sufficiently low to conceal some two hundred-odd homes, stores, warehouses, docks and shipyards composing Charles Town only a little over a thousand yards distant. They failed however to obscure the summits of two high hills rising at some distance beyond the town itself.

Even on the summit of Beacon Hill during the bombardment the air seemed to quiver; loose windowpanes could be heard rattling in their frames.

Sarah's mother's thin voice called querulously from her sick room. "What's going on? What is all that cannonading about? Oh dear, why doesn't anybody tell me anything?"

Sarah tossed strands of long golden hair back over her shoulders before deftly securing them with a becoming blue ribbon then she selected a fetching French peignoir from her clothes press. On hastening out from her room she encountered Papa looking drawn, wrinkled and quite aged. Except for a wig he was clad in the same breeches, waistcoat and ruffled shirt he'd worn to supper. He must have sat up all night.

"Look to your mother," directed the Major, "then invite your friends onto the back porch where we'll attempt to discover what in Hades is taking place." He then clumped off bawling for Toby and other servants to rouse and make themselves useful.

Sound of those regularly repeated broadsides stimulated the veteran's pulses almost as much as they had during the Siege of Louisburg. Damnation! If *only* there was some way he *openly* could participate in this affair, but here he was aged, rather decrepit and, worst of all, in the situation of being a professed neutral. Long ago he'd figured that by keeping his ears open around town he could be of more real help to the Cause of Freedom rather than by demanding a commission or by speechifying like so many windbags of his age.

Long a secret member of Boston's Committee of Safety the old man reckoned he'd really kept the public guessing through deftly avoiding answers to leading queries. Therefore, despite remonstrances from neighbors and associates, he'd continued to entertain British officers in his home.

Depending on the outcome of what now was promising to develop into a major engagement he wondered whether it would be possible to keep up his masquerade much longer. Since the first of June, Hilton had foreseen that a clash something like this was inevitable, but that the Patriot generals would be such inept fools as to attempt besieging the city from Bunker's and Breed's Hills and so risk getting cut off from their base in Cambridge passed belief. Surely, among the Colonials there must be enough seasoned veterans such as Seth Pomeroy, Israel Putnam and fat old Artemas Ward to avoid entering so obvious a deadfall.

After Sarah succeeded in reassuring her mother no immediate danger was threatening, she pattered back to her room to find Ellen half-dressed and kneeling beside her bed praying right out loud that whoever else might get hurt or killed, Brother Andrew must be spared. How awful this moment must be for him only she could guess. Because of the uniform he'd so eagerly elected to adopt, at this very moment he must be directing cannon fire on persons he had grown up among.

Once Major Hilton had settled onto a straight, ladder-back chair placed on a small porch facing slightly east of north he squinted through the powerful French telescope he'd fetched back from Louisburg and steadied it on a sturdy brass tripod set up by Toby. With great care Hilton adjusted the focus but soon discovered that smoke clouds lingering across the river remained so dense he couldn't make out much except the top hampers of men-of-war thrusting above shifting strata of fumes.

Once chairs had been fetched out for the ladies' benefit a maid passed a tray of crullers and a great silver pot of steaming-hot chocolate. It tasted fine since the sun still wasn't up and the air remained fairly cool.

The Oliver girl, a notably sound sleeper, appeared heavy-eyed but with dark-brown hair neatly brushed and beribboned. Stifling a yawn she knotted the belt of a yellow dressing gown around her distinctly chubby figure then addressed her host, "Sir, 'twas only when I waked and looked out the window did I realize the street below is so crowded by our troops on the march and that something must be amiss. Please excuse my tardiness."

The Major smiled only mechanically. Betty's uncle, Thomas Oliver, was a red-hot Tory and a former Lieutenant-Governor who nearly had provoked a dangerous riot in Cambridge last year through serving on the notorious Mandamus Committee until, under duress, he'd resigned.

"Miss Oliver, I'll wager Gabriel will have to blow his horn twice to awaken you come Judgment Day."

Nobody could be sure just where lay the loyalty of Benjamin Hilton, as a former British Colonial Army officer. Luckily, his bookshop lay on Cornhill Street near that of fat and jovial young Henry Knox whose store remained as a rendezvous for customers and scholars largely of anti-Royalist persuasions.

So intrigued by the voice and activity on the river was Sarah, she sipped through a treacherous cool layer of whipped cream covering piping-hot chocolate and then winced.

As for Ellen, she readily could visualize her brother striding back and forth across the deck and with unshakable calm directing his gun crews. Under stress Andy always had remained cool, complete master of his emotions.

All along Boston's northern exposure increasing numbers of people were appearing on rooftops, porches, terraces or any other point offering a fair prospect across the river.

Straightening from his telescope Major Hilton commented, "Wonder how soon that blockheaded Admiral Graves is going to quit throwing away ammunition."

"Why?" demanded the Oliver girl, shading large and somber eyes. "Have the Rebels run so soon?"

The old man cast her a penetrating look. "No, 'tis not that but, if you will notice, my dear, not one of those roundshot from the Admiral's Battery or any of the men-of-war has landed anywhere near that earthwork on Breed's Hill. All have fallen more or less short, only raising dirt and causing the defenders no harm."

His statement proved correct for, around nine of the morning of June 17th, 1775, the "cease-fire" signal fluttered up to the *Somerset's* signal yard whereupon the bombardment petered out as one ship after another stopped shooting.

Remarked Sarah's father, "I allow the King's men now are about to take a breather while General Gage and his staff try to make up their minds what they're going to do next. Tell Toby to fetch up a couple of my spyglasses so you ladies can see for yourselves something of what may happen."

Now that the smoke was clearing away Major Hilton directed

his attention on the redoubt and made out a mass of men in civilian garb furiously at work on parapets built of earth and logs. He counted five or maybe six embrasures; most had no cannon visible in them. Fields and pastures separating Breed's Hill from Bunker's Hill were dotted by contingents of Provincial troops moving about more or less aimlessly, or so it appeared.

He scowled into his instrument's eyepiece. The militia yonder were behaving just about as he feared they might and kept wandering around as if in search of units composed of friends or, failing that, for troops hailing from their own colony.

"Now I wonder," muttered the veteran more to himself than anyone else, "what the General is going to do about protecting his left flank. That's a damn' long gap 'twixt the Mystic and the fort. Ha!" He grunted approval when several bodies of Colonials hurried to take positions behind an irregular line of stone-and-rail fences and immediately began to heighten their breastwork by passing stones from up the beach one person to the next like people in a bucket brigade fighting a fire.

Sarah sighed and tightened her sash. "Well, Papa, since the first act of this drama appears to be over I think we girls had better go in and don more respectable garments." She giggled. "Blessed if Ellen, Betty and I don't look like a parcel of tavern wenches turned out during a raid!"

The old man chuckled, "You've never seen one; wish I could have been on hand if the girls were fetching as you. Tell Toby to look around and fetch up something fit to rig as an awning. Later on it's going to grow hotter than the hinges of Hell up here. Oh yes, and pray inform your mother she's not to fret. She's perfectly safe. I'll keep her posted should any development of a critical nature take place."

Downstairs, the front doorbell jangled impatiently, then a heavy tread presently could be heard ascending stairs leading to the back porch.

The caller proved to be lanky and beetle-browed Lieutenant-Colonel Brodnax Cameron of the Scots Guards; presently on detached duty as aide to Major-General Thomas Gage. Although barely forty years of age Lieutenant-Colonel Cameron, as a result of years of campaigning in a variety of unhealthy climates, appeared several years older. The whites of his small and cavernous dark eyes were yellowish and unattractive grayish tints showed in his otherwise red-brown complexion. In a wide canvas sling he was nursing what appeared to be a fractured right arm.

He bowed clumsily to the young ladies then, kilt asway, went over to greet Major Hilton as an old friend. "Hope, Ben, ye don't mind my using yer home as an observation post for the while. Really must obsairve what is about to happen to yon domned Rebels." He tapped his splinted and heavily bandaged arm. "You see, I ha' been invalided so I canna do a cursed thing about yonder bicker."

"Not at all, my dear Brodnax. You're indeed welcome. How come you've hurt your arm so badly?"

"Two days ago a mob of screaming mechanics attacked me whilst I was riding towards Headquarters. Some blackguard among 'em stabbed me mount's belly with a knife. The puir beast reared so sudden I got thrown headlong onto some confounded hard and dirty cobbles."

Cameron grimaced. "Surgeon says 'twas an uncommon bad break since a splinter of bone was near sticking through. However, he's cobbled me together sufficient to let me get aboot, but I'll nae be fit for duty for some time. Not that I'll be missed around Headquarters—too many bluidy self-important characters there who don't know their arses from their elbows. Aye, our High Command is clogged wi' stupid old-time servers and dandified Whitehall macaronis. I'd not say this to anyone else, Ben, but I fear Tom Gage finds himself surrounded wi' some few exceptions by a packet of brave but self-satisfied asses!"

Glancing at his host's telescope he raised a questioning black brow. "I've brought along a glass o' me own—mind if my orderly mounts it beside yours so we armchair generals can watch this battle, always provided the Rebels don't run off?" He glanced sidewise at his host. "Yet somehow, Ben, I dinna believe yer countrymen will quit wi'out putting up some sort of a fight. After all they're of British stock and behind breastworks to boot."

"By all means. Sit you down, my friend. Toby! Fetch some brandy; your orderly can rig a cushion to support that bad arm."

A fat and smelly orderly arranged a spyglass on a tripod to the Scot's satisfaction then clumped below just before the ladies reappeared.

Once they'd greeted the visitor with genuine warmth both Ellen and Sarah accepted pocket spyglasses and at once noticed that H.M.S. *Lively* was being towed on the ebb towards a new anchorage further off and very near to the river's mouth. Thus far those few smallboats which had appeared, loaded to their gunwales with Redcoats, were being rowed back to rest on their oars behind North Battery Point.

Acidly, Brodnax Cameron wondered why this had been done.

"They're waiting for the tide to come in," explained his host. "Some bright button on Gage's staff must have realized 'twould be impossible to put men ashore on the mud flats you see over there so nothing is likely to happen before noon or thereabouts. May as well get out of this infernal heat, go below and make ourselves comfortable. Come along, ladies, no point in damaging your complexions for nothing."

Once Major Hilton and his guests had enjoyed a light collation he and Lieutenant-Colonel Cameron returned to the hot shade of a striped awning rigged over the back porch. Similar contrivances were being slung to nearby rooftops while throngs of onlookers, guessing that an attack really promised to be made, collected upon every vantage point.

"Surely, Brodnax," Hilton commented, "Gage must have listened to practical and experienced officers like Pigot, Billy Howe and 'Gentleman' Johnny Burgoyne."

With deliberation Hilton traversed his telescope from one man-of-war to the next, watched well-trained crews running in their pieces then methodically swabbing out the bore before ramming home powder and roundshot. Fresh ammunition, he perceived, was being passed up from magazines and stowed in lead-lined chests.

Was it only because Hilton was aware that since Andrew's return to Boston the young fellow had been displaying an ever-increasing interest in Sarah or was it because H.M.S. *Lively's* gun crews were smarter in executing duties than those of other men-of-war? So powerful was his French telescope he presently was able to identify the tall, spare figure of Ellen's brother striding about and superintending preparations for a renewal of the bombardment. Would it end as it had at Louisburg?

Louisburg! Sighing, the veteran settled back in his chair. At first no one had recognized the fact that, on that cold and rocky Canadian peninsula, first had been sown the seeds of this bitter clash with the Crown. Goaded to desperation by the prolonged depredations on their shipping by French privateers and pirates based on Louisburg, New Englanders from three colonies, Massachusetts, New Hampshire and Rhode Island, had banded together for the first time and in doing so had relearned that in union lies strength—even for financially poor, underpopulated and widely separated colonies.

Somehow the Yankees had assembled a small army which they'd transported up to Cape Breton Island in their own ships and successfully had laid siege to Louisburg, that mighty fortress planned by King Louis XIV of France's most celebrated military engineer, Marquis Sébastien de Vauban, and had taken it without the help of a single British soldier!

Brodnax Cameron traversed his glass to the right, cried, "Och! Ben! There we come at last." From behind North Battery Point was rowing what appeared to be seemingly endless columns of small craft deep laden with red-coated troops whose arms flashed and glistened under the blazing sun. When more and still more boats hove into sight a griping sensation wrung Ben Hilton's bowels. Good God! Was there no end to this flotilla? By tens and twenties smallboats of all descriptions hove into sight on the slate-gray river but to Ben Hilton's silent satisfaction and Cameron's stupefication not one of them veered either left or right. All were rowed straight towards Morton's Point. Now that the tide was flooding its wide, level and treeless shores offered several ideal landing points on which troops could be marshaled without difficulty or danger.

Summoned from below, the girls, raising an excited babble, hurried onto the back porch. Betty Oliver burst out, "God bless the King's cause! What a grand sight!"

Ellen, less enthusiastically, demanded, "How many troops do the English have out there?"

"Near twa thousand I'd hazard," Cameron told her.

"Who will command this attack?" tensely queried Sarah's father.

Lieutenant-Colonel Cameron massaged his thin, wine-red

nose. "Last I heard the attack is to be made under General Sir William Howe wi' General Henry Clinton as his second-in-command. Once the assault begins Lord Howe personally will command the right wing whilst General Pigot leads the main body to attack the redoubt."

"Look!" burst out Ellen Hunter. "Something's happening aboard the *Lively!*" Through a short spyglass she could make out a pattern of dark figures clustering in regularly repeated patterns about the guns.

"What is she going to do?"

"Open fire presently," informed the Scot. "Where she lies noo her guns can enfilade both the slope of Breed's Hill and those breastworks wandering up frae the Mystic."

While the flotilla of smallboats was nearing the shore an intense bombardment delivered by all warships began. Concussion from repeated broadsides made windows rattle and dense blankets of smoke rise and partially obscure the far bank.

Ellen kept her attention on H.M.S. *Lively* anchored near the extreme eastern limits of Charles Town.

By the dozen, smallboats arriving at Morton's Point sent masses of scarlet-and-white figures splashing ashore. Without delay the boats then backed off and started pulling back to the Long Wharf for fresh cargoes.

Wincing, Lieutenant-Colonel Cameron eased his hurt arm then by way of relief gulped a tot of mellow Medford rum. " 'Tis good Gage has picked Billy Howe to command the attack. Clinton's good, too."

"What about Burgoyne?"

"His personal courage he has aplenty, but Johnny Burgoyne in an emergency just might get excited and mess things up."

The little group perspiring on Major Hilton's rear porch again leveled a miscellany of telescopes and pocket spyglasses of varying lengths and strengths.

Boom! Bo-o-om! Naval bombardment swelled towards a thunderous crescendo. Without comment the white-haired host noticed that, even from her new anchorage, H.M.S. *Lively*'s cannon balls plainly were visibly arching through the air only to fall more than halfway short of the summit of Breed's Hill. They then went skipping and bounding over the hay grass until gravity stopped them. Batteries on the other ships could do no better —or so it seemed.

H.M.S. *Falcon,* nearest to the landing areas, presently ceased firing probably because platoons, companies and regiments had begun to deploy over the fields.

Grunted Cameron to Betty Oliver, daintily using a lace-edged handkerchief to pat pellucid beads of perspiration from her brow, "'Tis thankful I'm no' carrying near a hundredweight of equipment up yonder hill on such a day."

"Then you'll admit," said Sarah while smoothing full skirts of pale-yellow lawn, "there *are* compensations for a broken arm?"

"Aye, and winsome lassies are among 'em."

Once the British order of battle commenced to take shape the group came closer about the Scot, especially when he started identifying various units.

"On our right ye'll spot the light companies frae all regiments. Can't mistake 'em in those short-skirted coats and low, brass-fronted hats. Grenadier companies are marching to their right."

"Why," exclaimed Ellen, "they seem like giants beside the light companies."

"Aye, lass, those tall, bearskin-covered hats are supposed to make 'em so huge they'll strike terror in an enemy."

In a taut voice Sarah inquired, "Please, sir, which regiments form the main body?"

Surprisingly her father, all the while peering through his telescope, supplied the answer instead of Cameron. "From right to left in the array are regular line companies from the 52nd, the 43rd, the 38th and the 5th Regiments and, finally I think, men from the 47th. That correct, Brodnax?"

The aide treated his companion to a penetrating glance. "Yes. Damme, Ben, for a civilian ye seem to ken a deal about our garrison."

Benjamin Hilton only grunted then hunched bony shoulders to train his glass on the redoubt. Um. Up there he saw men still making dirt fly. Also he noted that more groups of Colonists were hurrying over from Bunker's Hill to reinforce defenders feverishly working to raise and extend that stone-and-rail breastwork reaching down to the water's edge. Very few of the officers wore uniforms so remained indistinguishable from their men save for strips of varicolored cloth knotted around their left arms.

"Ha! At lang last there we go!" growled Cameron wincing over having forgotten about his bad arm. The Scot's burr became more pronounced. "I dinna doot this wee bicker will be settled come another half-hour."

A succession of shivers coursed the length of plump and dark-haired Betty Oliver's spine. At long last these sly, stiff-necked and uncouth Patriots were about to learn the folly of defying the Crown's authority. Nevertheless it proved unnerving for her to realize that amid those precise, straight lines, arranged like chessmen at the start of a game, there must be a number of English beaux and American neighbors—Tories she'd grown up among. Good! Before long traitors were about to be made to pay in part for the humiliation, anguish and loss of property too long endured by Americans loyal to their lawful sovereign, King George III.

On a hillock stood the glittering figure of Major-General William Howe together with a handful of aides. Through her small telescope Sarah saw the British Commander-in-Chief raise his sword; when he lowered it a bright blue flag was flourished and at once dozens of drums rolled "Advance." General Howe, erect as if on parade, himself moved out well in advance of his troops.

From watchers in Boston now arose a gale of mingled cheers, curses and shouts of defiance.

Across the Charles unfolded a sight no one present would ever forget. At precisely the same moment, those scarlet-and-white ranks moved out over the green fields, muskets carried precisely at the vertical; near two thousand bayonet points were sparkling under the torrid sun.

Major Ben Hilton's lips flattened against costly false teeth, carved out of walrus ivory, when Provincials who'd been at work in front of the stone-and-rail fence and outside of the redoubt, still lugging spades and pickaxes, scampered behind those defenses created with such incredible speed. Now, Hilton told himself, smoke and flame must burst from that handful of cannon on top of Breed's Hill and hurl devastating blasts of grapeshot or canister upon the King's men.

The steadiness of the British advance was infinitely impressive.

Bolt upright, the ranks moved off, elbow-to-elbow, line officers marching well out in advance. Still playing, red-faced drummer boys fell back on either flank of their unit in order not to hamper those deadly volleys which must come very soon now.

Formations briefly became disarranged when it became necessary to scramble over low stone walls separating pastures, but ranks promptly were re-formed by officers and serjeants into flawless alignment. They tramped on.

At the same time, on the British far left, a detachment of Royal Marines could be seen advancing on the two hundred-odd wooden buildings composing Charles Town, but still there was no shooting.

Step by step the long lines advanced more slowly because of the heat and the increasing grade. Many officers roundly were cursing the Senior Service for not having more effectively bombarded the enemy position, they of course being ignorant that gunports on the men-of-war had been so constructed that, under present conditions, cannon could not be sufficiently elevated to range the earthworks.

Why *didn't* the Rebels open fire? wondered Lieutenant Hartley licking dry and sunburned lips. From all he'd gathered such restraint wasn't to be expected from undisciplined troops. Still, no musket boomed above, not even by the time General Pigot's steady line companies had covered half the distance to the Yankee earthworks.

"Cor," panted a private pressing against Corporal Barton's right elbow, "this 'ere bloody pack's fair killing me. Weighs like a bleedin' anvil." Another growled, "I'd sell me soul for a swig o' cold water."

Out in front a major snapped, "Silence, you scum! Stay quiet till this job's done else I'll see the skin off yer backs!" The point of his sword was twinkling like a star of the first magnitude seen on a clear winter's night.

On the right, troops advancing along the Mystic's banks were ordered by General Howe to deploy out of column and into line abreast in order more effectively to assault Provincials seen lurking behind the stone and rail fence. Compared to the left wing ascending Breed's Hill his command was having a comparatively easy time for here the ground was fairly level and mostly of hard-packed sand or turf.

Along with Captain Angevine commanding the Royal Welch's Light Company, Lieutenant Hartley and other officers out in front of the line began to feel a trifle disconcerted; now that they'd advanced into easy musket range why wouldn't those damned Yankees begin shooting? Possibly, the undisciplined militiamen up there might already have run without firing even a single shot. Like many others, Gordon Hartley began to wonder whether the enemy hadn't become utterly demoralized by the sight of England's might on parade and advancing so inexorably to a shrilling of fifes and the thumping beat of many drums. Sea gulls at least had enough sense to wing away.

By the time they'd climbed nearly two-thirds of the slope men of the regular line companies were panting like hard-run fox hounds. Dark patches of sweat long since had stained their scarlet tunics while knapsacks dragged at aching shoulders and seemed to weigh twice as much as before.

A few officers felt somewhat contrite over striding along weighted by nothing heavier than a sword and a brace of pistols. Lieutenant Hartley was wishing he dared to wipe from his face trickles of sour-smelling sweat which kept stinging his eyes. But he didn't dare; before the men, it simply wasn't done for an officer to exhibit weakness, no matter how trivial.

Portly and bandy-legged Lieutenant-Colonel Gatsby's fat shoulders seemed to sag under the weight of heavy gold bullion epaulettes while advancing well out in front of the Royal Welch Fusiliers. The violence of his breathing could even be heard in the ranks. *Certes!* This was no day for a well-fed gentleman to overexert himself.

Moments later Hartley got a clearer view of a brownish bank of fresh-turned earth forming the redoubt's glacis. A sturdy figure wearing, of all things, a blue-and-yellow banyan was striding along the redoubt's berm and kicking up musket barrels leveled by overeager militiamen. He must be an officer from the way he kept shouting and pointing with what looked to be a dueling rapier but the steady tap-tapping of drums drowned out what he was saying.

Knee-deep in fragrant hay grass, Corporal Barton wheezed, "Why don't them bleedin' bastards up there start shootin'?"

Presently batteries aboard the King's ships stopped firing—probably gunnery officers had grown fearful of killing their own men.

Although they weren't sixty yards short of the summit officers out in front still marched with sword blades held erect. Now they could glimpse tense brown faces, hatless or wearing a weird miscellany of headgear, peering over the berm from behind a long row of musket muzzles. They didn't, thought Hartley, offer much of a target.

"B'God," panted Lieutenant-Colonel Gatsby, "damned if I don't believe those cowardly swine ain't getting ready to surrender without firing a shot!"

The foremost officers had arrived within thirty yards of the redoubt when it seemed as if a blinding, deafening volcano had erupted in their faces. The first American volley rocked the Royal Welch Fusiliers back onto their heels, beat faces with invisible fists through roaring walls of foul-smelling smoke.

The first to fall mostly were officers. Not in vain had Doctor-Colonel James Warren, commanding in the redoubt cautioned its defenders to "shoot at the prettiest waistcoats" or failing such a target to aim at that point where a Redcoat's white crossbelts joined. He was well aware that inexperienced recruits or even excited Regulars had a tendency to pull too hard on a trigger and so shoot low and waste charges.

In quick succession two more volleys flamed from the redoubt, hurled buck-and-ball into the tight-packed ranks of attackers, deafened and nearly smothered those red-clad figures under billows of burnt powder fumes. In this windless atmosphere such were slow to dissipate.

For what seemed an interminable interval Lieutenant Hartley remained so numbed and shocked he appeared frozen, swaying beneath his upraised sword, ears assailed by a hideous gale of mingled howls, unearthly screams and shrieks. A stricken soldier's musket fell on his instep and so hurt him he staggered but recovered and through shifting, bitter-smelling fumes recognized Captain Angevine who, instants ago, had been advancing only a few yards ahead of him. Hat and wig gone Angevine was sitting on the ground and using both hands in an attempt to stanch a wound in his left side. All the same jets of bright arterial blood with diminishing force kept spurting from between his fingers. A serjeant who'd been knocked over backwards swayed to his feet and, ghost-like amid gray fumes, attempted to use his halbert to drive forward dazed privates. Once, twice, thrice he gestured then, losing his cap, fell heavily forward to lie motionless among other bodies squirming or lying limp on raw earth at the foot of the glacis.

Similar volleys had torn great gaps in the ranks of the 52nd's, the 43rd's and the 38th's line companies. When drums and fifes fell silent ghastly, unearthly noises increased.

Through supreme effort Hartley had advanced only a few feet before a buckshot ripped off his second-best tricorn and burnt-powder grains stung his face like a swarm of midges.

Through the drifting smoke the Lieutenant glimpsed incredible sights. Like human ninepins Regulars were toppling sidewise, forward or backwards. Some, because the enemy were aiming low, as they'd been told, had been disembowled and, howling, were trampling their own intestines. Somewhere in the dim obscurity a hoarse voice was screaming with insane intensity, "Forward, for God sake! Come on, you bloody cowards! Follow me!"

Somehow, Gordon Hartley recovered sufficiently to face about and, using the flat of his sword, tried to help a bareheaded, smoke-blackened serjeant to beat the men into some sort of a line abreast. But it wasn't any use. Scarlet-clad figures wearing white crossbelts and dark-red facings had dropped muskets and, covering their ears, were reeling about as though drunk, until they also were cut down in struggling, tangled, howling and blood-smeared piles of mangled men.

Again the crude redoubt spouted death and destruction and the world appeared to degenerate into an incredible and confusing hideous turmoil.

Hartley, still on his feet and gasping like a fresh-caught fish, felt someone tugging at his leg in an effort to pull himself erect. It was a wounded private, who, his face coated by streaming blood from a wound in his forehead, only succeeded in pulling the officer down on top of him.

"My God," he whimpered, "get me out of here. Can't see!"

"Let go, damn you! Get up and follow me."

How Gordon Hartley managed to regain his feet he never could remember, the world seeming to have resolved into a spinning kaleidoscopic nightmare.

Although no recognizable order to retreat was heard redcoated men still on their feet commenced a slow retrograde movement despite the efforts of the few remaining officers and serjeants to make them stand firm and continue the attack.

Stepping over groveling, screaming wounded forms some of whom were headless or lacking a limb, General Pigot's troops commenced to fall back in ragged disorder towards Morton's Point on which strong reinforcements from Boston had commenced to come ashore.

Chapter 10 🦋

"ONCE MORE, UNTO THE BREACH, DEAR FRIENDS, ONCE MORE—"

FROM MAJOR HILTON's porch the host and his guests watched Major-General Pigot's command advance steadily up Breed's Hill without a shot being fired by either side. Drummers continued to beat "Advance" although line companies now found it difficult because of stone fences to keep step and alignment.

Complained Brodnax Cameron, "Why in Belial's name do yon bluidy Rebels hold fire? There'll soon be bayonets at work among 'em."

Only when white-wigged officers, marching ahead, had reached a point some thirty yards short of the redoubt's glacis and of that stone-and-rail fence meandering down to the Mystic, did the incredible take place. The redoubt, the stone breastworks and a couple of flèches, hurriedly dug higher up to protect the fort's Mystic side, spouted sheets of flame and whirling smoke.

Without removing his eye from his spyglass Lieutenant-Colonel Cameron squirmed on his chair. "It canna be! *It canna be!*" He relieved his feelings by ripping a volley of curses in Gaelic and other foreign languages.

Three crashing volleys delivered in incredibly quick succession had made the sky resound and reverberate above Boston and its harbor.

Only dimly did Cameron become aware that, so far as he could tell, not a single shot yet had been fired by the attackers. Why? *Why?* WHY?

Incredulously, General Gage's crippled aide shook his craggy, sandy head. He'd never heard of untrained troops being able to deliver three volleys in such rapid succession, being unaware of course that Doctor-Colonel James Warren, commanding in the redoubt, had caused his men to be disposed in teams consisting of three musketmen each. Once an initial volley had been fired the Number 1 man turned left and, carrying his still-smoking musket, pelted back to reload, yielding his place to the Number 2 man of his team. The Number 2 also fired low at the most brilliant uniforms or, failing that, let fly at crossbelts in a mass of Redcoats wavering not ninety feet below. They then ran back to reload with buck-and-ball behind Number 1, thus granting their Number 3 man opportunity to join in the carnage by which time Number 1 was ready to fire again.

Girls on the porch gasped, uttered low, anguished cries and both men choked in astounded incredulity when a vagrant puff of wind rolled aside the battle's smoke. Through glasses they could see the earthwork's glacis and the ground before the stone fence carpeted by heaps of limp or squirming red-clad bodies. Regulars still on their feet were holding their heads and staggering as if intoxicated until, to Cameron's dismay, they commenced slowly to fall back ignoring orders, pleas and beatings delivered by the flats of swords and spontoons wielded by a handful of officers and serjeants.

Despite all the confusion one astounding fact stood out; a planned assault, delivered in force by British Regulars, had been repelled by what so often had been referred to as a "mere rabble in arms."

Among hundreds of onlookers only a few could credit that the Redcoats actually were retreating not only down the long slope of Breed's Hill but also along the Mystic's bank away from those flame-spouting stone-and-rail breastworks.

To begin with, the King's men had commenced to fall back

only slowly but then the retrograde movement gathered momentum until, in great disorder, Regulars were running as fast as they could away from the fortifications.

Arriving on Morton's Point the fugitives, magnificently disciplined, soon found their units and re-formed ranks in obedience to an irregular rattling of drums and the efforts of those comparatively few officers who had survived.

Lieutenant-Colonel Cameron, features ashen beneath his mottled complexion, was panting as though he'd run a long distance. "Dear Saint Andrew, what ha' I done to desairve watching such a disgrace?"

Sarah Hilton noticed that Father's long and rugged face seemed to have congealed into what resembled an expressionless mask as, more to himself than to anyone else, he muttered, "That charge was magnificently mounted, Brodnax, but parade-ground tactics ain't sensible in this kind of war; anyone who's fought the French and Indians should have learned from Abercrombie's experience at Ticonderoga that massed frontal assaults against fortifications manned even by irregular troops can prove disastrous."

Sarah Hilton pressed trembling fingers against colorless cheeks while silently but fervently thanking the Lord that Andrew must be safe aboard the *Lively*. Ellen felt the same way but didn't say so, either.

Presently the men-of-war opened a second bombardment as noisy and as futile as the first one.

Meantime British commanders were wondering why not a single cannon had been discharged from the redoubt but thanked God their men hadn't been blasted by even a few discharges of grape or canister shot at short range or their losses would have been doubled.

As for Betty Oliver, she was praying that gay and handsome young Gordon Hartley hadn't been hurt. She shivered over the possibility his mangled body was lying among those motionless clumps of red-and-white across the river. Until this instant she'd not begun to appreciate how very deeply she'd come to care for that slim, eagle-featured young Englishman.

It was amazing that, inside of half-an-hour, the forces on Morton's Point once more stood drawn up in ordered ranks but no longer quite so spick-and-span. Some of the King's men were wearing bandages, a good many lacked headpieces and the white stockings of many sagged about their ankles. A few officers had lost not only their hats but gleaming white wigs as well. To Sarah these bareheaded men appeared a trifle grotesque in otherwise brave uniforms.

In sharp incredulity Ben Hilton shook his head. "God above! Surely Gage and his staff can't be such great fools as to attempt another frontal assault!"

Soon it became apparent that the British High Command intended to do just that. Through his telescope Sarah's father watched the officers and serjeants, tiny ant-like creatures at this distance, busily dressing ranks.

On the Long Wharf strong infantry reinforcements were scrambling into small craft even though there wasn't much chance of their participating in Lord Howe's second attack. In Cameron's opinion these fresh troops also would be led by Sir Henry Clinton, an undemonstrative but definitely sound if not brilliant officer who, whatever he was saying or doing at this moment, must be dead-set against repetition of so costly a mistake.

In perfect unison the long lines stirred, moved out in an unmistakable repetition of the first attack. Muttered Major Hilton, "They're magnificent, Brodnax, but this isn't war—it's murder!"

Again and yet again the rigid lines lost alignment but only while crossing fences. Purple-faced and drenched with sweat but still bearing cruelly heavy packs the Regulars sidestepped dead or dying comrades. Blood, spattered on the hay grass, was sketching long scarlet streaks across the men's pipe-clayed white gaiters and breeches.

The men-of-war now quit firing. No more cannon balls could be sighted bounding along well below the redoubt or rolling along the Mystic's shore till they lost momentum and lay still.

Almost unbearable tension gripped onlookers in Boston whether or not they were praying that this time British bayonets soon might be seen flashing inside that ridiculous little earthwork.

Ensued an unearthly stillness broken only by a shrilling of fifes and the febrile beating of drums across the river. Steadily the ranks, bayonet points twinkling, marched upwards but this time they frequently were forced to pick a course through windrows of sprawled dead and moaning wounded.

Again the Yankees held their fire. By now their never adequate supply of gunpowder was nearing exhaustion.

While witnessing the Army form for a second frontal attack Lieutenant Andrew Hunter felt as if invisible talons had begun to rend his bowels. So many conflicting loyalties had been tormenting him since H.M.S. *Lively* had fired her first shot to mark the start of this engagement.

The loader of Number 2 gun bit the linings of leathery cheeks while ramming a dripping sponge down the hot and still-smoking throat of the long 18-pounder he was serving. 'T'wouldn't do to leave a spark in the bore. He switched his staff to its rammer end and so drove home a fresh powder charge. A fellow easily could lose both hands and his eyesight if a premature explosion occurred. He stole a quick sidewise glance at several impressed Colonials serving the *Lively*'s starboard battery. Judging by the grim expression on their smoke-blackened faces he reckoned they too must be struggling to do their duty until, well—who knew what opportunity might not present itself?

Along the gundeck, despite choking, acrid smoke, orderly confusion prevailed; dull rumblings of gun carriage wheels being run in and out continued unabated.

Tom Izard muttered to another Marbleheader serving Number 4 gun, "If only there was *somethin'* we could do to hurt those damn' Bloodybacks."

Following a booming roar by yet another broadside Izard said from the side of his mouth, "Been talkin' to Fingers. He's on duty in the main magazine."

"Fingers can be trusted?"

"Yep. 'Tis five years since he got press-ganged off Nantucket Island but, Provincial or not, he's won promotion on account of he's uncommon handy with cannons. Claims he'll prove useful comes the right time. Look yonder." Izard inclined his head to one of several chests containing sausage-shaped muslin-covered powder charges. "Notice them ca'tridges showin' a little black dot on one end?"

"Yep," the loader muttered, "what about 'em?"

"Well, Fingers had those there ca'tridges only half-charged so balls they fires won't carry no great distance."

"Get your meanin'. Such shots jist might land 'mongst the Bloodybacks."

"Aye. 'Bloodybacks' they are!" Weals visible on Number 2's shoulders and back barely had healed from a flogging he'd suffered over some minor breach of discipline on the American and West Indies station. Not for nothing was Captain Purcell rated by fellow captains a brutal martinet.

First Lieutenant Saxeby snarled at Andrew, "Damme, Hunter, continually you put on airs over being an expert artillerist yet all I can say is that whilst no one can feel proud of the Navy's gunnery thus far, your guns have been among the worst served." Hard blue eyes narrowing, he rasped, "See to it once we reopen fire your marksmanship improves, else I'll prefer charges!"

Ellen Hunter's brother barely conquered a sense of outrage. Ever since this cruise had commenced, Saxeby had missed few opportunities to belittle him and other American-born crew members.

Imagine a Royal Navy lieutenant dressing down a fellow officer at the top of his voice before half-naked and powder-blackened gun crews. Even Captain Purcell wouldn't have approved so deplorable a breach of Service etiquette.

Lips compressed, Hunter through a pocket spyglass watched the Army for a second time breast the slope and advance over scarlet-dotted fields.

Briefly he wondered whether Sarah Hilton, Ellen, his father and that outspoken Tory, Betty Oliver, were looking on. Of course they must be. Rooftops on Boston's northwest side were dark with great clusters of onlookers. Some foolhardy spectators even had hired smallboats to row out to watch this extraordinary battle at closer range.

Presently he fixed his attention on a pair of crude arrowhead-pointed earthworks thrown in a feeble attempt to stop a wide gap between the beach breastworks and the redoubt. Incredibly it appeared that, exactly as before, the battered Grenadiers and the Light Companies were moving to attack them, as well as that same low stone-and-rail fence which little more than an hour earlier had spouted appalling death and destruction.

Running his eye along the deck Hunter, with detached satisfaction, noted that all his gun crews stood at their stations, sunburned and half-naked bodies glistening with perspiration. Many were wearing their hair in pigtails stiffened with tar and had bound bright-colored bandannas around their foreheads to keep sweat from trickling into their eyes and hampering their vision.

Vaguely Andrew again wondered as he strode stiffly back and forth behind the starboard battery how many impressed men British or Colonial might be serving the sloop's long 18-pounders. Some of the latter he'd long since identified, gunners like Tom Izard and Ed Littleton of Marblehead who last winter had been dragged out of Captain Ezra Tomkin's *Pitt Packet*. Theirs, of course, had been only one of several impressments conducted by H.M.S. *Lively* on patrol off approaches to Massachusetts Bay.

Thoughts on the subject came to an end when on peering over hammocks lashed onto the bulwarks to reduce splinter damage he realized that those distant red-coated ranks now were less than fifty yards short of their objective. His scalp tingled when at long last crashing volleys of musketry made the sky resound and swaths of red-and-white figures went down like wheat stalks struck by some invisible giant's scythe.

Through gaps in the battle smoke, for now a faint breeze had sprung up, Hunter watched officers' ornaments glittering, waving swords and keeping doggedly onward until killed or struck down into agonized helplessness.

Once more the attack lost momentum then hesitated. Under that deadly hail of lead the attackers started slowly to fall back in disorder. Situations such as this had not been covered in any of those drill manuals or books on tactics they'd been taught to respect only a trifle less than Holy Writ. This retreat towards Morton's Point was considerably faster than the previous one.

In several places attackers had fallen in readily discernible rows, like game laid out after a drive.

Even at her anchorage H.M.S. *Lively*'s company once more listened to a rising gale of horrifying shrieks, screams and yells.

"Leastways," growled a bald gun-pointer, "them fellers got no splinters to worry over."

"Why?" queried his Number 3.

"Splinter wounds be a heap worse'n gettin' hit by flyin' iron. Wood's jagged edges kin rip a feller apart nasty-like."

On Major Hilton's porch Lieutenant-Colonel Cameron heaved a shuddering sigh then gulped a deep, deep draught of rum-and-water "Swounds! Even a pigheaded ass like Tom Gage should ha' learnt the folly of ordering frontal attacks 'gainst an entrenched enemy!" The Scot glared at his host. "Tell me, Ben, why in Hell don't he, even now, order ships and troops to block Charles Town Neck?"

"No telling," the older man said. "Neither Braddock nor Abercrombie would learn, either."

"Oh, God!" gasped Brodnax Cameron. "I'm dommed if that great blockhead ain't going to follow the same tactics for *a third time!*"

The Scot gesticulated so violently he hurt his bad arm; the ladies covered their ears over the terrible way he cursed.

This time among the thinned ranks many went coatless and were wearing bandages. Survivors of the first two charges were forming into commingled regiments and companies. Only reinforcements under General Clinton, freshly arrived from Boston, wore complete uniforms and equipment as they assumed the traditional line formation. White-eyed, they looked apprehensively on battered troops gathering in less than precise formations. Even the dullest observer could sense that for them this attack wasn't about to be an exact repetition of previous onslaughts. Without regard to units, disorganized companies were marshaled into ranks, Grenadiers mixed with men from Light and Line Companies; even a few black-gaitered Marines were included.

A sigh escaped Benjamin Hilton. "At last someone's showing a grain of sense. D'you notice, Brodnax, even the reinforcements are being allowed to shed knapsacks and the wounded to peel off those damned hot tunics?"

Silently, the veteran of Louisburg prayed that the Provincials might still retain sufficient ammunition to beat off still another assault. Not long ago, he'd learned that a shortage of gunpowder was the local forces' most acute problem.

Naturally the Major couldn't know that even though a supply

of artillery cartridges finally had reached the redoubt, these were of no use since the balls wouldn't fit the fieldpieces' bores. Sulphurous curses were raised when it was realized that flasks, horns, pouches and hats couldn't be even a quarter filled with powder from cartridges hatcheted open.

Chapter 11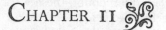

"—AND TRY, TRY AGAIN"

THROUGH A BRASS speaking trumpet gaunt and powder-blackened Lieutenant Saxeby barked from H.M.S. *Lively's* quarterdeck, "Charge all guns with carcases and fire at will on Charles Town. That Rebel rat's nest is to be burnt!"

Forthwith dozens of carcases—hollow iron spheres filled with sulphur, saltpeter, turpentine and other combustibles—were sent up from the magazine.

Through previous understanding Tom Izard and other impressed American Colonials took care not to waste precious half-charges on such shot. Carcases, they figured, weren't likely to kill many Britons, would only serve to set Charles Town ablaze.

Other men-of-war now opened fire using the same type of shot. Gracefully trailing comet tails of white smoke, carcases by the dozen arched up, up, then plunged into the doomed settlement before exploding. Almost at once blue-gray clouds of smoke arose from among the buildings and flames commenced to leap skywards.

Not until the town had been set well ablaze would come orders to use only shell or roundshot now that a third assault was getting underway. Unevenly this time the long red lines moved out to the rattling of drums—beat chiefly among reinforcements.

Andrew noted that on this occasion the British moved faster. Many soldiers had stripped to the waist and wore soiled white crossbelts supported only by raw, red shoulders. The officers—those few who had survived the first two attacks—as usual were marching well out in front of ranks with swords flashing, gold buttons and epaulettes glittering in the blasting sunlight. Many, striding stiffly along, went hatless and wigless; not a few were wearing red-stained bandages in place of headgear.

Over the crashing roar of broadsides Tom Izard muttered to Littleton, a fellow-townsman, "Ed, them dumblock Lobsterbacks orter ha' advanced like that to start with. God send our fellers on yonder hill won't run short of powder or buck-and-ball." The other nodded and, shoulders hunching, dipped his rammer's sponge into a bucket of water before driving it down the still-smoking throat of Number 2 gun.

A shout arose when the gunners noticed that Colonials defending the Mystic's shore had begun to quit their works. They either were running upwards towards the redoubt or retiring in the general direction of Bunker's Hill and Charles Town Neck.

H.M.S. *Lively's* Captain advanced to the break of his quarterdeck and through a bright brass speaking trumpet bellowed over a continuing thunder of broadsides, "Now that that rat's nest is ablaze order your gun captains, Mister Hunter, to load with roundshot, aim at their fort and fire at will. Miss, and I'll see the hides off their filthy backs."

The British no longer were advancing in well-dressed ranks with bayoneted muskets held rigidly erect. Now their Tower muskets were being carried horizontally waist-high. Halfway short of their objective, squads on command dropped onto one knee, shouldered muskets and dutifully fired in the general direction of the redoubt; there were no visible effects.

When no answering fire came the panting scarlet-coated attackers kept on, bent forward as if moving against a gale.

Officers, some decidedly obese, wheezed upwards picking a

course between piles and scatterings of motionless scarlet-clad figures as if they didn't exist.

Lieutenant Saxeby snapped at Hunter, "Now, my fine gunnery expert, I want to see your pieces range that cursed earthwork and hit it *hard!* No excuses will be accepted."

Throat constricting, Andrew Hunter curtly saluted then strode along the line of gun carriages. He instructed gun captains to remove all quoins and to aim at the redoubt although almost everyone was aware that, despite her new position, few if any of H.M.S. *Lively*'s roundshot could achieve sufficient elevation to range the target.

"Time for half-charges," grunted Gunner's Mate Tom Izard to Littleton. Both men selected powder bags each bearing on its end a small black dot.

Aware of and disconcerted by Lieutenant Saxeby's undeviating attention, Andrew Hunter halted behind Number 2 gun, ordered aside its grimy, gap-toothed captain. Then pushing his hat onto the back of his head he bent to sight the piece. Paying full attention to his task he failed to perceive that Number 4 gun also was being loaded with a black-dotted charge.

Once Number 2's crew had stepped aside he pressed a match glowing at a linstock's end against the long 18's priming; a jet of flame spurted skywards from its touchhole. The piece bellowed a split second before recoiling against its breeching tackle. Puzzled, Hunter wondered why the report sounded a trifle weak.

He, along with Captain Purcell and Saxeby, watched the ball arch high, higher over the river but fall short of the redoubt and go skipping and bounding along the ground into a group of Redcoats. At least half-a-dozen figures reeled crazily aside or fell limp and motionless on already blood-stained hay grass.

Purple-faced, Captain Purcell pointed at Hunter, shouted to the Marines, "Confine that officer in the brig! Clap the crews of Numbers 2 and 4 guns in irons and put them under guard in the forehold! Kill anyone who resists."

CHAPTER 12 🎔

NADIR

AIR IN H.M.S. *Lively's* little brig proved so hot, lifeless and evil-smelling Lieutenant Andrew Hunter at first felt certain he'd suffocate before long. Still stunned by the suddenness of what had happened he crouched, panting and shaking on an empty nail keg, this dark den's only item of furniture. Helplessly he clenched and unclenched sweaty fists. Thank God, the Marines, possibly because he held the King's commission and always had been just and friendly with all hands, had treated him well and hadn't manacled him.

A sense of despair such as he'd never before experienced numbed Andrew Hunter. How could it be that, in such a brief space of time, a man's career, hopes and aspirations could crumble and evaporate? He still couldn't credit Timothy Hunter's son under arrest and a prisoner until such time as a court-martial might be convened aboard the flagship.

Once his mind commenced to function after a fashion, the prisoner deduced that some person or persons serving Number 2 piece and perhaps other guns in his battery had contrived while reloading to substitute reduced charges of gunpowder. Common sense argued that those responsible must be impressed Colonials or mutinous-minded Britishers of whom there were many aboard. *Why* couldn't the ball from that piece he himself had trained have fallen into the water or in some clear space on the slope of Breed's Hill? As it was, Captain Purcell, Lieutenant Saxeby and others who'd watched the flight of that accursed projectile had seen it land where it must have slain or wounded more than a few infantrymen. Utterly astonished and horrified he'd witnessed the tragedy himself.

With regard to his immediate fate there seemed little room for hope—let alone justice. Probably tomorrow he'd be brought up for arraignment. No use attempting to deceive himself: beyond any shadow of a doubt he'd promptly be convicted of treason in the face of the enemy and forthwith condemned to dangle in a noose slowly hauled to a tip of H.M.S. *Somerset*'s main yard.

From all he could overhear Andrew gathered General Howe's third assault must have proved successful since the crackle of musketry on Breed's Hill had faltered and then gradually had died out, arguing that the defenders of the earthwork at last had been overwhelmed.

Not for a good while would anyone realize the cost of General Howe's victory. Of some 2,000 men wearing the King's scarlet forty-five percent had been killed or wounded, a high percentage of these casualties being officers. Later, Andrew would learn that the Colonial loss had amounted to 139 killed, 278 wounded and 36 missing or some thirty percent of a much less numerous force than those commanded by Sir William Howe.

Almost nothing could be seen by the faint light admitted through a tiny barred aperture let into the cell's stout door so Andrew stared blankly at its peephole. Now that H.M.S. *Lively*'s guns finally had fallen silent he could hear more of what was taking place above deck. For example, the sloop-of-war's smallboats were being lowered to ferry back to Boston what sounded like an appalling number of casualties.

Dully, the prisoner again tried to estimate his chances. Given time would, or could, Sarah Hilton's father do anything to help? Probably not. Ever since the Port of Boston had been declared closed that ever-cautious bookseller had taken pains to maintain a strictly neutral attitude. As for Sarah—what would she think once she heard that her most earnest and persistent admirer was likely soon to be hanged for high treason?

How would Father, Ellen and the rest of his family in Cambridge react once they heard about Captain Timothy Hunter's son having been executed by that same Navy in which he'd elected to serve?

A squad of Marines clumped below to relieve a sentry posted in a narrow passageway separating the brig from a storeroom opposite.

He heard the corporal in charge rasp, "Nah then, Dunning, look alive and make certain *nobody* is allowed to talk to 'e prisoner. Cap'n promises he'll have 'e bosun's cat peel 'e 'ide off'n 'e back o' any sentry who permits anything of the sort.

"Nah then, 'e rest o' you, go back on deck and find a place in some boat ye can handle a oar in, shake a leg. Lieutenant Saxeby's in a fine fury."

Someone growled while the relief was shuffling off, "Then 'tis truly that bad as they say?"

"Aye, 'e bloody Rebels blasted plenty o' Regulars into cat's meat but our loss would ha' even been worse if 'e bloody Rebels hadn't run short of powder or had had any bagnets to speak of."

Listening to random conversations on the deck above Andrew deduced that although Lord Howe's third attack had proved successful a majority of the earthwork's defenders had pulled out in time to retreat across Charles Town Neck, unthreatened by Naval gun fire. Lord Howe's battered infantry had been too exhausted to mount any effective pursuit.

Activities continued as orders were shouted and feet trampled continually back and forth. It was so infernally hot down here Andrew long since had pulled off a sweat-soaked shirt and blue serge tunic and even had debated removing his breeches as well. For all he tried to devise some action towards escape he got nowhere. Those Marines who'd manhandled him below had emptied his pockets and confiscated his clasp knife, so there was nothing to do save to sit and stare, unseeing, through damp strands of hair.

By the time darkness descended not a soul had come near this hutch of a prison saving a surly new guard who'd not even replied when he'd pleaded for a dipper of water; his throat felt dry and raw as if sandpapered.

Now and again smallboats passed in the near distance, their coxswains barking commands to oarsmen. Sometimes these craft came so near the prisoner could recognize cries of pain, moans and groans raised by wounded men being rowed back to that same Long Wharf from which they'd embarked so confidently earlier this same day—incredible though it seemed.

Vaguely, he pondered the fate of other men who'd manned Number 2 gun. How many Colonial-born seamen aboard now lay imprisoned in the *Lively's* stifling forehold? No telling. Andrew slumped, listless, against the damp, rough surface of the bulkhead and attempted to tie an invisible blindfold over his imagination.

He'd no idea how long he'd dozed before he was roused to a heavy *thud!* in the passageway loud enough to suggest that someone might have fallen out there.

Over the soft slap-slapping of waves along H.M.S. *Lively's* side he barely heard a hoarse whisper, "You in there, Mister Hunter?"

Andrew roused, croaked, "Aye. For God's sake, get me out of here else I'll go mad!"

"Aye, aye, sir. Easy does it."

Two bolts securing the brig's door at top and bottom *clucked* softly and then it opened just sufficiently for him to squeeze through and step over the sprawled form of a Marine guard. A soiled neckerchief and a seaman's kersey jacket were thrust into his hands. "Put these on, sir, quick, quick!"

The prisoner grasped the situation the instant he recognized the speaker as Boatswain's Mate Tod Fingers, late of New Bedford.

"Please, sir," Fingers urged, "git rid o' them shoes quick and go barefoot. Once we get on deck you're to line up with hands assembled to replace oarsmen who've been rowing wounded ashore since 'e battle ended. They're plumb tuckered out."

H.M.S. *Lively's* deck was illumined by only a few battle lanterns and deck officers, petty officers and seamen appeared dog-tired and only mechanically were doing what had to be done, Andrew reasoned, was why, undetected, he'd been able to follow Fingers, still clutching the belaying pin he'd used on the Marine, into a scene of orderly confusion. A thunderstorm appeared to be brewing so the deck proved providentially dark save when illuminated by the ruddy glare of tongues of flame spiraling briefly from ruins of Charles Town.

Walking bent-kneed and hunched over to disguise his unusual height, Andrew on spying an empty seat in a longboat bobbing alongside slid down a rope's end and grabbed an oar. By a sudden flare of the distant fires he saw several rowers smeared and splashed by blood from wounded men. Beneath his bare feet Light Infantry shakos, tricorns, bearskin hats and plenty of cartridge boxes, canteens, bayonets and other equipment littered the longboat's floorboards. The relieved boat crew clambering aboard the sloop-of-war moved heavily, uncertainly, like men in the grip of a bad dream.

Fingers called down softly even while Andrew, like the rest of the replacing rowers, raised his oar to the perpendicular, "Good luck. Join you soon's possible—others, too, maybe."

Almost simultaneously the relief coxswain yelled orders to shove the longboat clear of H.M.S. *Lively's* steep and dark-blue side. "Nah, then, ye clumsy barstards, when I gives 'e word to row, keep stroke, and put yer bleedin' backs into it!"

Throwing over his tiller the helmsman steered for Morton's Point where by light of the many torches, lanterns and dancing radiances created by huge bonfires disheveled soldiers were carrying limp figures or assisting walking wounded down to the water's edge. Some could be seen splashing out towards small-craft of deeper draft lying a few feet out, already the tide was ebbing.

Lowing sounds like those made by cows overdue for milking arose from among irregular rows of dark forms lying on the meadow above the beach.

A long time would pass before Andrew Hunter could forget the ghastly, nightmarish scenes he witnessed or participated in.

Taking care to keep locks of hair dangling before his eyes Andrew Hunter helped to lift aboard a succession of inert or feebly moaning bandaged but more often dripping bodies. Only a few wounded still were wearing scarlet regimentals; almost all were bareheaded.

Although the longboat already was loaded to capacity Andrew, just before shoving off, slid over the thwarts on noticing a white-faced drummer boy sprawled unconscious on the beach. Although the lad's head was roughly bandaged it kept on bleeding from that most sanguinary of all injuries, a scalp wound.

While gathering up the slight figure the warm drip of his blood on Andrew's hand prompted him further to disguise himself by donning a red-stained cap from the floorboards then daubing his cheeks with gore. No need to similarly smear his shirt and grimy breeches; already they were gruesomely marked.

Near one o'clock of this sultry night, very dark except when heat lightning played along the western horizon, the longboat bumped alongside lantern-lit Long Wharf, already crowded to capacity. Gently, Andrew lifted the drummer boy's limp figure onto the dock's splintery surface. An officer ordered him to deposit his burden onto one of several huge mounds of loose hay arranged in heaps near the end of Fleet Street. The pile to which Andrew was directed already very nearly was covered by wounded casually abandoned. Thinking fast, he mingled with a stream of oarsmen returning to their boats. He was tensing for action when a hand closed over his elbow, but relaxed when he heard a low voice he recognized as that of Tom Izard, Gunner's Mate and captain of the *Lively's* Number Six gun who'd been impressed off Nantucket almost two years ago. Muttering, "Follow." He pushed through the crowd, led into a dark and narrow lane giving off Fleet Street. Feebly lit, it reeked of garbage and stale urine.

Lightning flashed closer by and thunder rumbled and grumbled beyond the smoking ruins of Charles Town, reminded people of the cannonades heard earlier on. Finally a hard rain commenced to fall. Once they found themselves alone save for a few gaunt alley cats Izard, his long face barely visible in the gloom, said, "Sir, my brother, Jonathan, lives in Marblehead but when he puts in to Boston on business he always 'bides with our sister-in-law who lives in Beer Alley which is real nearby. With luck we'll find him in port."

"In port?"

"Yep. Among other craft Jonathan owns a sizable fishin' smack he uses mostly to carry lumber and salt fish here. Understand what I'm driving at?"

Andrew pushed back dangling red-brown locks. The falling rain felt fine on his sweat-crusted skin. "I do, and I'll never forget this. Can't begin to tell you, Izard, how mighty grateful I am."

"Don't try. Just follow me. Best grab a hold of the back of my belt lest we get separated."

Cautiously they advanced over slimy, foul-smelling cobbles between houses leaning so close together two men could scarcely walk abreast until they reached the alley's intersection with Middle Street. Holding their breath and pressed flat against a wall they watched a long file of fully armed Grenadiers slosh past, bearskins bent against the rain.

Said Izard, "Reckon our best chance of excapin' is while the port authorities are still at sixes and sevens. Doubt whether any kind o' vessel, large or small, will be allowed to sail come daylight."

It turned out that leathery Jonathan Izard, black-bearded, muscular and panther-lean, not only was at his sister-in-law's home but was desperately anxious to put to sea before Customs and Navy patrols recovered from temporary disorganization. He seemed mighty pleased over this thunderstorm and a succession of rain squalls pelting across Boston Harbor. In such weather folks weren't given to being extra nosy.

Thus it came about that by light of a gray and overcast dawn, the fishing smack *Polly Izard,* long since painted brown for reduced visibility, sloop-rigged and of about two tons burthen in dead silence was poled away from Izard's little private dock. Raising no canvas beyond a weather-darkened staysail and jib, Izard allowed his smack to be carried by the ebb then deftly steered her through a dark tangle of shipping congesting the inner harbor into the less crowded waters of the outer harbor. Silently and without being challenged the *Polly Izard* gained the comparative safety of island-dotted Massachusetts Bay.

Once the dark loom of Deer Island had been passed to port Jonathan Izard, in grim silence, shaped a course towards Gloucester and Marblehead.

CHAPTER 13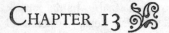

SEARCH PARTY

TILL NEAR DAWN Boston continued to resound with so many sounds of unrest little sleep was enjoyed in Major Hilton's handsome brick dwelling. An almost continual clatter of hoofs, the measured tramp of marching troops, the rasping of iron-shod wheels over cobblestones, the creaking of handcarts and wheelbarrows carrying groaning wounded, the occasional shouts and challenges of pickets on duty on Beacon Hill combined to make rest nearly impossible during this hot and rainy night.

Shortly after daylight the Major gripping a stout cane took a brief walk along Joy and Beacon Streets. Persons who recognized the bookseller either proved uncommunicative or hurried on, eyes averted. Why? Was he now considered an avowed Loyalist? All Sarah's father could be sure of was that the British finally had carried the redoubt but also that the bulk of its defenders had been able to escape over Charles Town Neck. Most accounts agreed that General Howe's troops had been so shocked by staggering casualties and had been so exhausted no pursuit had been attempted.

At present the defeated Colonists probably were retiring in the direction of Cambridge or retreating as fast as they could along country roads mostly leading north or westwards or anywhere beyond reach of Redcoat vengeance.

Hilton overheard a tall individual wearing a clerical collar solemnly state that around two-thirds of the King's troops had been either killed or wounded. Verily, the preacher concluded, Almighty God had smitten the Philistines hip and thigh.

On the other hand a lawyer of Major Hilton's acquaintance shook his head. "I know for a fact the Rebels killed or wounded less than a hundred British Regulars. Don't credit any rubbish about there having been a terrible massacre on Breed's Hill."

Of course Hilton knew this to be absurd—his telescope had told him that much. When, ever more often, the crash of improvised battering rams was preceded by noises of splintering wood and shrill, terror-stricken cries, the veteran hurried home and grimly made sure his home's handsome but sturdy street-level shutters were bolted shut and all outside entrances locked and barricaded as well.

For the time being no British Provost patrols had materialized to enforce orders so, once his dwelling had been secured, the veteran loaded his duck gun with heavy pellets such as he used on wild geese next primed a pair of silver and gold-mounted dueling French pistols picked up in Louisburg. Next, he unlocked a tantalus, selected a cut-glass carafe of fine brandy and took such a long swig he belched while mounting guard in a small library room adjacent to his front door. He came to the unhappy realization that not in years had he experienced so miserable a sense of indecision.

What would result from this amazing affront to the might of His Majesty's regular establishment? Inevitably, a steel ring swiftly would be forged around Boston and its environs and a thorough search for Rebel sympathizers would be implemented. Subjects known or suspected of disloyalty surely would be rounded up to be imprisoned or possibly hanged or shot out of hand.

Sarah and Ellen meanwhile lingered in Mrs. Hilton's sick room patiently enduring a torrent of querulous and generally unanswerable questions.

Sarah, usually ebullient, now resembled her father in adopting a restrained and thoughtful manner. As if she and Ellen had met only recently she now covertly considered Andrew's sister as, clutching a long lawn night rail about her, she peered intently out into the gray morning at the gradually quieting town. Whew! How still and terribly hot it remained indoors.

"Oh dear, I do hope Andrew, Gordon Hartley and the rest are safe."

From a quality in her friend's voice Ellen for the first time sensed that Sarah might be growing seriously attracted to Andy. If this were so, how would such an interest affect the Hunter family's immediate future, they being avowed Patriots?

Sarah, who also had come to peer out of the window was puzzled to explain a curious conviction that something very wrong had happened to Andrew. Oddly enough, while jerking a comb impatiently through disordered blonde locks, Sarah queried, "Tell me, Ellie, do you feel Andrew has come through this safely?"

Ellen, stepping back from the window, slowly tied ribbons supporting the last of three petticoats. "Why do you ask?"

Steadily, Sarah considered her friend. "Because I've the strange feeling Andrew is in deep trouble of some description."

"Strange you should say that, for I, too, have been worrying over the same possibility but, Sarah dear, there's small point to go on worrying till we hear something definite."

Ellen hesitated while lowering a billowing, blue-sprigged gown of light cotton over her head. "Tell me, what do you and your father intend to do if the British forces *have* taken a bad beating?"

Miserably, Sarah Hilton stared at the floor. "I swear, well, I just don't know where Papa stands. Ever since the Boston Port Act came into effect—and even before that—Papa has kept a neutral attitude. Now, I wonder how much longer it will remain possible for him to 'carry water on both shoulders' as our countrymen put it, since he's been a soldier of the King and is a home-grown Massachusetter at the same time."

Sarah guessed, but couldn't know, that at this moment a goodly number of long-unidentified Rebel sympathizers hurriedly were packing a minimum number of valuables in hopes of getting across Boston Neck before the British High Command could collect itself sufficiently to render any escape to the mainland out of the question. She'd never seen Papa look so grim as during Lieutenant-Colonel Cameron's quiet departure a while ago.

In subdued silence Ellen led the way below to join Sarah and her father for a breakfast of hot chocolate, scones and eggs consumed in a tense silence broken only when a violent hammering commenced on the front door and an angry voice began shouting, "Open up! Dammit, open this door immediately!"

Unhurriedly, the veteran wiped his mouth and tucked the pistols into his breeches' band before going down to where Toby hovered white-eyed and trembling over the incessant crashing of what must be musket butts against the door's panels.

"Open up! Open up at once, damn you! Else we'll break in!"

"Hold hard out there! No call to wake the dead!" Benjamin Hilton called then slid back massive brass bolts and raised a pair of stout wooden bars. Swinging open the portal he was confronted by the heated and suffused features of a youngish lieutenant wearing the Royal Marines' distinctive uniform. Sword gleaming, the officer burst in followed by a corporal and a trio of privates but checked himself in mid-stride before that tall figure in light gray calmly confronting him.

"You Benjamin Hilton?"

From the top of the hall stairs both young women, fingers pressed against lips, watched the veteran draw himself to full height, glare at the officer and then rasp, "*Major* Hilton to you, you ill-mannered pup! What the Devil d'you mean by damn near breaking down my door? Who are you?"

The officer, round-faced, sandy-haired and a sub-lieutenant by his single silver epaulette, checked himself but said hotly, "I am Lieutenant Dubose of His Majesty's ship *Lively*. Stand aside—sir!" He started advancing down the hall followed by his Marines who, hot and angry, held ready brass-barreled blunderbusses equipped with curious bayonets which at present lay folded back along the barrels but which could instantly be snapped into a forward position by pressure on a knurled iron button on the grip.

Unshaken, Hilton held his ground, leveled his pistols. "Since when have His Majesty's troops, lacking a warrant or any valid excuse, taken to breaking and entering the home of a peaceful British subject?"

Roared the Lieutenant, "Dammit, sir. I carry orders to search this house from roof to cellar!"

Hilton's steel-gray eyes narrowed. "In search of what, may I ask?"

The Marine officer, a chunky individual of below average height, snapped, "Sir, I've been sent to arrest a traitor and deserter named Andrew Hunter, formerly a lieutenant in His Majesty's Navy. He has been reported to be very welcome here."

"—And exactly what has Mister Hunter done to deserve such serious charges?"

Perspiring heavily, the officer lowered his sword. "Your pardon, sir, but I know nothing concerning that. I am merely obeying orders. Lodge any complaint with Captain Purcell of the *Lively* an you wish."

Deliberately the Major returned the French pistols to his waistband. "Very well, Mister Dubose, as an experienced former officer I know when to yield to superior force so I will escort you during your search of these premises. I ask only that you do not enter my wife's bedroom. You have my word that Mrs. Hilton is seriously ill and alone save for a black female attendant."

Lieutenant Dubose blinked, nodded then led his Marines, wearing short-skirted scarlet jackets, white breeches, black gaiters and low, pointed caps fronted by silvered plates bearing the inscription *"Per Terram, Per Mare,"* on a search which included all rooms save Mrs. Hilton's. They opened every closet, and wardrobe, peered under beds, even lifted the lids of clothing chests.

Mrs. Hilton's thin voice kept shrilling, "What's going on? Oh, Benjamin, don't let those noisy brutes harm our furniture!"

Meanwhile Sarah and her guest from Cambridge hovered uncertainly in the upper hallway, pale and clutching one another for reassurance. Ellen asked tremulously, "Wh—what can they want? Did you hear what that awful man said about Andrew?"

On drawing near, Lieutenant Dubose's manner relaxed a trifle, became almost apologetic, "Please, ladies, tell me the truth. Is— or has a Naval officer named Andrew Hunter been here recently?"

Sarah elevated and looked down an attractively short up-turned nose while her large, bright-blue eyes steadily regarded the intruder. "Yes, sir. Mister Hunter was our guest for supper last evening but was recalled to his ship before we had done dining."

"Indeed?" Dubose commented grimly. "Then he'd better not be discovered here."

"But wh—why all this pother?" Ellen queried, dark eyes snapping. "Of what crime does my brother stand accused?"

Dubose's next words chilled her to the depths of her being.

"—Of the worst! Treason in the face of the enemy. Hunter was arrested but somehow managed to escape the ship last night." Sarah barely suppressed a fervent "Oh, thank God!" as Dubose continued, "The evidence of his villainy is so overwhelming that when caught, Ma'am, he's bound to be hanged."

When at length the invaders had satisfied themselves that the fugitive wasn't to be found Lieutenant Dubose ordered his men onto the street to await orders. The moment the battered front door closed the Marine officer's manner underwent a remarkable alteration. Smiling somewhat sheepishly he removed his cap and frankly mopped a streaming red forehead.

"My deepest apologies, sir. But, since Andy—Mister Hunter, I mean—is or was a friend of mine, this has been a most distasteful task. I beg you to believe I'd no choice in the matter and I apologize for my previous behavior but felt it necessary to impress my men—some of whom have been acting surly of late."

Under a neat scratch wig Major Hilton's head inclined, "I understand, young sir; orders are orders, no matter how distasteful." He beckoned the Lieutenant into the waiting room then ordered Toby to fetch a decanter of his Number 3 sherry—just tolerably good.

Dubose followed but only after making certain that members of his search party indeed were loitering about the front stoop.

"Considering the circumstances this is most decent of you, sir," Dubose declared, openly impressed by the older man's unshakably calm manner. "I feel I owe you more of an explanation for this unhappy affair."

Benjamin Hilton struggled to conceal deep-rooted misgivings. "You do. Pray take a seat. Why were you ordered to search *my* home for Mister Hunter?"

"Well, sir," the Marine perched upon the edge of an occasional chair rather like a delinquent schoolboy about to be lectured by his schoolmaster, "aboard *Lively* I knew Mister Hunter fairly well."

"Good officer?"

"Yes, sir, one of the best; uncommon knowledgeable and curious concerning cannon of all descriptions; siege guns, swivels, mortars, coehorns—the lot. He was always inquiring, reading any manuals or textbooks he could discover on the subject of ordnance and its service."

With precision, Major Hilton refilled the delicate wine glass imprisoned between the Marine's stubby and none-too-clean fingers.

"I understand. Many's the conversation I had with him here concerning gunnery which bored the ladies no end, I fear." Hilton took a sip of his own wine. "Please tell me something about what chanced aboard the *Lively* yesterday?"

Uncomfortably, Lieutenant Dubose's gaze shifted to a celestial sphere which, with its companion terrestrial globe, flanked the fireplace. "Sir, I won't pretend to understand the truth of the matter, but for some time there have been suspicions voiced in our wardroom that Andy ain't entirely devoted to the King's Cause. Nothing definite mind you till yesterday morning when Mister Saxeby noticed that the fire of guns commanded by Mister Hunter was somewhat inaccurate.

"As I've already stated I know nothing about the rights of the matter, was much too occupied with my own duties. However, it was observed by several officers that balls fired from Andrew's Number Two and Number Four guns not only failed to range the Rebel redoubt but landed short and ricocheted a distance thereby causing serious casualties among our troops."

Benjamin Hilton stiffened on his chair. "D'you mean to say that Mr. Hunter deliberately caused his gunners to fire on His Majesty's troops?"

Dubose set down his glass, spread agitated hands. "Sir, I only heard that a number of half-powder charges for those and other guns of Hunter's division later were detected by Mister Saxeby."

"Um. Half-charges you say. No wonder some balls landed among the Brit—er—our troops."

"Yes, sir, but 'tis still to be proved that such treachery was done with Mister Hunter's knowledge or consent. Others may well have been responsible."

"'Others'?"

"On *Lively's* muster roll we have listed not a few impressed American-born and other disgruntled British subjects: the crews of Numbers Two and Four included several of these. Mister Hunter was seen by Mister Saxeby personally to have trained that Number Two gun which killed many of our troops, so ordered him arrested forthwith."

Sarah and Ellen sitting in miserable silence on the staircase heard the older man ask, "What else happened when those shots fell short?"

"Mister Saxeby ordered the entire crews of Numbers Two and Four guns into irons and caused Mister Hunter to be locked into the ship's brig pending court-martial."

Shivers trickled down Sarah's back and Ellen tucked a dark-red and full lower lip between white but irregular teeth as they entered the waiting room.

Said Ellen, "Sir, did I not overhear you state that my brother, Mister Hunter, has—has escaped?"

"Aye, Ma'am. That's why we've come in search of him."

In a strained voice, Sarah queried, "How did he get away?"

Lieutenant Dubose, looking both embarrassed and hot, finished the last of his sherry, said, "Why, Ma'am, 'tis thought Gunner's Mate Thomas Izard, an impressed member of our crew, during the transfer of wounded to Boston managed to go below and use a belaying pin on a Marine standing guard outside the brig. His blow was so shrewd the fellow's still unconscious—may even die."

"Let's hope he doesn't," interjected the Major. "What happened next?"

"Well, sir, as nearly as can be figured, Mister Hunter, on being released, made his way on deck and, aided by poor light, managed to mingle with a gang of oarsmen being assembled to relieve rowers who'd been pulling our boats for hours. 'Tis also thought Izard and several other traitorous rascals escaped in the same fashion.

"Because of this Captain Purcell has ordered all American-born seamen clapped in irons and confined below decks." Dubose put down his glass and looked solemn. "As an example, no doubt, four men—two each from Number Two and Four gun crews—have been tried by a drumhead court-martial and are condemned to die at sunset this evening."

An odd frigidity invaded Benjamin Hilton's being. "So they intend to hang them?"

"Until 'dead, dead, dead' as the magistrates say. On our other men-of-war all American-born hands have been placed, er—under restraint."

Muscles stood out along the veteran's jaw. Lest he say something unwise Hilton only commented, "Justifiable precautions no doubt. May I point out that you still have not explained why you were sent to ransack my house?"

Dubose's gaze shifted to Sarah. "Well, sir, 'tis a well-known fact in the wardroom that Andy—er, Mister Hunter—feels very taken with your daughter. Since he'd been entertained in your home on several occasions Captain Purcell and Mister Saxeby reasoned he might seek refuge with you. Obviously such is not the case so, with profound apologies, sir, I'll be on my way."

Once the search party had swung off along Joy Street's shiny brown cobbles a slow, shuddering sigh escaped Ellen. Well, at least for the moment Andrew was still alive! To know where he might have gone or for how long he'd escape arrest she'd have given five years off her life.

Sarah would have given more.

CHAPTER 14 ✺

CRUISE OF THE
POLLY IZARD

IT DIDN'T REQUIRE GRIMY, unshaven and otherwise disheveled Andrew Hunter long to deduce that Tom Izard's older brother, Jonathan, must be of considerably more substance than just the owner and skipper of the little fishing smack *Polly Izard*. This solidly built, beetle-browed and impassive individual also owned controlling shares in two large Grand Banks fishing schooners in addition to a freight dock and a sizable chandler's business in his native town of Marblehead. Also it appeared that he and his family occupied a modest but right-comfortable home built on Peach's Head on the outer rim of Marblehead's spacious but narrow-mouthed and rock-enclosed harbor.

Once the *Polly Izard* had left Boston's outer harbor astern barely sufficient light prevented her colliding with towering British transports and supply ships and impounded New England vessels anchored in the bay.

To render navigation still more difficult only a weak wind was blowing, barely sufficient to allow the *Polly Izard* steerageway. While she slipped ghost-like through the murk it came to the three Colonials as a meager consolation that so feeble a breeze would fill no canvas set in pursuit.

Soon it grew light enough to reveal in increasing detail not only the many islands dotting Massachusetts Bay but also, off to port, the dark and low-lying blur of the mainland.

Crouching, hungry and nearing exhaustion below the bulwarks amidships Andrew Hunter remained plunged in abysmal misery. Entertaining no illusions concerning his fate should he fall in British hands he made no effort to listen to the Izard brothers' low-pitched talk and wondered instead who might have been responsible for the making and use of those reduced loads, but of course that didn't matter now. Possibly Tom Izard, sucking hard on a short-stemmed and blackened clay pipe, might cast a light on the subject? Little time was required to realize that yonder lantern-jawed Marbleheader not only had saved his life but, more important, had settled once and for all the direction of where lay Andrew Hunter's loyalties.

On the other hand he foresaw doubts rising among the local citizenry once they learned that although he, Andrew Hunter, undoubtedly was New England-born and reared he'd nevertheless been serving in the Royal Navy since the age of fifteen.

Suddenly ravenous, he caught up a hitherto neglected bowl of cold codfish chowder and using fingers crammed it into his mouth at the same time striving to decide on an immediate course of action. Um. Right now it seemed only one factor might work in his favor. The Izard family, he'd gathered by now, had lived in or near Marblehead for several generations, also a branch of his mother's people, the Ornes. Originally her family had been known as the "Hornes" but in Marblehead the "H" had been dropped a generation or so ago, probably following some family row—a practice followed fairly frequently throughout the American Colonies. Members of the same family therefor might spell their patronyms with phonetic variations.

He now recalled his mother's having mentioned cousins who for a long time had been natives of Marblehead, but that branch of her family seldom had been mentioned. How closely related he was to the Marblehead Ornes he hadn't the least notion, but at best they could be no more than second cousins.

A fresh set of worries beset him. What would be the reactions of Sarah and the Major when, inevitably, they heard of his presumed treachery and escape? Come to think of it he'd fully intended, sometime during the evening of that unhappy supper party, to convey to Sarah as best he could—he wasn't glib or clever about such delicate matters—how tenderly he'd come to feel towards her.

In every way the Major's daughter appealed to him—her joyous disposition, her grace in speech and movement, also her tact. For a female, Sarah also seemed essentially practical. Now that her mother no longer had been able to cope, she, without fuss, quite efficiently had been running the house on Joy Street. How clearly now he could visualize Sarah's strongly handsome features.

Crouched, dirty and disheveled, under the starboard rail he remained overwhelmed by the incredible suddenness with which his career and ambitions had been wrecked. Mechanically, he used the back of a wide brown hand to wipe his mouth and bristly chin even while chewing a chunk of iron-hard ship's biscuit.

Andrew stiffened when he listened to Tom tell his brother how he, a gunner's mate, along with Johnny Bannock and Ed Littleton, also Marblehead men, had been able to make those reduced charges and plant them in the *Lively's* magazine.

Tom bit off a chew of tobacco before casting a quizzical sidewise glance at his former officer's untidy figure. Said he brusquely, "Don't suppose you'd recall Bannock and Littletons' bein' dragged aboard?" He almost added a "sir" but didn't.

"No. Probably because whenever impressments were made I, if in any way possible, stayed out of sight there being nothing I could do to help such luckless wretches."

"Shouldn't wonder," black-bearded Jonathan nodded. Although tall, gaunt and severe of aspect, Tom's brother usually wore a cheery, meaningless half-grin possibly to disguise a firm and penetrating mind.

Periodically, the *Polly Izard's* owner peered over a shoulder while talking with his brother. "Soon after the *Lively* reached Boston and we heard that you and other 'pressed Marbleheaders were aboard, the town went into an uproar. John Glover, Elbridge Gerry, Azel Orne and other members of our Committee of Safety got hot under the collar so 't was easy to brisk up recruitin' for the regiment they still haven't finished raisin'."

"How's it to be called?"

"Dunno for sure, Tom, but since it's mostly made up of officers and men out of the old 5th Essex County Militia, I presume 'twill be called the same—for the time bein' at least." Jonathan used calloused fingers to comb a round and greasy black beard before tapping dottle from his pipe on the rail. "Any others escape like you and your friend Hunter?"

"May well have. 'Twas near pitch dark aboard ship and everything was all at sixes and sevens. Yep. Some others must ha' got away."

Jonathan bent to ease the mainsheet at the same time keeping a watchful eye astern for a moment ago the tops of a two-masted vessel had heaved into sight coming from the direction of Boston. Most likely 'twould prove to be only another coaster fleeing like the *Polly Izard,* still she might just as well prove to be a Royal Navy patrol ship or a revenue cutter or something of that nature.

Evenly, Jonathan regarded his brother. "If you can, Tom, explain to me what happened aboard the *Lively* durin' the Lobsterbacks' second attack. How come the entire crews of two guns got clapped in irons so sudden and your officer friend here was chucked into pokey swift-like?"

"Like I've already said, those crews got spotted firin' reduced charges and Mr. Hunter had been noticed sighting Number 2 which killed a lot of Lobsterbacks." Slowly, Tom shook a shaggy head. "Weren't nothin' I could do so I kept out of notice till, later on, I seized a chance to go below and to knock out a Marine guardin' Mister Hunter."

Andrew cut in, "Since I'm no longer an officer of the King kindly forget the 'Mister Hunter.' I'd prefer you to call me just 'Andrew' or 'Andy.' Why'd you help me?

Tom grinned. "Reckon our side soon will need a mort of officers knowledgeable about Navy guns and artillery of all sorts, right badly."

Jonathan Izard continued to peer over the stern. "Damn this maiden's fart of a breeze! Go forrard, Tom, stiffen the jib. Don't fancy the way yonder stranger's closin' in. An he sails much nigher I'll put about and try for Nahant."

To the Izard brothers it proved grimly significant that on this particular morning practically no other sails were sighted, not even those of small coasters or skiffs or shallops such as usually were plentiful along this stretch of shoreline.

About the same moment it became evident this pursuer mounted at least two cannon; a small Union Jack fluttered up to her main truck. Instantly, the *Polly Izard's* owner pushed over his tiller and at what seemed like a snail's pace steered for a dim row of roofs, warehouses and wharfs composing the village of Nahant. Fortunately, just then, the topsails of what must be a considerably larger vessel appeared above a gray-white bank of fog moving in from the sea. The cutter—there now remained no doubt what she was—at once altered course to intercept this more promising prey.

Under present uncertain conditions it didn't seem advisable for Jonathan to venture into Nahant lying so near to Boston. The British might well have dispatched a force yonder in search of Rebel cannon and munitions. Tom and he lowered sail then dropped anchor in the lee of a small, uninhabited island where the smack wallowed unnoticed save by fishermen pulling lobster pots or hand-lining closer inshore.

Not until late afternoon after fog had crept inland was the anchor raised and sail made with Jonathan Izard sailing a compass course. But the fog thickened and then what little wind there was died out leaving the *Polly Izard* to drift and rock helplessly, monotonously on the broad waters of Massachusetts Bay.

Sometime during the night—no one aboard her had a watch—the fog lifted under a breeze out of the northwest which gradually stiffened until the smack commenced to flick spurts of spray over blunt bows while plowing in the general direction of Beverly and Marblehead.

By the light of a whale oil lantern Tom kindled a fire on a sand box set in the smack's hold empty but reeking of cargoes of long-dead fish. Since there'd been no opportunity for Jonathan to purchase those supplies he'd sailed over to buy, a pot of "Liberty" or sassafras tea was brewed, also an iron kettle of lobscouse—a codfish stew of sorts thickened with salt pork and ship's bread—

was put on to heat. A few cupfuls of well-watered Jamaica rum served to render the repast more palatable.

While they were eating, Jonathan at last found opportunity to consider thoroughly this muscular ex-officer with the firmly jutting jaw and small but clear and well-separated bright-blue eyes. By the light flames dancing on the sand box Jonathan remarked, "Know something? So far, you've yet to give me yer full name, where you hail from or whose kin you are."

"I'm Andrew Orne Hunter, born in Dorchester but my father shifted his shipping interests to Cambridge only a few years later; I grew up there."

Jonathan scratched under a grimy blue shirt of dowlas cotton. "Be you related to the Azel Ornes of Marblehead?"

Andrew swilled the last of his rum and set down a dented tin cup. "I expect so, Captain. Likely they'd be cousins of sorts. My mother was born in Marblehead but left there young and seldom visited in Marblehead, at least not that I know of. She was a daughter of Azel Orne born and raised in Gloucester and lived there till she married my father and they straightaway settled in Dorchester."

Jonathan nodded under a battered straw hat acquired in the West Indies. "Um. I've heard tell of some Ornes bidin' round those parts. Must have been a row of some sort 'twixt her branch of the family and the Ornes I know in Marblehead."

Andrew said wearily, "Let's hope after all these years they're ready to let bygones be bygones."

"Well, you'll soon be meetin' 'em so I hope they hold no grudges." Momentarily Jonathan fingered his beard, faced this fugitive with the piercing bright-blue eyes. "But your havin' served free-willing in the Royal Tyrant's Navy is going to take some explainin'."

He turned to Tom now yawning and heavy-eyed. "Wished to God I could learn how my other vessels be farin'. Both schooners were long overdue home from the Banks even afore I sailed over to Boston." He dislodged a shred of fish from between big, tobacco-yellowed teeth, which was remarkable since few men nearing forty retained many.

"Tell me, Mister Hunt—er, Andrew, how come Brother Tom bein' Colonial got raised to Gunner's Mate in that damned

Lively which, as you well know, has been pesterin' these shores for a long spell of patrol duty?"

Andrew's loose grimy shirt lifted under a shrug. "Possibly I might be held responsible to a certain degree. You see, like me, your brother is uncommon knowledgeable and skillful concerning the use of cannon of all calibres which gave me a plausible excuse for recommending him for promotion. Besides, Tom has an inborn quality for leadership." He smiled faintly. "He's used fists or a rope's end enough to prove that."

As the *Polly Izard* continued sturdily to plow through rising seas the elder brother nodded, "Aye, Tom's been daft over cannons ever since he was knee-high to a tadpole; he always was questionin', pokin' or pryin' at any piece of artillery on any vessel carryin' guns they'd let him come nigh to."

A smile broadened over the fugitive's wide, unshaven jaw. "I soon understood how Tom felt because I got bitten by the same bug at an early age. Expect that was why, even though I, a Colonial, won a commission early and got promoted to be the *Lively's* Gunnery Officer over some of my seniors who didn't relish that a little bit."

"I opine you couldn't have had an easy time of it in the King's ships," Jonathan commented.

"You opine correctly," Andrew admitted with a mirthless grin. "Somehow, I never have been able to fathom why so many home-grown Britishers tend to treat us American-borns like poor relations rather than equal fellow-subjects and useful allies."

"Ye're right there," Tom said. "We've supported England in every one of her wars over here with the French and the Spanish, and right up to the hilt, too. But that don't seem to count for tuppence."

Over the dull *slap-slapping* and sibilant hissing of waves along the smack's side Tom continued, "Tell me, Jon, has Johnny Glover by now got the Militia Companies equipped and drilled into usefulness?"

"Yep. Him, Eb Gerry, Jerry Lee, Azel Orne and others have licked our so-called minutemen what used to be the '5th Essex County Militia,' in which you'll recall we both served for a piece, into tolerable good shape. They've enrolled a lot of men last I heard. Right now they're called the 'Marblehead Regiment' but 'tis said they're soon to be listed as the 21st Regiment in the Army of the United Colonies. Sounds pretty impressive, don't it?

"Um. 'Army of the United Colonies.' It sure does. What sort of fellows are enrollin'?"

"Sailors and fishermen mostly but there are quite a few free, seafarin' Blacks among 'em. They're bein' accepted just like anybody else even if some folks don't fancy the idee. But, like a lot of others, I claim if a man aims to fight for liberty the color of his hide don't matter a mite.

"Our volunteers hev been strainin' their britches to go join in that general rally takin' place up to Cambridge."

While under a still-freshening breeze the *Polly Izard* followed an unusually long bowsprit in the direction of Marblehead, the brothers got caught up on what had chanced in one of most important fishing ports in North America since Tom Izard had sailed for the West Indies—and impressment—nearly two years earlier. Evidently quite a few events of importance had occurred. For example, on February 26th at noon of this same year, the British with a raiding force of 240 men suddenly had been landed at Marblehead and with bayonets fixed, drums beating and flags flying had set out to seize cannon and munitions reputedly collected in Salem and Beverly.

The Marblehead Regiment, Jonathan stated, had turned out in a big hurry but still were too late to stop the raiders' advance towards their objectives. They'd only been able to line the roads and stand ready to attack Britishers returning to their ship. Had the 'Headers received orders similar to those given at Lexington and Concord not two months later, blood certainly would have been spilt. However, outside of Salem local militia and minutemen had raised the North Drawbridge, the only communication connecting Marblehead with Salem and Beverly and so effectively had denied the raiders access to the latter village. So many Colonials appeared ready and able to fight that the British commander, Colonel Alexander Leslie, evidently a more sagacious individual than either Major Pitcairn or Lord Percy, at Lexington and Concord, had contrived a face-saving deal with the locals.

Provided the Rebels only would lower the drawbridge he pledged his word that his force would advance no farther than thirty rods in the direction of Salem. Having technically accomplished his mission, Colonel Leslie then had ordered his troops to about-face and in good order had retreated to Marblehead.

"You should have been there, Tom, to see a funny thing happen: when, behind martial music, the Redcoats marched back to their transport damned if our volunteers didn't form a column behind 'em and tramp along in step with the Lobsterbacks' band! I vow 'twas *that* comical I'll never forget it."

Towards noon a low and rocky coastline dotted with small islands loomed ahead. Not many trees were visible on glacier-scoured hills which looked as if they'd been planed smooth by an eternity of wild winter gales.

Here and there clusters of surf-spouting reefs showed smooth brown tops to which clung and swayed fringes of yellow-brown kelp. To Andrew, commencing to revive interest in his surroundings, these suggested the heads of balding Tritons on the point of surfacing.

Even before the *Polly Izard* had scudded past Cat Island on which had stood the smallpox hospital which had caused so much trouble before it recently had got burned down, and gained the harbor's entrance it seemed that news of the battle on Breed's Hill must just recently have reached Marblehead.

Even while Jonathan commenced picking a course towards his own dock through a dense tangle of moored or anchored shipping of all sizes and descriptions ragged bursts of musket shots could be heard—probably fired in mistaken celebration of victory. Loudly they reverberated about the town. Drums were rolling, church bells were clanging and great numbers of people could be seen milling excitedly about.

PART III
The Army's Navy

CHAPTER 15 🎐

MARBLEHEAD

THE MOMENT THE SMACK *Polly Izard* scudded past Marblehead Rock and entered the harbor's narrow entrance it appeared obvious that news of the conflict on Breed's Hill indeed must have reached this port only a few hours ago. This wasn't astonishing since by water Boston lay only little over nineteen miles away.

While the Izard brothers continually hailed rough-looking acquaintances for news Andrew Hunter was enabled for the first time to view this once-thriving fishing port at close range. Heretofore he'd only seen this port through a spyglass while, last fall and winter, H.M.S. *Lively* had patrolled this coast from Nahant to Cape Ann. In such fashion he was already familiar with the profiles of Salem and Beverly. The latter port reportedly was growing into an important shipbuilding center not only because timber could be more readily fetched there but also because this port, lying at a greater distance from Boston, was more likely to escape sudden descents by British landing parties. Defenders would be granted more time in which to muster should an alarm be raised.

Uneasily, Andrew once more speculated on the nature of the reception he might expect in Marblehead once news got about that he'd actually been aboard the well-hated man-of-war which, on three occasions, had intercepted vessels from this port and had impressed a good many husbands and sons before the eyes of outraged inhabitants. A cold, hollow sensation invading the pit of Andrew's stomach increased as gray-shingled and mostly white-painted homes and churches showed up in greater detail. White gull droppings splashed pilings and roofs of warehouses built along the shoreline.

Almost unbearable grew the stench of split fish in the process of drying on innumerable flakes erected in any open space among dwellings and other structures on a series of wide, gray-stone ledges climbing up from the water's edge.

Due to the blockade Marblehead's long and narrow harbor was jam-packed with Grand Banks fishing schooners, lumber scows, coasting craft and even a few tall, full-rigged ocean-going ships. These lay moored or often lashed together. Smallboats were pulling busily among them.

All at once a commotion broke out. Every one peered up at a bearded fellow who'd been working astraddle a topgallant yard. He kept pointing out to sea and yelling, "Damnation! Damn' Britishers are back on patrol!"

Sure enough a smart, black-and-white painted, two-masted ship, white canvas agleam, had appeared from the direction of Boston and had commenced to parallel the coast about two miles offshore.

Together with Andrew, Tom swarmed up to the masthead.

Jonathan growled, "Jesus! Them Lobsterbacks ain't wastin' no time! Which one is she?"

"By that new patch in her foretops'l," Andrew stated, "she'll be the sloop-of-war *Merlin*. Mounts eighteen 12-pounders, last I heard."

No further comments were made while Jonathan deftly picked a course through the shipping towards his own dock built near the eastern side of the harbor's entrance, complete with a powerful derrick and a sizable, shingled warehouse at its land end. It bore a weathered sign reading "J. Izard and Brother—Ship Suppliers."

"Yonder's my place." Tom's brother indicated a long and rambling, dark-red-painted one-storey clapboard house shaded by a few fruit trees and enclosed by a neat white picket fence. Decided Andrew, the Izard home rather resembled its owner—more solid and useful than decorative.

Jonathan spat over the side, said grimly, "Don't see neither my *Favourite* nor my *Eliza* tied up. Should have made port back from the Grand Banks a week ago at the least."

Since so few people were visible along the waterfront it stood to reason some matter of major significance must be taking place near the center of town—most likely on that Training Ground where, over generations, units of the 5th Essex County Militia had held musters and, fortified by plenty of fiery Jamaica rum, had drilled after a fashion. Yes. This must be the explanation for persistent shrilling of fifes and dry rattling of drums in the distance.

Once the *Polly*'s brown-stained mainsail had been lowered Tom jerked down the jib then made ready the forward mooring line before jumping onto a wharf among stacked and barnacle-encrusted buoys and lobster pots.

Jonathan didn't appear overly surprised when nobody came running down from his house. Usually his son Sam, a freckled, gangling fourteen-year-old, or Anne, his spindle-legged daughter of twelve, by now would have been jumping up and down on the dock shrilling welcomes. Nor did Deborah, his usually silent, plain and roly-poly but efficient and ever-devoted wife, appear on the front porch to flap greetings with an apron.

"Reckon folks must have gone to watch the troops assemble. Just afore sailin' for Boston I heard tell the Regiment had orders to be ready to march in short order."

Presently, a tall young woman whose abundant red-brown hair which seemed to bounce to her stride came running from a small cottage next to Jonathan's place. She hurried down to the wharf calling, "Uncle Jon, Uncle Jon! Thank the Good Lord you're back safe! What with all the news from Boston we've been *that* worried over you." Abruptly she halted staring as if at a phantom. "Tom! Can that really be *you?*"

He swept her off her feet and bussed her on both cheeks. "Sure is, Amy. My God, how you've grown up; kind of pretty, too." He turned, called to Andrew, "Make fast that stern line then come ashore and set yer feet on free soil."

Once he'd done so Jonathan Izard jerked a thumb towards the tall, auburn-haired girl. "Andrew Hunter, this here's Amy Orne, my niece by marriage. Her family mostly got carried off by a fierce plague of smallpox we suffered here back in '73; nowadays she lives next door with Widow Milburn; she's sister to my wife."

Amy Orne? All at once abysmally aware of his unkempt appearance, Andrew found himself diffidently shaking hands with this tall and pleasantly formed young woman. How very extraordinary that the first person he should encounter in Marblehead was an Orne; probably, she must be related in some degree. He managed a half-bow while declaring himself honored to make her acquaintance, more than ever wishing he wasn't looking so confounded scruffy.

Smiling steadily, Amy Orne returned his stare as if making rapid mental calculations. Um. This young woman appeared friendly enough, but how would the rest of the Marblehead Ornes react to a remote relative from Cambridge? Especially when they learned, as inevitably they would, that until a few days ago he'd been an officer of the Royal Navy?

Said Amy Orne, gaze still frankly occupied with this lithe but well-muscled stranger, "Uncle Jon, I know you're anxious because Aunt Deborah's not here but she will be once she learns of the *Polly*'s return. Although weary of so much parading and to-do, she went up to the Training Ground only to please Sam and Annie."

"What's going on?"

"The 21st Regiment is getting ready to set out for Boston early tomorrow, or so 'tis rumored."

Stooping to pat a big black-and-brown retriever Tom said, "Quiet, Sambo! What did you say the militia is called nowadays?"

"The 21st Regiment in the Army of the United Colonies. Sounds pretty grand, doesn't it? Nevertheless, everybody around here still names it the 'Marblehead Regiment.' I guess they always will."

"Who's commanding?" Jonathan wanted to know.

"John Glover is to be Colonel."

"Who are the other officers?"

"I don't know them all, but the Lieutenant-Colonel is to be Elbridge Gerry."

"Couldn't have made a better choice," Jonathan averred setting heavy sea boots onto the crushed-oystershell-paved footpath leading up to his home. "He's a good soldier but a better politician!"

The girl picked up gray, full skirts high enough for Andrew to catch a flash of neat-turned ankles. "By the bye, Colonel Glover has kept on asking where you are, Uncle Jon. Soon's you get freshened up you'd better go talk with him. His headquarters are in the Green Dragon."

"I'll bet," Tom said. "John always did like a tot handy-by. I warrant Harry Saunders and other tavern keepers are making a tidy packet these days and will so long as supplies hold out."

For Tom Izard it proved indescribably satisfying once more to find himself amid homely surroundings; even the pungent reek of drying codfish repugnant to most people save a true 'Header came as perfume to his nostrils. After his wife had perished during the smallpox epidemic of '73 and since there had been no children he'd rented his small house to move in with Jonathan and Deborah. How intimately he knew every detail of the long clapboard house and its surroundings.

Once the *Polly Izard*'s crew had consumed a meal of baked scrod, onions and Indian meal mush hastily prepared by Amy, Jonathan heaved himself to his feet and went to clean up a mite after announcing, "Well, reckon I'd best get up to the Training Ground and look up Johnny Glover. Maybe he can tell me what in Tunket is going on. Maybe you should bide here, Tom, and tell Deborah what's chanced when she shows up."

"Hell, no! I'm going with you."

"All right. Perhaps Amy can scare up shift-clothing that might fit Andy here and there. I'll come home minute I hear anything affecting us." He used the crisp, authoritative tones of a master mariner accustomed to prompt and unquestioning obedience.

Amy's small coral-hued mouth curved into a fetching little triangle as she said softly, "It will be a problem finding garments to fit Mister Hunter."

Tom thought Amy spoke as if she enjoyed what she was saying.

Before leaving, Jonathan led Andrew outside, spoke seriously, "Now listen, careful-like. Stay right here; if anybody comes by and looks sidewise at you or asks questions, act polite but don't grant information no matter what. Above all don't admit you've served in the King's Navy—let alone aboard the *Lively*—else you'll likely find yourself tarred, feathered and ridden out of town on a rail—if you're that lucky."

Once the brothers had tramped off through hot sunlight past successive racks of drying nets and rows of fish flakes, Amy set arms akimbo, tilted a shining reddish-brown head to one side and deliberately surveyed her companion. "I'm thinking maybe some of my late brother Abraham's garments might come close to fitting you, Mister Hunter. He too, was tall and wide in the shoulder."

"Ma'am, please, but will you call me plain Andy Hunter?"

She laughed and jerked a nod. "All right, but carrying yourself so straight and with that air of command, you'll never be plain Andrew Hunter to anybody with an ounce of discernment."

"Well, now," said he using fingers to comb back greasy locks of chestnut-hued hair, "that's handsomely said, Miss Orne—"

"'Amy' to you, sir."

"Very well, Miss Amy, Tom and I've just had a pretty rough time in Boston. Lady Luck surely was riding our bowsprit that we got here safe and sound."

Surprising how easy it was to resume New England accents and manner of speech. No more crisp, British enunciations for Andrew Orne Hunter. He reckoned his safest course for the moment would be to keep the Orne girl talking to fill him in on recent local events and politics in general and, most important of all, who he should be on his guard against.

How fine it was to stretch his legs, gaze out of open windows at flocks of gray-and-white harbor gulls wheeling, dipping and laughing over a small forest of masts sprouting from the harbor.

Soon he learned first news about Breed's Hill had arrived in Marblehead during the evening of the same night the battle had been fought. People had been mighty grieved to learn that two 'Headers, William Jackson and David Carmichael, had been seen sprawled stone-dead just outside the redoubt, and that several local men had been reported seriously wounded.

"Main thing is—" said Amy while pouring ale chilled in a spring bubbling back of the house, "—nobody knows for sure what happened, except that our side won but lacked a real victory. After all, they *were* driven in retreat over Charles Town Neck or so 'tis said."

Andrew passed a hand over bristles darkening his chin, didn't like the feel of them; if only there'd been a razor aboard the *Polly Izard*. "I—er—witnessed most of the battle. Later on I'll tell you what I saw of it." He looked appealingly into her handsome rather than pretty, strong-boned and lightly tanned features. "Meantime 'twould help me a lot if you'd tell me in more detail what's been going on in Marblehead lately."

Amy swallowed a sip of spruce beer—no ale for females—considered him over the rim of her mug.

"Well, Mister—er—Andrew, for weeks our Committee of Safety has been busy collecting guns and even a few cannon while recruiting, drilling and arming volunteers as best they can. A whole regiment of soldiers—"

"Soldiers?"

"Mostly ex-militiamen—everyone here calls it the 'Marblehead Regiment' even though a good many men from other towns have been coming in from all over the Essex County, mostly out of Salem and Beverly. Other volunteers are out-of-work local fishermen, artificers, sailors, shipbuilders and the like. It's going to be pretty dull around here for us poor females, married or single."

Her sigh lifted what appeared to be smallish but well-proportioned breasts beneath a shirtwaist of faded calico. Meanwhile Amy continued to study this curious friend of Tom's with undisguised interest and decided Andrew Orne Hunter looked as if recently he'd been run through a wringer, "hardish-like"—as Jonathan might have said. Naturally this newcomer's appearance would improve through use of soap, water and a razor. All the same those dirty, ill-fitting garments failed to disguise the attributes of a full-blooded man.

Having devoted considerable time as an assistant to Doctor Elisha Story, who last week had accepted a surgeon's commission in the new regiment, she'd found plenty of opportunities to observe at close range many male patients. Some of the younger ones she'd come to know fairly well, possibly too well, in the opinion of certain envious gossips.

Absently, Amy pushed a curl before lightly tanned features and a pert little upturned nose whose bridge was not unattractively speckled by a constellation of tiny, pale-brown freckles. "Ever since Parliament passed the Fisheries Act on top of the New England Restraining Act none of us along this coast have had an easy time—far from it! Trade and shipbuilding are at such a standstill many families are going on mighty lean rations or hungry to the point of starvation."

Amy's large and clear sherry-brown eyes flashed. "I declare I can't bear to see so many people looking downhearted and in rags; with so few vessels daring to fish the Banks this year, 'tis small wonder Colonel Glover and Mister Gerry have found little trouble in recruiting the Regiment even though John Glover has the reputation of being a strict disciplinarian."

CHAPTER 16 🍃

THE MARBLEHEAD REGIMENT

AMONG OTHER STERLING QUALITIES possessed by John Glover, forty-two and just recently commissioned Colonel of the 21st Regiment in the Army of the United Colonies, possessed an almost uncanny ability, regardless of surrounding confusion and distractions, to lower what he whimsically termed as a "mental blindfold" and so was able to devote entire attention to newly arisen problems of importance.

Now that long-anticipated orders for the Regiment to join the Army concentrating around Cambridge had been brought by a sweat-bathed aide, he and his staff had found their hands full and then some.

After tramping to the large second-floor bedroom in the Green Dragon Tavern serving as his command post, Glover momentarily closed small, wide-set and piercing gray-blue eyes before drawing a series of deep breaths as he generally did under similar circumstances. He became able to ignore noises beating through open windows: the pounding of drums, bellowed commands and ear-torturing sounds raised by ungreased axles belonging to an odd assortment of farm carts and wagons assembling to transport, on the morrow, the Regiment's scanty supplies and baggage to Cambridge.

He was leaving it up to thin and sickly but dapper Lieutenant-Colonel Gerry and well-stomached Acting-Major Gilbert Parkman to divide a noisy mob of newly arrived recruits into rudimentary squads, platoons and companies.

All the same, these grimly purposeful gentlemen weren't encountering half so much trouble as counterparts on duty at inland rally points. Here, most recruits were talking big about what they aimed to do to the Bloodybacks, had been seafarers and so long ago had learned, aboard ship, to obey orders promptly and without question, a merit which would go far towards rendering Glover's Marblehead Regiment highly respected throughout the Army. Indeed, General Washington, later on, frequently found occasion to compliment the Regiment and hold it up as an example of what efficiency and an inflexible but just administration of discipline could accomplish.

After brushing a speck of dust from his sleeve—the 21st's new Colonel always had been neat to the point of fussiness about his dress—Glover put down a tin cup of coffee liberally laced with Demerara rum then mopped a smooth and unusually high forehead while wiping a mental slate clean of other immediate concerns. He scowled when an orderly knocked.

"Sir? There's a Capt'n Izard outside. Claims he needs to see you straightaway."

"Which Izard? Town's crawling with 'em."

"Capt'n Jonathan, sir."

"Then let him in but don't allow anybody to disturb us till I bid you."

"Aye, aye, sir."

Glover arose from behind a kitchen table piled high with documents most of which he hadn't yet read. Impressive in a smartly cut tunic of dark-blue turned back in claret-red the Colonel, wearing a broad smile, strode forward offering a hard brown hand. "Damn my eyes, Jonathan, I'm *that* relieved to clap eyes on you! Feared the British might have scuppered you during your run over to Boston."

While advancing with a seafarer's roll to his gait the shipowner's yellowish teeth gleamed through round black whiskers.

"Well, John, how does it go? Or should I call you 'Colonel'?"

"Hell, no, old friend. My title is for official use only. 'Twixt us, 'twill always be John and Jonathan though according to the Bible I presume we ought to be called David and Jonathan."

Ignoring tumult outside he clapped his caller on the shoulder then, smile fading, he reseated himself and got down to business. "During your run over to Boston you must have seen and heard a lot I, er—we ought to know about."

"Hope so." Jonathan sat down without invitation, caught up a piece of cardboard and started to fan himself. "Watched all three assaults from a vantage point behind and above the North Battery."

"Did we really win?"

Jonathan nodded soberly. "Yes, and no. We lost the redoubt but everybody seems to agree we gave the King's troops a bad beating but I sure hope our folks ain't goin' to get puffed up about it. Wonder how many people realize we've only their dunderhead generals to thank for what happened. My God, those British regulars were brave, almighty brave! Never believed such discipline could exist anywhere but if our people hadn't run out of gunpowder I doubt whether the Redcoats could have stormed the fort which, come to think on it, was a blessing in disguise."

"Why?" Glover's eyes narrowed.

"Because the defenders surely would have got cut off on Charles Town Neck later on."

Glover's fist banged so hard on the table it made an inkwell jump and sent papers scaling about. "By the great leaping Jehovah! Gunpowder is our most desperate need! D'you know, Jon, it's been reliably reported right now there ain't above sixty-five barrels of the stuff to be found within a hundred miles of Boston?"

"My God, is our need *that* bad?"

"It is. Lacking sufficient gunpowder this rebellion will fail before it even gets started."

Jonathan nodded. "Also, I wonder even if we do get powder, where are we going to find cannons and sound firearms to use it in?"

Well-polished buttons securing Glover's tunic's lapels winked to his shrug. "We'll get some by God, and I think I know how.

145

First, take a slug of rum, then let's talk about the solution which is as obvious as the nose on my face."

Jonathan chuckled dutifully over this long-standing joke— John Glover's nose was prominent, long and as narrow as a butcher's knife.

"Since thanks to British Colonial policy and foresight none of our Colonies possesses iron foundries or powder mills worthy of the name I reckon we'll just have to force the enemy to supply us with munitions till we're able to make our own or to import what's needed from the French, the Spanish or maybe even the Dutch."

Someone tramped up to the door but in rough sea language the guard ordered the visitor to clear out. Flies buzzing through the open windows kept circling and trying to settle on the conferees' sweating features.

Jonathan waved aside a halo of the pesky insects. "You've hit the nail on the head, John. We've no choice but to supply ourselves from the British, but how are we going to go about that? We've no men-of-war."

"True, so I figure our only course is to select a number of small, swift merchantmen suitable for use as commerce raiders. We'll arm them and train sea-experienced soldiers as a sort of sea-going Army till Congress wakes up and authorizes a real Navy." He steepled fingers under his cleaver of a nose. "Of course such vessels couldn't and shouldn't try standing up to any of the Royal Pirates' regular men-o'-war but knowing these waters as we do we ought to be able to snap up enough unescorted or unarmed transports and supply ships to satisfy our needs for the time being."

"But where are you going to find an instructor to train your gun crews?"

Glover leaned forward. "I'll find someone, maybe in Salem. You any ideas?"

Once Jonathan had given a brief explanation of his return with Tom and Andrew Hunter, Glover frowned at hands locked on the food-stained table before him. "Um. So this feller and your brother escaped from the *Lively* along with other impressed men?"

"Yep. That they did, just as I've related."

"Tell me more about this fellow Hunter. Didn't you say his middle name is 'Orne'?"

"'Orne' it is. Seems his family quit these parts a long while ago. Andy don't know the reason but, anyhow, his folks moved to Dorchester then settled down for keeps in Cambridge. Andrew's Pa, I judge, ain't exactly poor."

"What's his profession?"

"Trader with the West Indies and before the Restraining Act with Europe, especially Scandinavia. Still captains his vessels on occasion."

"He reliable politically?"

"Yep. Always been a red-hot Patriot according to his son."

"Interesting. Explain to me, Jon, if his Pa's so anti-British why did young Hunter, a New Englander born and bred, elect to serve in the Royal Navy?"

Knitting bushy black brows the shipmaster replied, "Guess the only explanation is that Andy always hankered over ordnance. What he ain't learned 'bout cannons, mortars, howitzers, swivels and their service I don't expect would fill a extra-thick copy book. Fact. Tom told me that. Yankee or not, he got so expert he was appointed the *Lively*'s Gunnery Officer; t'was him who got Tom rated a Gunner's Mate. Claims Hunter in a quiet way always did what he could to advance or protect impressed men, Colonials or not. Don't doubt there are plenty of homegrown English who hate the Royal Navy like the Devil hates holy water. Possibly we can use some of 'em if ever opportunity offers."

"Um. So your new friend is due to get hanged an the enemy comes up with him?"

"Aye, if the Bloodybacks take ex-Lieutenant Hunter he'll dance the 'floorless hornpipe' sure as tomorrow's sunrise." Jonathan took a deep swallow of Demerara. "Now, John, enough on that subject, I didn't come here to jaw 'bout Tom or young Hunter. I came to ask back for my old rank of Serjeant in the Essex County Militia. Need be, Tom and me can be ready to march tomorrow; and I'm willin' to enroll as a private if it comes to that."

Frowning, Glover hunched over the paper-strewn table, spoke carefully. "Jon, me, Eb Gerry and others on the Committee of Safety have been thinking long and hard about you and other men of like worth and have decided 'twould be a sinful waste of experience, substance and leadership to allow many of our local overseas traders, shipbuilders and sea-wise people to join the Regiment." As was his habit when deeply in earnest Glover began successively to crack knuckle joints beneath his chin.

"What's your meanin'?"

"Sure as Hell's hot our side is going to be hard-put to find anywhere near sufficient cannons, muskets, flints, gunpowder, shot and arms of all sorts for a considerable spell of time. I know I'm repeating myself but I can't be too emphatic enough about this." John Glover sat back, laced fingers behind his big head. "So, as I've said, we've no choice but to arm some fast merchantmen and try to intercept enemy transports, ordnance and store ships. Luckily the British hold us 'Beastly Colonials' in such contempt they'll for a good while keep on sending such vessels into Massachusetts Bay unconvoyed or at best only feebly armed."

Tom Izard's brother looked hard across the table. "So you want fellows like me and some others to 'bide here and fit out commerce raiders?"

"Correct. Here, or perhaps over in Gloucester or more likely up to Beverly. I've learned Gen'ral Washington, our new Commander-in-Chief, Colonel Henry Knox and some other smart officers are like-minded."

"Knox? Who's he?"

Glover hesitated. "Don't know, really. They say he's already become one of General Washington's top staff officers. Maybe it's a lie but some claim he weighs close on three hundred pounds."

"He a professional soldier?"

"No, though he's held some militia commissions. By profession he's been a bookseller in Boston for quite a while. 'Tis reported Knox spent most of his spare time studying every book on European ordnance, artillery tactics and siege craft he could lay hands on. They say presently he's busier than a cat with its fur afire trying to scrape together a train of artillery of sorts, since right now we own very few useful field guns. Knox is forced to start from scratch with no help save for a few officers and men—some of doubtful loyalty—who learned to handle artillery while with the King's forces."

Somewhere outside a drunken brawl broke out. It was subdued with swiftness; Colonel John Glover's provosts, it would appear, were efficient.

"In other words," Jonathan commented, "you don't want me back in the old Regiment?"

"Of course I want you, you damn' blockhead, but to repeat, I want you, Nick Broughton, Ben Marston and Bob Hooper and other men of like substance to stay hereabouts long enough to select and arm a fleet of commerce raiders."

"I see, but 'twon't be easy, John, 'specially finding and mounting cannon and training gun crews. Can't foresee how our fellow townsfolk are going to fancy taking orders from a ex-Royal Naval officer."

Glover pursed thin, Cupid's bow-shaped lips. "Nor can I. Howsumever Hunter's part Orne at least, so I'll count on you and Tom to play that fact to the hilt and make our neighbors understand what it means to have our people trained under a professional if, as you say, he really *is* a Patriot." Glover's chair creaked when he settled back. "For a start, today I signed my brig *Hannah* over to the Continental Congress. She ought to be our first cruiser."

As always, thought Jonathan, Friend John ain't about to hide his light under a bushel to avoid favorable attention.

"I will do likewise and make over my *Favourite* to the Continental service," Jonathan said.

"Good." The Colonel leaned forward, small, gray-blue eyes intent. "Now I don't pretend to being any part of a grand strategist but I've soldiered long enough to foresee that, being so short of war-like supplies we'll likely lose this war before it gets really underway. So, Jon, old friend, bear that fact in mind when the Regiment moves out tomorrow."

Tom's brother solemnly offered a gnarled, brown-splotched fist. "I promise nothing except that me and the rest of us traders and shipowners will do our level best to do what you're aimin' at. We will, just as sure as you and the Regiment will to make the name of Marblehead known and respected clear down to Pennsylvany; maybe even beyond."

With so many able-bodied men absent, several days passed before life in and about Marblehead regained even a semblance of normality. Too few paying jobs were available and farming this rocky soil was unrewarding. Worse still, there appeared no means of disposing of hundreds of quintals of fish spoiling and stinking under clouds of flies on near five hundred flake racks. Too many old people, women and children literally were going hungry or wondering where their next meal might come from even though neighboring villages and communities lying at a considerable distance inland haphazardly sent in food and supplies of various sorts.

At once it became apparent to all sensible 'Headers that, to maintain order, a home guard detachment replacing the recently abolished Essex County Militia must be established; no easy matter since nearly every serviceable firearm appeared to have been carried off to Cambridge.

Captain Frederick Penniston, a sharp old lawyer and a veteran of the French Wars who, because of a gouty foot, hadn't been able to march away, was elected to command a rabble of half-grown boys, semi-cripples and old men still able to handle antique matchlocks, ponderous musketoons or long-barreled and nearly worn-out fowling pieces. Stiffening these were a handful of able-bodied shipwrights, carpenters, artificers and mariners which John Glover had left behind hopeful of converting coasters and fishing vessels into commerce raiders.

This motley collection promptly had named themselves Company B, of the newly reconstituted "Essex County Militia," a designation proudly borne ever since the community had been founded. Although members of this reconstituted unit were devoted Patriots to a man, only a handful had had military training of any description.

Jonathan Izard, happy to be home for a while with quiet, capable Deborah and their children, was in no great hurry to relinquish personal freedom of action although he sensed public opinion soon would make it wise. Tom and especially Andrew

Hunter, who could claim Cambridge, Massachusetts, as his hometown, must enroll with Company B.

To the Izard family's no great surprise Andrew Hunter, once his story got about, generally was accepted and fitted easily into the community especially after he'd volunteered to work as a common laborer on those gun emplacements he'd designed, a small demi-lune or crescent-shaped battery on Peach's Head to guard the harbor's entrance. He commenced, casually, to make friends among men proved intelligent, skillful and industrious. Such urgently were needed to complete the four-gun battery at top speed. No telling when the captain of some man-of-war, patrolling the coast from Cape Ann on down, might elect to dispatch a landing party to burn vessels bottled up in Marblehead's small harbor.

Increasingly, Captain Timothy Hunter's son grew relieved, over no longer wearing that uniform of which he'd once been so proud. Also it came as a relief no longer need he watch his accent or make sure certain observations he made now and then couldn't be misconstrued.

Ever more often he pondered a vital question: how were his father and the rest of his family faring now that Cambridge had become Headquarters for that fast-growing Continental Army? For a good many reasons they ought to be safe. Hadn't Captain Hunter all along been a stalwart, outspoken Son of Liberty? Hadn't he often voiced radical opinions to influential Loyalist neighbors such as the Vassalls, the Brattles and the Sewalls, to name but a few?

With increasing intensity he also conjectured about what might have chanced with Sarah Hilton and her father. Could they have become implicated in his escape? More and more he wondered in which direction lay Major Hilton's true sympathies. After all, he'd never once heard the old bookseller voice anti-Royalist sentiments, but then neither had he ever criticized Sam Adams, John Hancock or any other outstanding Radical. Was he affecting neutrality only to remain in Boston and conduct his book business perhaps as a cover for other activities? He wished he'd known Sarah and her father a deal better.

By all reports Boston now had become isolated from the mainland by elaborate fortifications thrown up across Boston Neck despite the fact these defenses might effectively be bombarded from Roxbury or Dorchester Heights. For some inexplicable reason the British High Command, although they'd finally fortified both Breed's Hill and Bunker's Hill, had left both heights undefended.

He'd give a lot to know Sarah's real sentiments concerning him. From the few times they'd been alone together he'd deduced she didn't deem him altogether unattractive for all his lowly rank. How odd he should feel much the same way about her. It was effortless to conjure up visions of large and luminous bright-blue eyes framed between golden ringlets and a small, full mouth the dark red lips which generally appeared to be wet and shiny.

Now that the battery on Peach's Head was nearing completion it had done him a world of encouragement to learn that, in a long-abandoned and tumble-down warehouse on the road to Salem, a half-dozen rusting 6-pound naval guns had been discovered together with their carriages. Unfortunately these mountings were seriously rotted in places but he calculated they soon could be rebuilt and become useful.

Seated on a bench set under a beech tree overlooking the harbor Andrew settled back comfortably puffing on a yard-of-clay pipe and feeling more at peace with himself and the world than in many a blue moon; it meant much to find so many soul-rending indecisions over and done with. In the naval forces being raised by the United Colonies, opportunities should offer themselves such as never could have arisen in the tradition-bound Royal Navy.

By dwindling twilight he made out Amy's tall, perfectly proportioned figure drawing near. He arose and, pipe aglow, ducked his head in greeting.

"'Evenin', Amy, glad of your company."

She smiled, "Indeed? How are you, Andrew? You seemed a bit tuckered out earlier on."

Grimacing, he held out hands swollen and raw with broken blisters. "I'm fine—except for these. Captain Jonathan sure drove us hard to finish fitting heavy oak braces under the *Favourite's* deck."

"My it's hot," she commented and, settling beside him, then without affectation several times blew down the front of her sweat-darkened calico gown. "Whatever does Uncle Jon want with extra braces? Why, his schooner's as solid as a brick meeting house and built not over two years ago."

"They're designed to support the weight of cannon—I hope."

She treated him to a serious look. "While shopping this afternoon I heard something I think maybe you ought to know about. Somehow, word's got about you not only served in the Royal Navy"—her expression hardened—"but also that you were aboard the *Lively* when she was patrolling this coast and impressed some Marbleheaders, which isn't likely to render you extra-welcome around here even though my uncles keep insisting you sometimes risked your career to help them and to ease the lot of impressed Colonials. Also, Uncle Tom tells anyone who'll listen how most shots fired by your guns at Breed's Hill mostly fell short and that one, aimed by you, yourself, slew a lot of Redcoats. Is that true?"

"Something like that happened although I didn't—"

Before he could finish Tom ambled out of the house picking his teeth after supper. He nodded amiably. "Howdy, Amy, cooler out here, ain't it? B'God, 'tis hotter than Tophet indoors. What're you two gabbing about?"

"We were admiring this lovely sunset," Amy lied.

"That's good. Don't cost nothin'. By the bye, Andy, afore we start work tomorrow mornin' Jonathan 'llows as how the three of us had best go and get enrolled in Company B. Says it don't look good to delay any longer, 'specially you."

"Think they'll accept me?"

"Sure," grunted the ex-gunner's mate. "The true story about your bein' in the *Lively* has been explained and credited. Besides, everybody with a grain of sense knows our people need real artillerists like damned souls crave a swig of ice water."

Amy nodded. "Likely you're right, Tom. Heard tell Captain Penniston is fair-minded, provided he's sober and his gout isn't afflicting him too sorely. But Andrew, I'd better warn you now there's one person you'd best be on your guard against. He's Caleb Twisden, First Lieutenant of Company B," she flushed, "an earnest admirer of mine. While Caleb's mannerly and good-looking above the average he's also shrewd and ambitious and, some say, er—a bit unscrupulous about getting what he wants."

Tom Izard winked. "Yep. Caleb's been more than a little sweet on Amy for a considerable spell."

"Can't fault him for that," Andrew observed and was startled when Amy's hand lightly brushed his.

Enjoying the moment Tom drawled, "Caleb's well-off, a real catch."

To his surprise Andrew demanded, "Do you indeed fancy Mister Twisden?"

Amy shrugged, looked out over the darkening bay. "I'm not quite sure. To be practical, as my father used to say, I find Caleb Twisden very charming when he chooses. Also, he has important connections in Boston and elsewhere whilst I'm poor as the well-known church mouse so, unless something happens soon, I fear I'll fade to a lone, lorn spinster."

"Perish the thought."

Although Amy Orne couldn't be much more than twenty or thereabouts, Andrew was well aware that, ever since British North America first had been colonized, even half-attractive girls caught themselves a husband before reaching sixteen, sometimes even younger, so urgent was the need in this vast empty land for the population to expand rapidly.

Flushing, Amy changed the subject. "Well, Andrew, how soon do you and the militia expect to complete the battery?"

Brows merging, Andrew deliberated. "Don't rightly know. Everything depends on how fast we can rebuild the carriages for those old 6-pounders, find suitable shot and ammunition. Gunpowder in these parts is scarcer than crowing hens."

Although his hands still burned and ached like fury Andrew Hunter at once dropped off to sleep that night unaware that come dawn H.M.S. *Lively* would appear to relieve H.M.S. *Merlin* and resume patrol duty along that same stretch of coast she'd blockaded so long.

CHAPTER 17 ✄

RECRUITS FOR COMPANY B

IN THE SMALL but neat white-painted and book-lined offices of Twisden & Marston, Barristers at Law, Caleb Twisden, thirty years of age and newly elected First Lieutenant, Company B, in the reorganized Essex Militia, stretched and yawned so prodigiously as to expose unusually long and sharp lower canine teeth set in reddish-brown, box-like features.

The sun, having barely lifted over the town's gray-shingled roofs sketched glowing red-gold ruler marks across piles of papers littering his desk, drew flashes from a double row of brass buttons on the dark red lapels or revers of his tunic.

Serjeant Jacob Marston, already at his desk, was fraily built and perpetually pallid of complexion. He was the next younger brother of Ben Marston, Twisden's partner who had deemed it wise last May, ostensibly on the firm's business, to depart for Halifax. He'd not returned, or even sent a word of explanation but there was no need since outspoken Tory views had made him powerful enemies. Also on hand was his legal assistant, acting-company clerk Corporal Joshua Denmead. He was a small, round-shouldered individual whose quick movements, alert little

155

black eyes and perpetually rounded cheeks put most people in mind of a squirrel unexpectedly clad in loose cotton trousers, dark gray waistcoat and a Quaker-brown knee-length coat to which he still hadn't affixed his corporal's shoulder-knot of dark-red worsted. Not surprisingly, his school nickname had been "Nutkin."

Queried Twisden, solidly built with widespread blue eyes and exceptionally long and muscular arms, "Say, Nutkin, how many 'listed men have we enrolled?"

Acting company clerk Denmead informed, "Forty-one. Need only nine more recruits to round out our authorized strength."

Snapped Twisden, "Why in Tunket can't you remember to say 'sir' when you address me on military matters?"

"Then don't call me 'Nutkin,' *sir!*"

Twisden grinned, "Fair exchange is no robbery, 'Corporal' it is."

B Company's First Lieutenant yawned once more while glancing out onto Mugford Street through the wide-opened twelve-paned window opposite his desk but saw only a few sleepy-looking boys herding cows out to pastures on the edge of town and a scattering of early risers trudging off to work.

Because the sun hadn't yet risen the all-pervading stench of drying fish hadn't reached its peak.

Marston, on peering out of the other window remarked, "Say, Caleb, early as 'tis seems like we're about to snare some fresh fish."

"Recognize any of them?"

"Aye, looks like Cap'n Jonathan Izard, his brother Tom and that mysterious friend of theirs. He's called 'Andrew Hunter,' I think."

"Oh yes, you mean the one they claim deserted the Royal Navy to save his neck?" Twisden queried just as if he, like most 'Headers, hadn't listened to more than a few conjectures concerning that presentable, chestnut-haired young fellow the Izards had brought over from Boston and who for the present was living with them. It also was known that this stranger had been much occupied with the refitting of Jonathan's *Favourite* as a privateer of sorts. Aside from that he was supposed to have designed that small demi-lune or crescent-shaped battery nearing completion on Peach's Head.

Marston commented, "So far, everyone admits Andrew Hunter knows what he's doing."

Characteristically Caleb Twisden also had obtained a good deal of information concerning the fugitive's family. They resided in Cambridge, Massachusetts, and had lived there for a long while; also that the Hunter family were all outstanding Patriots. For example Hunter's father, Captain Timothy, had been one of the original Sons of Liberty in that town.

Twisden watched the three men turn off the street and start up to his office. He felt especially pleased that, following instructions, the trio had turned up bearing arms. Both Izards were wearing seamen's wide, tar-flecked bell-bottomed canvas pants and worn-work coats over which they'd slung powder flasks, bullet bags, haversacks, even wooden canteens. The Izards were slouching along lugging short, brass-barreled and bell-mouthed blunderbusses. Their companion, however, strode along, straight-backed, shouldering in military fashion what looked to be an ancient fusil. Most probably, like so many old firearms in this part of the country, this weapon must have been fetched back from the Siege of Louisburg some thirty-odd years earlier.

After adjusting his stock and shooting greasy red cuffs Lieutenant Caleb Twisden straightening on his chair and assuming what he deemed to be a military manner while, succinctly, he instructed Corporal Denmead to admit the Izards at once, but to instruct the third volunteer to wait outside the gate till sent for.

Jonathan tramped in, weatherbeaten features forcing a grin barely visible amid the depths of his round black beard. He and his family never had set much store by any of the Twisdens since years ago, on a technicality, their firm had slapped a Royal Customs detainer on the cargo of sugar fetched from Antigua.

"Howdy, Caleb, or should I say 'Lieutenant?' Sorry me and Tom and some others have been so tarnation busy we couldn't find time to get here sooner."

The newcomers shook hands all round including thin-faced and scrawny Joshua Denmead only because he was a first cousin to Deborah, Jonathan's wife.

Announced Twisden, abruptly abandoning his military manner, "This won't take long, fellows. Just sign this muster roll after Jake swears you in." He smiled widely, "Thus automatically you'll become patriotic heroes and members of my Company which, by the way, has yet to be officially recognized though it will be any day."

Once Denmead's goose-quill pens had been used to scribble signatures, and the forms had been sanded, the clerk looked up, asked casually, "How is the battery coming on?"

"Guess we're makin' tolerable progress," was all Jonathan would admit.

"How much?" Twisden insisted.

"Wal, now," Tom drawled, "Andy thinks, with any luck we ought to be ready to mount some cannons come three—four days, provided they arrive from Salem on time."

Caleb Twisden arched bushy blond brows. "No sooner?"

Tom shrugged. "Never can count on them Salemites, but we'll get some cannons mounted inside a week's time. We'd all feel a heap better if the *Favourite* could get armed first of all, and she may be at that."

Twisden shot a quick glance at Denmead busily recording the conversation and sorting documents, then inquired of Jonathan, "You've located some cannon for your ship?"

"Think so. Andy Hunter can tell you more 'bout that—cannons being his specialty." Jonathan gazed at a dark square in the wall behind Twisden's desk previously occupied by an engraved likeness of King George III. "Whose phiz are you going to hang there now?"

Lieutenant Twisden grimaced, "Don't know yet. Maybe 'twill be John Hancock's or Sam Adams' or William Prescott's. If we lose, which God forbid, it will be George the III's again."

Once the Izard brothers had tramped out into increasingly malodorous Mugford Street where they found Andrew waiting at the gate, Tom muttered, "Remember you'd best not rile Caleb Twisden, no matter what the excuse."

Without being able to find a reason Andrew Orne Hunter somehow sensed that the impending interview might prove critical to his new career. Shouldering the ungainly fusil he marched into the law office and saluted smartly by brushing its lock with his fingertips whereupon, to his astonishment, Lieutenant Twisden arose saying pleasantly, "You may stand easy, Mister Hunter. After all, we must remember that our unit has yet to be officially recognized."

Young Jacob Marston all but gaped when his father's partner and his own classmate at Harvard, Class of '71, reached over his desk to offer a hand. "Heard a lot of good things concerning you from the Izards, Amy Orne and others."

"Thank you, sir."

"To be quite frank, Mister Hunter, at first some of us doubted the wisdom of accepting you as a volunteer but, since so many trustworthy citizens have voiced confidence in your loyalty, I stand prepared to enroll you as a private in Company B—a lowly rank I'm sure you'll not hold for long."

Andrew blinked. Damned if this was anything like the reception he'd been anticipating. What might lie behind this cordiality? "Thank you, sir," said he stiffening to rigid attention—no better way to impress an amateur officer. "You can count on my always doing my utmost in the service of our country."

Astonished over the Lieutenant's easy manner, Marston and Denmead pretended to study papers but all the same listened attentively over the rumble of farm carts and wains rolling along Mugford Street's dusty length. Some, Andrew hoped, might be fetching supplies for the *Favourite* and the demi-lune.

"Mister Hunter, *is* it true that during the battle for Breed's Hill you were serving on H.M.S. *Lively?*"

Andrew felt his breath check, "Yes, sir."

Twisden assumed a cross-examining lawyer's tone of voice. "You were her Gunnery Officer, I believe?"

"Yes, sir. I'd served in that capacity for almost a year."

Blond-haired Caleb Twisden's mouth momentarily flattened, and his pale-blue eyes narrowed while he settled back on his chair. "Tom Izard has informed me that your batteries maintained high records for excellent markmanship *except*"—he emphasized the word—"for a very poor showing during the engagement on Breed's Hill. Can you account for that?"

Andrew flushed beneath his deep tan and cheekbones jutting said evenly, "On my word, sir, I can offer no explanation attributable to me." No point mentioning those reduced powder charges he'd learned about later on.

"You are *sure* you, personally, did nothing to hamper your guns' marksmanship?"

More color flooded the ex-officer's already suffused features. "I've already given my word on that, sir. As an officer of the King that would have been impossible to do."

Twisden leaned forward, elbows on table. "I also have heard you are an uncommonly accomplished artillerist?"

"With all modesty I suppose that is true."

"Hmm. What weight and how many cannon can you mount in the Peach's Head battery?"

The tall figure in patched sea breeches looked even more unhappy. "Why, sir, I'd favor four 8-pounders but I've been given to understand only six old 6-pounders are available—which is a pity."

"Why so?"

"If the British decide to enter the harbor and destroy shipping such a pitiful array of pop-guns won't amount to a sniff in a gale of wind."

Joshua Denmead's little black eyes became extra-vivid amid the permanent pallor of his complexion. "Can sufficient gunpowder and enough balls to fit these guns be collected promptly?"

"Be quiet, Joshua," snapped the lawyer. "I am conducting this inquiry. Well, Mister Hunter?"

"To tell the truth, sir, thus far what powder we've got is of poor quality and in short supply, and we've only a moderate supply of suitable roundshot. Till more men and munitions arrive I doubt whether we could fire more than a dozen rounds per piece."

Already July's heat was making itself felt. After loosening a pale-blue sash Caleb Twisden instructed Andrew as, smartly, he shifted the brass-bound fusil from one shoulder to the other, "You can put down that silly thing; it wouldn't frighten an idiot child. Tell me this, Hunter, where do you expect to recruit gun crews and, should you succeed, how much time will be required for you to drill them into any degree of efficiency?"

"Locating sound men who aren't occupied on the battery or busy refitting the *Favourite* is our principal problem, sir. However, come a week's time, if Captain Penniston will furnish us with sixteen fit men for training right away we should be able to beat off a British landing party provided not too many of them come ashore."

"Good. I'll straightaway find out what can be accomplished but I doubt, even with luck, we'll come across more than a dozen men of the sort you need." Twisden's pale-blue eyes fixed themselves on Andrew's broad, sun-bronzed features. "How is work on Jonathan's schooner coming on?" He checked himself. "Oh, by the bye, at a Committee of Safety meeting last night it was proposed and carried that when she enters service her name be changed to *James Warren* after the officer who commanded the redoubt and got killed on Breed's Hill."

Using a faded blue bandanna Andrew mopped his forehead and somewhat relaxed his rigid stance. By God, he remained completely nonplussed by Twisden's ready co-operation. "Sir, her decks already have been reinforced, her bulwarks pierced for six guns, thickened and topped with elmwood against flying splinters."

"How soon do you expect to mount those guns?"

"Hold on, Caleb." Jacob Marston raised an ink-stained finger. "Clean forgot to mention that last evening Captain Penniston sent a note saying word's come from the Committee of Safety in Beverley that all armed merchantmen, well, let's call them 'cruisers' or 'privateers'—sounds more impressive, don't it?—for some reason are to be armed not here but in Salem or Beverly."

By the early sunlight illumining the offices of Twisden & Marston, Barristers-at-law, Andrew Hunter conducted a covert but comprehensive survey of his companions. One question still stuck burr-like to his imagination. Why had Amy Orne cautioned him against relying too much on this pleasant young lawyer wearing a lieutenant's sash slung carelessly over an outdated and somewhat moth-eaten tunic of the old Essex County Militia?

He was returned to present considerations by Caleb Twisden's stating as precisely as if he were addressing the Bench, "Although some 'Headers still are suspicious because of—er—your past service the all-important fact remains that your unique knowledge of artillery can be of unquestionable value to us particularly at this time. Therefore I am prepared to accept your enlistment. Here—" Crisply, Twisden said, "Nut—er—Corporal Denmead, administer the Oath."

He pushed forward Company B's stained and finger-marked muster roll.

The clerk stood to his scant five feet six and with dignity produced a battered calfskin-covered Bible. "Andrew Orne Hunter, raise your right hand. Do you solemnly swear to abjure any loyalty to the Crown of England?"

"Yes. I so swear."

"Will you obey any and all lawful commands from your superiors in the Service of the United Colonies?"

"I will, so help me God."

Still shaking internally over what he had done Andrew retrieved his fusil and was preparing to quit the law offices when Amy Orne's tall, curvaceous figure darkened the entrance.

"How delightful a surprise!" Twisden smiled widely. "What on earth brings you to town this early?"

"I've come shopping for necessities before they've all been snapped up." She beamed at Twisden, only nodded to Andrew and the others. "Also, Caleb, I'll admit I'm curious to learn whether you have accepted Mister Hunter's enlistment in Company B."

The Lieutenant indicated Andrew's signature on the muster roll. "Amy, er, Miss Orne, you have arrived just in time to witness Hunter's acceptance into Company B. May I add that your good opinion of him added to that of the Izards helped ensure his acceptance?"

"Thank you. You'll not regret it, I'm sure." She cast Andrew a fleeting smile before returning attention to the Lieutenant. "By the bye, Caleb, possibly you and Mister Marston would care to stop by at my aunt's home this afternoon to enjoy a dish of *guh!* 'Liberty Tea?' I venture Mister Hunter might be persuaded to show you around the battery and possibly what's been done towards refitting the *Favourite*."

Marston grinning like a cat by accident confined in a dairy guessed if anything lay in certain rumors there'd be a glass of something stronger than brewed raspberry leaves to be consumed. Said he, bowing, "We'd be delighted, Miss Orne. Mind if you include Joshua Denmead? He's a bit lonely these days what with his folks having moved away."

To Andrew, Marston's quick suggestion aroused a sense of

uneasiness. While it had been flattering of Amy to make sure his enlistment had been accepted why should she invite these people to view the new defenses and note progress on Jonathan's schooner?

Picking up his fusil Andrew asked, "Sir, when should I report for the Company's next exercises?"

A brief laugh escaped the lawyer. "Doubt whether one of His Majesty's Regular officers could learn much from a country drill master; but I'll give you ample notice when you are needed on the mustering ground."

For the first time Andrew Hunter ventured a question. "On short notice, sir, how many men could be counted on to man the battery?"

Twisden raised a brow in Marston's direction. "Guess about twenty-five militiamen live within easy running distance of Peach's Head. They could reach the battery within a matter of minutes of an alarm being given. That right, Jacob?"

"Guess so," he sniggered, "'Specially if they ain't sleepin' to home."

One eye on Amy, Twisden offered his hand. "Tell me, in your opinion, Private Hunter, can the *Favourite* make sail for Beverly inside a week's time?"

"Yes, sir." Lord, how silly he felt addressing this amateur as punctiliously as if he were an officer of the Royal Navy. "Always provided you send men suitable for gun crews. Training takes time, sir."

Exhibiting the faintest trace of mockery, Andrew Hunter smartly presented arms before marching, not walking, out onto Mugford Street.

For men who professed, and probably didn't possess, even a smattering of knowledge concerning artillery Amy Orne's guests displayed penetrating interest while being conducted about the fortification, a simple but solid crescent-shaped demi-lune constructed of logs, glacier-smoothed beach stones and boulders.

Escorted by Tom and Sambo, his big and exuberant black-and-brown mongrel retriever, the guests exhibited genuine curiosity over the construction of gun platforms made of freshly sawed planks. Andrew drew attention to a series of iron ring bolts forged by local blacksmiths and set into an embrasure's oaken frame then explained that a gun carriage's side-tackles eventually would be hooked onto these.

Caleb Twisden seemed especially pleased. "Indeed, Hunter, you and your men have accomplished much in a short time. My most sincere congratulations!"

"Thank you, sir." Andrew covertly studied the Lieutenant. Was this 'Header as truly ignorant as he pretended about cannon? To make sure the ex-Regular remarked, "I presume you have noted, sir, that I—we still lack preventer bolts?"

"'Preventer bolts'?"

"Eye bolts let into the deck to prevent a gun from recoiling too far and possibly hurting the crew or snapping its breeching tackle. Till we can rig some let's pray British men-of-war will conduct their blockade well off-shore and that their supply ships will continue to hug the coastline, like those out yonder."

Everyone's gaze shifted out to sea and for the first time made out specks of white barely visible on the horizon. Undoubtedly those were topsails of merchantmen sailing, independent of escorting men-of-war bound for Boston from Halifax, one of Major-General Gage's principal supply depots.

Shading his eyes, Caleb Twisden pointed to the distant vessels. "Tell me, Hunter, how soon may we hope to capture easy prizes such as those?"

"No telling. Everything depends on how quickly the yards in Beverly can get guns mounted."

Denmead trailing behind paused now and then to make a notation.

Sambo, ears flapping and barking joyously, raced about chasing plovers, sandpipers, beetleheads and other shore birds into brief and contemptuous flight.

While following the path up to the Izard home it proved difficult for Andrew, on such a lovely, warm and peaceful July evening, to realize that, across Massachusetts Bay, thousands of men must chiefly be occupied with planning how best to slaughter one another.

All through tea Amy Orne commanded Andrew's mounting admiration by the tact with which she directed conversation calculated to make her guests, himself included, feel equally important and at ease.

Once the tea things had been put away and perhaps because no wine or liquor seemed to be forthcoming, Jacob Marston remarked, "Even if Jonathan ain't here don't think he'd mind our taking a quick look aboard the *Favourite*. Once made a voyage in her down to Jamaica so I'd admire seeing what you've done to the old girl."

Of course everyone except Andrew knew the cruiser-to-be wasn't old; in fact, less than three years had passed since she'd slipped smoothly down well-tallowed ways into the water flaunting the Izard house flag—a white capital "I" centered in a scarlet diamond on a yellow field.

On her maiden voyage she'd cruised at an amazing speed down to the Sugar Islands of Dominica, Jamaica and Antigua. She also first had visited, quite illegally, certain foreign colonies, Guadeloupe and Martinique for example, where prices paid for lumber and salt fish were considerably more advantageous.

On her return voyage the *Favourite* usually would be riding deep with a cargo of indigo, molasses, sugar, rum and occasionally logs of mahogany, satinwood or dyewood which nowadays were becoming so costly that the practice of veneering was becoming necessary and adopted by even the finest cabinet makers in England.

Before long Andrew perceived that Lieutenant Caleb Twisden, although he apparently knew nothing about artillery, was quite knowledgeable about ships and their construction. This was understandable since Twisden & Marston specialized in maritime law, especially condemnation proceedings tried before Vice Courts of Admiralty which, in principally seafaring Colonies, were a power second only to the Throne.

Observed Twisden, "I expect Jonathan has relied a good deal on your experience with naval construction?"

Andrew shrugged. "That's as may be, sir. I haven't attempted drastic alterations, only those which are important." He looked Twisden in the eye. "What chiefly concerns me now, sir, is how lacking a single cannon am I to drill crews to serve this battery? This is a most urgent matter."

Unexpectedly the clerk Denmead interjected, "As I said earlier,

Cap'n Penniston's reported four cannons for the battery are on their way from Salem along with mountings or whatever such they are."

"Carriages."

"Carriages, then. At any rate they should reach town tomorrow sometime."

"Tell me," Twisden invited, "how soon after your cannons arrive do you and Jonathan figure they can be made useful?"

"Can't say, sir. Depends on how quick the locals learn how to handle artillery."

"It's not a quick or easy art, Caleb," Tom rasped recalling the stinging impact of many an officer's cane or a bosun's "starter" across his shoulders, "and that's God's own truth. All right, friends, judge it's time to stop in on Jonathan, ought to be home by now."

He was wrong. There was no sign of the *Favourite*'s owner. Had something gone wrong over in Salem?

Nevertheless, once the party entered Jonathan Izard's long, low and red-painted home Tom produced a stone jug of Barbados rum and dumpy, apple-cheeked Deborah Izard puttered cheerfully about heaping a platter with gingerbread cakes which, though much complimented upon at first, were ignored once the Barbados went to work.

All in all Amy Orne decided this occasion was going off surprisingly well. No one had proved more agreeable than Caleb Twisden. Only once did she notice a hardening of the lawyer's jaw line when he caught her casting a less than passing glance in Andrew Hunter's direction.

Only when Timothy Hunter's son wearily extended his wiry frame on a cot set up in a lean-to built onto the lee side of Jonathan's home did he attempt an appreciation of this afternoon's and evening's events. Certainly nothing had been said or done to raise doubts and yet, and yet, he recalled some leading questions of military importance raised by the visitors, and hadn't Joshua Denmead made copious notes?

Locking fingers under head Andrew lay stripped to damp and ill-smelling underdrawers on a thin mattress and again attempted to analyze his feelings concerning Sarah Hilton. Why should he, considering he'd not known the bookseller's pretty daughter either long or intimately? Come to think on it, he hadn't even held hands with her let alone bussed her cheek. Then why should thoughts of Sarah occur at unexpected moments, oddly enough mostly in Amy Orne's presence?

Sighing, he turned onto his side whereupon Sambo, who'd taken to him in no uncertain fashion, snuffled and raised his head to peer out of a rough board door at the moonlit sea before going back to sleep. This night was so very still the sound of waves breaking over small boulders strewn along the beach, Jonathan and Deborah's snorings on the other side of the wall could be heard.

Turning on sweat-dampened blankets Andrew realized a light still was glowing in the Widow Milburn's cottage only a few dozen yards distant. Could Amy Orne also be awake? Possibly. For a mere female she was an omnivorous and persistent reader; she also was unusual in other directions. Recently he'd come to notice contradictory facets in her disposition. For example she loved to tease yet, with unreasoning intensity, resented being even mildly joshed.

There could be no ignoring Jonathan Izard's niece's physical attributes. Where had she learned so demurely to lower her eyelids while at the same time slowly curving shiny, dark-red lips in such a fashion as to start a man's blood leaping like a frightened buck over a windfall? Her rather low-pitched voice at once was melodious yet crisp.

Why this growing attraction to Amy Orne? Was it because from the start she'd made small pretense of concealing her admiration of him? What complete contrasts were Sarah and Amy, who must be of about the same age. Unlike Sarah, Amy seemed to have grown up in decent but very modest circumstances. Attractive as Amy was, and full-blooded, too, why had she thus far resisted offers of marriage or some relationship possibly more financially rewarding though not sanctioned by Society?

Eyelids growing heavier by the moment, Andrew attempted to identify what most attracted him to this girl. Aside from her undeniable physical appeal this young woman's seeming lack of guile surely was to be admired. Unlike most females he'd encountered which, due to his previous profession, hadn't been numerous, Amy seldom directed conversation towards trivialities such as gossip, scandal, or the latest modes. In short, when Jonathan's niece added two to two the answer invariably came out four, not three or five as with so many females, depending on their mood. Furthermore, Amy, from what he'd thus far observed, appeared to be a shrewd judge of character. Just before falling asleep he came to the conclusion that Amy's way of thinking essentially was masculine.

Amy Orne also lay awake feeling rather pleased over the way this afternoon and evening had turned out. Hadn't she managed to bring two strong, intelligent but otherwise completely dissimilar men together without precipitating a clash of personalities?

Caleb, of course, she'd known for years. Once on a hayride when she'd been around seventeen he'd made bold to start exploring her petticoats and thereby earned a smart slap which, to her astonishment, he'd taken in good nature. He'd even chuckled while the hayrick rumbled along with other couples giggling and laughing: "I earned that, Amy, glad of it 'specially since sometime soon I intend advancing a serious proposal. But did you have to slap all that hard?"

A pity that the good-looking and witty young fellow hadn't enlarged on what exactly his "proposal" entailed. Later, she'd decided his legal training must be responsible but she'd never entertained illusions concerning Caleb Twisden, no matter how fond she was of him. As a young man he'd always been clever, hard-working but popular and politically astute. Nonetheless she sensed Caleb would never make a decision *contra* the best interests of Number 1. Not long ago she'd decided he might not make a bad husband provided she kept her wits about her and handled him with teasing subtlety. Caleb, she foresaw, was the sort bound to come out a winner no matter from what direction the wind blew.

She stirred, kicked the top sheet down to the foot of her bed. Lordy, weren't these sultry and windless July nights uncomfortable? As a born 'Header she sensed that before long there'd come a sharp change in the weather. Probably a brisk northern or a nor'easter would spring up and drive successive torrents of cold rain and banks of blinding fog in from the North Atlantic.

Presently she hiked up the hem of her cheap cotton night rail under her chin then several times blew over fairly small but erect and well-proportioned breasts.

Next she parted long smooth legs allowing air to circulate around and beneath her thighs. Why should thoughts of Andrew Hunter persist? What about his future? Beyond doubt this ex-British Naval officer was a real American, well-mannered and educated and, under normal conditions, socially entertaining. If only he'd laugh more readily, tell jokes or pose conundrums. All the same, she sensed that Andrew Hunter possessed a dry sense of humor but what had happened in Boston must have sobered him, temporarily at least. Only in part could she grasp what a shattering impact his disgrace and the ruin of a cherished career must have had upon him. Could he be worked out of this semi-frozen attitude? His being a distant cousin of hers possibly might explain why 'Headers were beginning to credit Tom Izard's account and even act friendly towards a former officer of the King.

Another element working in Andrew's favor was that not a few local merchants and sea captains either had dealt with or had heard of Captain Timothy Hunter, also that although he resided in Cambridge in a pro-Tory neighborhood he always had been a strongly anti-Parliament man even before the so-called "Boston Massacre."

Therein, mused Amy, lay her most critical and immediate problem. Following the hostilities at Lexington and Concord many admitted Tories had moved away from Marblehead and every day more were following them now that the Committee of Safety, headed by John Glover, Azel Orne, Jeremiah Lee, Elbridge Gerry and others, had purged the old 5th Essex County Militia of Loyalist-inclined officers and men.

Perspiring heavily, Amy turned onto her side then, for coolness, draped an arm and a leg over the edge of the bed. What might the next few weeks bring? Those few British Regular officers she'd encountered had voiced arrogant confidence in Britain's power ruthlessly, in short order, to suppress seditious combinations of any size or description. Likely they'd been correct about this. Right now it looked as if the Patriot cause didn't stand a chance of surviving any more than an unshielded candle's flame in a gale of wind. Utterly disorganized, ill-equipped and led for the most part by superannuated or inexperienced officers, what chance would the Colonial forces largely composed of unlettered farmers, ordinary mechanics and rough seafarers stand against the King's superbly disciplined and equipped forces?

What if, and it seemed an increasingly appealing idea, she were to encourage Andrew Hunter's attentions? What would Caleb do? Long ago she'd detected a jealous, faintly vindictive twist in his character. Yes. The lawyer could without effort find plenty of ways to removing Andrew from competition.

Um. For "Mrs. Caleb Twisden" no end of exciting possibilities presented themselves provided she took care always to remain subtle, astute and submissive when necessary. Why shouldn't Amy Orne Twisden someday rise to become a social leader in New England?

As "Mrs. Andrew Hunter" wasn't she likely to wind up penniless, with her husband fleeing for dear life? After all, didn't the Royal Navy have a hangman's noose waiting for Andrew Hunter? And yet, and yet, Andrew was so virile, so straightforward and strong-minded.

CHAPTER 18 ❧

DENMEAD GOES LOBSTERING

Two DAYS AFTER Amy's tea party a pair of extra-sturdy farm wagons escorted by a dozen un-uniformed but well-armed horsemen were raising lazy dust clouds while slowly they advanced towards Marblehead along the Salem road. Joshua Denmead, among other locals, noticed that on both these vehicles insufficiently greased axles were screeching under the weight of three cannon barrels. Everybody cheered when the procession halted to water weary, lathered horses then treated bearded teamsters and escorts to all the ale they could swallow before they mounted up and moved off in the direction of Poach's Head.

By a liberal use of elbows Denmead managed to get close enough to the carts to note that the dully gleaming iron tubes in them appeared in good condition, which was more than could be said about their carriages.

"What size shot do they fire?" he inquired of a driver.

"Dunno for sure, but once I heard somebody allow these cannons can hurl 6-pound iron balls."

Andrew Hunter really felt frustrated on discovering that repairs to the gun carriages had not been completed in Salem so now that these barrels had arrived nothing could be done for the present save to hoist, through by use of shears and blocks and tackles, the ponderous guns onto platforms of raw yellow planking. At once carpenters and shipwrights among the militiamen set to work. By grabs, they'd have these carriages completed for use inside of two days and once the first piece had been mounted he and Tom Izard could start drilling gun crews. Spirits soaring, he patted the smooth, warm iron and noted that, according to markings on the chase—a band welded just aft of the muzzle's flare—these British pieces must have been cast less than twenty years ago.

Amy Orne clutching a wide-brimmed straw hat against a stiff westerly breeze felt almost as excited as the men at work; soon Andrew would be able to prove his reputed skill with artillery. Moving around a milling throng of townsfolk and members of Company B she noted Caleb Twisden shaking Captain Penniston's hand. They were the only men wearing uniform; everyone else was clad in drab, often patched and sun-bleached work clothes.

Captain Penniston was saying, "Now, Miss Orne, I reckon we can put up a stiff fight an the need arises."

"A stiff fight?" Remembering a few remarks Andrew had made concerning the battery's feeble threat, Amy only smiled, said nothing; let the people go on believing that half a dozen insignificant 6 pounders could stand off the entire Royal Navy if necessary.

Joshua Denmead yelled as enthusiastically as anyone when somebody brought a roll of cloth to a flagpole rising beside the Izard's sail loft. Unfurled by the breeze it displayed a pointed and dark-green pine tree standing stark against a snow-white field, a design which by all accounts was becoming increasingly popular. Beneath it a motto read: "An Appeal to Heaven." Most people present felt confident that this, out of several designs, soon would become the official flag of the United Colonies. To the contrary many persons, especially in the Southern Colonies, were in favor of an ensign which depicted a rattlesnake with forked tongue extended, crawling diagonally across a series of red and white stripes above the motto: "Don't Tread on Me," but

172

there were plenty of objections by Patriots on the grounds that a poisonous reptile wasn't suitable as a national emblem.

Once the crowd had dispersed, Amy approached Andrew. "I'm so happy. I can only guess what the safe arrival of these cannons means to you."

He smiled, "After supper I aim to make a closer examination of the guns, must make certain none of 'em are even slightly flawed. Like to keep me company?"

"I'd be pleased to."

"Then I'll call right after we've suppered. You see, I'll need plenty of light."

"I'll be ready." She dipped the brim of her hat to eclipse a sudden sparkle in her eyes.

On that same evening Joshua Denmead casually informed his boarding-house keeper that he aimed to go out in the evening to pull a few of his lobster pots and maybe catch a mess of pollocks she could serve to her boarders so she needn't count of him for supper.

The sun was creating a molten glory on the horizon when Josh hoisted the sail of a small speedy skiff and steered for the harbor's entrance. Probably because most folks were busy with supper his departure went almost unnoticed. He took care, however, to wave, friendly-like, to the occupants of a few fishing boats belatedly making for harbor.

Once he'd sailed past the demi-lune on Peach's Head and saw it deserted Josh heaved a sigh of relief then, from between fingers, squinted into the flaming sunset until, way out yonder, he caught a faint flash of three topgallant sails. Um. So information from Boston had been accurate; H.M.S. *Lively* once more was patrolling this length of the seacoast.

Josh came into the wind only long enough to heave up a trio of lobster pots attached to bobbing buoys banded in yellow and green, his colors. By the time he'd finished unloading the traps and their contents of tail-snapping, olive-green crustaceans darkness really had begun to descend.

CHAPTER 19 🦢

SAMBO TAKES ALARM

ALTHOUGH IT WAS LATE—all of half-past nine—Amy Orne and Andrew Hunter continued to sit very close together behind a pile of sweet-scented pine planking destined to reinforce the bulwarks of the schooner lying at the seaward end of Izard Brothers' wharf. Wasn't it extra fine lingering like this, enjoying starlight and cooled by a moderate breeze blowing from the southeast?

Absently, Andrew rubbed aching, work-blistered hands but whenever he looked at Amy, unusually lovely by starlight, he forgot the pain.

"Sorry they hurt," she commented softly. "Seems as if you've almost literally worked your fingers to the bone—you and the rest of the men. What progress have you made towards repairing the gun carriages?"

"Three already are fixed and, if all goes well, the other three should be ready to receive barrels tomorrow."

"What were those loopy-shaped things on top of the cannon barrels?"

"They're called 'dolphins' because often a foundry will shape

174

them like one. They come in handy when it's necessary to hoist a tube onto a carriage or any other place; some are beautifully designed, especially on French or Spanish-made guns."

Due to an on-shore breeze the reek of sun-dried fish drifted inland over Marblehead Neck so for a change the night air smelt uncommonly sweet and fresh. Despite grinding fatigue Andrew more than ever became aware of Amy's strong physical appeal. Possibly she might have paid undue attention to her appearance before joining him on the wharf?

He noticed she was wearing a crisp frilled kerchief neatly and effectively crossed above her breasts but had pinned said kerchief just low enough to expose a *val* dividing what seemed to be small, well-rounded bosoms.

She smoothed a blue-and-white striped skirt puffed out by a yet undeterminable number of petticoats. Also, daringly for a community like this, Amy had done things to her wavy, red-brown hair. For one thing she'd trained a fashionable lovelock to dangle enticingly over her shoulder. Fortunately Nature had denied her the temptation of using cosmetics; her cheeks glowed a healthy pink-brown and her intriguingly full lips remained a luscious dark-red.

She'd even fetched in her hand basket a half-bottle of French claret smuggled into Marblehead not so long ago.

"Kindly draw the cork, Andrew."

After they'd twice drunk from thick glass tumblers Andrew grimaced. "Wish I'd had time for a swim but we toiled till 'twas too dark to see. Reckon I must smell like a cross between an old clothes shop and an overripe cheese."

"Honest toil like yours creates only pleasant odors," she laughed. "Now isn't that a truly patriotic lie?"

Lights were beginning to wink out all around the harbor and the town back of it. Never a lamp glowed in the Izard home nor in the Widow Milburn's cottage for even in normal times precious few 'Headers stayed awake very long after the sun went down. Nowadays lights were doused even earlier due to an ever-increasing shortage of whale oil and candles.

Said he, "I'll feel a heap happier once the guns are mounted and all their service utensils are here."

He watched her slim dark brows mount. "'Service utensils'? What on earth can such be?"

"Rammers, sponges, powder ladles, priming wires and the like, also quoins, tackle blocks and breaching ropes."

"For what?"

"Why, to run the guns in and out."

After sampling a third and final glass of claret he wound arms about Amy then drew her to him until the softness of her body became utterly irresistible. She voiced no protest; to the contrary slender but wiry arms slipped about his neck while she raised parted lips.

Hunger begotten by long months at sea and lack of female companionship other than that of waterfront whores engulfed him. They strained together hands probing and caressing. Sambo, who'd trotted down to the dock in search of his new friend, sat head cocked to one side looking on with a puzzled air.

Suddenly Andrew drew back, said thickly, "We've some extra-fine new duck canvas in the sail loft. Suppose we go and inspect it."

Once they'd arisen Amy paused to view the schooner lying with standing rigging sketched like sable cobwebs against the stars. "Looks mighty trim and speedy. How soon should she be ready to sail?"

"Ought to be fit for the run over to Beverly come a week's time."

Amy tossed disordered hair back over her shoulders. "Why Beverly?"

"That's where she's *supposed* to receive her cannon, gunpowder and other armament."

While walking along the cluttered dock, arms about waists, she said, "If your canvas is sufficiently light could you spare a few yards—enough so I could sew you—and Tom—some seamen's breeches?"

In the strong starlight Andrew's teeth glinted. "I—I'd be almighty pleased to have a pair, so would Tom."

The night, neither exactly dark nor light, felt blessedly cool after the day's sultry heat. No pretense was made about lighting a candle and nothing was said while Andrew led the way to the sail cutting room. Together, they sank upon a pile of fine duck yard goods and embraced fervently, crushing against one another as, once more, hands commenced to explore and caress. By now he could tell by the way Amy conducted herself that this well-mannered and well-spoken girl was no fluttery green virgin. He became aware of being enveloped by a peculiarly exciting aura of femininity.

"Certain-sure we'll be safe here, darling?" she whispered at the same time loosening her blue-and-white skirt's draw strings.

"Aye. Tom, Jonathan, neighbors, everyone long since will be snoring."

Everything seemed so preordained, so natural neither spoke while extending themselves on the soft and yielding duck. Fiery meteors and rainbows, visible only to them, commenced to dance and illumine the cutting room's spacious gloom.

On the stern locker of H.M.S. *Lively's* longboat Joshua Denmead sat jammed between Lieutenant Dubose of the Royal Marines and a coxswain who, gripping the tiller, strained to catch Denmead's instructions over the noise of waves surging lazily over barnacled kelp-covered rocks and reefs scattered along the eastern shore entrance to Marblehead Harbor.

For some time squadrons of high clouds had been obscuring light shed by uncountable millions of stars. So, only because he'd grown up hereabouts, was Joshua Denmead able to give orders, often at the last minute, to avoid half-submerged rocks.

The landing party, some fifteen Royal Marines and selected seamen, sat huddled together holding bayoneted muskets erect lest they stab one another. As many more men occupied the whaler rowing close behind the longboat and riding heavily over a succession of tired black rollers.

Sharply Dubose inquired, "Ain't we near that damn' beach?"

"Yes, sir," Denmead called over sea-sounds, "Come another hundred yards we ought to sight a gravelly beach hard by the Izard Brothers' wharf."

"You'd better be right," rasped the Marine, tapping the brass-mounted butt of a heavy boarding pistol jammed into his belt.

The Marines checked priming then straightened or otherwise reslung their equipment. Most were of the opinion that this expedition promised to prove a pretty dull business. Why, these damned stupid Rebels hadn't even bothered to post lookouts or to patrol the harbor's narrow entrance.

"That the battery?" Dubose growled, pointing to a dim low outline just visible above the shoreline.

"Yes, sir, that's it. No need to worry, sir. Doubt they've got a single gun in serviceable condition, let alone manned."

But Lieutenant Dubose did worry. By now he'd learned that all too often Rebels had proved smart when they were supposed to be stupid, and on their guard when expected to be careless, unalert.

Denmead said, pointing to a dim white streak, "Yonder's the beach. B'God, we're closer in than I thought. This light can fool you."

"Another mistake will be your last," snapped Dubose. "Way enough!"

At the coxswain's order seamen stopped rowing, tossed dripping oars and allowed the longboat's momentum to carry it halfway up a narrow, pebbled beach until it ground to a stop.

Holding muskets high to keep charges dry Marines and seamen scrambled over gunwales and commenced to wade ashore.

About that moment Sambo, snoozing comfortably among stacks of lumber on the Izard's wharf, awoke to hear the splashing of many feet and sniff the odor of bodies too long unwashed. The retriever didn't know quite what to make of this, only that the master he'd adopted still was lingering in the sail loft where he'd been for quite a while. But once he heard a musket barrel go *clink!* against another Sambo leaped to his feet and started a commotion fit to waken the dead. On a still night like this the racket he created covered a considerable distance.

The couple in the cutting room hadn't intended to dally so long in their euphoric state so sat up staring wildly about the semi-darkness.

"Oh, dear Lord," gasped Amy frantically pulling down skirt and petticoats, then her perspiration-soaked blouse in the opposite direction. "What can Sambo be barking at?"

Instinctively Andrew knew on recognizing the clank of equipment, the tread of many feet and sounds of ill-suppressed voices.

"Raiders!" In a frantic haste he did up his breeches' buttons.

"Can't be anything else. Stay here and count slowly to a hundred before you make for home."

Andrew dashed out of the sail loft's rear entrance yelling at the top of his lungs to distract attention from the wharf and raced towards the Izard home. Thinking this must be some new game Sambo pranced about, kept up his frantic barking.

He continued shouting, "Turn out! Turn out! British are landing near battery!" until in most nearby houses lights began to glow.

Because people living hereabouts had existed in a state of perpetual apprehension for so long no more than a few moments passed before most 'Headers were ready for action. Someone commenced to sound a tocsin contrived of a discarded cartwheel's iron tire suspended from a tree branch. When struck with any object fashioned from bronze or iron it gave off loud, shivering and far-carrying notes.

While nearing the Izard house he encountered Tom stuffing a nightshirt into his pants with one hand and cocking a blunderbuss with the other.

"What the Hell's goin' on?" yelled Jonathan, hair and beard disheveled and naked to the waist.

"Redcoats landing on beach near your dock."

"How many?"

"Too dark to make sure but it sounded like around thirty or forty men!"

Jonathan caught up a brass-barreled blunderbuss and slung on his powder horn. Tom did the same while Andrew grabbed his old French fusil which, like most firearms in this vicinity, had been kept loaded and ready ever since news had arrived about the encounter at Lexington and Concord. Fervently Andrew wished he too were armed with a blunderbuss—so much more deadly at short range, especially when loaded with buck-and-ball, than a long-barreled fusil's heavy but lone bullet. Small children awoke and, bewildered, raised shrill, persistent clamorings because Sambo and the neighbors' dogs kept on barking excitedly as if they'd never shut up.

As usual during a crisis Deborah Izard kept her head and in addition to other alarms sounded her personal tocsin, a tin dishpan she beat with an iron ladle. By the time Lieutenant

Dubose's party was forming up along the shingle beach blear-eyed Colonists even in the dark were lifting firearms from pegs driven into walls near doors and, just as they'd been instructed by Andrew Hunter, started pelting towards the Izard place, the farthest outdwelling on Peach's Head.

Joshua Denmead, guiding the detail, recognized the flash of Amy Orne's blue-and-white striped skirt and petticoats when she lifted them knee-high to start scurrying up to the Widow Milburn's cottage.

Corporal Denmead grinned to himself while the raiders, muskets held at the ready, advanced towards the dock and the schooner's dim outlines. So *that* was where the high-and-mighty Orne girl had been nesting! He bet he could name that tall figure he'd glimpsed bolting out of that same building seconds earlier.

Cursing and panting militiamen appeared singly or by twos and threes and fell all over themselves while in the dark trying to form up behind stacks of barnacle-whitened lobster traps.

Andrew, catching his breath, assumed that the main target for this foray must be the demi-lune and its cannon but, on second thoughts guessed that the enemy, undoubtedly informed by some spy, must know that the demi-lune's defenses were incomplete so posed no immediate danger so sensed that the real objective of this expedition was to ensure that the *Favourite* would never set sail.

A light mist had arisen and lingered over the shingle beach on which the raiders' boats had been pulled up. Only a hundred yards separated the water's edge from the battery, Jonathan Izard's home and the Widow Milburn's cottage, lying a hundred more paces farther inland.

"This way, *Lively!*" a shrill voice kept yelling on the demi-lune's seaward side. "Get moving, you clubfooted baboons. This way, on the double!"

The first minutemen, some still wearing night clothes, and members of Company B arrived. Following Captain Penniston's and Lieutenant Twisden's bellowed commands, they attempted to form a ragged double rank behind Jonathan's house. When nearly seventy men had arrived breathless and began banging musket barrels against each other, Captain Penniston, half-choked with excitement, ordered an advance on the battery. He and Jonathan then had a sharp disagreement.

"Can't you understand, you gol-durned ninny-hammer, them Lobsterbacks ain't here just to destroy our battery." The rest of his remarks became lost amid rising tumult. Lieutenant Twisden added to the confusion by shouting, "Captain Penniston's right! It's the guns they've come for!"

"Like Hell!" roared Jonathan. "These Bloodybacks are here to cut out or burn my schooner!"

Just before the militia commenced a disorderly advance on the demi-lune, Lieutenant Dubose at Josh Denmead's insistent urging detached half of his force to make for the wharf and the unrigged and helpless *Favourite*.

Led by Lieutenant Dubose, Marines and selected seamen, easily recognizable by the cutlasses they wore and by bell-bottomed pants halted, closed up and on command leveled firearms at figures dimly seen beyond the battery's parapet. Brief dazzling jets of flame and booming reports followed, made the militia less eager to advance, especially after a couple of their number screamed then crumpled to the ground kicking senselessly or moaning and groaning.

Although Penniston and Twisden pleaded with the men to keep on the militia took a few wavering steps forward then halted the instant the enemy fired more shots.

Andrew, having run out ahead on the right of line, leveled his fusil and with a few others fired point-blank into a knot of dimly seen figures swarming over the battery's parapet. Shrieks and cries resulted but after reloading he found himself alone. Protected by clouds of burnt powder smoke he waited until some ten or fifteen locals at last heeded their officers and again advanced slowly and more cautiously.

"Shoot low," Andrew warned. "Come on! Can't let 'em take our cannon."

From the moment he recognized the *clang clang!* of hammers striking iron he knew there was now no point in attempting to defend the demi-lune. God almighty! The raiders were spiking his precious pieces! Weeks would be required to drill out a spike which when driven deep into a touchhole rendered the piece useless for a considerable length of time.

The air grew opaque when drifting gun smoke mingled with the mist. Since the Colonials had only a few bayonets among them any attempt at hand-to-hand fighting was likely to prove suicidal. Very soon the enemy, their goal attained, fired a ragged volley then fell back and started for their boats.

At the head of maybe a dozen panting and sweat-bathed militiamen, Caleb Twisden ran up to Andrew. "Rally your men, Hunter! Can't let those Lobsterbacks go scot-free, come on! Come on, damn you!"

Having already retreated halfway to their boats the Marines greeted the pursuing 'Headers' approach with a volley pointed in their general direction. The resultant damage was small but it caused a musket ball to graze Jonathan Izard's shoulder. A few stout-hearted New Englanders now ran up and blindly fired into layers of low-hanging bitter-smelling gun smoke. A buckshot knocked off Lieutenant Leonard Dubose's cap and another, grazing his skull, dropped him senseless into a gully between a pair of recently repaired gun carriages where he lay inert and hardly visible.

Only after realization that his guns indeed had been effectively spiked did Andrew heed shots and excited voices rising in the direction of that wharf from which he'd bolted not half an hour earlier.

"Follow me!" he yelled and then at a run led a party of militiamen along the shore and towards the wharf now swarming with dark figures. His anxiety grew, sharpened when he saw that the raiders, as was customary in the Royal Navy under such conditions, had fetched along some dark lanterns. An icy fist seemed to crush his heart with realization that Jonathan had been right. The British had come principally to capture or set fire to the schooner.

Marines on order from their Serjeant leveled bayonets and quickly drove back a shadowy mob of half-dressed and wild-eyed Colonials. Lacking even a semblance of discipline there was nothing Caleb Twisden could do when Andrew's men ran up but to shoulder his musket and fire in the Redcoats' general direction. Although he couldn't possibly have known it, his bullet was the one which nicked Joshua Denmead on the side of his neck just deep enough to start bright arterial blood pulsing through his fingers and onto the dock's splintery surface.

The Marine Serjeant commanding paid no heed to the gurgling wretch's feebly diminishing struggles, because the informer was wearing civilian clothing.

Andrew Hunter from a low ridge behind the dock and sail loft noticed torches being kindled from dark lanterns. The men carrying them made straight for the schooner and scattered the torches over her chip- and sawdust-littered deck. Plenty of pitch and turpentine being available it didn't take the raiders long to set fires crackling at strategic points not only fore and aft but below decks as well.

Soon the whole scene, dock, sail loft and even houses on the rise behind, quickly became revealed by a flickering red-and-yellow glare.

"Nah then, you sods, fall in," the Serjeant barked once he'd made sure the flames were spreading rapidly along sun-dried timbers. The bright tongues of fire lapped at shrouds and other recently tarred standing rigging then raced hungrily aloft creating strange bright patterns amid clouds of pungent and oily black smoke.

Satisfied that this Rebel vessel never would question the Crown's authority the Serjeant led his party at the double along the shore back to the boats and in so doing encountered that detachment which had rendered useless the battery's guns. All cursed with impatience to rejoin H.M.S. *Lively* before broad daylight. Not until the raiders had helped their wounded into the boats and were preparing to launch did anyone notice that Lieutenant Dubose was missing.

"Where's the Lootenant?" the Serjeant shouted.

A chorus of voices denied having sighted him since the demilune had been taken.

"Christ! Let's get out of here. Look up there!"

A dark mass of men in a wavering line were trotting towards the beach. Presently they halted and opened fire. After two of his men were hit the Serjeant yelled, "Shove off!" then quite unnecessarily added, "Row like Hell!"

Amy, trembling and desperately anxious, went to peer through a window in Mrs. Milburn's sitting room. The widow herself had stayed upstairs, which was just as well. Lord above! Who could ever imagine that so many disasters could strike in so short a time? Her body still glowed, reminiscent of raptures shared in the cutting room, then when a rattle of musketry became intensified a terrible question arose. *How was Andrew faring?* Next, occurred a sickening fear someone might have observed her flight from the sail loft.

Further anxieties shook her when towering spirals of flame and sparks began rising in the direction of the dock. Soon it appeared that Uncle Jonathan's vessel would never harass or capture any British supply ship. It was just as well, considering Amy's state of mind, she couldn't be aware that in retreating to their boats the British had left Joshua Denmead slowly dying on the dock.

Although there didn't seem much chance of saving the schooner a party of militiamen headed by Lieutenant Twisden shielded faces from the heat and ran onto the dock which had taken fire at several points. By now high-soaring flames had combined with dawn to illumine all of Marblehead.

While retreating from the conflagration Caleb Twisden only by chance noticed the outline of a man lying sprawled and half-concealed between piles of pine strakes stacked near the dock's land end.

"My God, Denmead!" he choked but because of the roaring flames no one heard him. Shaken by implications raised by his clerk's presence here under such conditions he bent over the round-shouldered figure, appalled by the extent of the blood puddle in which Denmead lay.

"Josh. Oh Nutkin, what happened? You still alive?"

"Only just—feel cold—so cold—"

"Was it you who informed and guided the British?"

"Yes. I—a whole Tory not—half-hearted—like some I know." He coughed, spattered blood into Twisden's face. All the same the lawyer bent lower over the gore-spattered man he'd known since boyhood.

The ashen-faced figure gasped, "When we came—saw Amy Orne run out—knew her striped skirt—from sail loft—soon after— tall man—looked—Hunter."

Twisden lowered an ear close to Denmead's bloodied quivering lips. "You *sure?*"

Bubbling sounds drowned the rest of what Joshua Denmead might have said.

CHAPTER 20 🦢

CASUALTIES

WHILE RALLYING MILITIAMEN and other confused defenders running aimlessly around the demi-lune Andrew Hunter, revealed hard-eyed and wildly disheveled by a flaring, dancing glare cast by the burning schooner, heard voices in the direction of the shore shouting, "Mister Dubose! This way, Mister Dubose! Where are you, Mister Dubose?"

Hell's roaring bells! Undoubtedly it was the officer commanding H.M.S. *Lively*'s Marines they were calling for. Leonard Dubose must be leading this raid customarily a task for Marines. What could have happened to Dubose? Too bad if he'd been killed or badly hurt. He'd been on far better terms with him than other English-born officers.

He sighted corpulent Captain Penniston amid a dark crowd of men milling uncertainly about. He was limping as if his gout was bothering him.

"Sir! Sir!" he yelled. "Let's go to the beach and shake salt on their tails!"

Now that dawn had brightened, red-coated figures in the act of shoving off offered promising targets. By dint of much shouting and gesticulating Penniston, Twisden and Hunter succeeded in forming skirmish line of sorts which, at a brisk trot, started for the beach. The Marines fired a few poorly-aimed shots while the seamen were getting out their oars. Some 'Headers checked their advance and stopped to shoot back but were so excited and short of breath they couldn't sight properly; their bullets only raised brief plumes of water around both boats just as their oarsmen settled down and began pulling steadily towards the dim silhouette of H.M.S. *Lively* standing under easy canvas about a mile offshore.

Reckoning that for some reason Lieutenant Dubose hadn't made it back to his boat Andrew ranged about the demi-lune along with Tom Izard and a handful of 'Headers.

"Hi, Cappen! Come on overhere," shouted a gray-haired man with a powder horn slung over a billowing nightshirt. "By grabs, I've found a damn' Lobsterback." The Marine Lieutenant was lying sprawled and unconscious in a shallow gully between gun platforms.

"Damn' Bloodyback looks dead," someone grunted. "Lookit at all that there blood runnin' out his head."

Andrew stooped, tested a thick, limp wrist then glanced over his shoulder up at Captain Penniston. "This man isn't dead, sir, but he's been hard hit. Shall we have Mister Dubose lugged up to the stable?" Only a fraction of a second too late did Andrew realize the seriousness of the mistake he'd just made.

"Oh, so you recognize this fellow," coolly snapped Twisden.

"I knew him when I—well, when I was serving the King. You know about that."

"Oh, yes, I'd forgotten. Well, fetch a shutter and let's carry him up to Mrs. Milburn's stable."

When Dubose was brought in Amy appeared, hair hastily combed but still wearing a rumpled striped skirt. She was dressing Jonathan Izard's hurt shoulder which she quickly realized was no worse than a deep but painful flesh wound. When the wounded Marine officer was being lugged into the stable she shot Andrew a single agonized glance before setting to work. His expression remained quite unchanged.

Quick checking up revealed that, so far as could be told, the amount of blood spilled in repelling this raid had not been excessive. Only one 'Header was reported killed outright and five others had been wounded, one probably mortally in Doctor Bond's opinion.

On the other hand, as near as could be ascertained, when the attackers had departed they'd been seen carrying three limp bodies. Opinions varied, but almost everybody agreed that the enemy likely had suffered three times that many wounded.

Throngs of wide-eyed, angry townsfolk kept flocking out from town to gaze in morbid curiosity on a dead Marine's body lying so very flat under a horse blanket and already attracting swarms of bluebottle flies.

Tom growled, "Goddammit, an the wind keeps blowin' out of this quarter we're going to lose the schooner and most of our wharf!"

Caleb Twisden, along with townsmen and some militia, quickly organized a bucket brigade from Jonathan's well to the fire; they worked hard, aware that sparks and brands landing on the Izard home's sun-dried roof shingles would set the place ablaze in no time.

While passing what seemed an endless succession of slopping buckets Twisden, in a cold fury, recalled implications raised by poor Nutkin's dying words when he glimpsed Amy's blue-and-white striped skirt moving about the stable ministering to groaning wounded sprawled on trusses of hay. Although he'd only Denmead's statement to go on he felt convinced that beyond doubt none other than Andrew Hunter had been with Amy in the sail loft.

By now throngs of 'Headers, including a good many women and children, were milling excitedly about Peach's Head. Those men who weren't busy passing buckets gaped in awe and wretched helplessness on soaring flames consuming the *Favourite* especially onlookers who in one capacity or another had worked on her. Furious curses arose when news spread that all six cannon in the cherished battery had been spiked, rendered useless.

Anxious to make certain about this, a number of singed and smoke-blackened selectmen urged Andrew to conduct a thorough inspection and give an expert estimate of the damage.

About the only encouraging result of the raid came when

Andrew, after careful probing of the plugged touchholes, straightened up saying, "Seems to me those spikes they used are just a shade too small in circumference to plug the touchholes efficiently; shouldn't be too difficult to extract provided proper drills can be found and if—"

The balance of what he was about to say became lost amid ringing cheers which swelled and spread over Peach's Head and sent alarmed flocks of gulls and terns to screaming out over the harbor.

Even before the *Favourite* on burning to the water's edge had disappeared under clouds of mingled smoke and steam rumors commenced to circulate that the Izards' friend, Hunter, formerly of H.M.S. *Lively,* was in truth a clever spy who deliberately had brought death and disaster upon a community which had sheltered and befriended him. Others thought it possible, even probable, that Hunter was no spy but that the British, informed of Hunter's whereabouts had come to seize him while at the same time wrecking the battery and burning the schooner. Why not try killing three birds with a single stone?

Other men were equally convinced this attack had been simply another of those harassing raids which during the past year had occurred with increasing frequency along this strategically important stretch of the coast.

Not before the schooner had sunk and nearly half of the Izards' dock had been consumed were fires brought under control. Only then did Andrew, singed, grimy and hollow-eyed, make his way through the crowd and between racks of fish flakes up to the stable in which Lieutenant Dubose was recovering a degree of consciousness. Realization that Amy no longer was visible came as a huge relief.

Hawk-faced Doctor Nathaniel Bond, having attended wounded 'Headers, now knelt beside the prisoner and pursing thin lips set about examining the large and freely bleeding hole in his left thigh and next a shallow scalp wound which had streaked Leonard Dubose's pallid features with crimson.

Captain Penniston, redder of face than ever and mighty self-important, presently ordered militiamen to disperse with the exception of Caleb Twisden, Tom Izard and Jacob Marston. Andrew, not daring to think what Dubose might say, straggled out with other townsfolk into glaring sunlight. The Lord alone knew how these 'Headers might react to whatever Dubose would state.

Meantime Penniston knelt above the prisoner, demanded not ungently, "Your name and rank, sir?"

"I—I—Leonard Dubose," mumbled the supine figure, "Leftenant commanding Marines aboard—*Lively*."

Jacob Marston then posed a question all present were keen to hear answered. "Why was Marblehead selected for attack?"

Eyes sagging and heavy-lidded, Dubose breathed, "Largely because a rebel sailed out to *Lively* last night—reported you—harboring former officer of ours. He—not only—deserter but traitor, too."

"Who was this informer?" Penniston demanded curtly.

"Fellow—called self 'Denmead,' I think."

"Joshua Denmead!" Twisden appeared completely staggered.

"Yes. That was name he gave."

"Well, I'll be damned!" Marston burst out. "Who'd ever have suspected poor little Nutkin capable of turning his coat? What, sir, is the name of that deserter you mentioned?"

"Andrew Hunter. Admiral Graves—Captain Purcell—have vowed—see him swing from—main yard."

After looking hard at his Lieutenant, Captain Penniston asked, "What other information did Denmead give you?"

"Reported—battery unfinished—but ready—few days' time. Also—schooner buildin'—harry our transports—supply ships."

"Always did suspect Hunter," unexpectedly put in Jacob Marston. "We'd better arrest and try him straightaway."

Tom Izard, waving his arms, shouted, "Let's not act overhasty, boys. You all know Andy Hunter's been amongst us several weeks and no one can rightly claim he didn't lay out our battery real fine and toil harder than most in buildin' it. Think a minute. If Andy really is a spy is it likely he'd bring on an attack and risk falling into British hands?"

Twisden suggested loudly, "He may have—he knew our defenses were nearing completion. He might have done whatever he did aboard the *Lively* just to make himself appear a bona fide deserter."

Tom Izard balled his fists. "You callin' me a liar, Caleb Twisden?"

"No, but—"

"Then shut up. I've already told you what I *know* happened in Boston!"

Captain Penniston commanded, "Calm down! Calm down! Andrew Hunter shall have his day in court. Remember, we're not a pack of savages but law-abiding—" he started to say "British subjects" but switched to " 'Christians.' Now somebody find Hunter and say I order him to report here at once!"

CHAPTER 21 ✣

AFTERMATH

THE DAY FOLLOWING the raid proved dismal in that the entire area had been enveloped by a fog so dense a body could "shingle onto it," as New Englanders were given to saying. Effectively, this dank, sea-smelling blanket obscured the battery and mercifully concealed the Izards' wharf. However, all hands were at work salvaging still useful gear and lumber from the dock's undamaged section. The sail loft building had remained unhurt beyond blistered paint on its door and windows and a few small holes burnt through its roof.

Only because Amy Orne was familiar with every foot of this area was she able to find her way towards the battery among tufts of marsh grass and half-buried boulders. No horizon was visible and the fog grew so cold and opaque she felt as if death-chilled hands were stroking her face by the time she encountered a party of workmen looming through eddying mist. Obviously they were straggling homewards, their day's work at an end. She approached a ghostly figure and called out, "Is Mister Hunter still at work?"

"Yes, Ma'am, but he was fixin' to quit. He can't be more'n a few dozen strides behind."

The shipwright proved right. Somehow, she sensed Andrew's nearness when after a few moments he approached looming gigantic amid this shifting gray atmosphere.

"Andrew? Andrew!"

They stepped off the path and exchanged a hurried kiss.

"What in the world are you doing here?"

"Come to fetch you. Doctor Bond thinks the prisoner hasn't much longer to live and Mister Dubose urgently begs to speak with you. Tell me," she breathed, "does, does anybody suspect about—about us last night?"

"Don't believe so. So far, I've heard no talk of anything save the raid."

Trembling in his embrace she burst out, "Oh darling, my darling, I'm so vastly relieved! You can't begin to imagine how worried I've been both on your account—and mine."

"What about Mrs. Milburn? She's a queen gossip in a town overburdened with such."

"Don't worry, dearest. Aunt Elizabeth is hard of hearing, and asleep, she can snore through a whole gale."

Voices in the gloom sent them back onto the path leading up a low bluff lying behind the battery. They found the Widow Milburn's cottage dark save for lamps in the kitchen and another in the parlor window creating dim halos through the fog.

Before a side door Andrew halted, gripped her shoulders and crushed her to him so hard she almost cried out before his mouth closed over hers. "Dearest, I believe we're safe for the moment but should matters take a bad turn be sure I'll not abandon you."

She pressed a cheek against his as he queried, "Where is the prisoner now?"

"Just before I set out to find you on Doctor Bond's suggestion they'd carried the Englishman up to Mrs. Milburn's spare bedroom."

"Just where is it?"

"At the head of the stairs rising from the kitchen."

In the kitchen they found Doctor Bond, Serjeant Jacob Marston and Mrs. Milburn acting so uncommon jolly Amy reckoned she must have been sampling some of "Penobscot Sachem's Elixir," a powerful cough mixture she favored. A small fire was crackling in the fireplace, just big enough to heat a big iron teakettle slung to a crane.

Doctor Bond, a lanky, loose-jointed individual, advanced with a pleasant smile decking smooth, pink and almost cherubic features. Said he in unctuous tones, "Ah, Mister Hunter, glad Amy found you. Fear my patient is almost sped, he's lost far too much blood."

Mrs. Milburn sniffed, cocked her head sidewise like a robin eyeing a promising worm-hole. She wore thin gray hair skinned back into a small chignon. "You may well say so, Doctor, because that—that Royal pirate's blood already has spoiled two pair of good linen sheets. The Lord only knows if I ever can get out them there stains."

Beyond perfunctory greetings Amy only took time to unhook and hang her cloak to a peg before silently disappearing upstairs. Down the short corridor she saw a vertical beam of lamplight emanating from the "extra" room. Without lighting a lamp she settled onto her bedside and, heart still thumping, attempted to calm herself and decide her next step. While listening to undertones rising from the kitchen she realized she'd felt like this before. Oh, Lordy! Cheeks growing hot, she recalled that time she and Jared Sparks had gone blackberry picking and in a secluded birch thicket that brisk young fellow awkwardly had harvested fruit of a different nature. Again, there was that time at Amos Winslow's barn-raising when, while others were making themselves useful, she and Peter Lufkin had slipped away to raise something else. Providence only knew why she'd experienced no unwanted results from either encounter. Could it be she was barren?

If only she could be completely certain that that interlude in the sail loft really had gone unobserved she'd have raised silent hosannas of joy. Only then did she recall that only a thin lath-and-plaster wall separated her room from the next.

On occasion she at first had been embarrassed then intrigued to discover that quite clearly she could overhear everything being said or done next door. For example there was that occasion last May when Mrs. Milburn had invited her nephew, Jesse Beasley, and his bride to spend their nuptial night there. Such eavesdropping had proved stimulating and informative.

She heard the front door unlatched and Jacob Marston's voice saying, "Well, gentlemen, I'll be making tracks for home. By the way, Hunter, Captain Penniston said you're to report to his office tomorrow morning at nine."

Once Marston had departed Doctor Bond looked thoughtfully at Andrew before saying, "Whatever the prisoner has to say must be said quickly and to the point. When I saw him a short while ago I scarce could find his pulse."

Amy roused at the sound of weighty footsteps ascending the staircase's twelve treads; she'd counted them shortly after coming to 'bide with her late mother's widowed sister, Aunt Elizabeth Milburn. Sitting in the musty-smelling dark Amy debated whether in all decency she shouldn't grant Andrew and the dying officer complete privacy but ended up by reasoning she'd a right to eavesdrop on the grounds that what might be said next door could decide her own and Andrew's immediate future.

Andrew sank onto his knees beside the bed which despite the summer's heat was covered with a "Jacob's ladder" designed quilt and took one of Dubose's icy hands between both of his saying gently, "Leonard, Leonard!"

The wounded man slowly opened his eyes. "Who—who—you?"

"Andrew Hunter. Why do mischances have to overtake both of us?"

"Fortunes of war, Andrew m'boy," replied a voice so weak Amy could scarcely distinguish it. "Glad you—here. I—I—" he coughed briefly.

"Why now of all times, do you want to talk with a so-named traitor and deserter?"

"Because I, and some others in *Lively* refuse—believe you'd knowledge of—weak ammunition but didn't dare—voice our opinions. Oh, my friend, why this cruel, senseless rebellion? It promises to grow into a dreadful civil war; nothing could be worse for both sides. Damn the King's advisers!"

Amy overheard Andrew's deep voice, "Agreed. Isn't there *anything* I can do to help?"

"No, my fine American friend—my diary describes my most secret feelings—is still on *Lively*. Might help you."

Dubose coughed again, more weakly. "—Something to tell you. Recall Major Hilton and his daughter Sarah?"

Amy's already keen interest sharpened. Who might Sarah Hilton be?

A trifle too quickly, Amy thought, Andrew added, "Yes, but what of that? Sarah and I have enjoyed each other's company—nothing else."

"Nothing else? I wonder—" Dubose's breathing was becoming harder, slower.

"Yes," Andrew said. "While Sarah Hilton is well-placed in Society and a very charming hostess, to my mind she's not a wholly convincing Loyalist."

"Even so, after you—er—escaped, why would she keep on inviting colonels, generals, admirals—all perishing from boredom —along with me, a mere leftenant to her father's house?"

"Wish I could answer that, Leonard."

"—Told her, you and I close friends in *Lively*. Seemed—interest her."

"Is her father a real Tory?"

Although Amy pressed an ear harder against the wall's cold surface, she missed the next few words.

"Towards—Tory side even more. Fact, when we last sailed— heard the Hilton home's—rendezvous for Bostonians favoring King."

"Strange." Andrew's voice sounded thick, unfamiliar. "Somehow, I fancied the Major's true loyalty lay with the other side, or to say the least he was playing both ends against the middle."

"Mistake. Why should Hilton entertain so many—our officers —captains of ships fetching in supplies or reinforcements?" Bubbling noises interrupted the dying man. "Enough of that. Sent for you because Sarah Hilton said she refuses—believe you traitor, wanted—learn your whereabouts."

Amy, curiosity soaring to new heights, listened so intensely she thought she could hear her heart beat.

"Ten days ago—Rebel fisherman captured off Salem informed Captain Purcell you busy buildin' battery here. Purcell flew into fury—swore he'd never rest till—you—executed." Leonard Dubose's speech sank so low Amy could hear only the voices of the Doctor and her aunt conversing in the kitchen below. She pinched her lower lip between her teeth. Sarah? Sarah Hilton? Who might this female be? Her attention reverted to the room next door when the stricken Marine's voice again became audible.

"Said I'd try—oblige her but I'd no means—communicating. She spoke of a Doctor Clague—friend of her father's whose skill —devotion saved lives of many of our officers and men after Breed's Hill—has been granted permission—pass through our lines any time. Seems he also tended—Rebels wounded.

"Last time—saw Sarah—she gave—letter—case—came across you."

"Where is this letter?"

Had a sudden note of urgency entered Andrew's voice? Amy wondered.

"On—ship. She showed me—letters to be carried by Doctor Clague to Cambridge—finally asked—tell Doctor Clague 'Onion crop here looks good.' Strange, can't imagine—" Again he choked. "Asked to read Sarah's letters—make sure no dangerous information included—kept on asking where you were. 'Course I'd no notion till—captured sailor from Salem spoke of you buildin' battery—Marblehead."

"If I prop you up a bit higher you might be able to talk better. Are you convinced the Hiltons are Tories?"

"Must be. Should see Sarah playin' up to handsome— especially titled—field officers."

Amy's worst misgivings commenced to wane. If this unknown was such a flirt why worry?

"Sarah wanted to locate me?"

"I—I—" Dubose commenced a series of wet-sounding coughs. When he next spoke it was in clearly recognizable accents. "Old Bones is drawing close. God help you and your Cause. Think there's much right in it."

Andrew's voice sharpened. "No! Don't try to sit up. Just lie back and rest."

Amy heard a gurgling sound, then Leonard Dubose gasped, "God save the King!" then forever fell silent.

CHAPTER 22 🍃

REINFORCEMENTS TO
CAMBRIDGE

NEXT MORNING, precisely at the stroke of nine o'clock, Private Andrew Orne Hunter diffidently halted before a stout door opening onto Fore Street and bearing the legend "F. H. Penniston & Co., Customs & Insurance Brokers" engraved on an unpolished brass plate. He could recognize the voices of Company B's officers but wondered to whom the third voice might belong. While knocking he experienced a fleeting tremor just as if he'd struck his "funny bone" hard against some hard surface.

"Come in," directed Penniston's deep voice, then in lower tones added, "Act military, you know how."

Behind a wide, paper-littered table and looking as solemn as if they were about to conduct a court-martial sat three uniformed officers and a wooden-faced clerk in civilian clothes holding a goose-quill pen poised over a pewter inkpot. Captain Penniston occupied the central chair, to his right and sitting bolt upright was a sparely built officer Andrew never had seen before. He was clad in new and smartly cut regimentals consisting of white riding breeches and waistcoat and a brass-buttoned navy-blue tunic the dark-red revers of which emphasized the spotlessness of his stock and white shirt.

Quickly it turned out that this sharp-featured smallish gentleman with the long, red-veined nose was none other than Lieutenant-Colonel John Gerry of the 21st Massachusetts Regiment of Foot or the "Marblehead Regiment" as Colonel John Glover and almost everybody invariably referred to said unit.

Somewhere in the vicinity of the Training Ground a drum kept on beating a complicated rhythm, but what this signal was about Andrew hadn't the least notion. After closing the door behind him he stood to rigid attention conscious that his best suit of Sunday clothes didn't fit at all except where it touched his tall and wiry frame.

While merging heavy cinnamon-hued brows Captain Penniston noisily cleared his throat, snapped, "Stand at ease, Private Hunter. A serious matter is to be discussed—it may take time."

Heart leaping like a frightened buck over a windfall, Andrew queried, "What is this, sir? Am I facing charges of some sort?"

"Quite the contrary," Lieutenant Twisden put in peering at Andrew as if he'd never before beheld him. "We have only commendation for your conduct during the British attack. Count yourself fortunate that disclosure of Joshua Denmead's villainous treachery effectively clears you of any and all charges of spying or double-dealing."

For a fleeting second Andrew wondered why, with the traitor working daily in his law office, a man as smart as Caleb Twisden hadn't come to suspect his clerk in one way or another.

Deferentially, Twisden addressed the stranger, "Colonel Gerry, in view of present circumstances does your request for this man's transfer to the 21st Regiment still stand?"

Like his much better-known brother, Elbridge, Lieutenant-Colonel John Gerry was lean and short of stature but, being so well proportioned, didn't lend the impression of being as small as he actually was.

Steepling large-knuckled slim fingers under his chin Gerry fixed penetrating, deep-set dark-brown eyes on Andrew Hunter and narrowly surveyed him a long moment before turning to Captain Penniston. "All right, Captain, I'll take him. Seems fit for field duty so an what you've told me concerning his abilities as an artillerist proves accurate I'll 'list him among the recruits and replacements I've been ordered to bring to Cambridge." Half smiling, he diverted his attention to Andrew Hunter standing hot and uncomfortable before him. "What say you?"

"Sir, if ordered to accompany you, I, as a duly enlisted private soldier, must obey for all I can't fathom the reason behind such haste."

"That is unimportant. I can tell you're no ordinary recruit so that my mission is with all haste, to enroll here, and in the vicinity of Salem, sixty sound men with good teeth and, heh-heh, morals to match. Captain Penniston has informed me you are still being energetically sought by the Royal Navy. Further, your officers here both have assured me that a good many townspeople in this area have the feeling your continued presence here seems likely to provoke further raids and even attacks in force on Marblehead. From what the late Lieutenant Dubose deposed on his deathbed we are aware that the Royal Navy is determined to hang you. Therefore, I concur with these officers and will rid Marblehead of your trouble-causing presence but in an honorable fashion."

Twisden inclined his narrow, blond head, "Private Hunter, you understand the situation?"

"Yes, sir, but may I not be granted a little time to—to, well, settle personal affairs?"

All in an instant, Lieutenant-Colonel Gerry's manner became frosty. "No, Private Hunter, your private business will have to wait. I still have to recruit in Gloucester and Beverly before returning to Cambridge. My brother is of an impatient nature and a strict disciplinarian intolerant of excuses."

Twisden treated Andrew to a steady look while observing, "Wasn't it fortunate for our side, Hunter, that you chanced to be up and about so early on the morning of the raid?"

Andrew felt an icy rivulet cascade down his spine. So, somehow, the Lieutenant had learned about that rapturous romp in the sail loft. Although the realization struck him with the force of a roundshot he managed to keep his expression impassive. How could Twisden have learned about the rendezvous? "Yes, sir. Where shall I report and when?"

"By two o'clock on the dot on the Training Ground."

In short order Captain Penniston's clerk drafted orders to the effect that as of August 15th, 1775, Private Andrew Orne Hunter had been relieved of duty with the Fifth Essex County Militia and had been transferred to serve with the 21st Massachusetts Regiment of the United Colonies Army.

Summoning a bleak smile Lieutenant-Colonel Gerry offered his hand. "Young man for some reason I feel confident in Cambridge your talents, such as they are, can be more usefully employed towards beating the British, than were you to remain here."

Thoughts in utter disarray Andrew swung along New Meeting House Lane faster than an average man could trot. On reaching the edge of town he hurried between rows upon rows of foul-smelling fish flakes and presently sighted the Widow Milburn's gray shingled roof and that of Jonathan Izard beyond it. Bitterly he noticed no visible activity in or about the demi-lune. Um. How soon could those spikes be drilled out and the little battery rendered useful?

On reaching Mrs. Milburn's cottage he learned that on this— of all days—she'd sent Amy on an errand taking her to the far side of town.

"Mercy me," clucked the Widow on learning Andrew's orders. "Seems like that song 'The World Turned Upside Down' is all too true. Well, Well," she dusted plump, flour-whitened hands. "So, quicker than a scared cat, ye're off to Cambridge and the Siege of Boston?"

"Aye, Ma'am. We recruits are ordered to assemble by two of this afternoon. How soon do you expect Amy back?"

The Widow sighed; this likely young fellow looked so bitterly disappointed. "Sorry, can't say. Likely she'll tarry trying to find Doctor Bond and, failing that, she'll seek medicines, dressings and bandages." Again she clucked like the fat brown hen she resembled. "Poor Jonathan's wound has turned that purple and angry-looking we're all of a fret. Ah me, what sorry times we live in."

"Thank you, Ma'am. I'll go see how he's faring. Please, Mrs. Milburn, when Amy returns tell her what's happened, ask her to hurry to the Training Ground before two o'clock."

Jonathan was sitting up in bed, his brown, black-whiskered

face more florid than normal. Under a clumsily applied mass of bandages his wounded arm lay propped upon a mound of pillows and bolsters. Said he after Andrew had announced his transfer, "Know something? These orders may prove a blessing in disguise for you."

"How so?"

"Certain noisy Patriots in town still are suspicious and don't want you lingering in these parts. You'd best clear out leaving a clean slate. See what I mean?"

Once Andrew had tucked his few personal possessions into a canvas ditty bag he lifted down the ancient fusil after slinging on powder horn and an ammunition pouch containing extra flints, a bullet mould and a half-bar of lead. As he approached the door Deborah Izard suddenly flung pudgy arms about him and, eyes filling, bussed him heartily on both cheeks.

"God bless you and preserve you, Andrew. Whilst Jonathan and I ain't known you extry long you'll always be as welcome under this roof as any relation who dodn't want to borrow something."

While extending a broad brown hand, Jonathan stifled a groan. "Good fortune to you, friend Andrew. Seems about time you enjoyed some after that sorry business in Boston and now this." He cocked a furry brow. "Am I mistook or ain't Amy Orne going to miss you dretful bad? Anything I can say to her?"

"Pray tell her, Friend Jonathan, I'll write to her and you, too, the moment I know for sure what lies in store for me. If for some reason I can't communicate pray convey to her my most sincere compliments and—and enduring affection."

Stony-faced, Andrew set straight a battered, rusty black tricorn hat which had belonged to Jonathan's father then, without once looking back set out for the Training Ground where on arrival he had to push his way through excited throngs of people milling about.

Near this parade ground's worn and yellow-green center stood bantam-like Lieutenant-Colonel Gerry together with Company B's officers. Andrew sought a corporal fingering a list of names and again fell to wondering why Caleb Twisden and certain other sturdy 'Headers hadn't volunteered to join the Marblehead Regiment. Certainly, the lawyer was in fine physical condition and just as robust as Serjeant Marston who worked in the same office. Didn't that give one to think especially since they'd been in daily contact with Denmead? Captain Penniston, of course, being afflicted with spells of gout, usually convenient, wasn't fit to take the field at present.

Dogs barked, women laughed and chattered in spurious vivacity, barefooted and freckle-faced boys raced about whooping and teasing little girls until Captain Penniston, wearing a dress sword and acting mighty important, ordered Company B to form up. "Attention!"

Sweating and untidy the militiamen formed double ranks. Many wore hair in pigtails stiffened with tar and were wearing blue jackets, striped shirts and bell-bottomed canvas trousers. Quite a few were armed with blunderbusses and business-like brass-guarded cutlasses slung to broad leather belts. Momentarily, as they shuffled forward to form up, they more resembled picaroons than soldiers.

Little Lieutenant-Colonel Gerry smiled inwardly. B'God, one month from today wouldn't these sunburned fellows offer a very different picture? Another realization struck him. Most of these seamen were looking serious, damned serious, even those who'd obviously lingered in some taproom.

In obedience to a sign from Captain Penniston a perspiring drummer boy flourished sticks extra high over his head then quit beating.

Twisden stepped forward, shouted, "The following men will take two steps forward."

The men in ranks dressed any which way and carrying a weird miscellany of firearms, stood hot and uncomfortable while names to the number of fifteen were read off.

Lieutenant-Colonel Gerry alert as a squirrel and dapper in new regimentals scanned the roster. Onlookers quieted when he fingered the gilded hilt of a dress sword and drew a deep breath. Said he briskly, "Fellow 'Headers, I am impressed by such evidence of *practical* patriotism. Be sure friends and relatives already in Cambridge will welcome you with open arms and—" he stuck his thumb in his mouth, simulated swallowing "—heh-heh, maybe a swig of Medford rum!

"You can fall out now but inside of twenty minutes see that

you reassemble before the Crown & Sceptre on the Salem Road. Make sure you bring plenty of water in your flasks and a mite to eat—we mayn't reach Salem afore dark."

Carrying his sword tucked carelessly under one arm, Twisden approached Hunter, said with convincing earnestness, "Here's wishing you swift advancement and the best of luck in Cambridge, er—Andrew. Hope you don't mind the familiarity. Were Amy present I'm sure she would share my sentiment. Presume you'll keep in touch with the Izards?"

"Yes," said Andrew, still standing to attention. "They proved very kind when I most needed help."

In the act of turning away the lawyer paused. "Know something? I've just had an odd premonition that, before long, I'll be joining the Regiment in Cambridge."

Militiamen fell out of ranks to join families and friends, mostly displaying little or no emotion since for generations 'Headers had grown accustomed to bidding their men farewell often for the last time.

As for Andrew he lingered where he was, his fusil's slim, octagonal barrel gripped unnecessarily tight between sweaty fingers till he foresaw that, on such a long and hot march, it might be wise to prime himself with a jack of ale. On counting coins in his pocket he found they totaled all of one shilling and sixpence. Nevertheless, he continued on towards the Crown & Sceptre and noticed that an angry splash of black paint had been daubed obscuring the crown on the swingboard. He was about to enter the tavern when his name was called by a voice which halted him in his tracks.

Amy must have run a considerable distance she was that disheveled, sweaty and breathing so hard. Infinitely relieved, Andrew started to throw arms about her but restrained himself. With all these people about there was no point at all in feeding rumors so he merely grasped her hands. "Oh, Amy! Amy! I was about ready to give up hope. We've only a very few minutes, let's seek a quieter spot."

Ignoring occasional stares from passers-by he led her into a narrow lane and shared a fleeting embrace.

"What are we to do?" she panted while using the bight of a muslin scarf to dry her brow.

Arms tightening about her shoulders he peered into large, sherry-hued eyes. "My mind's in such a confounded flux it's impossible to decide, but this much is certain: Caleb knows about us. Tell me, isn't there somebody you could take refuge with if you're forced to leave town?"

Nervously, Amy dabbed aside dark-brown ringlets clinging to her forehead. "Let me think. I've a first cousin, Deborah Palfrey, living in Salem. I know she's trustworthy and we were great friends till she married and went to live in Salem. Recently I've heard that her husband was killed at Breed's Hill. Deborah lives somewhere on St. Peter Street, where I don't know—but you shouldn't have trouble in locating her."

To make sure he'd got things straight he twice repeated Mrs. Palfrey's name and address, then said, "I'll write you in her care soon as I find what's to be done with me. Should you not join Mrs. Palfrey, be sure to leave a forwarding address with her."

"I will, but oh, dearest, how I loathe being separated like this!"

"Remember, my sweet love, no matter what chances we'll marry the earliest possible moment."

"Oh, darling, take care and let it be soon. I don't just love you, I—I adore you!"

The brittle tattoo of a drum beating "Assembly" started people moving in the general direction of the Salem Road. Behind the drummer, a scantling-legged and pimply youth of about thirteen, together with the fifteen other replacements, shouldered arms and moved off behind jockey-small Lieutenant-Colonel Gerry astride a rack-ribbed bay gelding hired from Paul Newbald's livery stable. The rest of Company B lining both sides of the well-traveled road and, serious of mien, presented arms as well as they could till the replacements had disappeared under drifting clouds of yellowish dust.

Amy bit her lips to keep from weeping on noticing quite a few women with tears streaking their cheeks but none of them sobbed audibly or otherwise complained so, blindly, she mingled with a scattering of solemn-looking townspeople turning into Rope Walk Lane.

So much of portent had occurred all at once that for a while she couldn't collect her wits, just allowed her feet to carry her past the entrance to Norden's Lane; normally she would have followed it out to Peach's Head.

She wondered how many girls had been proposed to under such unromantic conditions. The important fact was that he'd actually asked for her hand.

From behind a man's voice called, "Amy, aren't you going home?"

Amy caught her breath and, turning, beheld Caleb hot and dusty in his old-style uniform. He was smiling while he came striding up between long rows of drying fish. Without comment he guided her into a side lane saying, "You look *that* shaken up, my dear, you must be rather fond of somebody who's just marched off."

Caleb's condescending manner brought a flush of annoyance. For sure, this ambitious young lawyer hadn't allowed grass to grow under his feet before capitalizing on her lover's departure. Stomach tightening she recalled Andrew's words: "Caleb knows." Once they'd paused in the lee of a rickety tool shed she attempted to rally, but to her astonishment Caleb Twisden's expression now held no hint of ill-will. Instead, his strong and well-proportioned features were forming a wide smile. Presently he announced, "We will now proceed to my office where we can discuss a pressing and delicate matter. On this particular afternoon no one will disturb us there."

Amy managed to look him straight in the eye but could find no hint of threat behind his steady and calm gaze. Said she, "I would go with you but—but Mrs. Milburn was feeling poorly when I left. Yesterday's excitement has left her in a tizzy and undone. Besides, I'm overdue to change dressings on Jonathan's shoulder. May I go?"

"No," said he in flat tones. "Mrs. Milburn and Jonathan Izard must wait a while; I promise I shan't keep you long." Twisden offered his arm. When Amy ignored it he spoke sharply. "Take it —if you know what's good for you. To be seen in my company at this particular time just might quash the spread of certain rumors."

Amy went scarlet and caught her breath then her manner underwent a change worthy of an accomplished actress. Said she in subdued tones, "Very well."

Nothing for it but to act unconcerned as they strolled along Mugford Street. She permitted her hips to swing a little and, clutching her companion, casually greeted preoccupied friends and acquaintances.

When Caleb bent to unlock his office's door Amy ran fingers through her hair, smoothed her dress and assumed what she hoped would pass for a cheerful expression. Leading the way, he bowed a little, indicated a wooden armchair once occupied by the late Joshua Denmead.

"Excuse me a moment. I believe a tot of sherry would do us both good."

"Thank you, Caleb, but please, I don't want—" she stopped short and dropped her gaze when Caleb strode over to tower above her as she sat perched on the edge of her chair as if preparing for flight.

"Amy, look at me," he directed in clipped accents. "You must understand that, from this moment onwards, what you want or don't want is no longer of importance. When you hear what I have to say I believe you will agree that *I* must decide what is best for you—for us. Do you understand?"

"Yes, but not without reservations."

"I'll chance that." He laughed a little. "Come, Amy, smile a bit —I'm no part of an ogre."

Us? Amy's full, dark-red lips quivered while he crossed to a cabinet bulging with documents and from it produced a cut-glass decanter and two small glasses.

Seating himself, Twisden took a sip then surveyed Amy over his glass's rim before raising it. "Well, here's good luck to the both of us, dear Amy. Relax, you've nothing to fear. Haven't we known one another for a donkey's years?"

"I—I guess so—Caleb."

"Wager you've no idea how often or how deeply I've yearned for you ever since that hayride when you slapped my face. Remember? Reckon that was when I first realized how much I've wanted you."

She nodded, struggled to sound convincing. "Please believe, Caleb, you've really held a most important place in my thoughts. You're so smart, good-looking and so—so determined."

Slowly, he revolved his glass by its stem. "I will now forget, *forever,* you having indulged in a bit of nonsense and games with Jared Sparks and Peter Lufkin."

Amy made a valiant effort to sound and to look indignant. "Wherever did you hear such dreadful lies?"

"For years I've made it my business to learn what's going on here and in Salem. For instance, I'm aware that your first cousin, one Deborah Palfrey, who used to live in Salem—"

"—*used* to live there?" Amy's eyes rounded and her heart seemed to contract. How unlikely that this man at the moment calmly unbuttoning his uniform's tunic and waistcoat should know about Deborah!

"Where is Deborah now? Why—why did she leave?"

"I've no answer to either question. All I know is that when she learned her husband indeed was among those Patriots killed at Breed's Hill she apparently went to pieces. Recently, she's let her house and departed for God knows where."

"Didn't she tell *anyone* where she was going?"

"Not so far as I can ascertain."

For a moment Amy felt as if she were about to slip into an ice-rimmed spring hole but rallied after taking a deep swallow of sherry then managed to say steadily enough, "Caleb, can't you give me any pleasant news?"

Smiling he leaned forward, placed a hand on her knee. "Yes. You, that Hunter fellow and I are the only ones who *know* what chanced in a certain sail loft on the eve of the raid. Since none of us stands to gain anything should this—er, indiscretion become public knowledge I propose on one condition to keep that secret between ourselves."

Amy realized all at once that Caleb's manner of speaking at this moment resembled that of a barrister pleading an important case. Somewhat like a patient about to have a painful tooth extracted Amy gripped her chair's arms. Oh dear! With every passing moment Andrew must be marching ever farther away. She somehow wasn't too surprised to hear her voice ask, "What is your condition?"

"Don't take on so, my dear." All at once Caleb's voice sounded surprisingly gentle and his hand slipped a few inches higher above her knee before he got to his feet, stood towering above her. "Listen to me, Amy Orne, and know that, come what may, I intend to marry you."

"I've been more aware of your—feelings than you might think," she murmured.

"I would have sued for your hand long ago had not my law practice and, uh, certain other ambitions delayed a declaration."

"But, oh please, surely you *must* sense how I feel towards Andrew Hunter and—"

"Enough!" He snapped his fingers. They sounded almost as loud as a pistol shot in this quiet office. "From this moment on you will employ the past tense in referring to Andrew Hunter." Glaring, he moved his face within inches of hers. "You have only imagined yourself in love with him; think things out and you'll perceive all this sudden infatuation has brought you is naught but embarrassment, grief and insecurity. The fellow's penniless. Moreover, I suspect that, if and when he reaches Cambridge his family who, by all accounts are ardent Patriots, won't exactly greet the prodigal son with open arms."

Amy burst out, "Oh, they surely will once they learn the truth about his—well, his quitting the King's Service."

"I question that. Too much explaining would be required." Caleb lifted his sherry glass, took a sip then, in no way threatening, offered a broad smile. "Well, my dear Amy, what have you to say anent my proposal?"

Amy's bottom squirmed imperceptibly on the wooden armchair and her fingertips commenced to tingle as invariably they did when confronted by a major crisis.

She put a hand over his. "Please, Caleb, grant me just a little time to think. This is—must be the most important decision I'll ever have to make in my lifetime."

"Amy, aren't you even a bit fond of me?"

"Oh, yes, yes!" To her surprise she managed a genuinely warm smile.

"Well then, why cavil? Best remember, lacking my protection your future bodes to become uncertain to say the least."

"Yes." Amy thought fast again appreciated that this earnest young lawyer in uniform was far from unattractive mentally or physically. Another side of her nature commenced to influence her. Come to think on it, why shouldn't Caleb Twisden, properly handled, prove a most satisfactory husband? Wasn't he definitely well off, well bred, ambitious and with an untarnished past?

"Caleb, please try to understand, I—I—well, right now I don't know what to say."

"In that case," came his incisive comment, "I will make your mind up for you. So listen and then do exactly what I tell you. From here you will return to Mrs. Milburn's cottage acting as though you'd done nothing more than bid farewell to a soldier marching off to war—one you thought highly of—" his expression hardened "—to say the least."

Hands clenched behind him the lawyer commenced to pace back and forth without glancing in her direction. "I have considered this matter from all aspects and have decided what course you must follow. You will continue to stay with Mrs. Milburn until circumstances permit us to announce our intention to wed and then—" he broke off.

"And then—?"

"—We will go over to Salem or Beverly and have a quiet wedding. I understand a good many such are taking place nowadays. The sooner you start preparing yourself for becoming 'Mrs. Twisden' the better. Do you understand?"

Numbly she nodded but somehow didn't feel as outraged as she ought to have. "I will marry you, Caleb, provided you keep our plans secret."

"Very well, I understand. Till the banns are published I will call on you and expect you to accompany me on evening walks— er, in order to achieve a more intimate understanding of one another."

When he kissed her she responded with a warmth which surprised and delighted him and astonished herself.

Chapter 23 🐚

SALEM

DUSK WAS ABOUT to set in when the detachment of recruits following Lieutenant-Colonel Gerry reached Salem's Common. On it cooking fires were flaming cheerily before a dozen or so ill-assorted and carelessly pitched tents. Many volunteers had appeared from nearby towns making Salem's elm-shaded streets crowded and noisy with armed men. From the way most newcomers walked, talked and dressed, Andrew Hunter reckoned that, like his companions, they must be mostly seafaring folk. Quite a few wore a small gold ring in their left ear and carried long sheath knives buckled to wide leather belts.

Lieutenant-Colonel Gerry now knew his recruits numbered seventy-eight men and well-grown boys, which pleased him no end because Colonel Glover had issued orders for him to bring back a total of sixty sound volunteers. Yes, sir, this small surplus was bound to prove mighty welcome.

Gerry conferred briefly with a Major Crowninshield, the local militia's billeting officer, who said, "March your boys over to Jonathan Mason's Place. 'Tain't far, only across the Common yonder. He's got a pretty sizable house and barn in which your

210

men will find plenty of marsh grass for bedding. Also, our Committee of Safety has readied some rations for distribution behind the Town Hall. Meantime, Colonel," Crowninshield sputtered occasionally because his false teeth didn't fit extra well, "you're welcome to 'bide with me and my Missus." He lowered his voice. "By the way, I've a jug of better than middling Barbados rum tucked away. Comes in useful in case of snakebite and it's a sure cure against fatigue."

"I'd gladly accept, Major; if you don't mind that my men and I must turn in early, Colonel Glover expects us to reach Cambridge by midafternoon tomorrow."

Once he'd made a bed for himself in Mason's barn Andrew sought his commanding officer, saluted smartly. "Sir, request permission to call briefly on friends living nearby."

"Friends? What friends?"

"The Palfreys who live on St. Peter Street."

"Their place lies only two spits and a jump yonder—beyond the church," remarked Crowninshield, pointing northwards. "'Tis of white clapboards with two chimneys."

Said Gerry quietly, "Very well, Hunter. You've my permission to go calling provided you give me your word you'll report back within the hour."

As if by prearrangement St. Peter's church bell struck eight sonorous notes. Feeling infinitely pleased that Lieutenant-Colonel Gerry so readily had accepted his word Andrew saluted and marched off, fusil correctly sloped against his shoulder.

It proved simple to identify the Palfrey residence. The first person he addressed said, "Yes, sir, you'll find the Palfrey house third one on your right beyond the church."

Andrew nodded thanks then hurried on. Arriving at his destination he found the front door standing wide open probably because of the evening's humid heat so was able to hear voices of people in a white-fenced back yard conversing so loudly he was forced to knock several times before a tall, white-haired and lantern-jawed individual appeared. He was carrying a smoldering pipe and looked annoyed.

"Hold hard! No call to knock a body's house down."

Andrew drew a deep breath. "Please excuse me, sir, but there's so much noise on the street I couldn't tell if I'd been heard. Is this Mrs. Palfrey's residence?"

"Was hers."

"*Was?*"

"Yep. I'm Donnell Smith, a tanner by trade. Bought this place a fortnight back on account Dorcas and me hev a pack of young'uns and my own place over near Lynn got burned to the ground by a passel of drunken militiamen we got billeted on us. They was on their way to Cambridge or so they said."

"But Mrs. Palfrey—has she left Salem?" Andrew queried, heart in throat.

"Yep. When the pore soul got the news her husband had sure enough got himself kilt in that big battle hard by Boston she kind of, well—don't know how to say it, but she went all cater-wampus. At any rate, she sold me this place, packed a few things then lit out for God knows where. She looked *that* distracted I ain't sure she knew herself."

A sudden clamor of children playing in his back yard caused the tanner to break off. "Hush yer fuss back there else I'll take the butter paddle to you!"

Andrew asked tautly, "You're sure you've no idea where Mrs. Palfrey went?"

"Like I just said, I dun't know. She only hinted she might be headin' north—mebbe to somewheres in Noo Hampshire."

"Has she no family here?"

"Nope, none I ever heard tell of, anyway."

The tanner drew a whiff from his blackened and evil-smelling clay pipe. "Yes, sir, Mrs. Palfrey cleared out so sudden she didn't tarry longer than to collect my down payment. 'Course her lawyer will hear where she is when my next payment falls due."

Oh Lord, thought Andrew, if this didn't put cream on top of his bottle of misfortune.

Through a cloud of smoke Donnell Smith demanded, "Why be you so dead-set on findin' Mistress Palfrey? You related?"

"No, but a close friend of mine, Amy Orne, is her cousin. She was expecting to live with Mrs. Palfrey for a while. I've arranged to write her at this address for as long as I'm serving in the Army."

The old man frowned, exposed a few snaggle teeth to increasing moonlight. "I'd ask you to stay here but me and Dorcas hev agreed not to billet passing troops no more—not after what happened in Lynn." He shoved out a gnarled brown hand. "Howsumever, I'm wishin' you good luck, young feller, which dun't cost anythin'! An you're so minded, write anyhow. Not promisin' a thing, mind, but I'll see what I can do for you. Good night."

So saying old Mr. Smith closed the door leaving Andrew to stand staring blankly at St. Peter's Church looking so simple, pure and silvery in the moonlight.

Several times on his way back to Jonathan Mason's barn he questioned passing townspeople but none said they'd any notion of where Mrs. Palfrey might have betaken herself. The last person he addressed was a noticeably pregnant young woman wearing a poke bonnet and a Paisley shawl. "Sorry, Mister, I don't know, even though I'm a near neighbor and belong to the same sewing circle as poor Deborah. I was *that* thunderstruck at the sudden way she took off. Don't think she was in her right mind after she learned for sure Silas had been slain at Breed's Hill."

CHAPTER 24 🎐

NEWS FROM BOSTON

DOCTOR HENRY CLAGUE didn't intend to tarry at "Fair View," Captain Timothy Hunter's handsome two-storeyed house of red brick at the foot of Spring Street but did.

"Here's another gossip sheet for you," said he handing Ellen Hunter a slim letter carefully sealed with black wax. At once she recognized Sarah Hilton's immature handwriting.

Behind square-lensed, steel-rimmed spectacles Doctor Clague's pinched features assumed an anxious expression. "Pardon, Miss Hunter, but I must repair straight off to Medical Headquarters. I believe they now are situated in the Henry Vassall mansion?"

"Yes, Doctor. Your services will be badly needed yonder. This morning Mother and I worked there and, oh dear, there's so much sickness about, besides injuries accidentally inflicted by men unused to handling weapons. Please, Doctor, how are Sarah and her father faring?"

Bulging leather medicine bag in hand, Doctor Clague lingered just inside "Fair View"'s handsome front door shaking a nearly bald head. "I—well, to tell the truth, Miss Hunter, I'm becoming a bit alarmed concerning them. You see, in her last letter to you

Sarah included certain information which could only have been available to officers in the British High Command. Somehow the enemy came to realize this, so inquiries are underfoot." He had to raise his voice a little when a company of Rhode Island infantry, mostly clad in homespun, noisily appeared on Spring Street. They were followed by a fiddler playing "Drops of Brandy" and escorted by yapping curs and screeching children.

"Therefore, for their sake, yours and mine, we must abandon this means of communication for the time being—except in a case of extreme emergency." He blinked. "You can have no notion of how many real or suspected spies the British are executing every week. Strangely, I don't relish the notion of being hanged."

Pulse quickening, Ellen accepted the letter. "You mean the enemy have begun to suspect where the Hiltons' true loyalty lies?"

He resettled the steel-framed spectacles on a bony nose and peered cautiously about. "I fear so. We of the Committee have urged the Major to quit Boston as soon as possible for even if the British don't like 'em, they're like to suffer from misguided Patriots who believe them to be red-hot Tories."

Ellen queried softly, "You passed Sarah my last letter together with my affection and esteem, didn't you, Doctor?"

"I did. She reciprocates. But, to repeat, 'twould be dangerous for us all to continue transmitting information in this fashion. After all, onion juice writing is easy to detect by anyone experienced in intelligence matters."

Skirts flying, Ellen hurried upstairs and returned carrying a slim letter composed after considerable thought. Her missive written in clear horizontal lines dealt with trivialities such as the hopelessness of obtaining modish raiment or millinery, or perfumes or silk ribbon of any description. Also she'd dwelt on the prohibitive cost of sugar, spices of any kind, not to mention the nonexistence of tea or coffee.

Her secret message was written vertically and would remain invisible unless heated at the right temperature.

Doctor Clague examined the sheet of stationery with care, held it up to the light. "This looks innocuous enough. Let's hope the British on Boston Neck will agree. May I add, my dear, that

215

we of the Committee deem you one of our most reliable sources for information. Small wonder you're nicknamed 'Foxy.'"

"Thank you, although I'm truly not sly or foxy at all." Always she'd hated this sobriquet.

"Pray present my respects to your good mother." The Doctor broke off, looked grave. "Tell me, any word come concerning your father?"

"No, sir, we fear the worst since both he and the *Rising Star* are now long overdue in Newport. 'Most everybody fears his brig has been captured now that the British have extended their blockade to include Rhode Island and Connecticut."

The Doctor put his hand on the silvered-glass doorknob. "Let us hope, my dear, that Captain Hunter has been taken prisoner, for all his lot as a captured Rebel sea captain won't prove agreeable; recently our enemies have been treating captured Colonists like dangerous animals."

Ellen nodded, quickly changed the conversation. "Mamma will regret not seeing you, sir. She's out drawing rations to feed some officers who've been quartered on us; they've all got hearty appetites."

In the act of turning away the physician checked so sharply his bag of medicines and instruments rattled, swayed like a pendulum. "Oh, I near forgot! Have you heard aught concerning your brother, the Tory one, called Nathan?"

Ellen's pointed features stiffened. "Nothing except that he and his fellow King-lovers are garrisoned on Spectacle Island—the one in Boston Harbor of course."

"What of your other brother?"

"We've received vague information that Andrew's been recognized in the vicinity of Marblehead—please inform Sarah to that effect. Presumably, my brother for the time being is well and safe."

The physician pulled out a huge gold watch. "Dear me, I must leave but, before I go I must warn you that this may prove the last occasion the British will allow me through their lines." So saying Doctor Clague departed into the late August sunlight, a drab figure in rusty-black almost a trademark for the medical profession. Almost immediately he became lost to sight amid lazy clouds of dust raised by a wood-cutting detail of Connecticut militia whose farm carts were moving in the opposite direction.

Somewhere in the distance fifes shrilled and drums thumped and rattled. Lordy, wouldn't Cambridge ever again enjoy scholastic somnolence, unhurried peace and quiet? Every day it seemed the streets were becoming more filled by groups of shaggy-haired but earnest brown-faced fellows carrying a weird assortment of weapons. Volunteers such as these almost never appeared in uniform or even parts thereof.

The Henry Vassall residence was occupied by General George Washington. New Englanders were coming to agree with some reluctance that though a Virginian this tall, red-haired gentleman knew his business all right and so was becoming increasingly respected—if not admired.

By this time all those imposing homes along what now was called "Tory Row," where the Sewalls, the Brattles, Judge Joseph Lee, Thomas Oliver and Colonel Ruggles had lived, had been taken over.

Mrs. Hunter and Ellen were glad that four commissioned officers had been billeted in "Fair View." What with so many hundreds of undisciplined volunteers not to mention common rogues now swarming in and around Cambridge their presence offered insurance against robbery or rape.

In particular Ellen favored lean and saturnine Colonel Jason Roberts from the Maine district of Massachusetts. Then there was a smallpox-scarred but otherwise personable young captain named Edward Mott who hailed from somewhere in the Hampshire Grants and had been among the Green Mountain Boys who'd been along with Colonels Ethan Allen and Benedict Arnold when they'd surprised Fort Ticonderoga.

Such was the density of traffic in Cambridge it seemed, to a good housekeeper's despair, everything indoors and out bore a heavy coat of dust. When in ever-increasing numbers detachments of militia came straggling in from all over New England, New York and Pennsylvania, odd assortments of tents appeared on lawns or in any vacant space. There also appeared a regiment from Virginia including Colonel Dan Morgan's tough but highly individualistic riflemen clad in comfortably practical fringed buckskin hunting shirts; most ended about their knees.

Units which couldn't be accommodated in the already jam-packed dormitories of Harvard College, Hollis, Massachusetts, Holworthy and smaller structures lived in roughly contrived shacks and shelters erected about the so-called "Yard."

Fingers trembling on Doctor Clague's letter Ellen sought the kitchen where Betsy the ever-cheerful and plump mulatto cook was baking. Her neatly braided kinky gray-black hair was secured by a yellow bandanna. In the sunlight it glowed bright as a golden sovereign.

From the back of the stove Ellen selected a flatiron, wet her finger with spit and tested it to make sure the iron was hot but not too hot for her purpose before she sought her bedroom upstairs. Hurriedly, she bolted the door before breaking the wax seal securing Sarah's letter and scanned it rapidly since the missive wasn't lengthy and dealt with trifling generalities. After noting that, whenever possible, Sarah expressed Loyalist sentiments she placed the letter face-down on her dresser then covered it with a piece of heavy brown paper before passing the hot iron over it while silently counting to twenty by which time onion juice used to pen a secret message should have turned brown and become legible. It did.

> *Two supplie ships, Brigateens* Triton *and* Grampus *are expeckted to arrive from Halifax next weak. Reported to be unarmed and laded with Field Cannons, powder and Weapons of all sorts. Also they are carrying Replasements and food for Troups already Quartered hear. Next month is eagerly expected the arrival of a brig named* Nancy *from England. Papa hath learnt She is fetching a grate number of Muskits and Shot of different Sizes and many peaces of Artilery.*

Hurriedly Ellen tucked the folded letter down the front of her gown then perfunctorily ran a comb through dark-red-brown tresses. She thought she still looked messy but the sooner she reached Colonel Glover's quarters the better.

By now it was well known that many of Colonel John Glover's well-disciplined regiment, mostly composed of seamen, were as familiar with the coast of Nova Scotia clear down to New York as the fingers on their calloused hands.

It was nearing noon when she approached a small but well-proportioned dwelling in which Colonel Glover had established Headquarters for the 21st Regiment of the United Colonies. Four cutlass-bearing guards wearing dark-blue shell jackets, flat, broad-brimmed and well-tarred hats and dirty bell-bottomed white duck pants only grinned and waved Ellen straight inside.

Enjoying the comparative coolness indoors Ellen again noticed that the handful of officers present all were in neat uniforms. Not for nothing had Colonel Glover become known as such a stickler for discipline, clean equipment and personal cleanliness that recently General Washington had ordered a platoon from the Marblehead Regiment assigned to his personal bodyguard.

At the age of forty-two John Glover had small, alert gray-blue eyes. Wide-jawed and clean-shaven he wasn't large but lent an impression of being so since he held himself so erect and always kept shoulders squared. People who knew him well said the man seemed utterly tireless, radiated unbounded energy.

Once an orderly announced Miss Hunter's presence his incongruously-shaped Cupid's-bow lips parted into a slow smile as rising behind his desk he said in a large but not unpleasant voice, "Ah, Miss Hunter, how good to receive you once more. Do I presume correctly you're fetching news about the doings of our 'friends' over in Boston?"

Miserably aware of her untidy appearance Ellen bobbed a curtsy. "Yes, sir, I believe you will be particularly pleased with intelligence conveyed by my friend."

Once he'd read and reread the message written in onion juice he bobbed a balding head several times. "Thank you, Mistress Hunter, thank you indeed! This information is of first importance. Possibly something can be done to intercept the *Grampus* and the *Triton,* but I doubt it since they're due to make port so soon.

"From other sources we've learned that several more troop transports and other supply ships, among them one called *Nancy,* are expected during the latter part of September. Will you attempt to discover the probable arrival dates of these as soon as may be?"

A small frown creased the girl's smooth forehead. "About that, sir, there can be no telling at this time. It's rumored that some of our sources have fallen under suspicion."

"God forbid!" Golden epaulettes winked as Glover motioned her to a chair. "You can have no conception, Miss Hunter, of how highly we esteem information on such matters." He tapped Sarah's letter. "I will bring this to the Commanding General's attention at once and feel confident he will act upon it promptly. But what can be accomplished lacking a regular Navy which the Congress still denies as necessary? The General is doing everything possible with money and men to help me and others to fit out as speedily as possible certain merchant vessels suitable for conversion to commerce raiders which, in short, will have to serve as the Army's Navy.

Lips pursed he reread the message. "About the first two transports mentioned; I fear not much can be done but the *Nancy* which sounds like a floating arsenal ain't due till sometime in the early autumn; seasonable line storms and equinoctial gales may still further delay her arrival.

"Dear me, I near forgot to ask whether you've had word about your father?"

"No, sir. Never a word. But my mother and I remain confident we'll hear from him before long. There is great power in prayer, sir."

When she hesitated, Glover said quickly, "What of the other members of your family? To spare unnecessary embarrassment I must inform you we've heard all about your brother Nathan's having gone over to the enemy. But what news is there of your older brother, the ex-Royal Navy officer?"

"We recently have learned that Andrew's alive and free, but more than that we know nothing, sir."

Glover took her hand then with unexpected grace bent to brush her knuckles with those curiously shaped lips of his.

Once the brisk, terrier-like commander of the Marblehead Regiment had escorted her to the head of the stairs Ellen started downwards. Almost the first person she beheld among sunburned men crowding the hall below was the familiar tall and muscular figure of Andrew Orne Hunter.

CHAPTER 25 ✤

COLONEL JOHN GLOVER

THE MARBLEHEAD REGIMENT recently had been moved to occupy tents or barns or sheds in an area along the Menotomy Road running north and west from Cambridge Common while their officers had been accommodated in private homes nearby.

Private Andrew Hunter encountered no difficulty in obtaining from Lieutenant-Colonel Gerry permission briefly to visit "Fair View" on the banks of the tawny Charles. He'd no notion whatever of the nature of the reception he'd receive.

Following General Orders that with exception of men on duty soldiers must not bear firearms in town, Andrew gave his fusil into the keeping of a lanky Congregational lay preacher from Swamscott with whom he had struck up a promising and apparently sincere friendship.

The moment Mrs. Timothy Hunter beheld her oldest child's tall and wiry figure all but filling "Fair View"'s front doorway she blinked then gasped and flew to him. Sobbing softly she hugged her oldest-born closer than ever she had since he'd been a small boy in need of comforting.

Ellen cried a little too for all she'd kept her emotions pretty well under control till now.

"Oh, Andrew! Andrew! Bless the Good Lord, you're here. Ellen and I've been *that* upset over not hearing from either you or your father for so long—then over the way Nathan has disgraced us by running off to join the Tories. Oh, my darling! You —you come as a safe refuge amid a sea of troubles."

Andrew's eyes brimmed and he choked up so badly he couldn't say anything for a while, could only press his mother closer.

Wiping eyes, she then said, "Andrew, you'll be eager for something to eat. Come to the kitchen. Once you're fed I want you to settle, for good and all what really chanced on board the *Lively*."

"Of course, Mother. What about Father?"

"We still don't know anything definite one way or another," Mrs. Hunter said. "It's only that his ship is now a month overdue in Newport."

Andrew tried to sound confident. "He may have made for some southern port where enemy ships aren't so many. Again, it's so close to hurricane season he may have been driven far off his course, so don't take on, either of you. Pa's smart." He hoped he sounded more confident than he felt.

"Now what was that you said about Nathan running off to fight for the Tories?"

Ellen sniffled and looked aside. "We'd no notion what Nat was up to. He just disappeared one night and left a note saying he was off to do his duty and fight for his King."

Andrew commented, "Well, Ellie, you haven't changed a mite since that afternoon at the Hiltons'."

"But you have, Bro. Heavens, you look ten years older." Hastily she added, "but handsomer than ever—doesn't he, Mamma?" Ellen continued, "To begin with some of our neighbors felt bitter over your being in the King's Service but then word got about why and how you deserted the *Lively*. Then for a while we heard nothing till somehow we got word you'd reached Marblehead and were building a battery there for our people."

"All the same," Mrs. Hunter added sadly, "some evil-minded folk believe you're still a Loyalist at heart."

"They won't when they learn the truth." Concisely, he then de-

222

scribed main events up to the date he'd been transferred to Glover's regiment. Never once did he refer to Amy.

As of old he tore like a starving sailor into the substantial meal Betsy improvised until, wiping crumbs from his mouth, he stopped eating and said he must hurry back to his unit.

"What's your colonel like?" Ellen demanded while knotting scraps of food into a napkin.

"Well, Foxy, John Gerry's able and devoted to our Cause but many fear he's too frail in health to take the field. You see, he coughs a lot and sometimes there are specks of blood on his handkerchief. An it proves at all possible, I'll return home this evening because, aside from seeing you both I'd like to poke through my things unless they've been tossed out."

"They haven't been," Mrs. Hunter observed. "Nothing of yours has been touched—except for cleaning."

"Good, I'll need certain books and other articles."

Fully in command of herself once more Andrew's mother patted his hand. "Try to eat with us—Betsy will hold supper in any case. I imagine you'll enjoy meeting one of our lodgers, Captain Edward Mott of the 6th Connecticut Regiment."

Ellen inclined her small rusty-red head. "I'm sure of it. Captain Mott displays considerable interest in artillery. He served with Ethan Allen's force when it took Fort Ticonderoga last spring. Guess I'd best leave him tell you about that."

Beaming, Betsy padded in clutching a large, cloth-covered basket. "Please, Misto Andrew, mebbe these eatments will come in handy till yo' gets yourself joined to a reg'lar mess; some o' dem is just that—messes!"

"Why, why thank you!"

The warmth in Betsy's large and rather bovine dark eyes prompted Andrew to cross over and lightly kiss the cook's round brown cheek. The freedwoman started as though touched by a hot iron, briefly rubbed the spot then, eyes brimming, said, "I'll pray good and hard tonight, Misto Andrew, de good Lawd won't never quit watchin' over you." As quietly as she'd entered the mulatto, sniffling, retired to the kitchen.

Andrew eased the grimy band of his shirt's collar, made a transparent effort to appear casual.

More than ever resembling her nickname, Ellen's small and

close-set bright eyes peered narrowly at her brother when he said while fastening pewter buttons securing the brown tunic he'd been issued in Salem, "I can't recall whether Major Hilton ever declared himself an out-and-out Tory. Do you know anything of this?"

"I really don't know," Ellen lied out of sheer force of habit. "So many wild rumors are circulating these days."

"—And what about his daughter? Wasn't she named 'Sarah'?"

"Oh, come off it, Andy, you very well know that's her name."

"—And so?"

"I hear from Sarah now and then. Seems she's as gay and giddy as ever; writes that she and her father often entertain high British officials and officers."

Andrew's hands sought and tightened on his sister's sloping shoulders. "I admire your caution, Ellie, but tell me the truth. *Have* the Hiltons really turned Tory?"

Ellen looked straight up at Andrew, said seriously, "Very well. Now that Nathan's finally gone over to the King's Cause I can speak out. Till this moment only Mother and I and a very few high-ranking officers here in Cambridge are aware that Sarah and her Papa are two of the most reliable informants we have in Boston."

Momentarily, she bit her lip. "I also must tell you that a Doctor Clague, who acts as a go-between, was here only a short while back. He said he fears Sarah and her father may have fallen under suspicion lately—which God forbid!"

"Has Sarah, well, ever inquired concerning me?"

"Oh, yes quite often. She wastes valuable space in her letters begging to hear something of your whereabouts and state of health. To my mind Sarah's rather taken with you. Lord knows why," she added with a small giggle.

Striding along, Andrew found difficulty in relating to these crowded, bustling streets with the academic atmosphere and bucolic simplicity prevailing in the surroundings among which he'd grown up.

During his absence many new houses, shops and warehouses had arisen along the Charles and on the outskirts of Cambridge. In these large and handsome dwellings spaced along "Tory Row" he noticed that beyond missing picket fences and a good many trees chopped down for firewood as well as a few smashed windows temporarily repaired with oiled paper, little damage had been suffered by the residences of Loyalists. Mildewed tents of all sizes, shapes and descriptions stood on wide, elm-shaded lawns surrounding most such edifices.

Despite the heat everybody seemed to be in a hurry. Sweating military runners and mounted couriers kept yelling for people to get out of their way. Andrew had just passed the Courthouse's steps when he realized that dapper little Lieutenant-Colonel Gerry was beckoning.

Acknowledging Andrew's precise salute Gerry said, "I was getting ready to send the Provost's men after you though your pass won't expire for another half-hour. Come along." Striding briskly along, he added, "Can't imagine why John Glover is so interested in you except possibly he's done business with your Pa."

Colonel John Glover, erect and always spruce with regard to apparel, commanding the 21st, formerly the 23rd, Regiment of the Army of the United Colonies, had established his headquarters in a spacious elm-shaded house facing red-brick and ivy-covered buildings composing Harvard College now used as receiving barracks for newly arrived militia.

Golden afternoon sunlight was beating through the windows of a large, gray-shingled and two-storeyed house distinguished by lead-diapered glass windows and a portico supported by four slim, white-painted Ionic columns. Before the entrance lounged a squad guard armed with carbines and cutlasses. They were wearing the Marblehead Regiment's distinctive uniform of rakish-looking stocking caps, dark-blue pea jackets with flat yellow buttons, striped blue-and-white jerseys and bell-bottomed trousers—so distinctive people commented on them, not always favorably since long ago it had been established that most mariners were a drunken, licentious and irreligious lot. Mothers often sent nubile daughters scurrying out of sight the moment Glover's men were seen advancing. One matron's warning became widespread: "Them's sailormen! Git, girls, and mind you fetch along that scrubbin' brush, sailors will ravish anything with hair onto it."

On recognizing John Gerry's rank both sentries flanking the doorway drew themselves up and presented arms so precisely

Andrew was reminded of British Marines. Drawing himself up to his scarcely impressive five feet, four inches of height, Lieutenant-Colonel Gerry instructed an orderly to report his arrival. The fellow disappeared to return almost immediately averring that the Colonel would be mighty pleased to receive Colonel Gerry in exactly five minutes.

"'Exactly five minutes'! That's typical of Johnny Glover," Gerry commented brushing dust from a wrinkled coatee. "I vum that man measures his time with a chronometer, moreover, he's nowise patient over insubordination, tardiness nor excuses of any description no matter how good they sound."

From the floor above rang the biggest voice Andrew had ever heard. It was loud enough to make the whole busy hallway resound, but strangely there were no angry overtones to it. "Tell you again, Glover, goddammit, we've somewhere *got* to collect a train of field and siege artillery guns else we'll lose this damned war before the year's out!"

"That," remarked an infantry officer, "sounds like Henry Knox at his best. I know, once worked in his bookshop for a time."

Colonel John Glover's voice colder but less penetrating carried down the stairs. "Takes no ghost from the grave to tell me that."

Colonel Knox's bellow of laughter was something impressive to hear. "My God. I own you have many fine qualities, John, but I'd never have taken you for a student of Will Shakespeare."

"You might be surprised," came the crisp reply, "to hear how much I've learnt about military arts through study. In any case, aside from some trifling service with the militia, I'm in complete agreement. Just tell me where in Tunket are we to find these cannon, let alone men fit and able to serve 'em?"

"A good question. Manley, Broughton and I daren't approach the Commander-in-Chief on the subject, patient and courteous as he is, till we can offer some workable solution."

Henry Knox could be heard speaking deliberately for once. "Been doing a deal of thinking on that subject. Since us Colonists for a long time ain't been permitted by the Home Government to forge any worthwhile number of cannon, I guess till we can cast our own we'll have to capture what we need to create a real train of artillery—including siege guns—if we're ever to drive the King's troops out of Boston.

"So," boomed Knox, "it behooves us and you know damned well we've *got* to reopen that port to survive."

"Correct." Glover said, "Gen'ral Washington agreed when first I opined it might be a good idea for seafaring merchants to fit out some fast vessels as coastal cruisers able to snap up unguarded transports and supply ships. Damned if I understand why those nit-picking ditherers in the Continental Congress obstinately refuse to authorize a regular Navy."

Knox's voice rumbled, "We should be able first off to capture a lot of field guns on the sea but where in God's name are we to lay hands on siege cannon weighty enough to bombard Lord Howe out of Boston?"

They overheard Glover say, "Don't yet know—" The rest of the conversation became lost when a group of officers, spurs jingling, took to the staircase, came clumping downwards.

Frowning, Gerry beckoned an orderly. "Present my compliments to Colonel Glover and tell him twice five minutes have passed since five o'clock."

Almost immediately the orderly came running from the floor above. "Colonel says he's sorry, sir, and please to come up at once."

Gerry turned to Andrew. "Come along with me. Let them decide how much you really know concerning artillery of various weights and descriptions. You should find a willing listener in Colonel Knox; with him cannon and their service long have been a passion."

It was typical of contempt for military etiquette prevailing in most units composing the recently designated "New Establishment of the Army of the United Colonies" that Lieutenant-Colonel Gerry, on entering, merely offered a curt head-bow to a pair of colonels seated behind a document-littered table facing the entrance. They broke off reading only long enough to wave vaguely.

Andrew however stood to attention and remained so until Colonel Knox, noticing, drawled, "You can stand at ease. By God, you at least know how to act like a soldier. We could do with more like you."

Covertly surveying these two well-known staff officers Andrew decided it would be nearly impossible to encounter two more entirely dissimilar figures. John Glover, the Marbleheader, was short and spare but muscular and with wide shoulders. His strongly modeled features were dominated by a powerful box-like jaw, a long slim nose and small but piercing gray-blue eyes.

By contrast Colonel Henry Knox, former bookseller and some-time militia officer, devoid of field experience but reputedly a devoted student of military arts, was gigantic. He stood six feet four inches in stocking feet and at the moment was tipping the scales at seventeen stone, as most New Englanders reckoned. The Bostonian's large, round and gray-blue eyes radiated good nature disguising remarkably shrewd discernment. His heavy cheeks and jowls were as jolly and rubicund as any Kriss Kringle's.

About the only point the two held in common was that both were wearing smart uniforms cut from materials of fine quality.

Knox stood up, offered Gerry his good hand—the left lacked two fingers due to a hunting accident, an impairment about which he always would remain unduly sensitive. "Well, John, and how is the Gerry tribe doing these days?"

Hastily smothering a cough the other replied with a wry grin, "Last I heard we're still for the most part out of jail and unhanged."

"Seen Elbridge recently?"

"Aye. He's well and, as usual, busy as a fox in a hen roost."

"Tell us," Knox rumbled; even when suppressed his voice resounded like someone tapping a bass drum, "what about this soldierly-appearing fellow you've brought to our attention?"

Gerry smothered another cough before stating, "Well, my friends, after what I've heard about him I figured he just might prove useful to one or both of you."

"Who is he?"

"Andrew Hunter, an ex-Royal Naval officer but a native of this very town and the oldest son of Captain Timothy Hunter." His gaze shifted to Glover. "You heard of him?"

"Hell, yes; done considerable business with Tim on occasion. Good man, better trader."

"Possibly you've heard something of young Hunter? He's the man who designed and built that battery at Peach's Head and

228

led the militia in driving the enemy back to their boats. He's also rumored to be knowledgeable about artillery of different sorts."

Beneath his tan Andrew flushed, miserably aware that one of many fleas was crawling above his neckband. He shouldn't have; here in Cambridge nearly everyone was infested by lice, crabs or fleas.

"So you've some knowledge of gunnery?" Knox queried sharply before a smile widened heavy and shiny red features. "Since I'm not entirely ignorant on that subject I'm going to pose a number of questions."

"Not now, Henry." Glover started pacing rapidly, taking short steps like an uneasy terrier. "We've a shoal of unfinished work on this table. Remember?"

"Expect you're right." Colonel Henry Knox sighed but didn't remove an attentive stare from the sloppily uniformed figure standing so erect before the table desk. "But I need time to question this fellow at length."

Crisply, Glover spoke. "Private Hunter, report to my private quarters at precisely eight o'clock tonight and I mean *precisely*. Dismissed."

CHAPTER 26 🦋

EXAMINATION

AT MRS. HUNTER's dinner table lingered Private Andrew Orne Hunter and Captain Edward Mott of the 6th Connecticut, other officers billeted in "Fair View" having departed on a variety of duties or amusements. A loud rapping preceded the appearance of a breathless young militiaman.

"Gents," he panted, "Mister Hunter, Cunnel Glover wants I should show you the way to his private lodgings at eight o'clock —sharp." Uncertainly the messenger faced about. "Mister, be you Cap'n Mott? They said you was livin' here too."

"I am. What of it?"

"Well, my boss—the Lootenant, I mean, says you, too, are to come to Cunnel Glover's place."

Mott snorted, looked annoyed. "That's odd. Since when has Colonel Glover been in command of Connecticut troops?"

"You be a cannoner, ben't you, Boss?"

"Yes."

Exuding nauseous odors from clothing unwashed for weeks on end the badly sunburned messenger blinked. "'Tis Cunnel Knox hisself says for you to come along of Mister Hunter."

"That's different. Run like Hell and say we'll show up as ordered."

Once the runner turned and hurried off without saluting, Mrs. Hunter sniffed, told Betsy to open a couple of windows. By now she should have become accustomed to the variety of stinks prevailing in and about Cambridge whenever people gathered—but wasn't. Soap, never in great demand, now had become all but unobtainable.

Ellen remained absent having been recalled to Medical Headquarters. A serious outbreak of camp, jail or ship fever as this disease variously was termed and later described as typhus—along with other epidemic diseases—was taxing its hard-worked staff beyond endurance, let alone efficiency. Indeed, sometimes it seemed as if every newly arriving unit brought with it some disease such as putrid fever, dysentery and smallpox, also contagious ailments all but unrecognizable to hard-working but often ignorant doctors and inept volunteer assistants.

To many medical men it came as something of a surprise that militiamen who proved to be most vulnerable to infection were not stunted measely-looking fellows raised in towns but the brawny, and ruggedly built specimens recruited along the frontier or in backwoods hamlets.

After dusting his shapeless brown tunic and, purely through force of habit, running a rag over its flat pewter buttons Andrew sighed, "B'God, Cap'n, you'd think even red-hot Patriots would have the grace to let a fellow stay home on his first night back."

Andrew's mother, smiling, fetched a platter covered with wedges of golden-brown pumpkin and plunked it down without comment. Long ago she'd learned that silence often is an effective questioner.

Mouth full, Andrew leaned over the table, directed his attention to the Connecticuter's shrewd, smallpox-pitted and rather pinched-looking brown visage. "Captain, d'you mind tellin' me as much as you can about those cannon you noticed at Ticonderoga —including the ones they hauled over from the ruins of Fort Crown Point? Did many appear to be of foreign make?"

The Connecticuter sighed, wiped his mouth on the back of a black-haired hand. "Don't know. Never got a chance to really examine 'em. I know little about such. Besides, my company got ordered to march north with Colonel Arnold's force almost directly after we'd occupied the fort."

He laughed, tilted more thick, yellow cream over his pie. "By the way, can I tell you, in confidence, that that business at Ticonderoga wasn't anything like the heroic victory you hear described in songs and ballads. The poor damn' British garrison, only forty-four in number, a lot of 'em invalids, were sound asleep when we struck. For a fact Allen and the rest of us were kicked in the arse by Lady Luck to have captured the place with nary a man killed—or the enemy, either."

Andrew grunted, dislodged a piece of meat from between strong but uneven teeth. "In what sort of shape would you say the guns you noticed were in?"

The Connecticuter shrugged. "Blessed if I could tell—most were rusting half-buried under rubble. Some smaller ones have been used for snubbing bollards on the supply dock or as counterweights on scales. The rest lay out in the weather or were tumbled any which way into ammunition bays beneath parapets."

"About how many kinds of foreign guns did you recognize?"

"Don't know. I'm only familiar with English-cast cannon so the heft likely have been forged in foreign parts."

To Andrew's annoyance a nearby church bell sounding the hour of half-after seven effectively terminated the conversation.

The surroundings of Colonel John Glover's quarters proved comparatively quiet. Only a few squads of soldiers were squatting across the street occupied in cooking over small and smoky fires.

Captain Mott checked brass buttons securing his tunic's lapels while Andrew did his best to adjust that ill-fitting dark-brown tunic he'd been issued in Salem. Strange, how thirsty he was feeling, for all Mother had provided him and his guest with plenty of ale.

It was not to a staff room that the callers were conducted but into a private dwelling and a stuffy little library whose walls were lined with books and cluttered with maps. Entering they heard Colonel Henry Knox growl, "God's blood, John, I'm fair roasting. Mind if I ease meself?" Without waiting for a reply the giant cast loose a long line of gilt buttons securing a turkey-red waist-coat over a vast belly.

"Aye. No use standing on ceremony."

After mopping a very high and smooth forehead Glover followed Knox's example and told his subordinates, "Make yourselves comfortable, too. May have to linger in this hot-box some little time."

A small, great-eyed and very pregnant tabby cat appeared from nowhere and went over to undulate against Henry Knox's plump calf. He stooped to pat the animal with a surprising gentleness.

Once tallow dip candles, smelling something like badly scorched beef, had been trimmed by an orderly who promptly withdrew, Glover directed his attention to Captain Mott. "Sir, pray give us as accurate and detailed a description of those cannon barrels you observed in Fort Ticonderoga." He turned to his huge companion. "Please direct your replies to Colonel Knox."

Once Mott uneasily admitted to only limited knowledge concerning cannon, Knox emitted a whirling gust of gray-white smoke from the pipe on which he'd been sucking noisily then smiled that peculiarly warm and winning smile destined to endear him to thousands of American troops. Not for seveal generations would another American general, Dwight Eisenhower, be endowed with so disarming and engaging a magnetism.

Once the Connecticuter finished talking, Knox rumbled, "Thank you, Captain Mott, 'specially for making us aware that a large number of foreign-made cannon are among those from which we hope to create a useful train of artillery. Now tell me, sir, have you any idea how many siege guns might become available?"

"No, sir. As I've said, I'm no part of a trained artillerist and hardly can tell a howitzer from a mortar. I can offer no further information on this subject."

Glover offered his hand saying briskly, "In which case we will not detain you longer, thank you."

Once the Connecticuter had disappeared Knox chuckled. "Well now, John, ain't that first-class news about all those gun barrels up to Ticonderoga?"

Glover sighed. "You're such an incurable optimist I hesitate to remind you that said guns you're getting so excited about, at the moment, lie way up in the New York Colony, near three to four hundred miles from this spot. So far as I know there aren't any bridges, canals, or roads useful for transporting heavy guns through a thinly populated wilderness over a Hell's mint of mountain ranges and high hills, 'specially when such a movement would have to be attempted in the dead of winter."

Knox frowned briefly, tapped his pipe's amber mouthpiece against large yellowish teeth. "That's all true, I'll admit, but those guns have *got* to be fetched here. Presume you've already sounded out the Commander-in-Chief's views on such a project?"

"Aye. General Washington not only recognizes the difficulties you mention but, no less, our need for heavy ordnance without which we can't hope to bombard the British out of Boston and gain a major port to handle supplies from abroad—supplies without which we can't hope to continue."

For a long moment Glover narrowly studied the tall, wiry and chestnut-haired soldier standing ramrod-straight before him. "Henry, suppose you interrogate this man who, incidentally, is reported to be a well-trained gunner."

Slowly, the massive Colonel's head swung in Andrew's direction. "You can stand easy, soldier, whilst I pose a number of questions which you are to answer briefly and accurately. What military authorities on the subject of ordnance have you studied?"

Although becoming aware that he had begun to sweat from more than just the heat in this stuffy little library Andrew spoke succinctly. "Sir, whilst on duty in Southampton on various occasions I secured access to the Royal Navy's library and was fortunate to enlist the interest and friendship of an assistant librarian named Captain Desaix, a specialist in the study of ordnance."

"Desaix sounds French," Glover commented. "How'd he come to be where he was?"

"Sir, his family were Huguenot refugees who arrived in England in 1590 or thereabouts. He advised me to concentrate on certain volumes selected by himself."

Reassured by an encouraging gleam in Knox's large and heavy-lidded gray-blue eyes Andrew relaxed a trifle.

Knox again bent to stroke the pregnant cat. "Which authorities did you study especially? May have read some of 'em myself so be careful about your replies; what of modern tactics and grand strategy?"

"Sir, Marshal Saxe and the Duke of Marlborough have no equals. On the subject of military engineering Captain Desaix directed my attention to the writings of Messers Clairac, Muller and Pledell.

"With regard to the design of fortifications, ballistics, logistics and related subjects he recommended the works of Messers Vauban, Belidor and Coehorn. He insisted that on the subject of ordnance Messers Muller and Holliday are the most reliable sources."

Knox's reddish moon of a face lit. "By Cod, Hunter, your mentor really knew what he was about. Now tell me, on which volume did you concentrate?"

"On John Muller's *Treatise on Artillery*, sir. I expect you know it's about the only manual written in English on the subject."

"Excellent! Answer a few more questions in such fashion and I'll grant you full marks. Tell me, along what precepts are most French fieldpieces built and served?"

The reply was instantaneous. "On the Système Vallière, sir."

"And how are the weights of pieces to be recognized?"

"Sir, by ornamentations on the cascabel of a tube. On 4-pounders a lion's head is embossed; on 8-pounders an ape's head and a rooster's head on 12 pounders. Also there often is ornamentation on the chase behind the muzzle's swell such as the motto: *Ultima Ratio Regum,* meaning as you gentlemen no doubt are aware, 'The Ultimate Argument of Kings.'"

Knox's chair creaked when he sat as upright as his thick body permitted and, cackling, watched Glover lean so far over his desk the Marbleheader's breath caused candle flames to waver. "How about howitzers?"

"Sir, such pieces generally are cast from brass or bronze and mostly are designed to fire 8-inch and 5½-pound shells. They fire charges of canister and grape, also solid shot, but only at close range in case of emergency since a howitzer's barrel is not long enough to ensure accuracy over any great distance."

Knox clapped a hand on his thigh so loud the round-bellied cat skittered off casting reproachful looks over one shoulder. "That shines, really shines! Well, John, what do you think?"

Glover's pink lips formed a wry smile. "Well, I'd say I feel something like a minnow swimming in the wake of a whale." He settled back in his chair, fingertips massaging a high, smooth forehead which at the moment was glowing in the candlelight as though carved out of pink marble. Said he, "So far so good, Mister Hunter."

His use of the title "Mister" wasn't lost on either Knox or the ill-dressed soldier standing before the desk.

Glover cocked an eye at Andrew. "Since I know little beyond the service of small-caliber naval guns I'd like to have your opinion on what weight of guns are best suited for use on small men-of-war such as schooners, sloops, corvettes and brigs."

"Sir, in the Royal Navy a main battery of 4-, 6-, or 8-pounders plus a few 12-pound pieces have been found to be a generally satisfactory combination."

"—Their effective range?"

"Much depends, sir, on the size of shot used and the charge propelling it. Properly handled some types can develop a muzzle velocity calculated at around 900 to 1,300 feet per second."

"Maximum range?"

"Twelve hundred to two thousand yards, sir, but, due to lateral deflection caused by the drift of a spherical ball, it is difficult surely to hit a small target at anything over 1,000 yards—even when roundshot is employed. Other types of projectiles are less effective and only at considerably reduced ranges."

Knox got so interested he forgot and held up his left hand so for the first time Andrew noticed it lacked its third and fourth fingers. "On land and in open country what is the extreme *accurate* range for a fieldpiece—say on an 8-pounder?"

"Sir, grape or canister is effective at about 500 yards on small targets such as advancing troops, enemy field artillery and the like. Larger targets such as earthworks or buildings can be hit with accuracy at near 2,000 yards."

Knox and Glover exchanged glances. Said the latter, "It would appear our friend here *does* understand a something concerning artillery. Thank you very much, Serjeant."

Andrew's rather heavy reddish brows shot up. "Serjeant, sir?"

Glover's hitherto austere expression relaxed, "As of this moment you are appointed to that rank and will serve my headquarters."

Knox growled, "Come, come, John! This man's far too knowledgeable to waste his understanding of heavy artillery tinkering with such ridiculous pop-guns as you'll have to mount on your so-called commerce raiders."

For a moment glacial silence descended, only ended when the Marbleheader snapped, "Colonel Knox, granted there may be considerable sense to your objection, my need is grave and *immediate*. Since Serjeant Hunter already is duly enlisted in my regiment he will remain with the 21st until further notice."

Chapter 27 🕊

NEWS FROM MARBLEHEAD

EARLY ON A cold and stormy morning unseasonable for mid-September, a little party of horsemen splashed out from behind a series of raw earthworks supposedly defending the approaches of Cambridge. The horses clumped dispiritedly along, heads held low since the highway to Salem, Beverly and Gloucester. Much used it frequently was fetlock-deep in mud and dotted with wide, rain-speckled potholes.

At the column's head Colonel Glover wore a weatherbeaten boat cloak belted tight about him and had pulled an ordinary seaman's round hat low over his forehead. Beside him and feeling equally as uncomfortable rode Colonel Joseph Reed, efficient if acidulous military secretary to the Commander-in-Chief and presently responsible for the proper equipping, arming and manning of merchant vessels being bought or chartered for use as commercial raiders.

Also riding in this sodden little column were blustery Colonel Stephen Moylan, Mustermaster-General of the Army and temporarily appointed to assist Glover's mission in every possible manner.

A few lengths behind Glover trotted Captain John Manley, a hard-bitten Marblehead sea-captain who enjoyed an enviable reputation for always getting the best out of a ship and its crew. All the same, Manley, like most seafarers, was proving as awkward a horseman as the dozen-odd noncommissioned officers and soldiers detached from duty with the 21st Regiment, now splashing along in his wake.

Rain continued to descend in a succession of furious squalls until Andrew got so chilled he began to shiver violently beneath a short and inadequate poncho and his uniform's thin jacket. Alternately cold then fiery rivulets began to course down his back, causing his seat to become soaked. He recalled a friend's saying, "My spirits stay as high as my arse is dry." Seldom had he experienced such a depressed state of mind due, among other causes, to the fact he'd received no communication from Amy Orne. Another disconcerting factor was awareness that Sarah Hilton's correspondence with Ellen had ended with ominous abruptness.

Worst of all was the fact that, so far, the family had received never a word from Pa, especially now that the hurricane season was advancing. What *could* have happened to so able a captain and his well-found brig?

Only one encouraging factor remained: he could rely on John Glover's support. For a fact, the Marbleheader had touted his abilities so highly before Colonels Reed and Moylan he'd flushed with embarrassment and for the first time had come to appreciate how desperately this improvised Navy stood in need of experienced officers.

The gale kept wrenching at the new tricorn hat Mamma had given him on parting and only stayed on through having been secured by a sodden scarf knotted under his chin. Would a letter be waiting for him at the Widow Palfrey's former residence? Had beetle-browed and surly Donnell Smith kept his promise about preserving such a missive? Of course if Amy had learned about Deborah Palfrey's departure for parts unknown he needn't expect to find any communication.

It was early afternoon before the bedraggled group of riders finally splashed into the sprawling outskirts of Salem to discover that, despite abominable weather, the Mayor and a handful of selectmen still were lingering in the North Meeting House to greet them.

For Yankees they created a considerable fuss over Colonel Glover and his dripping companions and informed them that quarters for senior officers had been provided in the comfortable homes of the Honorable William M. Brown and Colonel Sergeant, both of whose homes were located close to the Courthouse.

Characteristically, Glover demanded, "What about shelter for the enlisted hands?"

"Why, sir," said the Mayor, "they're expected to sling hammocks and live aboard the schooner *Hancock* which, as you likely know, used to be Tom Grant's *Speedwell*."

Everyone anticipated Glover's next question—a critical one. "Any reports concerning" (he almost said "my") "the *Hannah?* She made any prizes?"

"No word, sir," a gaunt and heavily spectacled selectman informed, "but we're expectin' to hear from her any day."

"Has Captain Selman made port with the *Franklin* yet?"

"She's due tomorrow, John. By all reports Selman's mighty keen to get ready for action."

Glover crooked a stubby, big-knuckled forefinger. "Serjeant Hunter, march the crewmen down to Cap'n Webb's Tavern straightaway and stand 'em to plenty of hot buttered rum—on my account."

"Y-y-yes, sir." Despite himself, Andrew couldn't check a persistent chattering of his teeth. Strange, he also was commencing to experience unaccountable, brief small muscular twitchings in his limbs.

Once the party had gulped plenty of hot rum a local man led them down School Street in the general direction of Captain Marston's cluttered dock above which darkly loomed the former *Speedwell*'s topmasts and rigging. Through the downpour crewmen noticed someone had started to paint the name *Hancock* in white across the schooner's stern board but had got no farther than H A N C O—before this storm must have struck.

"You'll only bide here in Salem but a short while," the guide informed. "Come a day or so you and the *Franklin* will sail over to Beverly to take on guns, powder and provisions." He winked.

"Suppose you fellers know Johnny Glover just happens to own the best and biggest shipyard over yonder?"

That no discipline of any description prevailed aboard the Army's *Hancock* became painfully evident when Andrew failed to locate any officer or man responsible for granting shore leave so, without challenge or hindrance, took his way across the gang-plank. In his mind's eye he already could visualize the plain but well-proportioned façade of what once had been Deborah Palfrey's modest home of white clapboards.

Due to the storm darkness closed in early but, while tramping along School Street, Andrew overheard several anxious conjectures as to how the Army's *Hannah,* the 78-ton brig, might be faring. Also he learned that John Glover, in addition to being a true Patriot, was such a shrewd merchant he'd sold this vessel to the Army way back in August—possibly so he could claim credit for supplying the first American armed vessel to challenge the Royal Navy with a battery of six 8-pound cannon and twelve swivel guns mounted along her rails! At best, she constituted a first faltering step taken in a direction deemed by George Washington absolutely essential for keeping his Army in being.

Bowing his head into the rain while making his way down St. Peter Street, Andrew encountered a couple of Marbleheaders who'd served under him on Peach's Head. To his infinite relief both waved and called greetings arousing recollections of that chaotic skirmish way back in July. Especially, he was eager to locate Tom Izard, dependable as sunrise and much shrewder than his speech or manner suggested. Then, while tramping along through thinning rain, it seemed the ground appeared to shift beneath his sodden shoes even as a severe headache commenced to pound his skull. What in blazes was happening to him? Yes, sir, if he didn't feel a deal better come morning he'd better go on sick call, much as he dreaded the prospect.

Almost before realizing it he was using a dolphin-shaped brass knocker on what had been Amy's cousin's white-painted front door.

Bolts clicked then through a crack peered a scruffy twelve-year-old girl in pigtails. "What you want, Mister? Pa's at supper. Can't be disturbed."

"Please tell your Pa Andrew Hunter is back to pick up an important letter he's been holding for me."

The child's red-rimmed eyes widened. "Oh. So you're Mister Hunter?"

"Who's that?" yelled Donnell Smith. When told the bandy-legged tanner appeared at once, bristly jaws still working.

At once Andrew sensed something must have happened since they'd last met; why, Smith's manner was almost gracious when he offered a horny fist. "Come on in out o' the wet, set you down, eat and mebbe drink a tot of somethin' real warmin'. See by that green worsted knot on yer shoulder you've made serjeant."

"Even smart officers can make a mistake," Andrew attempted to joke.

Donnell's wife appeared, a plump, big-framed woman with lank black hair and bosoms large enough to accommodate two females of her dimensions. "Mercy, what ails you, Mister? Your eyes look *that* pink and swollen."

"Must be coming down with a cold, Ma'am."

Six young children wearing coarse homespun gawped and remained grouped in the background while the tanner pulled back a chair up to a cluttered supper table standing before a cooking fire.

After gulping a mug of steaming clam chowder and a tot of watered applejack Andrew gathered courage to put the critical question, "Have, well, have any letters come for me?"

"Yes. One came just two days ago," Dorcas Smith stated. "I'll go fetch it." She clumped upstairs leaving her children to gawk at this intruder who although soaked to the skin remained important-looking despite poor dress and lead-hued features.

On recognizing Amy's clear, flowing script Andrew's heart leaped like a speared salmon.

Unexpectedly Donnell Smith drawled, "Reckon since that there paper is of import suppose ye go into what used to be the library where ye can read private-like. Two of the nippers sleep in there but they wun't be beddin' down for a while yet."

"Thank you very much."

Seated in the cluttered little room Andrew lifted Amy's letter to the light of a single sperm oil candle and in acute suspense delayed momentarily revolving it between chilled and trembling fingers, aware this missive very well might shape the course of his life. At length he drew a deep breath, thrust a dirty thumb-nail beneath a coarse flying seal of embossed paper then held the letter closer to the candle since, for some reason, Amy's carefully formed words appeared to blur and merge:

YE 15TH DAY OF SEPTEMBER 1775

My Heart's Own Dearest Darling,

How many Times have I not penned and rewritten this, the most important Letter I have yet composed. Before you read further, never forget, Dearest Andrew, that I will forever ADORE you and that so long as Breath enters my Body my Heart will beat only for you.

Andrew sharply caught his breath; his chills became more acute.

I fear you will find it Difficult to credit the above Declaration after reading what the Circumstances beyond my control force me to Relate.

The very Afternoon of the day you marched off with Colonel Gerry and the other Voluntiers Caleb Twisden Approach'd Me and firmly led me aside.

Before my pen travels farther I must admit that, in all Honesty, Caleb has not prov'd to be quite the Black-Hearted Rogue we both deemed him.

Despite his hard and Pracktical Manner and occasional suspicious Actions I find he really is a warm-hearted Person. Nor have I ever suspected how long or how deeply he vows, on his Honour, he has worshipped me from a Distance.

Also Caleb has informed me (possibly to encourage his suit) that my dear Cousin Deborah Palfrey has suddenly departed Salem and gone to no one knows where. I would have doubted her vanishing without Writing a Word to me except that others have confirmed this. I penned her a letter of Condolence over her husband's untimely Death in Battle, which has not been answered.

243

Feverish currents racing down his back forced Andrew to intensify efforts to focus his gaze. Worse still, a splitting headache was rendering it difficult to grasp even the essence of what Amy had written. Steeling himself, he read on:

> In any case, my Beloved Andrew, Caleb also informed me on the Day you went away that come what may he is determined we are to Marry. When I told him I LOVE YOU alone and always will Caleb pointed out, quite Decently, that were I not to akcept his Offer it would prove well-nigh Impossible for me, with a certain tarnished sail loft reputation, to continue dwelling in Marblehead. There is also another reason for my taking this decision Dearest Heart—I must confide that our love-making, brief as it was, will bear Fruit therefore I had better get married as soon as may be. Caleb need never know who is responsible for My Condition since he agrees with Certain Ministers of the Gospel who averr that a married couple's first child may be born at any Time after they become join'd in Holy Matrimony, strangely, all other Babes require a Nine Month Term.

Groans of indescribable agony escaped Andrew when the possibility occurred that this pregnancy, real or false, might serve only as a subterfuge to excuse Amy's defection. If only he'd known her longer or understood her better and could talk with her right away—but with this sickness growing worse such a possibility seemed unlikely.

Straining swollen eyes he read on:

> Within the next few Days Caleb and I will travel over to Gloucester where we are less known than in Salem or Beverly. There the Nuptial Knots are to be tied, but for me they will feel no better than Iron Fetters. Oh, my Beloved, how my Heart quails at this Prospeckt. How can Fate prove so pitiless?

Here, tears had splashed and dimmed Amy's penmanship.

I implore You to Believe that I am doing only what I must for, not Knowing where you are, or how to reach you, no alternative remains for me to adopt.

I shall pray for your safety in this Dreadful War and wish you as much Happiness as lies in God's Power to grant you. I implore you, Dearest LOVE, never to forget that forever I worship the very Ground on which you tread.

Your Distracted but ever Adoring,

Amy.

CHAPTER 28 ❧

FEVER

THE EQUINOCTIAL GALE continued to rage so violently broken branches flew about while trees, the earth at their roots softened by rain, crashed over. Outhouses were tipped over, roofs were ripped off, shingles and slates flew through the air at such a rate Dorcas, Donnell Smith's robust spouse, shrugged. "Reckon the poor fellow will have to 'bide here. Wouldn't do to turn out even a Injun or a sick dog in such a storm—'tain't Christian."

"Right, though I don't fancy the way that flush's spreadin' over his face. Sure as death and taxes the feller's comin' down with some heavy sickness."

Dorcas Smith's wide mouth, showing a faint but perceptible mustache, flattened into a tight line. "Donnell, 'tain't sensible to keep him here in this house—suppose what he's took with is catchin'?"

"—And so?"

"Why dun't you and the older boys rig a cot in the new tool shed; 'tis nigh weather-tight."

Andrew blinked, tried to steady his swimming gaze and ignore a dizzying headache. "Please, good people, don't put yourselves out on my account. I—I can make it back to the ship."

"Fiddlesticks! You couldn't even cross the street. Whoa! Take it easy!" The tanner lunged to steady the tall man swaying and still clutching his crumpled letter. "Now just set you down. Come mornin' I'll go see if there's space for you in the soldiers' pest house."

"But we haven't been paid yet—I haven't money."

"Money be damned!"

Dorcas started. Never before had she heard her husband say any such a thing.

Smith then added, "Right now you'll do what you're told, Mister Serjeant Hunter. Dorcas, send Isaac runnin' for Doc Price and see if he kin find him though I doubt it—he's *that* busy nowadays." The tanner then turned to his eldest daughter, instructed the pigtailed girl who'd answered the door, "Hester, go carry a bolster and all the second-best quilts we got out to the tool shed. Oh—and yes, put a chamber pot neath the cot.

"Tim. Kindle a fire in the chimney piece out there fastest as you can. Git!"

Clearly, Donnell Smith was accustomed to giving orders and having them obeyed promptly.

Andrew, sitting by the kitchen fire, felt so much worse he barely noticed someone hammering on the front door.

"B'God, what now?" grumbled Smith. A great gust of misty, salt-smelling wind seemed to literally propel indoors the familiar figure of Tom Izard, stalwart black-bearded, brown-faced and beetle-browed as ever.

Dripping wet, he could be heard shouting over the booming wind, "Just heard tell you've a shipmate o' mine here."

"Could be," Dorcas sniffed. "but the feller's a poor bargain; acts awful sick."

"Let me see him," the Marbleheader snapped. "Heyo, Andy. Just heard you been assigned aboard the *Hancock*."

"True, but seems I—I comin' down with some ailment. Can't seem to manage my legs."

"Lemme see if I can figger out what ails you; once served for a while as a loblolly boy in the goddam *Lively*." Squatting onto his heels the big mariner first tested the stricken man's pulse rate

247

but couldn't tell much except Andy's heart was racing and his forehead felt hot as the hinges of Hell. Next he opened the other's damp shirt, noticed tiny red welts beginning to form.

"Stick out yer tongue, Andy."

When the sick man complied and Tom saw how brown and thickly coated it was, he felt nigh certain about the nature of Andrew's ailment but still wasn't ready to go on record.

"There a doctor livin' nearby?"

"Only old Doc Price. Sent for him just afore you got here. He's about the only sawbones left; younger ones hev all shoved off to serve in the War." Donnell Smith looked more anxious than angry. "What's yer friend's trouble?"

Tom lowered his voice. "Dunno for sure but 'ppears like he's been took by a fever called by a number of names."

"—Such as?" Dorcas's voice sounded taut.

"Wal, depends where you be. Some calls it jail, ship or camp fever. Strikes mostly when folks gets crowded too close together and can't or won't wash. Hungry men die quickest, so do oldsters. Bugs, lice and fleas are supposed to have somethin' to do with this sort of thing but nobody knows why."

"Mercy!" quavered Dorcas. "Camp fever's catchin', ain't it?"

"Can be but not in a clean place like yours."

At the end of half an hour Tom and Donnell lugged the patient, delirious and struggling feebly, out to the tool shed in the back yard, placed him on a pallet filled with wheat straw then covered him beneath a good many old patchwork quilts.

"What can be done to keep the rest of us from takin' what he's got?" Dorcas stolidly inquired while starting back towards the house.

"Nothin' except fetch soap, towels, a wash rag and a couple of pails of steaming hot water. Mister," he told the tanner, "I'll strip, shave and wash him from head to toe, meantime you'd best boil his garments and later on burn the bedclothes an you have to. Say, hadn't you good people better hit the hay?"

Smith answered promptly, "Wal, sounds like good advice if we can't help none. Come along, Dorcas." After the Smiths had disappeared Andrew attempted to talk but his speech remained slurred save for a lucid moment during which he mumbled, "Wha' 'bout Amy?"

"Nothin' that'll please you."

The sick man's swollen eyes rolled upwards. "P-please speak up."

"You'll hear sooner or later so I'll tell you. Last week Amy Orne and Caleb Twisden went over to Gloucester and got spliced. By my reckonin' ye're damn' well rid of her."

First thing next morning Tom Izard made a beeline for Colonel Glover's headquarters and explained what had happened to this serjeant his fellow-Marbleheader appeared to hold in such high esteem.

The 21st Regiment's Colonel looked and acted deeply concerned but wasn't taken completely by surprise.

Work on the gunboats was suffering all along the line even though men who remained well redoubled their efforts. Dysentery, smallpox, lung fever and venereal infections increased and appeared to spread more rapidly whenever new contingents of men reached town. There had been hardly ever any physical examination of prospective recruits beyond making sure they enjoyed reasonably good eyesight, didn't suffer from hernia and had retained enough teeth to bite off a cartridge's end or to chew tough Army rations.

As a result of Tom Izard's visit Glover promptly sent to the house on St. Peters Street a Doctor Scott, the medical officer attached to his headquarters. Wearily the military physician conferred with old Doctor Price, palsied, half-blind and nearly toothless.

"Ain't no doubt about it," the older man stated. "I figure this young feller's been took by the camp fever. Tongue's thick-coated, brown as leather, his eyeballs look badly conjuncted and, as you can see, he's sweating like a dray horse; suffers from nervous twitchings, too."

Doctor Scott nodded, pulled out a huge nickel-plated watch, took the patient's wrist. His expression tightened once he'd counted around one hundred and thirty beats to the minute.

Anxious to learn the truth, Dorcas and Hester, her eldest daughter, were hovering about the doorway although Donnell and the other children had heeded Tom Izard's advice and kept well back.

Doctor Scott straightened, looked Mrs. Smith in the eye.

"Sorry, Ma'am, for two reasons. This patient will have to stay right here for a spell; first, because he's too sick to move and second, there's no space left in the pest house, the poor house or in the Army infirmary. I will recommend to the Colonel that Seaman Izard here be granted temporary leave to help you out as a sort of a nurse. He's been to sea a lot, seems familiar with this kind of sickness."

Tremulously Dorcas demanded, "How long is—is this poor fellow likely to stay in such a state? Are we likely to take the fever?"

"No, Ma'am. Not if you steer clear of his clothes and bedding and soak everything he touches in boiling water."

Old Doctor Price cackled, "To answer your first question, Dorcas, he could remain bedridden anywhere from two to three weeks maybe less, he's still young. 'Tis oldsters and hungry folks who die quickest."

"And that's all true," agreed Doctor Scott. After putting away his watch he picked up a battered black medicine bag. "By tomorrow little red spots likely will appear on his face, wrists and possibly the soles of his feet. He's recently been washed, I take it?"

"Yep," Tom grunted. "'Fore I came lookin' for you I holystoned Andy down to the bone. You'll note I've already whacked off most of his head hair and I'll shave off his private hairs soon's he quits thrashin' around."

The physician stared. "Why are you listed only as an A.B.? You should be transferred to duty in an infirmary somewhere. God alone knows how badly we need men like you."

Tom flared right up. "I will like Hell! Mister, I've got a goddam heavy score to settle with the Britishers, 'specially since they've made such fools of the poor old *Hannah* and her pick-up crew."

Everyone in the town was hopping mad because the Army's first cruiser, the *Hannah*, had put to sea a few days earlier only to be almost immediately chased into Beverly by H.M.S. *Merlin*, the sloop-of-war presently patrolling this length of the coast.

Doctor Scott heaved a gusty sigh. "Have it your way, Mister Izard, but don't you dast quit this place till the Colonel grants you leave."

"Don't intend to, Doc. Save I've got to make a quick trip over to Cambridge and let his folks know what's chanced."

CHAPTER 29 🎀

FLIGHT

A MOMENT AFTER Major Hilton had locked his front door Sarah appeared, realized she hadn't seen Papa wear near so grim an expression since they'd watched that battle on Breed's Hill. "Sarah, come into the library. I've heard grave news. We must act accordingly and at once."

The young woman's tapering fingertips for a moment pressed hard against her lips then, her father's daughter, she said steadily, "Papa, what has chanced?"

Employing precise movements the Major stalked over to hang his tricorn on its rack. "My dear, a short time ago a ranking officer at General Howe's headquarters let drop that this afternoon a Doctor Clague, on his way to Cambridge, has been arrested and charged with spying."

"Papa! What can have gone wrong? He's been passed through the lines dozens of times."

"Don't know. Didn't dare discuss the matter for fear of raising suspicion." His jaw line tightened and his gaze became penetrating. "Tell me, Daughter, did you last night give Doctor Clague a letter for Ellen?"

Shocked and paling she nodded. "It was found?"

"All I know is that the Provost Marshal's men have grown far stricter about suppressing espionage. Only yesterday four wretches got hanged, two the day before on slimmer evidence than your letters to Ellen Hunter."

"Papa, do you think anyone will suspect onion juice was used?"

"Much depends on what other incriminating evidence might have been found on poor Clague's person. Our only hope lies that those dolts in the Provost Marshal's office mayn't suspect that letter contains such writing. Clague was arrested around noon but as we know the British ain't given to moving promptly so go pack a bag of useful clothes."

"Why don't you do the same, Papa?"

"I must remain to continue—well, what we've been doing."

"I *won't* leave without you."

"Sarah, as always, you will do as I order. If I'm questioned I may possibly be able to convince certain friends at Headquarters that you were only a scatterbrain girl acting on your own— without my knowledge."

Major Hilton didn't believe his own words, but felt it important to lend Sarah some measure of self-assurance. For the moment Benjamin Hilton felt unfeignedly thankful his ailing wife had gone to her reward over a month ago. What an emotional if not hysterical outburst poor Emily would have indulged in under present circumstances!

Said he sharply, "Whilst you're getting your things together I'll send word to Billy Gorham to ready his skiff. He knows what to do. I've spent plenty to keep him ready to sail either or both of us over to the Cambridge shore come dark."

"Please, Papa, I thought we were in this together."

Major Hilton's voice barked like that of a testy drill serjeant. "Daughter! Do as ordered. Do I assume rightly you'll take shelter with Ellen Hunter?"

Numbly, Sarah inclined her narrow, gold-blonde head. "I'll pack right away; won't be long."

"Good, but don't let the servants see what you're about." The old soldier in him prompted him to add, "Best put bread and cheese in your bundle. God knows how long 'twill take to slip past those damn' patrols on the river even if Billy Gorham knows their system of reliefs as well as he claims."

Bad as things looked Major Benjamin Hilton found it vastly encouraging to have fathered a daughter who, free of feminine fantods, megrims and tears, almost had taken the place of that son he'd yearned for but never had sired.

Once Sarah disappeared upstairs he crossed the room, mounted a set of library steps and from a topmost shelf removed a row of false book backs and without hesitation made a selection of documents to be burned in the fireplace.

Next the veteran pulled aside a sliding panel from a bookcase and unlocked a small iron-bound chest. From it, he selected a small, brown-leather bag; it clinked when he emptied its contents onto his desk. Methodically, he commenced to stack gold sovereigns in piles of ten each. Um. Should things go really wrong for Sarah near a hundred pounds, gold, ought to keep her free from want for a reasonable time.

Oh damn, *damn,* DAMN! Why did this silly, needless war have to commence? Before, England and her American Colonies had been flourishing and probably still would be growing save for that well-meaning but stupid German Oaf in Whitehall and his pack of often degenerate self-seeking ministers.

He scribbled a note to Gorham: "Prepare skiff immediately. Stand ready till further notice." He then dispatched a young black footman who couldn't read running down towards Barton's Point, a thinly populated suburb beyond Mill Pond.

Flushed and breathless, Sarah re-entered the library carrying a striped ticking bag such as the family customarily used for sending out heavy laundry. The Major smiled fleetingly on noticing that Sarah had changed into a dark-brown serge dress and was wearing a black poke bonnet hat secured by a ribbon knotted under her chin.

"B'God, Daughter, wonder how many young females would have thought to change into such hard-to-see garments. How many stout shoes have you taken?"

"Three pair, Papa, with low heels, some strong, knitted string stockings and—er—warm underpinnings."

"Good. You always were a sensible little baggage. Now go stow your bundle in the hall closet." He drew himself up, stalked over to a mirror adjusted the lace jabot at his throat, then straightened a snowy scratch wig before ringing for Toby. "Go down cellar and fetch up a—no, two bottles of the '35, no '32, amontillado."

Once the butler had departed, Ben Hilton put into Sarah's hands the small but weighty bag of soft-tanned leather.

"What is this, Papa?"

"Enough hard money to keep you going till—" he smiled wryly, "—till I can get things sorted out. Take it."

Sarah knew better than to hesitate so slipped the bag into a black-netting reticule.

Once Sarah had closed the door Benjamin Hilton shrugged only slightly bent shoulders wishing to God he felt free to run while the going was good. But too much lay hazard; tomorrow, if things went as usual, he should be able to secure a tally of troop reinforcements and supplies now overdue from Halifax.

A casual observer watching the Hiltons dine could never have suspected anything wasn't as it seemed. Carefully Toby offered a dusty bottle of amontillado for the Major's inspection then, on a nod of approval, filled long-stemmed glasses.

Once the light supper had been consumed the Major took his customary stroll along Joy Street. Everything appeared normal. Somewhat reassured, he returned home.

From his writing desk he removed and grimly inspected a pair of pistols for, if his time indeed was running out, Major Benjamin Hilton had no intention of quitting this existence unaccompanied by enemies, be they French, Indian or, alas, British; such wasn't his nature. Briefly he debated whether to give Sarah a handsome little Spanish-made pocket pistol but ended by deciding not to. Were she arrested with it in her possession things might go hard for her. How was it possible for the secure and gracious living he'd worked so long and hard to establish to end like this?

He smiled quietly on his agitated daughter. "My dear, since darkness won't set in for some time shall we indulge in a game of picquet?"

It did his heart good to see how quickly Sarah quieted, took off her hat and pulled a chair up to the card table they generally used.

"Of course, Papa. Better watch out, I intend to beat you and even our tally." This was a standing jest between them; over several years they'd played picquet and had kept a record of winnings and losses. Most times Sarah won through sheer ability but, on occasion, should her interest appear to flag the Major always managed to allow her a victory.

Once twilight had faded and real darkness had set in Benjamin Hilton said calmly, "Put away the cards. Should there come any intimation of a visit from the Provost's men grab your bundle, speed out the back door and make for Billy Gorham's fishing shack. As you'll recall it lies beyond the Mill Pond on Barton's Point. 'Tis a lightly settled community.

"When you reach Cambridge, pray present my compliments to Mrs. Hunter and congratulate her that her eldest son is safe and is now serving his County ably, or so I've heard." With steady hands Major Hilton lit a pipe from a candle on the table, "'Twill be interesting to learn exactly how young Hunter managed to escape the *Lively*."

Through an open window beat the cadence of marching men approaching but, things being as they had been in Boston for so long, this in itself didn't mean much. On this occasion, however, someone rasped a command for a squad to halt before 10½ Joy Street.

"Sarah, *git!* An things go well I'll communicate through Ellen."

Sarah pecked her father's florid cheek, grabbed her bundle from the closet then sped below thankful that the cook and Toby had gone to bed as early as usual. While running she crammed the black poke bonnet on at a crazy angle before opening the basement door a crack. Thank God! No one seemed to be in the back yard but out on Joy Street somebody was roaring, "Open up! In the King's name, open up!"

By the time Sarah had reached an alley paralleling the river she heard repeated hammering noises ending in a very loud crash of splintering wood. Always a good runner she hiked skirts and petticoats knee-high then sprinted as she never had before.

From somewhere behind her came the reports of three or four gunshots but it proved impossible to tell in exactly what direction the shooting had taken place.

CHAPTER 30 🙋

FLIGHT II

PROBABLY BECAUSE SHE took care to slow her pace to a hurried walk whenever a British patrol hove into sight no one challenged the Major's daughter while she made her way along the Charles's crowded, malodorous waterfront until, gingerly, she was able to set foot on a walkway leading onto Old Billy Gorham's ramshackle and gear-littered landing stage.

How indescribably reassuring it was to glimpse a feeble ray of yellow-red light shining through a crack in one of the shack's window shutters—also to note, bobbing beside the stage, a small dark-painted skiff lying with sail unstopped and ready for hoisting.

Billy Gorham, slightly built, bent and white-haired, blew out his house light and materialized before Sarah had advanced even halfway out on his landing float.

"Thank Heavens you're ready, Mister Gorham," Sarah panted, peering nervously about at a shadowy tangle of masts, yards and rigging traced between the dim outlines of several boathouse roofs.

Squirrel-quick for all his advanced years Gorham hurriedly

grabbed her bundle then handed her into his craft. "Keep yer voice down and stay below the gunnels out of sight." While casting off he added, "Good thing a breeze is springing up."

Sweating and breathing wildly Sarah flinched while crouching in an inch or so of cold water covering the skiff's floor boards. Next, she noticed that the night steadily was growing darker; only a few stars shone briefly between ragged low banks of hurrying clouds.

Once his skiff, carried by the tide, started to drift away from his landing the old man sank onto the stern sheets and gripped the tiller after tucking between his knees a conical-shaped dark lantern fashioned of tin.

"How could you be ready so quickly? Papa only sent word a short while back."

"Heard about Doc Clague's gettin' picked up yesterday so even afore I got yer Pa's message so I figgered you or the Major might need me in a hurry. Your Pa's been payin' me for weeks agin a moment as this. Scrooch still lower down, Missy. Mustn't be noticed."

Still breathless and aware of warm rivulets of perspiration creeping down her back and between her breasts and buttocks, Sarah sprawled flat on the skiff's bottom miserably aware of a chilly dampness spreading fast through her garments.

Not until the tide had carried the skiff out over a hundred yards of restless, jet-black water did the silver-haired waterman slowly hoist his skiff's patched and dingy leg-of-mutton sail. At once the little craft came alive, commenced to gather speed and become buffeted by rising waves. Only then did Gorham inquire what had happened.

She told him briefly, concluding, "The Redcoats were smashing down our front door as I fled."

"Pray God your Pa can win free of this. He's mighty able, and a true Patriot if ever I've seen one and I've met a heap of 'em since Concord and Lexington. Eh? What is it?"

"There's a tiny speck of light showing from your lantern."

Instantly the waterman covered it with a strip of tarpaulin. "Thanks, Missy, can't risk no giveaways. Not tonight. Plenty of Lobsterback patrol boats abroad—seen 'em settin' out come sundown."

Repeatedly the skiff heeled over so hard no doubt remained that a real breeze was making up, fortunately up-river.

"Good thing ye're bonnet's dark," Gorham's thin voice commented over an ever-mounting *slap-slap* of waves. "Now raise yer head till you just kin peek over the rail and keep a sharp lookout. Me eyesight ain't so keen as it uster was. Sight anything suspicious kick my foot then point."

Faster and faster the skiff sped until in increasing quantities flicks of spray spurted over its bow.

All at once Sarah kicked the waterman's foot as he crouched low over the tiller. She pointed off to port. "Big rowboat over there, not far off. I can see one mast and a swivel gun. Looks like her crew are trying to raise sail."

Without hesitation Gorham altered course for a low, marshy point on the far shore which, topped by a row of low trees, barely was visible through the gloom.

"Still see her?"

"No, she's disappeared. Where we going?"

"Peck's Point, lies straight ahead and has one of our batteries onto it. An all goes well I'll signal her come 'nother few minutes."

Fervently Sarah hoped it wouldn't take long. Water on the bottom was rising and, for early autumn, felt icy. When her teeth commenced to chatter she tried to warm hands in her bundle of clothing. Lord above! What might have happened to Papa? Certainly that angry smashing of his front door didn't augur well at all—at all. Oh dear, 'twas a good thing he long had cultivated influential officers serving at British Headquarters. If *only* she could know what evidence, other than her letter, might have been discovered on Doctor Clague's person.

Once trees along the Cambridge shore commenced to assume more distinct outlines the old man was forced to ease the leg-of-mutton sheet—too much water now was cascading into the skiff. He steered for a slight rise in the shore topped by what seemed to be a low and flat embankment.

"Missy, I be too busy steerin' so you'll show the recognition signal." He pushed his dark lantern forward, indicated a small lever on one side explaining it was designed to manipulate a set of metal shutters.

"What is the signal?"

"When I give the word, blink twice, pause, then three more times. Men in the battery will be on the lookout. Understand?"

"Yes. Two, then three times." The lamp's warm metal felt fine under her chilled fingers.

"Now!"

The moment Sarah pressed the lantern's shutter lever but it stuck just long enough to allow a gust of wind to blow out the candle. Sickened, Sarah heard someone shout, "Halt! Go about, else we fire!"

Gorham through cupped hands at the top of his lungs shrilled the password, "Marblehead! Marblehead!" But the wind proved too strong. A line of brief red-yellow jets of flame sparkled along the shore like giant fireflies.

Something went *ta-chunk!* into the rail on a level with Sarah's ear a second before her bonnet went whirling off into wind-filled darkness. Another musket ball hissed by close enough to sever a lock of hair, though at the moment she didn't notice.

Gorham stood up waving arms and screaming, "For God's sake *don't shoot* more! We be friends, *friends!* Marblehea—"

He broke off and swayed, convulsively clutching his right shoulder until his legs gave way and he slumped over the tiller, gasping and groaning but nevertheless maintaining his course.

Major Benjamin Hilton's daughter didn't hesitate, jumped up shrieking, "Marblehead! Marblehead!" in such penetrating, high-pitched tones they must have been heard ashore for almost at once the shooting faltered then died out. Then, rather like a crippled goose, the skiff drifted on till it blundered aground on a muddy, sedge-lined beach.

Out of the darkness someone yelled, "Marblehead ahoy! Give the countersign!"

Gorham rallied, "Gerry! You damn' dumblocks! *Gerry!*"

Moments later the skiff, single sail flapping crazily, was hauled up on the beach by a knot of shadowy figures carrying slung muskets. Someone in authority rasped, "What the Hell's the matter with you, Gorham? Whyn't you shine the recognition signal?"

Sarah spoke right up. "'Twas my fault. The blinker's shutter jammed long enough for the wind to blow the candle out."

"Gorham, how bad you hurt?"

"Dunno. Can't hardly move me right arm."

259

More dimly outlined figures splashed up.

"Who is this wench?" demanded a towering fellow wearing a farmer's broad-brimmed hat.

Gorham grunted, "This here's Major Hilton's daughter, no wench. Get us ashore fast! Spread word Doctor Clague and maybe Major Hilton have been arrested!"

Unceremoniously Sarah, legs wide parted, was lugged piggy-back through heavy clumps of reeds fringing this sand spit and set down. If, as a well-bred young lady, she was expected to faint, she proved a disappointment. Apparently she wasn't exactly the delicate and exquisitely sensitive blossom to which several poetically inclined admirers had compared her.

A tall fellow wearing a seaman's stocking cap and a cutlass handed over her bundle.

Said a cultured voice, "Sorry, Mistress Hilton, didn't dare take chances; been warned all week to watch out for a British night attack. If only Gorham had shown the light when he should have."

"How badly is he wounded?"

"Can't tell much yet, but at first glance his hurt don't look grave—just a flesh wound."

CHAPTER 31 🙠

THE FATES' DECREE

BY THE TIME she'd bandaged Gorham's wound after a fashion and the waterman had been carted off to the nearest field hospital, Sarah Hilton had become so exhausted one of two ragtag privates who'd escorted her up from the beach had to use Captain Hunter's dolphin-shaped door knocker. Lordy! What a sorry spectacle she must present with lank hair falling over her face and shoulders, her blouse sagging open in disorder and her shoes and brown skirt streaked by slimy, gray-blue mud. While waiting she heard her bundle dripping water.

Once Ellen Hunter had unbarred the door her sleep-heavy eyes flew wide open. "Sarah! Dear God in Heaven! What can have happened?"

"Sorry to impose, Ellie, but I, I well—I've no choice." Sarah's knees gave way, buckled so quickly that the pair of unshaven infantrymen from the 21st, recognizable by their seamen's wide petticoat breeches, were forced to half-carry, half-haul her over the threshold with feet trailing.

One remarked, "Now don't go and git all foamed up, Mistress. She really ain't hurt, only nigh pooped out."

The other waved a vague salute, said gravely, "Sorry, Mistress, us has orders to report back to the Cap'n right away."

Once they'd deposited their charge on a bench in the hall they swung off towards a brilliant early-autumn sunrise with a seaman's distinctive rolling gait, muskets slung slantwise.

After pushing her friend's damp blonde hair back over her shoulders and wiping mud from her face Ellen shrilled for her mother and Betsy. Although she said nothing to that effect Ellen more than half-suspected what might have happened over in Boston. Once the three women had assisted Sarah into the Captain's study Mrs. Hunter briskly ordered hot tea laced with a tot of rum. Not a sea captain's wife for nothing Sally Orne Hunter was aware that, despite religious scruples to the contrary, a tot of alcohol administered at the right moment could prove a remarkable restorative.

Once a touch of color returned to her features Sarah muttered groggily, "W—where—Andrew—Captain Hunter?"

"Tell you later," Mrs. Hunter replied quietly. "First tell us what's happened to bring you here in such a state—not that you aren't welcome, my dear."

Mrs. Hunter and her daughter, kneeling beside the bedraggled figure, listened to a brief and at times somewhat incoherent description of events leading to her flight from Joy Street.

"What can have happened to Doctor Clague?" Sarah queried tensely. "We've only just heard about his arrest."

Ellen pushed a pillow farther under Sarah's tangled hair. "He is to be tried by a court-martial today. I fear we can foresee its verdict."

Mrs. Hunter queried while gently stroking Sarah's grimy hand, "Your father. Did—did he escape?"

Sarah blinked, stared upwards unseeingly. "Don't know. Papa insisted 'twas his duty to remain—rely on friends in high places and so perhaps continue to forward information."

Ellen tried hard to make her voice sound confident. "I'm sure he'll be all right. After all, your Papa is a veteran soldier and mighty resourceful. Now, dearest friend, come up to a real bed."

She, Mrs. Hunter and Betsy had to half-carry the disheveled refugee up a narrow flight of stairs, a real task. Sarah was tall and much heavier than most people might think. Once they'd undressed her Mrs. Hunter said almost sharply, "Get some sleep, Sarah. We can talk more sensibly later on."

"Wha—wha' 'bout Andrew?"

"He's safe. Let that suffice for the moment."

"No. Must know more—"

Mrs. Hunter shook her head so hard gray locks still in whalebone curlers swayed. "As I've said, we'll tell you more in good time. Meantime I will try to decide what had best be done."

Sarah slept as though felled by some Indian's *casse-tête*, remained blissfully unaware that two important events had occurred.

First off burly Tom Izard, dusty and ill-smelling after a hard ride over from Salem, rode up to "Fair View" and tied a lathered, angular nag to its hitching post. Once he'd identified himself, the black-bearded seaman was made much of, especially after it appeared that he, personally, had been responsible for Andrew's escape from H.M.S. *Lively*. He also spoke of the British attack on Peach's Head and Andrew's part in partially defeating it. Patently ill-at-ease in this handsome dwelling, Tom perched uncomfortably on the edge of a delicate armchair until he arose blurting, "Sorry, can't linger. Got to report back aboard the *Lee*—my ship. Besides, Andy's mighty ailin'."

Ellen's and her mother's eyes rounded. "Andrew sick! With what?"

"Like plenty of others he's come down with what us seafarin' folk calls 'ship fever.' Reckon maybe you've heard speak of it?"

Ellen's narrow head inclined. "Yes, 'tis the same as 'jail' or 'camp' fever. I see cases of it every day."

"Now do tell. How come?"

Succinctly Mrs. Hunter explained. "For some time my daughter has been assisting physicians in charge of the principal military hospital here in Cambridge. They depend on her a great deal, therefore I feel—"

Ellen broke in, "How bad off *is* my brother, Mister Izard?"

"Let's say his state ain't so pretty good. The fever keeps so high his face stays red all the time and he throws up anything given him. He's begun to pick at his bedclothes which they tell me is a bad sign."

"Merciful God," burst out Mrs. Hunter. "What sort of attention can he be getting in a little port like Salem?"

"Not extry good, Ma'am, and that's a fact. Right now Salem's swamped with mariners, contractors, troops and shipbuilders; ain't but two sawbones left in the hull town."

"Where is my brother?" Ellen demanded.

"Andy took sick in the house of a rough-and-ready tanner called Donnell Smith. Think maybe you'd best ride back to Salem with me? Andy sure can use better care. Ma Smith's got a flock of young'uns underfoot."

Ellen got to her feet. "I'll go pack a few things and be ready to leave right away."

Mrs. Hunter also arose, thin pink lips flattened ruler-straight. "Not so fast, Ellen. True Andrew *is* your brother, but he's also only a single human, so you 'bide here where dozens on dozens of sick men need your attention just as much." She wheeled about. "Ellie, could Sarah be of use in this pinch?"

Distractedly, Ellen's fingertips compressed thin, almost olive-hued cheeks so hard they paled under the pressure. "I can't say for sure, Mamma, but I know Sarah's uncommon level-headed and cared for her sick mother a long while so she should understand something about invalids. Besides, she knows Andrew and was quite taken with him until that dreadful battle on Breed's Hill." Despite strong contrary impulses Ellen announced, "Mister Izard, as my mother has pointed out, I agree my first duty lies in Cambridge. I'll send Sarah over to Salem tomorrow, er—provided she's well enough and willing to go."

" 'Well enough'?" Izard repeated. "Is she sick?"

"No, only worn down to a frazzle. When you hear what's happened you won't be surprised." Briefly Ellen described how a flow of invaluable military intelligence from Boston abruptly had become cut off. She concluded by inquiring, "Where in Salem does this tanner, Donnell Smith, dwell?"

Tom described the house on St. Peter's Street at the same time wondering how Andy might be faring under Dorcas Smith's well-intentioned but haphazard ministrations.

He heaved himself to his feet, said gravely, "Pleased to have met you, ladies. Reckon all you Hunters must have been run out o' the same mould; duty first. Like I said, you should ha' seen

Andy the night that damn' British landing party raided the battery he'd built on Peach's Head. Tell you all about it sometime. Goodbye for now."

He offered huge hands marked by old gurry sears. No fancy drawing-room bows for Tom Izard. Without further ado he then tramped out to untie the shaggy saddle horse waiting with blunt head drooping before Captain Hunter's hitching post.

Once he'd departed Sally Orne Hunter rolled eyes ceilingwards. "Oh, Ellen, blessed if it don't seem as if all the world we know is crumbling apart." This was said early that evening before someone shoved a note under Captain Hunter's front door, knocked, then took off as if pursued by the Devil himself.

Shakily Ellen unfolded the oblong of paper and on reading it felt a succession of icy currents chill her being. Someone had written in an educated hand:

> *Doctor Clague sentenced to be hanged this morning.*
> *Major Hilton after killing two soldiers was shot dead*
> *last evening while resisting arrest.*

CHAPTER 32 🙦

ST. PETER'S CHURCHYARD

THE FOURTH DAY after Andrew had quit his bed and was able to move about a little bore out what Doctor Scott always maintained—there is nothing like youth as an ally in health matters—especially when youth is aided by unremitting care. Due to having found lodgings almost directly across the street from Donnell Smith's dwelling Major Hilton's daughter had been able to be in almost constant attendance.

Day in and day out she did whatever might be done towards speeding recovery; unpleasant, unromantic tasks such as cleaning vomit, changing and boiling Mrs. Smith's patched cotton sheets, quilts and the patient's nightclothes. Tirelessly she'd sponge sweat from his face and body—above the waist, of course. Also, she'd rubbed onto angry scarlet rash soothing ointments prescribed by Doctor Scott, wherever it broke out on an often delirious patient's face, arms or legs.

Only a little less than Doctor Scott had Sarah been relieved when no indications of jaundice appeared since the physician had declared it responsible for carrying off a majority of ship or jail fever patients. Only briefly did Andrew suffer fom what the

Doctor described as "dementia" or "melancholia," therefore, towards the end of his first week's confinement, the patient proved able to retain gruels and certain other nourishing fluids instead of immediately vomiting.

Once Andrew became able to retain solids his recovery accelerated so rapidly that, at the end of a fortnight, considerable strength returned and little remained to mark his ordeal beyond hollow cheeks and eyes and a sprinkling of pink splotches on his face and limbs marking former locations of maculo-papular eruptions.

Although fatigued Sarah rejoiced not only over the speed of Andrew's recovery but also increasing manifestations of his interest in herself. When that he no longer was bedridden his regard appeared ever more intense; why, this very afternoon when out the yard when one of the Smith youngsters began to play a tune called "Spanish Ladies," long a favorite of the Royal Navy, the invalid had sung a verse or two—decidedly off-key.

Next evening when the setting sun commenced to sketch flaming gold and scarlet tints among the few leaves remaining on sugar maples surrounding St. Peter's Church, Andrew suggested that he and Sarah take a short stroll through the churchyard. They occupied a bench fairly well secluded from surrounding lichen-grayed and yellowed headstones.

For the first time in a very long while Andrew was beginning to feel pleased with life.

But by now the fact had become confirmed that Sarah's father had been shot and killed in his own hallway after pistoling a British subaltern and another member of a Provost's detail come to arrest him. Also it had been confirmed that the career of that quietly courageous Patriot, Doctor Henry Clague, had terminated at the end of a hangman's rope.

For early October this day had been so pleasantly warm it encouraged Sarah to don a becoming pale-blue printed gown of fine challis which by the effective sunset's rays set off naturally curly but rather coarse golden-blonde hair.

They then discussed the note she'd received from Ellen describing the lack of intelligence following the death of her father. Lacking information of any sort she wrote, it now appeared likely, in the opinion of most responsible persons, that Captain

Timothy Hunter and his ship either had been overwhelmed by a hurricane or even more likely had been carried by some of the many pirates known to infest the Leeward Islands. Mrs. Hunter could offer no plausible alternatives to such grim possibilities. The Captain ever had been close-mouthed concerning business affairs.

Perceptive of his unhappiness, Sarah's rather large but well-formed hand closed over his. "So, Andrew, we've one thing in common. We both stand close to losing everything of material value."

A fever-thinned arm encircled her. "Oh, Sarah, Sarah! How right you are."

Since a majority of Salem's population now was occupied with preparing or consuming supper the maple- and elm-bordered streets were uncommonly quiet. In St. Peter's Churchyard he drew her closer was stimulated by that softness peculiar to a female's body. Suddenly the realization occurred that Sarah's figure wasn't at all like Amy's being more yielding and more fully rounded in the right places.

Presently she peered up into his gaunt, still pallid features. "Surely, my dear, by now you must have guessed how, well, how fond I—I've grown of you?"

"Aye and by the same token I have come to appreciate more and more of your warmth, no less than the patient care you've given me, your tenderness, your rare sweetness, lively humor and understanding." He laughed softly then stroked her hand. "Now isn't that a rare tribute? Might have made a poet, eh, what?"

"You are one, without being aware." She tilted her face upwards. "At any rate what you've just said is the finest compliment I have ever been paid."

That they should kiss not hard or long didn't seem strange in the least.

Once their mouths separated Sarah lowered her head laughing softly, "Dear me, Andrew, 'twould appear you are really recovering rapidly, so I'll confess this isn't the first time we've kissed."

"What?"

"While you were only half-conscious I discovered that a kiss on your cheek or forehead somehow appeared to ease your dementia." Color mounting, her hands tightened between his palms. "Once, dear Andrew, you strained upwards to return my caress so, despite all of Doctor Scott's warnings, I couldn't resist meeting your lips."

He chuckled, heaved an exaggerated sigh. "To think I wasn't fit to capitalize on such fortune! There's my bad luck again."

In sudden confusion they broke off, glancing upwards at an attenuated "V" of Canadian geese pursuing yet another leg of their long southward journey and creating wild music against the sounding board of the sky.

At length Andrew said, "Sarah, if matters stood differently I, well, d'you think we might consider a serious understanding?"

Slowly, she looked aside. "I understand, Andrew. At the moment we both are all at sea with no safe harbor, no sure future in sight." She drew slightly apart. "Besides, before we talk further, there's something I wish you'd clear up; for me it's rather important."

He faced her sunken eyes intent. "What in the world can you be talking about?"

Her gaze sought the church steeple. "Perhaps 'tis of no consequence but often in your delirium you kept pleading for the—for the—the love, and I gather, intimate caresses of someone named 'Amy.'"

"Amy!" The bench appeared to shift under him. "Amy? Aye. Amy."

"Who is Amy?"

"A young woman who befriended me when I landed in Marblehead a miserable, hunted fugitive. Amy proved kind and, well, understanding of my situation." Recollections of iridescent moments in the sail loft sent traces of color into his pale cheeks.

"Care to tell me more?"

"Only that Amy was a warm-hearted lady who, very like you, granted me kindness and understanding when I most stood in need of such." His hands tightened on hers. "However, my dear, all that lies forever buried in the past. Please let's not pursue the subject."

"You must be referring to Amy Orne?" There now was an edge hitherto absent to her voice.

"How did you know that?!"

"Tom Izard told me that, well, you once felt rather tenderly towards her, which I believe because in your delirium you so often called for her."

"Sometimes Tom talks too much. In any case, my sweet, that matter is over and done with and Amy is now a married woman."

CHAPTER 33 🙐

"A SPECIAL DUTY"

OF ALL THINGS when they returned, somewhat subdued, to Donnell Smith's place they discovered the tanner comfortably guzzling beer in his kitchen with none other than black-bearded barrel-chested Tom Izard. The moment he sighted Andrew and noticed the extent of his recovery he vented a string of delighted oaths and bear-hugged him so hard Sarah sharply warned him to desist.

Tom obeyed, smothered a beer-belch. "Well, Miz Hilton, must say you've helped my friend recover quicker than quick. Ever I get took with a misery I'll send for you straightaway."

Recollections of Izard's mention of Amy Orne allowed Sarah only a faint smile. "Thank you. I—I really must get back to my lodgings for supper." Flinging on her cloak she hurried off without a backward glance.

Once she'd disappeared Tom's manner changed. "Brought some news for you."

"Hope it's good. I've listened to about all the ill-tidings I can stand for a while."

"Wal, might call it good news; you feel sufficient hale enough to travel over to Beverly?"

"Maybe. Why?"

"Colonel Glover's there and in a fine foam over that there mutiny they've had aboard the *Hannah*."

"Mutiny?"

"Yep, broke out soon as her crew learned a Court of Admirality refused to condemn the *Unity* as a lawful prize so they stood to lose prize money for her capture."

"But why?"

"'Twas proved that, sure enough, she ain't British owned. Belongs to a feller name of John Longdon from somewhere up in the Hampshire Grants." Tom's expression hardened. "What makes matters worse is that the *Unity* first was taken by the goddam *Lively*."

"Well, I'll be damned!"

"When the *Hannah*'s men boarded they found she'd had a small prize crew out of the *Lively* aboard."

Andrew fingered his chin a moment. "I see. The Court's classed the *Unity* a recaptured American vessel. Is that it?"

"Yep. All hands are hoppin' mad."

Tom scratched at his big shaggy head. "They say Gen'ral Washington and his Marine Committee ruled, some time ago, recaptured vessels can't be condemned as lawful prizes provided 'tis proved the ship and cargo are American-owned."

After Smith had refilled all three earthenware mugs Andrew asked, "So then what happened?"

Tom Izard snorted so hard he blew a fleck of froth off his drink. "Mutineers wuz arrested and marched over to Cambridge under guard where a court-martial of some sort condemned 'em to floggin' and dishonorable discharge."

"Good God!" Andrew growled. "Now where will the Army find soldiers willing to serve in the new cruisers *Franklin, Hancock, Lee* and the rest?"

Donnell Smith blinked like a sleepy dog. "Damn' if I'd sign up. Is it fair to ask a feller to risk his neck and get only legal farts in exchange?"

Tom sipped the last of his ale. "Belay there, friend. You ain't heard the whole of it."

"What else?"

"Wal, by now ye should know, Southerner or not, this Gen'ral Washington's smarter than a den full of vixens with cubs. He commuted all sentences save for a couple of ringleaders and ordered that a sum of money is to be divided among the *Hannah's* company." The ex-gunner's gaze shifted. "Andy, this is where you come in."

"Me?"

"Yep. Colonel Glover's sent word ye're to get over to Beverly fastest you can. Seems like he's fittin' out the *Lee* for a crack ship; she was Tom Stevens' topsail schooner. Wants the best of everythin' for her. 'Tis claimed she's extra speedy, fairly new and well found. Glover wants you should look him up early tomorrow."

Deliberately Andrew sipped ale. "Why me?"

"Don't know too much about it, but heard tell he's rigging some sort of a fancy commission in yer name. Reckon he wants you for a special duty which I allow will be to command the *Lee's* guns and drill her gun crews."

When Andrew sat up in his chair a throbbing started in his fingertips, as always when deeply moved. Who ever would have guessed that that brief talk in Cambridge last summer should have stuck in John Glover's mind?

"Well," Tom commented. "I'd say 'tis too good a chance to miss, provided ye're strong enough to travel over yonder— Beverly ain't that far."

"Not so sure I could ride a horse but I'll go to Beverly if I have to hire a chaise."

Donnell Smith grunted while scratching at an armpit. "Don't fret yerself. I'll borry Jed Coffin's shay. No point in yer fallin' off and goin' back to bed." He grinned. "—Lest you aim to keep that pretty Hilton gal nursin' ye a while longer."

Tom chuckled. "Wouldn't blame him; Mistress Hilton's a rare, sweet and capable creature."

They talked on till the church clock boomed six sonorous notes. When Tom heaved himself erect his black head brushed fly-blown plaster ceiling built only six feet high to conserve heat during cold weather. "Allow I'd best make tracks back to Beverly and tell the Colonel you'll come see him tomorow." In the doorway he checked himself. "Oh, by the way, Andy, who d'you suppose has been appointed to be the *Franklin's* Lieutenant?"

"Stop funning. Who?"

"None other than our dear neighbor, Caleb Twisden. They say he's become the most fiery Patriot round Marblehead of late; really is working damn' hard and gettin' results."

The bottom seemed to drop out of Andrew's stomach but he only grunted, "In that case good luck to him."

Watching Izard drive up to Donnell Smith's place in a ramshackle chaise drawn by a rack-ribbed nag, Sarah Hilton suffered uneasy premonitions. Why? Following their return from the churchyard Andrew had made bold to put an arm about her and kiss her again in the hallway—yet all the same she sensed suppressed turmoil in him. Before long she sensed his malaise; it must be due to her having mentioned Amy Orne. Yes. That was it. During his illness she'd inferred that something perhaps not altogether creditable might have chanced between them. However, one comforting fact remained, the Orne girl, whatever she might have been, now was married to one Caleb Twisden, a lawyer residing in a community where marital infidelity, let alone divorce, never had been tolerated.

Just after Tom Izard helped his companion onto the chaise's seat he'd made a pretense of adjusting the nag's breeching strap, long enough to note how Sarah and Andrew were peering at each other as if they'd just met.

Once Tom slapped reins and the chaise had commenced to move Andrew waved to Mrs. Smith. "Please keep a bait of victuals warm for supper. Should be back by sundown." But he wasn't. The moment Colonel Glover spied Andrew's gaunt figure enter his quarters he strode forward smiling, broad brown hand extended.

"Fine to see you up and about again. Congratulations on your quick recovery, Serjeant, or should I say, 'Brevet-Lieutenant Hunter'?"

"'Brevet-Lieutenant'? What in God's name is that rank, sir?"

Glover chuckled. "Why 'tis but a temporary grade the Commander-in-Chief has devised for the benefit of gentlemen like you who are awaiting issuance of a regular commission. While it isn't the same as a commission it entitles you to the same pay, rights and responsibilities as a lieutenant in the Continental Army. Likely, you're the first of the breed in our Army's Navy."

A commission in the offing? The room swam so strangely about him Andrew for the moment feared a recurrence of fever.

Glover frowned. "Well, sir! You don't seem overimpressed. Colonel Knox and I have gone to considerable lengths to obtain the Marine Committee's consent for the creation of this stopgap grade."

Andrew stiffened to attention. "Sir, please believe I'm truly and immensely honored and taken aback you should pose so much confidence in a person of—er—unproved character."

"Needn't be. I'm told you did pretty well in Marblehead. You see, Hunter, although quite a few former British Regulars now hold commissions in the Continental Army practically no Royal Navy officers have turned their coats. Therefore the Naval Commissioners and I are reposing special confidence in your knowledge by posting you to the *Lee* but, alas, not as a Naval officer." He summoned a wry smile. "You will serve aboard her as an Army officer on detached duty from the 21st Regiment." He slammed one hand into its mate. "Why *won't* those nit-picking fellows in the Congress vote to create a regular Navy?" He answered himself. "I suspect they fear such a move would sound too much like an outright demand for independence."

"Sir, what of this ship I'm joining?" Andrew held his breath.

"The *Lee* is a tops'l schooner, belonged to a friend of mine, Tom Stevens of Marblehead. I can tell you, she's fast, well built and fairly new. If possible I'd like to see her become flagship for our infant flotilla."

A warm sensation pervaded Andrew. God above! What it meant not only to be enabled to use knowledge accumulated over the years.

What was Glover saying? "Now, because of that—er—trouble with the *Hannah*'s crew, I intend the *Lee* to be manned by a crew hand-picked from among seamen serving in my Regiment. Your captain will be John Manley from Marblehead, another old friend of mine. He's a first-rate mariner and a fighter from 'way back. Recently he's been commissioned captain in the Army so's he can command the *Lee*. My son Jack—John Glover, Junior, that is—will serve as her first lieutenant. Feel he's too young to hold a command of his own—needs more experience. You'll act as Second Lieutenant and Gunnery Officer. I expect Manley will depend heavily on you, trained cannoneers are as scarce along this coast as virgins on a waterfront. You'll supervise the *Lee*'s conversion with regard to the proper mounting of her guns. 'Twill also be up to you to select the proper site and protection for her shot lockers and magazine."

"How many guns, sir?"

Soaring hopes were dashed when Glover replied, "Oh, around a half-dozen or so."

Andrew blinked. "And of what will the main battery consist?"

Glover smiled over his use of the word "main." "Six 8-pounders. Not much weight, true enough, but sufficient for the purpose of this cruiser. Don't look so glum, Hunter, this is only the first step towards greater ends for, by God, if we survive, we intend to construct a real Navy.

"You will be given a fair supply of roundshot and issued enough gunpowder for this cruise, provided it ain't wasted." His hard gray-blue eyes fixed Andrew. "Inside of a week can you whip half-a-dozen gun crews into some degree of competence?"

"Yes, sir, provided you enlist a few experienced gunners of Tom Izard's sort."

"I'll see to it. The Marine Committee is expecting great things from the *Lee*."

"Great things?" Andrew struggled to conceal his dismay. What sublime temerity to send out a schooner displacing only 76 tons, armed with only six light guns and expect her to perform miracles. Hell's bells! She'd be forced to run before even the lightest regular man-of-war on the North America Station.

Glover's deep voice queried, "Well, Serjeant, do you accept the assignment and that—er—provisional commission?"

Andrew stiffened to attention as he had not since fleeing the King's Service. "Sir, I am more than honored to accept this brevet rank. To whom do I report and when?"

John Glover's smile came as a warm ray of sunshine. "From this place, Lieutenant Hunter, you will proceed immediately to my construction wharf where the *Lee* is being completed and report to Captain Manley. He will be expecting you and, incidentally, he's been informed concerning certain—er—facts about your past. Somehow, I feel you and John will get along well enough, with you doing most of the 'getting along.'"

"One request, sir?"

"What's that?"

"I'd like to have Thomas Izard enrolled as the *Lee*'s Master Gunner."

"Couldn't pick a better man. Being a Marbleheader I've known Tom since we both got switched by the same schoolmaster." Glover straightened shoulders under a neat, brass-buttoned and dark-blue tunic turned up with claret red cuffs and revers. "And now, on your way, Lieutenant."

Andrew saluted, about-faced, then sought Tom Izard. He found him, as expected, in the nearest grog shop. Briefly he described his talk with John Glover and spoke about the *Lee*'s complement.

The big 'Header's amber-tinted teeth glinted in the depths of his round and ragged black beard. "That shines, Andy. Oh, s'pose as I ought to address you as 'Mister' Hunter again."

"Only on shipboard, damn your eyes!"

"I'll be that tickled to serve guns under you again!"

Andrew stared then, laughing, wrung the other's horny hand.

Tom then unwound reins and slapped the somnolent nag's back so hard little puffs of dust arose when the vehicle started bumping and jolting over uneven brown cobbles towards Glover's rigging dock among horsemen, farm carts, drays and yokes of oxen dragging baulks of timber towards the waterfront.

Alighting among lumber piled alongside the *Lee*, Andrew said, "Tom, please explain to Miss Hilton why it's become impossible for me to return even long enough to collect my things— not that they amount to much. You can fetch 'em along when you return."

Tom looked his new superior hard in the face. "And what d'you expect me to say to Mistress Hilton?"

"Explain as best you can about how I've just been sort of commissioned and ordered for immediate duty. Present my sincerest apologies, Tom, and tell her I'll be over to see her first possible moment."

CHAPTER 34 🎗

AMBUSH

ON THE TWENTY-EIGHTH OF OCTOBER, 1775, in Beverly's crowded Inner Harbor, the topsail schooner *Lee*, 76 tons, set jibs and topsail then swung slowly, almost reluctantly it seemed, away from her moorings with Captain John Manley in command. Her first officer was young John Glover, Junior; folks agreed Jack deserved a heap of credit for having passed up command of a lesser vessel in order to gain experience aboard this smart new cruiser.

Then there was tall and still scrawny Brevet-Lieutenant Andrew Hunter. Normally he would have ranked as second officer but his commission still hadn't appeared. Of course no Britisher would recognize his brevet rank as valid.

Serving as the *Lee*'s Master Gunner was bandy-legged and black-haired Tom Izard. The rest of the new cruiser's complement numbered thirty-eight, every one sea-experienced privates or noncommissioned officers on detached duty from Glover's 21st Massachusetts. Many claimed to have served aboard privateers or swore they'd been impressed into some ship of the Royal Navy. Andrew soon suspected some of these must have told the truth since the conduct of gun drills increased in efficiency with astonishing rapidity.

While the *Lee* was standing down channel from her main gaff streamed an expertly contrived ensign sewn by patriotic ladies. It depicted a pointed green pine tree centered on a snow-white field; beneath it had been embroidered the pious motto: "In God We Trust." Throngs of people waved and cheered, a few salutes were fired from various half-finished batteries which scared clouds of sea-birds to wheel and flee, screaming, out to sea. Undoubtedly there would have been more salutes fired if gunpowder hadn't been so hard to come by.

Following the Captain's orders Andrew caused the three small guns comprising this schooner's starboard broadside to be run out, but the magazine being not even half-full, only a single 8-pounder was fired in acknowledgment. At length the *Lee* pointed her long bowsprit towards Bakers Island and the wide reaches of Massachusetts Bay.

When the shoreline had faded to a low-lying sandy blue-green streak and the cruiser had commenced to dip and roll smoothly, rhythmically, Andrew experienced a sense of exhilaration such as he'd not enjoyed in too long a time. He turned to Tom Izard, who, like the rest of the crew, was wearing worn and patched workaday garments—only Captain Manley and young Glover, Junior, wore uniform coats of plain, dark-blue serge. Grinning, Andrew remarked, "Damned if we don't look like a parcel of rag pickers."

Off Salem Neck a strong slant of wind increased the schooner's speed until her wake fairly boiled and water hissed crisply along her beam. Grins widened on many faces.

No doubt now the *Lee* probably could outrun any vessel save the fast sloops-of-war such as the *Lively*, the *Merlin* and the *Nautilus*.

Here and there the wide, lead-hued expanse of Massachusetts Bay was dotted by groups of small, rocky and generally uninhabited islands.

In response to Manley's hail lookouts reported but a single flash of canvas low on the horizon and apparently making for Boston.

How glorious felt Andrew once more to tread a real man-of-war's deck, to direct a battery of carriage cannon—even a handful of 8-pounders—quite a comedown from those twenty guns he'd commanded aboard H.M.S. *Lively*.

Once land had all but faded from sight Captain Manley exchanged his uniform coat for a pea jacket and a warm and comfortable brown scarf. Gladly Jack Glover followed suit, he was growing chilled to the bone.

Great flocks of sea ducks, scoters, coots and eiders sped by low over the water, but dark snarls of black ducks, mallards and widgeons skimmed by well above the schooner's straining topsail.

During the next few days of the *Lee*'s maiden cruise no possible quarry was sighted but on several occasions ominous clusters of sails—beyond a doubt those of British men-of-war—were sighted. Invariably, John Manley altered course, painfully conscious that even a single, weak sloop-of-war could blow the *Lee* out of water long before her battery of 8-pounders, even double-charged, could range a target accurately at over 1,000 yards' distance. At short range, however, the schooner's armament when charged with grapeshot and properly handled could cause serious damage. Time and again a chase had to be abandoned as soon as Manley had made sure the strange vessel carried too much weight of metal to risk closing with, which nowise helped to raise the crew's spirits.

As a rule the schooner patrolled the coast fairly well in-shore from Salem, beyond Marblehead and Gloucester and out towards the very tip of Cape Ann—a maneuver calculated to intercept vessels following a course usually favored by ships bound for Boston from Halifax or Europe.

Usually towards nightfall the Army's cruiser would heave to in the lee of any one of these many groups of rocky and generally uninhabited treeless little islands.

Andrew kept his guns ready to be run out on a moment's warning. Lookouts blessed by extra-strong vision were sent aloft to maintain a chilly vigil on the crosstrees.

Six days after clearing Beverly dawn was becoming more than a presentiment when the foretop lookout shouted down, "Ahoy, below! Two sails to the nor'-nor'-east."

Manley roused from the locker on which he'd been sleeping, cupped hands and yelled up, "How do they steer?"

"Seem to be standing straight into the bay, sir!"

At a nod from the Captain a red-headed, freckled younker commenced to swing a rattle. Men tumbled out of tiny bunks and, mostly barefoot, swarmed on deck with Izard in the lead spouting orders.

Andrew, heart pounding, ran up the fore-ratlines then clung monkey-like to the shrouds leveling a spyglass. Canvas was set even before the dripping anchor had been catted. Everyone looked happy as foxes in a hen house on sighting what promised to be pretty much what they had been waiting for. From the direction of Cape Ann and about a mile off-shore a big brigantine was plowing along in company with a more distant and smaller black-painted brig. Both were under easy canvas and following a course parallel to the coast. Excitement swelled when spyglasses revealed that neither vessel appeared to be armed with anything heavier than a few "murthering pieces" or swivel guns mounted along their rails.

A freshening off-shore breeze set yards and booms to creaking louder, heeled the *Lee* well over to starboard as, gathering speed, she raced from her ambush behind the island.

Now Andrew's seemingly endless gun drills under varying conditions proved of value. Swaying to increasing motion gunners ran to their stations to snatch up loading implements from racks. Others tailed onto training tackles; gunport lids banged up; matches were ignited from a pot of coals always kept smoldering in the galley, and attached to linstocks. The Pine Tree Flag was hoisted, snapping briskly, to the main gaff; the schooner's canvas strained under a steadily increasing wind until, like a greyhound closing in on brace of hares, the *Lee* sped to intercept the quarry.

As morning brightened and the range diminished, spirits rose higher aboard the little commerce raider for, beyond any shadow of doubt, yonder bluff-bowed brigantine, although flying a British Naval red ensign, was a sluggish, round-sided merchantman undoubtedly chartered as a supply ship or possibly as a troop transport.

Tom Izard grunted, "She's as slow as a boy going to Sunday school on a fine morning."

The other vessel, half a mile farther off-shore, was a brig named *Saucy*—if Jack Glover had read her name right through his glass. She was proving to be a rather better sailer than her consort and her master must be more alert for the moment he sighted the schooner's Pine Tree Flag standing out from the lee of a rocky little island, he at once ordered signal flags sent up but received no acknowledgment from the larger ship.

On order, the *Lee*'s gun captains commenced to blow on their matches. Andrew remained in a torment of anxiety for, to conserve powder, there'd never been target firing aboard the *Lee*.

Finally, the larger vessel hoisted a signal whereupon the black-painted brig spread more sail and steered for the open bay. Perhaps because her bottom was foul, one could see long streamers of green weed wavering along her beam—she moved so slowly John Manley calculated it shouldn't take long to overhaul her. Ruddy bulldog's features gone redder than ever Captain Manley returned attention to the brown-painted brigantine, now wallowing along not three hundred yards away; a regular floating barn if ever there was one.

"Mister Hunter!" he directed. "Fire a shot across their bow but take care you don't hull her. Looks like she'll surrender in a hurry so no need risk damaging her cargo."

Horatio Bullock, the ex-merchantman's short and enormously fat captain, was still only half-awake thanks to a rousing night-long bout with kill-devil rum punch, so he ignored the schooner's warning shot, raising a brief waterspout some fifty yards in advance of his bowsprit. But when Andrew Hunter personally aimed his Number Two gun and splintered the brigantine's weatherbeaten figurehead Bullock struck his flag in a hurry and ordered his cumbersome craft into the wind, so presently the *Lee*'s company were able to read the brigantine's name: *Nancy of Liverpool*—a name which wouldn't quickly be forgotten either by the Continental Army or British forces.

Manley, who'd climbed higher into the main shrouds, was hailed by Jack Glover. "Sir, sir! What about the brig? Shan't we give chase? We can overhaul her, easy."

The Captain's attention however was fixed upon two sets of

large and snowy topsails now lifting higher above the horizon. Dangerously they resembled those of British sloops-of-war.

Harshly, Manley called down, "Mister Glover, best recall thet adage about 'a bird in hand.' We'll be doing well enough to fetch so plump a capon as this into Gloucester."

The moment Captain Manley watched the brigantine's ensign hauled down and having satisfied himself that her high bulwarks indeed were not pierced for cannon he positioned the *Nancy* to windward.

A veteran at this sort of thing Manley sensed time indeed was of the essence so while his longboat was being lowered and manned he named young Glover prize captain and Brevet-Lieutenant Andrew Hunter second-in-command, with orders to head for Gloucester at the best speed this ungainly prize could manage.

Body yielding rhythmically to the pull of the longboat's oars, Andrew probed his memory. Nancy? NANCY? Where had he heard that name before? Then he remembered. A while back Ellen had made mention of a ship by that name in a letter delivered by the late Doctor Clague. What was her importance? Why had she been mentioned? Try as he might he simply couldn't recall the connection.

Due to the almost incredible ease of this capture John Manley commenced to experience serious misgivings as to the value of her cargo. Surely, if Admiral Graves and General Howe had been anticipating the arrival of essential supplies they'd never have failed to dispatch at least one or two regular men-of-war to escort this store ship into Boston. Or was that the mission of those still-distant sloops-of-war?

The sea had commenced gradually to make up before the longboat, crammed with wildly excited boarders, reached the brigantine wallowing with slack sails slatting. Judging by the scaling of her paint work and the grayness of her tarred standing rigging Andrew decided the *Nancy* indeed must have been at sea for a long while.

Meantime, her consort, the black brig sailing considerably farther out to sea had all but disappeared.

Young Jack Glover, Acting Prize Master, didn't much resemble his father except in coloring. He was taller and broader in the shoulder yet all the same he'd inherited much of his parent's common sense and was displaying an innate air of command.

That the *Nancy* indeed was but a chartered and overaged merchantman became inescapable the moment Andrew peered over her rail and viewed the shabbily dressed and hangdog crew waiting with hands uplifted, only a few pikes and cutlasses lying scattered about their bare feet. Beyond doubt these unsavory fellows were waterfront scrapings: shifty-eyed stupid-appearing foreigners, or sullen, impressed Englishmen or Colonials. Nimbly, Andrew followed Jack Glover up a ladder lowered from the prize's waist.

A few men snickered when, purely out of habit, Andrew saluted the quarterdeck and a grossly fat figure who, scarlet-faced, wigless, sleep-tousled and wearing a half-buttoned Naval officer's jacket, appeared, swaying, at its break and groggily demanded to know what was going on.

In a clear, carrying voice Jack Glover demanded and at once received surrender of what proved to be His Britannic Majesty's ordnance vessel *Nancy*, commanded by one Horatio Bullock whose name certainly fitted him for the fellow had no perceptible neck and his belly and rump were simply enormous. His waistcoat and breeches were stained by food, liquor and tobacco juice.

Andrew's hopes plummeted. Surely not even the most hardened embezzler at the Admiralty ever would have dispatched, unescorted, a cargo of any value across the Atlantic in a hulk like this.

Following a brief pause the Prize Master then ordered all the brigantine's hands to assemble before the mainmast and drop concealed weapons of any description. Sluggishly the *Nancy* rocked on long low swells till Jack Glover ordered sails trimmed and ordered a local man to take the brigantine's helm and shape a course for Gloucester—no easy task since the low-lying coastline barely was visible as a dim blue outline.

Scarcely had the *Lee* and her prize gotten underway when a fast fishing skiff scudded parallel to the victor's counter long enough for her owner to yell, "Get the Hell out of here."

"Why?" bellowed Manley.

"We've sighted that goddam *Lively,* the *Nautilus* and another sloop-o'-war steerin' this way."

John Manley, destined along with John Paul Jones to achieve fame, bellowed thanks. The fisherman's skipper then diverted attention to the prize.

"Hi, there! Clap on every stitch this damn' hooker kin carry. Make for Gloucester, Beverly or Salem fastest you kin!"

Jack Glover, Andrew and the balance of the prize crew, long since having satisfied themselves no one aboard the *Nancy* had any intention of offering resistance, ordered more canvas set.

Hasty inspection of the prize's papers revealed that the *Nancy* had cleared the supply docks of Woolwich Arsenal nearly two months earlier. Also, it had been purely by chance that, a few days earlier, she'd joined company with the little black brig.

Of sullen, pudding-faced Captain Bullock, Andrew demanded, a fist cocked, "Speak up! What is the cargo of that brig you were cruising with?"

Bullock's blubbery lips created flatulent sounds. "Don't know anything beyond she's called the *Saucy* and is loaded to her gunnels with gunpowder which I hope will blow you blasted Rebels to perdition!"

The moment he heard the word "gunpowder" Andrew hailed the *Lee,* made bold to suggest to Manley that he order the cruiser in pursuit.

"Gunpowder! Oh, God!" groaned Manley. "Too bad, but goddammit I daren't chase with those bulldogs so close by. We'll keep course for Gloucester."

He was wise for by now the *Saucy* was well away and standing straight towards ominous clumps of topsails every moment showing up in sharper detail.

The morning brightened cold and crisp with a rising wind luckily quartering out of the southeast and driving cruiser and prize past the murderous ledges of Norman's Woe Reef, then by Ten Pound Island and Rocky Neck and into the entrance of Gloucester Harbor. Reducing sail, the *Lee* and her prize then hove to in Freshwater Cove in the lee of the harbor's western shore and under cover of batteries thrown up on Dolliver's Neck. Only then did Captain Manley board the prize and order Captain

Bullock to produce his manifest and all invoices and bills of lading.

He'd glanced at them only a moment before he sharply beckoned Andrew. "What do you make of these?"

On scanning the first few bills of lading Captain Timothy Hunter's eldest son felt as if the *Nancy* had been struck by a tidal wave. Lips tightening, he read aloud: "Says here they have aboard 2,000 muskets with bayonets and other fittings, 100,000 fine musket flints, 62,000 musket balls, 20,000 roundshot and nearly 500 bomb carcases and that's not all!"

Manley demanded sharply, "Sure you're reading right?"

"Yes, sir."

"What else?"

"Listed are 8,000 fuses and 20 barrels of gunpowder."

"God above!" Manley burst out. "Anything else?"

"Why, sir, the list says there are in the holds ten 9-inch siege mortars and iron bases for such." Supreme excitement broke through his tone. "Then, sir, there's a brass siege mortar of 13 inches bore! Can't believe it!"

How utterly incredible the Admiralty should dispatch so priceless a cargo across the Atlantic *unescorted!* He could scarcely credit his eyesight when he read on. Manley and Jack Glover also looked happily incredulous.

"Also listed are 7,000 of roundshot cast to fit cannon of 8 and 12 pounds."

As if to heap riches on riches—provided these manifests proved accurate—down in the foul-smelling hold reposed barrels and carriages for a dozen 8-pound field guns and nearly as many cannon barrels forged to fire 12-pound shot!

Thought Andrew, Colonel Knox himself couldn't have indented for a choicer selection of munitions.

Only after initial jubilation had commenced to subside did Andrew perceive that this otherwise invaluable cargo included *no* cannon of heavy calibre or regular siege guns capable of battering British fortifications and naval anchorages.

CHAPTER 35 ✖

GUNS FROM THE SEA

BECAUSE CAPTAIN MANLEY had sent his longboat scudding ahead into Gloucester to spread news both of the *Nancy's* capture and of the presence of three British men-of-war not far offshore preparations of varying descriptions immediately were initiated.

Church bells clanged, drums rattled and banged and trumpets shrilly and discordantly kept on sounding "Assembly" whereupon militiamen quit whatever they were doing, hurried to arm themselves and ran to predetermined concentration points. Gallopers were sent pounding frosty roads over to Beverly, Ipswich, Marblehead, Wenham, Salem and lesser communities, ordering all armed men immediately to rally on Gloucester.

Colonel Glover at once dispatched to Cambridge a slim young ensign astride "Starlight," Captain Henry Pike's prize-winning racehorse, riding hell-for-leather to convey the great news to General Washington's headquarters.

Andrew personally instructed the dispatch rider to apprise Colonel Knox of this incredible windfall. Above most other staff officers that giant would appreciate what might become possible once the *Nancy's* cargo had been safely conveyed beyond reach of the sloops-of-war.

A series of small and generally unfinished batteries thrown up on Stage Head, Duncan's Point and Watch House Point guarding the approaches to Gloucester Harbor were manned helter-skelter. Miserably scant supplies of shot and powder were distributed to best advantage.

Townspeople, man, woman and child, cheered themselves hoarse once the prize, followed by her captor, reduced canvas and slowly entered Freshwater Cove where the *Lee* dropped anchor but the *Nancy,* on Manley's orders, kept on until she could be tied up to the Long Wharf thus obviating the necessity of hoisting out her cargo then ferrying it ashore, a dangerous and time-consuming procedure.

To Andrew it proved a pleasant sight to see the Pine Tree Flag fluttering above the *Nancy's* red ensign, yet somehow it struck him that another design might better express a spirit so rapidly spreading throughout the sadly disorganized, poverty-stricken Colonies challenging the world's mightiest military and naval power.

Once Andrew had finished reading the *Nancy's* manifest to a group of red-faced, often breathless senior officers and local leaders, realization came that enough armament was about to become available to equip quite a few of those ill-armed regiments in the vicinity of Cambridge. One item stuck, burr-like, in Andrew's mind: some 30,000 roundshot of weights suitable for field artillery reportedly now were being hoisted out of the prize's hold.

Andrew caught Manley's attention, held up a hand. "Sir, does the manifest state the weight of the roundshot?"

Manley frowned, sought and found the page he needed. "Well, Mister Hunter, says here most of the shot have been cast to fit 8- or 12-pound cannons. Also, there are some 10,000 balls cast to fit 4- or 6-pound cannon."

Again a shout arose, not so loud as the first because most present couldn't comprehend the enormous significance of such a seemingly trivial detail.

Captain Manley's deep voice continued. "'Tis already verified there are quite a few iron mortar beds aboard." His glance circled the tense faces about him. "Also, there is a brass mortar listed as weighing 10,000 pounds though I scarce can credit the existence of a piece of so vast a calibre. About the rest of these artillery supplies I reckon Lieutenant Hunter can tell what's especially useful."

Andrew, still gaunt features taut, queried, "Aside from that big mortar, sir, you've just mentioned are there any 24- or 32-pounders, siege guns?"

Manley shook his blue-black, bullet-shaped head, bristly and close-cropped since he was wearing no wig.

A runny-nosed captain of militia demanded, "What you bitchin' about, Hunter? Ain't you made a extra fine haul?"

"Sir," Andrew explained, "Colonel Knox will be gravely disappointed. His greatest need right now is ordnance pieces of long range."

Jack Glover put in, "Life's full of disappointments. Mister Hunter, why can't you be happy with what we've taken? Haven't we seized sufficient field cannon to equip a train of field artillery?"

"What does such amount to?" demanded a scholarly-appearing individual whose face resembled a weathered spine wearing square-framed spectacles. "Who's to command it and what's this here train supposed to amount to?"

For a moment Manley fingered an unshaven jaw. "Guess Henry Knox will be its Colonel; may be made a general before long. I know 'cause I helped him plan a train. He'll rate in his command a lieutenant-colonel, eight captains, nine captain-lieutenants, eight first and seventeen second lieutenants." He paused, peered about the *Nancy's* stuffy little captain's cabin. "Also a adjutant, a quartermaster, a surgeon and his mate, a commissary, twenty-six serjeants and corporals and fifty-two bombadeers forty-nine gunners and field music plus some two hundred-and-sixty matrosses, but likely this here table of organization will have to be altered to suit conditions."

Manley turned to Andrew. "What d'you call siege guns such as Knox keeps hollerin' for?"

"Aside from mortars, sir, he needs cannon to fire 24- to 32-pound shot, or other calibres useful at long ranges."

"'Long range'?" someone asked. "What d'you mean by that?"

"Say from Roxbury or Dorchester Heights into Boston, or to any of the Fleet's regular anchorages."

Jubilation became somewhat muted when it became known that the *Saucy* had escaped laden with gunpowder.

Colonel John Glover, intercepted on his return from a council-of-war convened in Cambridge, galloped into town enormously elated over the *Nancy*'s easy capture. All the same, he got right down to brass tacks, warned the celebrating and semi-drunken local authorities, military and civilian, "This is all fine and dandy, but it's our responsibility to get these munitions overland to Cambridge fastest possible way. Moment Lord Howe learns of this capture he's bound to risk everything to recapture supplies he needs 'most bad as us."

It was not surprising therefore that within thirty-five hours, through frenzied efforts of relays of volunteers, the *Nancy*'s holds were emptied and her cargo loaded into carts, wains and wagons of all descriptions brought in from the countryside. These then had been started towards Cambridge under heavy guard from Glover's 21st Regiment. Garments flapping under a chill wind, the convoy set out to cover the thirty-odd miles to Cambridge.

At irregular intervals more detachments of armed men joined in an increasingly riotous triumphal procession to escort the munitions beyond possible reach of the enemy.

No one had worked more efficiently, more tirelessly than John Glover, together with Mustermaster-General Colonel Stephen Moylan and Andrew Hunter—no longer brevet but a full lieutenant now that his commission had arrived. It was he who exercised special care that cannon barrels were properly cushioned with sailcloth between piles of straw or salt water grass. Also he saw to it that no gun carriage suffered damage.

Personally, Glover and he had supervised the operation of cranes used in hoisting the precious, ponderous tubes out of the brigantine's hold and lowered onto conveyances.

To his immense satisfaction H.M.S. *Lively*'s former gunnery officer made note that all these captured pieces were in good condition, also many were new judging by the King's intricate cypher freshly engraved atop.

What had captured special attention of workers and onlookers alike was the arrival of that huge brass mortar in Knox's artillery park just outside of Cambridge.

General Israel Putnam, still an able and dependable veteran of the last of the French and Indian Wars, clambered up on the mortar and, somewhat unsteadily, splashed a mug of rum down its gaping throat shouting, "If Tom Mifflin will consent to stand godfather, I hereby christen this here beautiful monster 'Congress'!"

Not until three days after delivery of the *Nancy*'s cargo did Andrew find opportunity to ride over to Salem and seek Donnell Smith's home. Although on the verge of collapse through fatigue the new lieutenant nonetheless felt pulses quicken the moment he started up the brick walk leading to Deborah Palfrey's former home but the expression on Dorcas's face when she opened the door snuffed out the flame of high spirits like a sudden gust of wind.

"Sarah? Is she here, is she well?"

"No, Andy. She left here two days before the *Nancy* was captured. She's left a little letter fer ye." Dorcas waddled indoors, reappeared fingering a small, neatly folded square of paper.

Hands shaking so violently he found trouble in focusing his gaze, Andrew read:

My Dearest Heart,

You are constantly in my Thoughts and Prayers, especially now that you have sailed to fight your former Comrades. God forbid you ever should be taken Prisoner by them!

My Father indeed is dead and all his Properties have been Confiscated by the Royal Authorities—so am now an object of Charity, so to speak.

I trust you will be able to read this before long.
Tomorrow I depart to spend a brief Visit with your Mother
and Ellen whilst I attempt to Decide where my Small
Talents as a Doctor's Assistant can most usefully be
employed. God bless and protect you, Darling One!

Yours till the End of Time,
Sarah

Dorcas waited until he'd finished reading and some of the stunned look had faded from his features. Then, somewhat archly she remarked, "By the way, Andy, 'twas only yesterday a kind of pretty young lady whose hair hung down in pretty ringlets stopped by here and asked for you. She sounded mighty keen to discover what had become of you."

"What did this lady look like?" Even before Dorcas had half-finished describing large, sherry-hued eyes, curly reddish-brown hair and heart-shaped features he knew who had inquired his whereabouts.

"She looked mighty respectable—quietly dressed. 'Llowed she was Mrs. Caleb Twisden."

Amy! Why should she have come looking for him here in Salem? Then he recalled that Deborah Palfrey had been Amy's cousin. Caleb, he'd heard, presently was at sea, serving as Lieutenant in the Army's cruiser *Franklin*. It was lucky perhaps that Sarah Hilton had departed before Amy's appearance.

What he needed to know but didn't dare to ask soon came out when Dorcas Smith confided she'd noticed Mrs. Twisden's pregnancy from the moment she'd sighted her.

"Aye, Mister Hunter. I hazard she'd be 'bout four or five months along."

"She talked as if it was about something important?"

"Aye. Mrs. Twisden sounded *that* upset when I 'llowed as how, only three days earlier you had sailed in the *Lee* to fight the Royal Tyrant. I invited her in to take a dish of tea—which like you know is mighty skurce nowadays—but polite as pie she refused. All she told me was that her home lay in Marblehead but said she couldn't make plans till her husband's ship returns. You know how 'tis with seafarin' people?"

"Ought to. Did Mrs. Twisden act easy-like?"

"No. Seemed more like she'd a load on her mind. Come along, Andy. I'll fix you a mess of vittles. You look like a starvin' scarecrow."

Chapter 36 🪻

GUNS FROM THE NANCY

Soon after a galloper on a badly blown mount arrived to spread news that the *Nancy's* cargo had been discharged and was on its way to safety within the Continental Army's lines. There were plenty of exhibitions of sober patriotism and more of bibulous enthusiasm. The town buzzed like a bee tree knocked down by a honey-hungry bear.

Soldiers, seamen, clerks, mechanics, farmers and civilians alike came flocking in from camps and the countryside eager to view the spoils with their own eyes.

Troops belonging to undisciplined units promptly quit drilling or abandoned duties to line the Gloucester-Menotomy highroad and fairly yell their heads off.

Only General Washington's personal bodyguard and a few other dependable regiments such as the 5th Rhode Island and Glover's 21st lined Menotomy Street under fixed bayonets. They kept in position even if forced now and then to use musket butts to drive back drunken or overexcited civilians. Most obstreperous in the crowd were Morgan's Riflemen, easily recognizable by their knee-length hunting shirts. Lord! What an unearthly racket these frontiersmen created, raising war cries, scalp yells and the like.

The British High Command soon had become aware of their ordnance ship's capture so, veteran American officers reasoned, the enemy would make *some* attempt either to recapture the *Nancy*'s cargo or at least to deny the Continental forces the use of it.

Not far in advance of the first wagons, mighty stiff and dignified rode Mustermaster-General Colonel Stephen Moylan; Colonel Glover with his favorite son, Jack. After them trotted square-jawed Captain John Manley whose appearance raised resounding cheers—especially from the Marblehead Regiment.

On the *Lee*'s Captain's near side rode Andrew Hunter happily conscious of a new tricorn adorned by a large cockade of black ribbon hastily stitched together by Dorcas Smith and, even more, of a hastily fitted dark-blue tunic showing the light-blue ribbon-knot of a lieutenant fluttering on its left shoulder.

Once the supply train's advance guard hove into sight Ellen Hunter, teetering on a crowded granite door stoop, joined in the cheering and hand clapping.

Ellen's eyes overflowed the moment she glimpsed Brother's tall figure bumping astride a ribby gray—he'd never been a good horseman—riding about a horse's length behind Captain Manley.

Sarah, joyfully brandishing a scarf, wept unashamedly. Andrew had returned gaunt but seemingly unharmed. By dozens hats, caps and bonnets sailed into the air.

"Andrew! Andrew!" Sarah screamed jumping up and down and brandishing a green kerchief in spirals.

Andrew abandoned his impassive manner long enough to lower his tricorn in her direction. Sarah, by God! Wasn't she a delight to look at? Before replacing his hat he blew a kiss in her general direction and promptly felt ashamed. What would subordinates make of so flagrant a display of emotion?

As John Glover's staff rode by looking very pleased with themselves Sarah for the first time in her life yielded to overwhelming impulse. She ran off the stoop then used elbows to drive her supple figure through the crowd until she could reach Andrew's mount and clasp his dusty booted leg. Casting military dignity to the cool November wind the new Lieutenant bent in his saddle, flung an arm about Sarah Hilton and to delighted yells from the crowd lifted her clear of the ground. He bussed her twice before setting her down.

Someone in the crowd, undoubtedly a seafarer, shouted, "Hi, there, Lootenant! Don't abandon so pretty a prize so nimble-like!"

Andrew laughed, bent to kiss Sarah once again. "There now. You've destroyed my image as a heartless disciplinarian. Tell Mother I'll come home first moment I can escape Headquarters. It may be difficult so she's not to fret if I don't show up right away."

Throngs of boys kept prancing around the carts; many scrambled onto the creaking vehicles to straddle or pat iron, brass or bronze cannon barrels. A few exuberant females made bold to run forward and kiss some ugly black muzzles.

Seemingly endless cheers arose while sweating farm horses hauled the spoils towards the Army's first real artillery park, a hayfield Colonel Knox recently had ordered cleared of tents, shacks and other encumbrances.

That impressively tall and reserved Virginian named George Washington, together with his staff, waited quietly on restive mounts near the center of this frosty, muddy and deeply rutted area. Nearby loomed the huge rotund figures of General Israel Putnam, that much admired veteran, and of Henry Knox. The latter remained a colonel although supposedly he was overdue to become a general officer any day.

Gravely, the Commander-in-Chief raised his hat in acknowledgment of John Glover's brisk salute and those of his companions.

Presently the first carts carrying the *Nancy's* plunder appeared, axles whining and groaning, and were directed to various stations. Munitions mostly were being transported in ordinary farm carts drawn by plow horses but the great mortar and similar heavy loads had been loaded onto wains hauled by spans of slow-footed brown-and-white oxen.

On the outskirts of the crowd Sarah hastily wiped wetness from her eyes. "Oh, Ellen, isn't this almost too good to be true?"

"Well, 'tis true, thank the Lord! Now we'd best hurry back to duty. Sick men can't celebrate till we tell them what's going on!"

"Of course, but tell me how—how soon do you imagine Andrew might—well, might reach home?"

"No telling," Ellen replied tonelessly. "I've just begun to learn that waging a war takes up a sight more time on paper than in the actual marching and fighting. Somehow, I suspect Brother, being so knowledgeable about artillery, will be in demand round Headquarters."

CHAPTER 37 🎝

MISSION OF THE FIRST IMPORTANCE

DURING THE TIME required to classify and allot the *Nancy's* cargo to best advantage the weather turned much colder; skim ice formed on puddles and firewood was in such short supply that many troops quit drilling and sought all-too-rapidly diminishing woods in the immediate vicinity. In Boston the shortage of fuel had become so grave that unoccupied houses were being pulled down; picket fences long since had vanished.

Troops from the more southerly Colonies such as Colonel Daniel Morgan's Regiment of Riflemen recruited in Virginia and Pennsylvania, lacking warm garments, commenced to suffer from the cold. Many Rangers wore ordinary woolen blankets draped around them, Indian-like. Desertions from among them increased despite brutal punishment when a runaway was apprehended.

No one was busier than stocky Major David Mason who, since early autumn, had been serving as Adjutant on Colonel Henry Knox's staff. Knox's problems and responsibilities had become all but overwhelming now that the Commander-in-Chief had named this huge Bostonian to be Chief of the Continental Army's pitiful train of artillery. Long since, Knox should have received his General's commission but someone in Congress—still a badly confused and uncertain body—had neglected to forward it.

Major David Mason right away recognized Lieutenant Andrew Hunter as one of the few officers who understood how captured guns of various sizes, shot and ammunition should be allotted to best advantage. Tacit regard between the two increased daily.

Major David Mason who hailed from nearby Wenham was only in his early thirties but, being nearly bald, appeared much older. His little round eyes were widely spaced and of so dark a brown that in a poor light they appeared black. His brows were heavy, dark and all but formed a single line above a short, thick and straight nose. Although not badly scarred, he obviously must have suffered smallpox at an earlier date.

In an odd way David Mason reminded Andrew of his father, so long unreported everyone was sure he and his ship must have been lost with all hands—God alone knew when, where or how. This major had the same chunky build as Pa—being broad in the shoulder, solid without being clumsy and supported on rather short but well-formed legs. Why these two got along so well might have been difficult to explain save they both came from near Boston and were descended from long-established New England families—for whatever that might be worth. Both understood ordnance and the uses of artillery as did few others.

Having allotted the last of so many 6-pound roundshot and carcases to such and such a battery and 8- and 12-pound shot to others, Andrew, towards dusk, suggested that Mason take in a hot toddy in "Fair View" and led the way through light, sifting snow over half-frozen fields in the direction of the Charles.

They halted. In the distance a tumult characterized by screechings and Indian-like whoopings peculiar to Colonel Daniel Morgan's all but uncontrollable Virginia and Pennsylvania Rangers. To identify their encampment it proved easy since numerous rough wigwams fashioned from bark or odd bits and pieces of cloth of any description loomed like miniature pyramids amid European-designed tents or rough wooden shacks.

That something unusual was going on was inescapable;

Rangers, mostly garbed in knee-length wamus shirts of linen, dowlas or deerskin, worn under Dutch blanket coats, were waving long-barreled rifles, flourishing war hatchets, long skinning knives and yowling as they milled about a tall wooden tripod of halberts to which had been tied a lean, brown-skinned and yellow-haired fellow who, despite freezing wind, had been stripped to the waist. Nearby, a burly serjeant holding a heavy stock whip tucked under one arm was rolling up his sleeves. Although an independent and quarrelsome lot these intractable fellows had proved invaluable; they could shoot with incredible accuracy, even picking off British officers at ranges of well over 300 yards after which they'd brag loudly, outrageously and interminably. Compared to them, champion warriors like Achilles and Hector, were rank amateurs when it came to the business of killing a fellow-man.

David Mason halted. "Don't want to interfere, Hunter, but that brawl looks dangerous."

Once he neared the prisoner Andrew noted he'd rather an Indian-like countenance with dark skin, and high cheekbones flecked with smallpox pits. Save for coarse and long dark-yellow hair he might indeed have passed for a Redskin.

"Hold on, fellers," he was pleading. "Didn't try nawthin' till that little wench, after I give her some shillings, swore she were sixteen, spread her legs and told me to go ahead. So I shoved it to her, balls and all, but then she squealed like a piglet and the Provost's men came a-runnin' and claimed I was rapin' a child."

The frontiersman glanced desperately about at this punishment detail from the 5th Rhode Island Regiment until he realized Rangers in the background were beginning to unsheath big-bladed knives.

"I sway 'fore God," the prisoner shouted, "that sly vixen really vowed she were above sixteen."

"Shut up, you goddam savage!" A rake-thin serjeant-major in charge of the punishment detail smacked Jake Razors' face then beckoned forward the man with the whip.

Livid curses arose from an ever-increasing, milling mob of riflemen. Here and there the cold glint of steel became increasingly visible when more Rangers wearing hunting shirts of buckskin or heavy linen came running up, yelling like jaybirds being picked alive.

Abruptly David Mason snapped, "Come along, Hunter, something's got to be done and fast. Fellow may be guilty as Judas but we can't tolerate more disorder; discipline in this Army's already rotten enough."

He strode up to a noncommissioned officer—a serjeant-major by his shoulder knot who seemed to be in command of the punishment detail—then shoved aside the soldier carrying the coiled stock whip.

Andrew had to admire the quiet way Major Mason took charge of the situation. He appeared visibly to grow in stature.

"Precisely what are the charges against this prisoner?"

"Rape of a very young gal, suh." The Provost's serjeant-major had been around Cambridge long enough to recognize the importance of that single silver epaulette and the dark green sash slanting across Mason's tunic front. Jesus! This officer was serving on Gen'ral Washington's own staff! What really counted with him was knowledge that the Commander-in-Chief was no blue-nosed New Englander but a true Virginian, like most of Dan Morgan's Rifle Regiment.

A shout rang in from the background of the shifting mob of Rangers. "You whup Jake and we'll have yer skelps smoke-dryin' 'fore ye know it!"

Little clouds of snow commenced to fall, veiled the scene.

Dark eyes snapping, Mason demanded, "Can you swear this man has been properly tried and convicted by a regularly convened court-martial?"

The Serjeant-Major's gaze shifted beyond a veil of breath vapor. "Naw, suh, cain't hardly do such. What Razors got was a drumhead trial 'fore the Provost's captain."

"Fine, any witnesses, any convincing evidence against this man?"

"Naw, suh, 'twas only a case of her word agin hisn."

Mason strode over to confront the still-struggling, half-naked prisoner dangling under the tripod. "What's your name? You a Virginian?" He felt a measure of encouragement when the man panted his answer.

"Jake Razors, sir. I ain't no Southron. Me and quite some others here are Vermonters."

"Vermonters?"

"Yep. Us was so keen to get in some licks 'gainst the Redcoats we joined Colonel Morgan's war party whilst they tarried overnight near Great Barrin'ton. Honest, sir, I didn't go for to do the lass no harm; 'twas only when she took my two shillin's she cozened me 'bout her age."

Andrew, anxious to back up the staff officer, shoved into a small cleared space surrounding the tripod. "Razors, whereabouts in Vermont you hail from?" Silently he wondered how this fellow had come by so unusual a patronym.

"Why, sir, purty nigh to Pawlet which lies near straight acrost Lake Champlain from Fort Ti' in N'York."

At that David Mason reacted quickly. "You know that country well?"

"Orter, sir," the other cried, slanting jet eyes wide with appeal. "Been trappin', fightin', and tradin' round them parts since I growed knee-high to a crawdad."

Mason's gaze bored into the eyes of the prisoner whose long mane of yellow hair had begun to stir under an increasingly icy wind like the war-shredded banner of some veteran regiment.

In silent admiration Andrew wondered why his friend's attitude had undergone a noticeable change.

The crowd quieted a little when Mason turned to the Serjeant-Major in charge of the punishment detail, said, "I am Major David Mason, aide to General Washington. By virtue of my rank I will now take custody of this prisoner to make sure real justice is done. The Commanding General is becoming very strict in matters of this sort that the accused shall be assured a fair trail."

The chunky Major turned to survey leathery fierce faces ringing him in. "Don't doubt, my friends, that if Razors is found guilty he will be hanged. Turn him loose!"

Surprisingly the Serjeant-Major did just that and a cheer arose from among the snow-sprinkled Rangers.

As Jake Razors was being untied Major Mason cocked a brow at Andrew and, frowning, stroked a large and solid chin. "Officially I presume he's been dishonorably discharged from Morgan's Rangers so he's now unattached and is our responsibility in a way."

"'Our'?"

"Yes. From something I just heard this fellow might prove useful. Don't ask me now. I'll describe the project later on.

"Don't know as much about paperwork as I should, so I'll have to take this matter up with Colonel Knox once I'm assigned to his staff."

Jake, hugging rags about him, said through chattering teeth, "Believe me, gents, I'll gladly die tryin' to thank you for savin' me that whippin'."

Andrew arched a brow. "Did you *really* think that girl was sixteen years old?"

Razors shrugged, looked away, "Like I said, sir, didn't know what to believe. Never could count extry good 'specially when I come across a tasty piece of baggage, but I *did* figger she *was* as growed up as she claimed."

Before Captain Timothy Hunter's home Andrew held Jake back suspecting Mother mightn't take kindly to the presence of a wild-looking, dirty and, most probably, verminous stranger. All the same he then motioned Razors inside. "Come along. We'll find you a hot dish and something warm to wear."

The frontiersman's strong but irregular and tobacco-stained teeth showed in a wide grin framed in a blond three-day beard. "Well, sir, thanks a-plenty. Food I could do with—ain't et nothin' in a day's time but I won't need clothin' on account of my mate, Paul Thebaud is keepin' Jenny, my rifle, a Dutch blanket coat, my possibles bag and the rest o' my gear in camp. He 'listed with Morgan same time as me and don't fancy this peaceful kind o' war round here no more'n me. We're set to light out for where *real* fightin's goin' on."

Heavy-set Major Mason fixed on the frontiersman a long and penetrating look. "If you mean what you said about being grateful, you won't desert. We can understand why you Rangers can't take to this European sort of warfare but I guess you can prove mighty useful along some frontier—especially in Vermont and around Ticonderoga where you know the lay of the land."

"Yes, sir. That's a promise. Me and Paul will come first thing tomorrow morning ready for duty any kind you need so long as you can use prime marksmen."

Mason hesitated, glanced at Andrew. "If it's all right with you,

Hunter, suppose Razors and his mate report here?" He lowered his voice. "By then I should know more about what's in the wind."

Colonel Knox's new aide returned his attention to Razors shivering in the doorway. "You aware that no scalping is tolerated by our Army?"

"Yes, sir. But it shore limits a feller's ambitions."

Andrew demanded, "Which camp is yours?"

By the snowy afternoon's fading light Jake's Indian-like cheekbones and the slight tilt of his eyes appeared more pronounced.

"Dunno its name, sir, but I sure know where it lies."

Mason inquired quietly, "How well d'you know the Green Mountains and the country around lower Lake Champlain, Ticonderoga and Fort George?"

"Like I said, sir, I was borned, brought up and first bedded thereabouts. Might you be headin' that way?"

"Too early to say. Very well. Come in and eat some hot vittles. Be here tomorrow morning by seven o'clock sharp," Andrew instructed. "If it so happens I'm not here wait till I show up. Can I rely on you?"

"Yes, sir. Sure as sun rises tomorrow me and Paul will turn up armed, provisioned and rarin' to go."

After consuming biscuits and a steaming bowl of clam chowder the Ranger departed, his scuffed and stained moosehide shoepacs creating no sound on the snow-covered brick walk.

Once David Mason had departed, explaining he was due to attend an important grand council to be held at General Headquarters, Andrew sought the kitchen where he found Ellen alone and looking a bit flushed. Obviously she'd been eavesdropping and was feeling guilty.

She asked in soft tones, "Who was that handsome officer friend?"

"Major David Mason. He's from Wenham."

"Why didn't you invite him to supper?"

"He'd an important staff meeting to attend. I'll invite him to supper tomorrow if Mamma don't object."

"Ma's ailing but it'll be all right."

"Anyhow, Dave Mason's just told me he's been transferred from Headquarters for special duty as an aide to Colonel Knox, our new Chief of Artillery. And believe it or not, he thinks I'm about to be promoted to Captain and posted to Knox's staff."

Ellen's darkish V-shaped face lit. She flung arms about his neck and kissed his cheek. "Glory! High time your work is recognized."

Andrew was hanging his snow-flecked cloak to an elkhorn coat rack in the hall when Sarah appeared from above clad in her Sunday "go-to-meeting" gown and wearing a fetching yellow bow tied about her short, very white neck, an attribute which in the past had attracted compliments from British officers of all ages.

Since Mrs. Hunter apparently had a streaming bad cold only three sat about the kitchen table illuminated by a single candle.

Sarah dabbed full and dark-red lips with a ridiculously small lace-trimmed handkerchief then, eyes drawing golden tints in the candlelight, cried, "Oh, Andrew, I—we've been counting the minutes for your coming."

"Would have appeared sooner," he explained, gaze on Sarah, "but for some fierce arguments over division of the *Nancy*'s cargo. Every commanding officer claimed the lion's share."

Ellen, under the pretext of carrying supper to her mother, disappeared upstairs and tactfully lingered with the invalid. The moment she'd departed Andrew hugged Sarah, treated her to such ardent kisses the girl gasped before crushing fragrant lips against his bristly mouth.

After a few moments she stepped back. "Oh, Andrew, you look so much better than I've ever seen you since the day before that dreadful battle on Breed's Hill." Eyes shining, she moved closer. "Dearest, you'll never understand how very much, how deeply I love and admire you."

"Don't wager too much on that," he laughed. "I feel—towards you—" Many lingering and moist kisses terminated conversation.

As autumnal darkness descended street noises diminished due to deepening snow's muffling hoofbeats, wheels and the tread of passers-by.

Coals in the kitchen fireplace had commenced to grow gray around their edges before Sarah murmured breathlessly, "Think I'd better repair above before, well—" she flushed scarlet, hurriedly dabbed lustrous strands of hair back into place, "—before inclinations get the better of me." She smiled, "You'll remain in Cambridge a while longer, won't you?"

"'Man proposes, God disposes.' I've no notion what my orders may be till I speak to Major Mason. I'm sure he'll have news affecting both of us."

While smoothing skirt and blouse Sarah commented, "Papa used to claim 'tis a very good idea for a responsible man to keep a journal, a diary or whatever such is called. He did, right up until the—the day of his death. It often proved useful in establishing facts and dates. I hope you will do so too, Andrew, so you can tell me exactly what you were doing when, where and how. Perhaps future historians may find it useful to read an account of what really happened and not to have to depend on hearsay or old recollections no matter how the teller recalls what he honestly *thinks* happened long ago. Will you do that?"

"Yes, darling, but you'll probably be the only one who'll ever read it." He stepped back, heart beating a tattoo. Lordy! Physical contact with Sarah was proving almost as deliciously maddening as that with Amy Orne.

At the foot of the stairs they again embraced briefly before, managing full skirts, Sarah hurried aloft, with difficulty shielding a candle before her.

Andrew was preparing to put the cat out for the night when an insistent rapping commenced on the front door. On raising a lamp to identify the caller he realized that a real blizzard was starting—whirling snow was coming down so hard Major David Mason had to brush a liberal coating of flakes from a triple cape before entering and bringing with him an aura of cold air. Smiling, the aide hung up his cape.

"Fix me a hot drink, my friend, and one for yourself."

"Sure, but why are you grinning like a horse collar?"

"Because you'd better brace yourself for glorious good news!"

Only through a great effort was Andrew able to control himself. God above! Recently, good news had been scarcer than crowing hens.

Once he'd chunked up the kitchen fire and flames had begun to create golden patterns on the ceiling did Andrew snap, "Damn it, man, what's up? You're cruel to keep me in suspense."

Mason extended hands to the fire, said over his shoulder, "Jot

307

this date down in your memory, Andrew, my lad; as of tomorrow you have been transferred from the 21st and assigned to duty on Colonel Knox's staff. Moreover, you lucky oaf, you've been commissioned a captain of artillery!"

"D'you mean John Glover actually is willing to transfer me?"

Mason's balding head inclined. "Matter came up before a meeting of the General Staff. Seems Colonel Knox, after his interview with you some time ago, directed searching inquiries into your qualifications. He must have found them so valuable he's bound and determined to use 'em, come what may. He dwelt on the capable part you played during the evaluation and division of the *Nancy*'s cargo."

Only vaguely he heard Mason say, "John Glover, of course, created an almighty row before agreeing to your transfer and gave in only after the Commander-in-Chief himself pointed out that officers possessing your special training and knowledge are mighty scarce. He added that Colonel Knox, having been ordered on a mission of supreme importance, felt your capabilities could be more usefully employed by him than in the mere outfitting of gunboats. Should have heard Glover bellow over that! But Knox remained steadfast and General Washington backed him up."

David Mason, after swallowing a gulp of rum laced with sugar and scalding water, coughed explosively. "It was most unfortunate, the Chief of Artillery pointed out in that smooth way of his, that, although the *Nancy*'s cargo had proved otherwise invaluable, she'd not been transporting siege guns."

Mason continued, "'Tis the general opinion that although lacking formal military education, Henry Knox is a natural-born organizer and general if ever there was one. Nathanael Greene promises to be another. During my brief service I've never observed a calmer or more persuasive staff officer. What Knox doesn't know, theoretically at least, concerning ordnance, the proper service of cannon and supplies required wouldn't fill a nutshell.

"The lid really blew off when 'twas announced plans are being made to transport those heavy guns Knox requires from Fort Ticonderoga."

Andrew stared, drink poised, "Ticonderoga! Why, don't that

fort lie somewhere way up to Hell-and-gone in the Province of New York?"

"Yes. Something like three hundred and fifty miles from here to there. Anyway, we've been ordered there to fetch 'em here, one way or other."

"When do we start?"

"Colonel Knox plans to leave tomorrow or the day after at the latest."

"What! With cold weather coming on?"

"That's just what General Lee and plenty of others have pointed out. They claim such an expedition just isn't possible in mid-winter."

"How, they ask, is heavy artillery, some pieces weighing hundred of pounds, to be dragged over steep mountains lacking bridges or even rough roads through thinly settled country infested by hostile Indians without the help of trained military engineers?"

Once rum and the heat of the fire had commenced to take effect Mason shrugged, loosened his collar and shook his head. "Between ourselves, I agree 'tis a harebrained scheme at best and doomed to failure—save for one thing. Until now Henry Knox has proved he knows what he's about. They tell me Washington's been planning such a project for a good while. Since our Army lacks siege guns he's determined Colonel Knox's staff will procure some, come what may.

"In any case, tomorrow, you will be relieved from the 21st to Colonel Knox's staff and promoted to the rank of Captain in the Regiment of the Continental Artillery."

Beads of sweat glistened on Andrew's forehead. "David," said he, "Colonel Knox is expecting too much of me. Probably, I'll prove incompetent."

While the blizzard rattled windowpanes, Mason said gravely, "You won't, and I'm coming along to help see that you don't." He raised an earthenware mug. "To your health and success, Captain Hunter!"

PART IV

Guns from the Land

CHAPTER 38 🎕

TOWARDS NEW YORK CITY

To UTILIZE THE handsome brass-and-copper pen case Sarah Hilton had presented on the eve of his departure from Cambridge on November 14, 1775, to make daily entries in his journal proved unexpectedly difficult. Although well schooled in the writing of official reports and in addition enjoying a natural facility with his pen, Andrew soon discovered his chief trouble lay in deciding which happenings were of sufficient value to be recorded. Conditions being what they were, following a long day's ride a bone-tired man had little inclination to record personal impressions. Andrew reported only noteworthy facts.

For example, he made no effort to record sensations he'd experienced on parting from his mother, Ellen—and Sarah because a messenger had ridden up to "Fair View" summoning him to join Colonel Knox's party at once so they'd only time for the briefest of farewells.

Ellen Hunter remained outwardly unemotional—only a faint quivering of lips betrayed anguish over this, another departure and perhaps a final one. Long a sea captain's daughter by now she'd learned how to dissimulate convincingly. Save for suspiciously full eyes Ellen counterfeited a complete lack of emotion even while bestowing a sewing kit complete with a blob of beeswax, needles, thread, buttons and patches of cloth of various sizes and colors.

Once Sarah and Andrew momentarily were left alone they stepped into the library where she'd made him the compliment of a small diary.

Since his family and others were looking on Andrew was able only once to kiss Sarah almost fiercely and whisper, "Don't fret, my darling, I'll be back before long."

Colonel Knox, astride what resembled a dray horse—few animals were capable of supporting his huge weight—gathered his reins. At his elbow rode his red-haired younger brother William, solidly built but by no means equaling his elder's dimensions. Also there were a few aides including square-jawed Major David Mason.

Andrew Hunter clambered ungracefully onto a bony saddle horse led up for his use. Among the escort he was pleased to sight Jake Razors and his saturnine, brown-bearded friend, Paul Thebaud. Riding near the short column's rear they slumped in their saddles, long rifles slung slanting diagonally across their backs.

Gravely, the Colonel raised his hat towards the ladies huddled in the door stoop then wheeled his mount and arm-signaled the little cavalcade to move out in the direction of the road to Marlboro, New Haven and eventually to the City of New York—still struggling to reach parity in population and importance with Philadelphia, largest city in the revolting Colonies.

That same night in a tavern in Marlboro, Captain Hunter blew on frost-stiffened fingers and prepared to write in his new diary. Although he wasn't aware of it this would be the last entry for several days but was descriptive of the party's start on its nine-day journey.

The general commanding in New York made Knox and his people quite comfortable—alcoholically and with female companionship. He also offered advice since Henry Knox was deeply concerned on how best to solve multiple problems that must confront him along the route to far-off Lake Champlain and Fort Ticonderoga.

On the evening of November 28th in a chilly little bedroom in Albany Andrew sat on his hands till they warmed sufficiently to permit writing:

Nov. 28, 1775

> *Bitterly cold here save for the warmth of Major-General Philip Schuyler's Welcome and that of the Inhabitants. Albany is somewhat larger than most of us had imagined. This Town looks and is prosperous. Many of its buildings show Dutch influences.*
>
> *So unremitting is General Knox's haste we just now have received Orders to set out at dawn tomorrow for Stillwater, Saratoga, Glen's Falls then on to Fort George which lies at the northern tip of a Lake by the same name.*
>
> *Jake Razors says despite depth of snow this Road is well used and not too bad as most in the Parts.*
>
> *Nevertheless we will have some forty-odd miles to cover so should gain Fort George in about two days time always Provided the Weather don't worsen again.*
>
> *Arrived yesterday in Albany despite severe cold only because our Mounts bear up well thanks to good care and plenty of corn to eat.*
>
> *In my humble opinion Gen. P. Schuyler appears a General Officer of the First Rank. He and Colonel Knox have got on famously from the start. Gen. S. is doing all within his Power to speed our departure for Fort George where he hopes to join us ere long.*

Nov. 30, 1775

> *Arriv'd Ft. George at dusk. Found the place already so Overcrowded we officers including Col. K., have been forced to find Accommodation in farmhouses built close to the Fort. The enlisted men are sheltering in barns where hay and bonfires keep them fairly warm.*

Even though a fire of sorts blazed in a smallish fireplace framed with blue-and-white Dutch tiles the room remained so cold Andrew was forced frequently to warm fingers beneath armpits. Finally he gave up and went below into the sitting room where his attention at once was drawn to the handsome figure of one John André, a young British major and staff officer. Amusingly, he told how he'd been captured a month earlier in Fort Chambly by General Richard Montgomery's troops on their advance towards Quebec. He now was on his way to New York for exchange.

Despite his situation, Major André, dapper in well-cut scarlet regimentals, proved so witty and genteel he commanded Colonel Knox's attention and sympathy, especially after the Britisher's servant had circulated small glasses of arrack, a strong but palatable drink, from Major André's traveling liquor cabinet. Swiftly, effectively, this good-looking man gained the attention of his enemies—especially that of Colonel Knox who, having cast loose brass clasps securing a voluminous gray watch cloak, lingered before the fire glass in hand.

Nobody present could have guessed that the next time these two met would be some years later: General Henry Knox as a member of a court-martial which, albeit regretfully, had to order death by hanging for this same gracious Major André, caught out of uniform while entering into treasonable negotiations with Major-General Benedict Arnold, then commanding highly strategic fortifications in and around West Point on the Hudson River.

Later Andrew retired and wrote:

DEC 5, 1775

Today Razors and Thebaud informed the staff we should Arrive below Fort Ticonderoga by tomorrow's Sunset! Everyone is pleased and Surprized over the Prospeckt of attaining our Goal so speedily despite freezing weather and all manner of hinderances. However, no one can decide whether our Expedition, ordered to enter rugged Wildernesses at mid-winter, is not pure folly.

Fort Ticonderoga 'tis said lies indeed Extremely well-sited on Heights commanding the Junction of Lake George with Lake Champlain. Here, the Waters run up from the South towards the Northwards, a fact of which I and many others have not been aware. Alas, a series of

*Exceeding Furious Rapids connecting these two Lakes
renders necessary land transportation over a short but
difficult "portage."*

*Am all of a Froth with impatience to observe
personally the Condition of these Pieces which I have been
informed have suffered Years of Neglect.*

DECEMBER YE 7TH, 1775

*Today I accompanied Col. K. his Brother, Major
Mason and other gunnery officers in making a rough tally of
Cannons, Mortars and Howitzers of almost every Weight
and Calibre stacked without order or plan in brick bays
supporting the gun platforms on the Fort's South-East and
South-Western Bastions. Tomorrow am ordered to survey
and Determine the State of pieces, especially Siege Guns to
decide how many are flawed or worn out.*

*David Mason meantime will address his Attention to
the State of Caissons, Gun Carriages and Beds for Mortars.*

*Col. K. remains all a-fire to start this hodge-podge Train
of Artillery on a fearful Journey over scantily populated
Country, across swift Rivers through dense Forests, over
high ridges and tall Mountains.*

*Today Colonel K. has directed my friend, Razors now a
Serjeant, to select a corps of Rangers to scout around and
protect our flanks, also to bring in forage and game. Jake
will be in command and also termed "Chief Scout." This
step has been taken because the Col. has received word
parties of hostile Indians and Tories are eager to attack
strays or careless parties of our People. I say "People"
because the vast Majority are not Soldiers at all—not even
Militia—only patriotickally minded civilians giving to our
Cause the best they have of Property and of themselves.*

*Tomorrow I shall present for the Colonel's inspection a
list of Pieces William his Brother, Dave Mason and I have
determined to be sound and of the useful Weight for our
purpose. Much depends on how great a supply of shot can
be found to fit our Selections since none can be had
elsewhere.*

317

CHAPTER 39 ❦

DEPARTURE INTO
WILDERNESS

ALTHOUGH THE TEMPERATURE in this smoke-filled wigwam, fashioned of elm bark strips, hovered a degree or two above freezing Chief of Scouts Razors was feeling more contented with life than when he'd last slept with Nellie Noisy Bluejay. Also pleased was Paul Thebaud, the bandy-legged half-Dutch and half-Mohegan, Jake's sworn blood-brother since the time the pair of them one daybreak two years ago had surprised a marauding band of Nipmucks sleeping off a drunken carouse. They'd been selling inexperienced settlers land the Redskins didn't own. Between them they'd lifted five scalps.

For the moment Jake's attention was directed on using a razor-sharp skinning knife to trim fingernails grown almost as long as those of Mohawks who allowed such to grow into talons able to tear out some enemy's eyes or rip his skin into gory ribbons.

"Wal, now, Paul, what's yer thinkin'?" Gapped leather thrums swayed on Razors' buckskin leggings when, employing a heel, he shoved log ends towards the center of a fire, over which pemmican, along with a potful of elk marrow bones, was cooking.

"My Brother, lacking but two men I'll bet this here expedition will wind up no better'n frozen wolf bait."

"Meanin' who?" Jake inquired as if he didn't know.

A cloudlet of rank gray smoke drifted away from Paul's red clay pipe. "Our Cunnel and Gen'ral Schuyler. Never did hear or see a pair of men, let alone officers, half so smart, far-seein' and so damn' near tireless."

Razors spat, "Hope ye're right, my Brother, but still I don't fancy our chances. Durin' that two-day cast you and Tim Berkeley made nor'west o' the fort see any sign worthy of note?"

The half-breed's oily head inclined under its lynx-skin cap. "Yep and no."

"That ain't no answer."

"Mebbe so, but I chanced on a band of friendly Agawams a while back. They 'llowed as how news of our intended march ain't spread far as yet but when them English-lovin' Mohawk sachems hear what's up we'd best think real good and act sharp else there'll be plenty of plain and fancy killin' goin' on afore long." From a gourd dipper the half-breed swallowed a big gulp of hot pemmican stew and belched so hard his breath went whirling clear across the wigwam.

"Anythin' else?"

"Wal, over Shoreham way, 'bout five mile from here, I came across a plump and likely-lookin' young squaw cabined up with a stringy old buck." Thebaud leered. "She were nigh as purty as Nellie Noisy Bluejay."

Jake shook his head. "Doubt it. Anyhow, right now there ain't no time to tumble a squaw—purty or not. Notice anything else?"

"Yesterday me and Tim Berkeley cut the tracks of a little band of Indians and white men circlin' to the northward o' here and workin' this way. Funny thing, some o' them whites didn't walk like no woods people, feet in line, they marched like reg'lar soldiers else I'd ha' come home and told ye. I'd hazard they're a band of British deserters and some stray Injuns out for easy pickin's."

"How many was they?"

"Only round a dozen, no more; not 'nough to raise a real ruckus if they're really actin' on their own."

"Let's hope so," Jake said pulling moccasined feet under him.

"Soon's we've stuffed our guts we'll go inform Cap'n Hunter. In a way 'tis lucky the most of our number are frontier-trained milishy but we ain't got not near enough to protect the line o' march. Good thing the Cunnel's hirin' so many locals who should know this neck o' the woods. There'll be others like 'em hired further on; should be familiar with the lay of the land thereabouts. Good-will on the part of locals and their oxes and horses are about our only thin hope of haulin' them damn' cannons any distance."

Thebaud elevated a furry brow. "What you hear from the Vermont side?"

"Only a mighty few folks are settled over. They're skeered stiff of British and Injun attacks and are makin' tracks for Ticonderoga fastest they kin. Cunnel's playin' up to such plenty, promises good pay—twelve shillin' a day for every team of sound hosses or a span o' sturdy oxes. Gen'ral Schuyler's agents also are out in the backwoods offerin' fancy prices for sturdy wagons, sledges and sleighs fit to carry heavy loads acrost rough country."

The two huddled closer over the fire, hiked a blanket higher over heads and shoulders.

"Tell me, honest, Jake, what d'you figger our chances are of fetchin' them damn' great heavy brutes o' iron down to Albany, let alone to Boston?" Thebaud spat a brown arc of tobacco juice. Briefly it sizzled among the coals.

"About the same chance as findin' a virgin in a whorehouse. What you think?"

"About the same. From what I hear from Cap'n Andy the train will have to cover no better'n three hundret miles across the Taconic Mountains, then there are the Berkshire Hills with never a real road or bridge to help anyone acrost. This time o' year most fords will be choked with ice but worse—what happens if a thaw sets in when we've got acrost lakes, ponds or rivers? If such happens our pickaxes and crowbars will get wore out widenin' Injun trails, or else the Cunnel's got to find a easier path, even if it takes more time. B' grabs, things would go easier if the Cunnel wasn't in such a goddam tearin' hurry."

"Wonder why he is?"

"Reckon that's between him, God and Gen'ral Washin'ton. You and me and other timber beasts will make out, but I'm sure wonderin' what's going to happen to them milishy and reg'lar soljers and officers used to comfort round Headquarters."

When somebody scratched at the wigwam's entrance both leaped up, rifles ready, but lowered them once the caller proved to be Major Mason, squarish face gone gray-pink with cold. Heavy black brows, almost merging, were whitened by frost.

Mason said, "Jake, Colonel wants you should come up to the fort right away—Thebaud, too." Before backing out the engineer officer held hands above the fire a moment then tightening a scarlet-and-gray-striped muffler which, knotted under his chin, held a battered three-cornered hat in place.

"Hell," Jake grunted slinging on gear, "sounds like them high-falutin' people in Command feel like mebbe they're strayin' out o' their depth. Be that so I wouldn't wager a clipped shillin' how far this crazy expedition is goin' to travel, 'specially comes a thaw which in these parts is possible at this time o' year, believe me or not. That happens, you'll see good guns sinkin' under the ice quick, like beavers when someone slaps water with a paddle. Yep, for my money, come spring, foxes and wolves for miles round are goin' to git fat and there'll be a mort of scalps smoke-dryin' in wigwams."

Thebaud finished strapping on knife and tomahawk over a dingy brown Dutch blanket coat. "Wal, Brother, 'ppears to me like you and me had best talk serious-like with the Cunnel and Gen'ral Schuyler. What say you?"

"As I see it, everythin' depends on how many people livin' round here feel like us about Rebellion. For another thing, who knows for sure that Tories, from Major Skene on down, ain't this minute raisin' Loyalist milishy and talkin' Redskin sachems into sendin' out war parties?"

When the Rangers silently entered the fort's General Council chamber big fires were glowing at either end; it was pleasantly warm but reeking of wet fur and bodies too long unwashed. Among so many uniforms and generally tarnished gold lace Jake felt like a mud hen alighting among a flock of mallard drakes.

As usual, Colonel Knox, despite his booming but not unpleasant voice, remained polite; he even arose behind his table desk when his Chief of Scouts and Thebaud were shoved forward. As usual he held his crippled left hand behind him. "You're mighty welcome here, boys! Right now we need help like a damned soul wants ice water."

The former bookseller's round, rubicund features broke into that broad and genuine smile which had won him a host of friends and many a serious argument. His gaze circulated over this motley company crowding the Council Chamber. Henry Knox was called fussy over his appearance under all conditions so his epaulettes of gold braid fairly sparkled amid this gathering largely composed of local civilians wearing drab but warm garments. The handful of militia officers present rather pathetically were attempting to appear soldierly despite stained, patched and faded uniforms of various hues. Most numerous of all was a group of shaggy, greasy-looking officers of the Green Mountain Boys. These were squatting Indian-like on their heels in the background and making little or no attempt to conceal contempt for so much dangerously showy braid, brass, buttons and polish.

"By now," Knox boomed, "you must have realized that time is of the essence for the success of our expedition. Therefore, first thing tomorrow, General Schuyler, Captain Hunter, Major Mason, I and a few others will inspect all ordnance deposited here and finally select pieces most useful to serve our needs." He turned, indicated tall and wiry General Schuyler whose sallow features were dominated by a long, thin beak of a nose. "The General here long since has dispatched advance parties along the route we mean to take to contract for or, if necessary, commandeer horses, oxen and vehicles and above all men willing and able to help move our train across and out of this confounded wilderness.

"Gentlemen," his resonant voice made the Council Chamber resound, "I want you to remember one all-important fact; I don't intend we should attempt to conduct this march by following European-style rules." His wide-set and slightly bulbous blue-gray eyes roved about. "Orders are to be obeyed promptly and to the letter, but I want everybody no matter what his rank to address soldiers and, more important, civilians as friends and equals. Always hearken to advice from locals although you don't necessarily have to heed it. All of us must do all we can to keep our men and beasts well fed and healthy and to seek no greater consideration for ourselves than our men enjoy. That's all I have to say right now."

CHAPTER 40 ❧

SELECTIONS

BY THE WAVERING light of a box lantern lighting some junior British officer's former snug quarters in Fort Ticonderoga, Captain Andrew Hunter swallowed another draught of steaming Medford rum and in so doing lost enough of weariness to permit making another sadly delayed entry in his journal. For the first time in days he was feeling comfortably warm. Snow melting off heavy, country-made knee boots had started forming dark puddles over the floor of light-blue tiles, the work of expert French builders.

A good thing David Mason, sharing these quarters, was fast asleep and making noises like a circular saw biting into a knot of wood. After sharpening his quill's point he dipped into the leaden ink bottle and wrote:

> *God send I don't suffer many more Days like this! Since*
> *Daybreak, Colonel Knox, his Brother William, Majors Mason*
> *and Lamb and I have been tramping the length and breadth*

*of this great Fort with great care and, from various points of
view surveying Pieces as are deemed fit for use. General
Schuyler had already ordered Guns to be more or less
collected according to weight of Shot.*

*Wm. Knox devoted his attention chiefly to the supply of
Projectiles suitable for each Type selected whilst I again
inspected the condition of each Piece with the greatest of
care.*

*Already Gen. Schuyler has plotted, only roughly to be
sure, what seems the best and most Practicable Route from
this Lake down to Fort George and thence to Glen's Falls,
Saratoga and Stillwater to Albany where, probably, an
attempt will be made to ferry our Train of Artillery across
the Hudson; how or when only God knows. In fact Gen. S.
and Col. K. have planned our Travels all the way to
Claverack, a village lying close by the Border to
Massachusetts where, holding New Yorker Commission, Gen.
Schuyler's Authority ceases.*

*I hear that Col. K. and his Aides now are busy
considering possible Routes across the Taconic Hills and
then the Berkshire Mountains. It is in conquering these
Heights we anticipate our greatest Difficulties and Dangers.
God send no Hostile forces, British, Tory, or Indian, will
attack to compound our troubles!*

Silently Andrew prayed for sufficient energy to write in more
detail and send love to his mother, Ellen and Sarah. Next he felt
to wondering what might have chanced aboard the *Franklin* during her cruise off the entrances to the St. Lawrence. Could a
nonprofessional seafaring man like Caleb Twisden quickly learn
his duties and otherwise measure up to a naval officer's responsibilities? Most likely Caleb would make good or even better.
After all, Amy's husband always had proved capable, shrewd and
inflexible when it came to serious matters. Besides, as Jonathan
Izard once had remarked, young Twisden possessed a rare ability to ignore unimportant details in order to concentrate on essentials.

What of Amy? Unseeing, he stared into coals gradually paling in the fireplace. By now, she, poor girl, must be advanced in pregnancy. Time and again he pondered whether it lay within Amy's nature ever to admit to Caleb that the child she was carrying was not his. Lord. How often nowadays he suffered pangs of remorse. Imagine it. The baby would be of his own blood; that of a very old and reputable New England family.

In the far distance a wolf set up eerie, prolonged howls immediately answered from various directions; some sounded disconcertingly near. Chafing badly chapped and grimy hands, Andrew crossed to a small diaper-leaded window to peer down on the moonlit *place d'armes* and survey a group of field-gun barrels he'd tentatively selected. They lay ranged on the snow like so many dark and lethal logs.

Long before reaching Ticonderoga he'd decided three factors must dictate his selections: first, a tube under consideration must be unflawed in any way; second, its calibre must be limited to projectiles for which a liberal supply of fit ammunition was available. Not by half had he anticipated the wide variety of ordnance found lying, hit or miss, in those brick bays beneath the fort's massive parapets. Everything from small coehorns and howitzers to ponderous siege guns and a weird variety of mortars had been found, but Henry Knox remained chiefly interested in possible siege pieces. Aside from cannon cast in England, field guns ranging from 1-pounder to ponderous 18-pounders were of French, Spanish or even Dutch origin.

The ideal weight of shot for field artillery, so desperately needed for the Continental Army, Knox stated, ran from 6 to 8 to 12 pounds. Fortunately, Will Knox, the Colonel's long-jawed and generally taciturn younger brother, had mastered the art of correctly estimating almost on sight the weight of piled solid balls, shell and charges of grape and canister and bar shot.

Major Mason, too, was accomplished but in a different direction in that he quickly was able to select sound or suitable traveling gun carriages and loading equipment. Together with Major John Lamb, Andrew Hunter squatted on his heels, brushed away snow and with meticulous care examined each brass, bronze or iron tube considered for transportation.

Most of the cannon were decorated with handsomely carved apes', roosters' or lions' heads in addition to coats-of-arms or Royal cyphers. Firmly, he condemned a tube on detecting of rusting, serious pitting or the existence of hairline cracks. Quite frequently trunnions, indispensable adjuncts which supported the gun on its carriage, were found to be cracked, flawed or missing.

To Andrew's no great surprise his portly Colonel's principal interest remained centered on cannon of siege calibres. Also he very closely examined chunky mortars cast from iron, brass or bronze designed to lob heavy shells clear over an enemy's highest defenses and so wreak havoc behind them. What gave inspectors food for thought lay in the fact that such mortars were extremely heavy, not readily transportable.

That evening, Colonel Henry Knox for the last time summoned principal officers to the drafty Grand Council Room where plenty of toddies, long on Jamaica rum, sugar, nutmeg and cloves, but rather short on boiling water, stood waiting. In his great voice the former bookseller boomed, "Gentlemen! I think no one rightly can claim any of us have been idle." When he extended a foot towards the fireplace's brass fireguard Andrew noticed a sizable dark hole worn in the sole of its boot.

Knox turned to his brother William, now seated at a camp table set up comfortably close to the roaring fireplace. "Bill, you've completed a tally of ordnance selected for transportation?"

"Sure, Henry."

"Then read it out loud."

Briefly William Knox knuckled smoke-reddened eyes then spoke in measured tones. "Listed here are a total of 59 pieces of artillery of all descriptions. Of these 43 are iron fieldpieces including a few cast in bronze. There are also mortars; 8 of them brass—considering their size such mortars are goddamn weighty."

"How heavy?" someone inquired.

"Bronze ones round 150 pounds each but iron mortars average closer to 300 pounds which I think is too much considering what lies ahead of us."

When he took a deep swallow General Schuyler's thin and reddish beak of a nose protruded over the brim of his pewter mug. "Any notion what will be the total weight of this ordnance?"

William Knox looked uncomfortable. "Can't vouch for it, sir, but I allow the total weight of this lot can't run short of 120,000 pounds. If I'm any judge 'twill be closer to 150,000 pounds."

On the morrow Knox, watch cloak fluttering in freezing wind, announced a further examination of siege guns finally to decide which pieces would be selected for transportation: such as the double-forted 18-pounders. Since these ran from nine to ten feet in length and weighed between 4,000 and 5,000 pounds apiece only a few could hope to be transported some three hundred miles across a mountainous wilderness.

After untying a long woolen muffler and kicking off snow-sodden boots Andrew Orne Hunter shed an evil-smelling uniform jacket just before burrowing beneath a heap of musty blankets topped by a coverlet of moth-eaten black bearskin. He fell asleep long before his weary body commenced to generate heat under the weight of his coverings.

By the end of the third day following the arrival of Henry Knox's party, plans for transportation during early stages of the journey were well in hand, largely thanks to General Schuyler's remarkable foresight by ensuring that along the line of march provisions had been stocked to feed the expedition.

Recently dozens of rough-clad civilians bringing draft animals and wagons, pulled mostly by horses, appeared anxious to assist the handful of regulars and militia in hauling guns and munitions over a short but very difficult portage paralleling unnavigable rapids down to Sabbath Day Point where the waters of Lake George emptied into Lake Champlain's southern end. Fortunately, very little snow had fallen since the party's arrival from Albany and held off while the portage was being negotiated.

Heavy guns were dispatched first and painfully lowered by groaning blocks and falls into a small flotilla of gundelows and Durham boats. Field guns were dispatched next. Sometimes, four tubes of light calibre might lie bedded on hay like bundling couples in a single creaking wagon. There wasn't as much confusion as Andrew and many others anticipated, aside from occasional disputes and fist-fights over precedence in loading; undoubtedly this was due to weather which remained fair but extremely cold.

So accurate had been Philip Schuyler's estimates that wagon masters, sent on in advance, usually had rounded up plenty of food, fodder and shelter to provide for volunteers who kept coming in singly or in small groups all afire with patriotic zeal—for the time being at least.

Chapter 41 🎋

MASSACRE

FOLLOWING ORDERS TO thoroughly scout regions northwest of Fort George's landing dock on Sabbath Day Point, Serjeant Jake Razors selected from his command some thirty hard-bitten trappers, timber cruisers or experienced woodsmen. Long ago he'd learned that for a task of such scope and importance his command should best be broken up into parties numbering no more than four or five. Controlled by a leader who knew his business, small bands in a single day could cover and survey an amazing amount of territory.

Because Thebaud was his blood-brother Jake included the half-breed in his own party. Logically, Paul should have been leading another unit but there were plenty of other experienced scouts available so he didn't waver on this decision.

Ranger units were ordered to send runners back to the fort the moment they detected suspicious signs. Jake ordered his parties not to attack hostiles unless conflict became unavoidable.

At the first hint of dawn on the ninth of December, 1775, Jake Razors, accompanied by Thebaud and three other scouts, quietly paddled themselves over to the Vermont shore and concealed their canoe before fanning out into a line-abreast nearly a half-mile in width. They moved in a northwesterly direction through dense forest composed largely of giant hardwoods carpeted by snow not yet deep enough to require the use of snowshoes.

Jake shifted Jenny to his other shoulder, studied the sky a long minute. "Hope to Hell comes on to snow before long."

Paul nodded. "Yep, my Brother, such would cover our tracks."

"—And other people's," commented a lanky young Ranger armed with a fairly new Deckert rifle.

No one could feel sure there mightn't be more than a few packs of hostiles ranging this steep and rocky countryside. Following instructions, Jake knew his first duty was to protect parties of settlers hopefully seeking security in Fort Ticonderoga. Because homesteaders in this territory were claiming huge property rights they pretty soon would finish off already badly depleted fur-bearing animals and edible game. Already, Jake had heard British agents had been busy pointing this out to sachems among the Wappingers, Mohegans, Nipmucks and remnants of other broken tribes inhabiting this vicinity. Said they, their livelihood was endangered by an ever-increasing flood of land-hungry Yankees—an old-time Indian corruption of the term "English."

At a space-eating dogtrot Serjeant Razors selected a tortuous but time-saving course across a succession of steep rocky ridges crowned with tall beeches, chestnuts and conifers. Because winter hadn't struck hard yet Jake glimpsed some few red foxes, squirrels and raccoons and a good many deer. The moment they sighted or smelt humans the white flags of their tails went wigwagging into deep woods away from underbrush they'd been feeding on.

Loping along with Jenny cradled in the crook of his arm Jake felt increasingly satisfied with life, as always when removed from crowds. If he knew how to sing he would have—softly, of course.

Traversing a ridge running parallel to Lake George the Rangers encountered a rough wagon track showing fresh wheel marks, the spoor of two cattle and of as many horses. They also identified three sets of human footprints. After backtracking a short distance Jake beckoned in his companions. They agreed

331

that a heavy wagon drawn by a pair of sizable horses was being followed by a cow and a half-grown calf, probably heading for the fort.

A Ranger wearing long black hair braided into a pigtail drawled, "Wal, Jake, reckon there ain't more'n three people travelin' on foot; two men and a boy. Of course mebbe a woman and some sprats are ridin' the wagon."

Bluejays screamed, darted off brilliant flashes of blue-and-white among stark and leafless branches. However, neat and saucy little black-capped chickadees, some of them feeding upside among frost-killed weeds, made no effort to fly away, only eyed these shaggy strangers in mild curiosity.

Breaths creating silvery cloudlets about their heads Jake's party were fanning out when, on the far side of a steep ridge and at no great distance, sounded the deep-throated bellow of a musket being fired, almost at once it was followed by a scattering of shots.

A lanky and runny-nosed youth wearing a red fox-fur cap the tail of which kept bouncing between meager shoulders commented, "Sounds like folks up ahead hev done gone and gotten 'emselves caught in a ambush."

"Now do tell," rasped Thebaud. "Stow yer gab, Bub."

While checking flints and priming Jake and his companions agreed those shots had come from beyond a low, birch-grown ridge lying to the southwest.

When two more reports boomed in the distance Jake waved forward. Twice, three times they raised shrill scalp yells. Somewhere at the back of Jake's mind, dim memories commenced to stir but assumed no recognizable pattern.

Silent as embodied ghosts the party, about fifty feet apart, sprinted among the birches. They kept abreast of Jake who alone followed the wagon tracks, Jenny's long and nut-brown barrel held ready. B'God, pretty soon he aimed to kill somebody; this wasn't any damn' fool European fight.

At the end of ten minutes whooping shouts and the faint, shrill screaming of a woman in pain grew louder, then ceased, left a vacuum of sound in the wintry wilderness. Obedient to Razor's hand signals Rangers on reaching the ridge's crest quickened stride down a gentle slope ending where the wagon trace had entered a dense stand of black-trunked sugar maples. Beyond it a cloud of blue-gray smoke had commenced to climb. Razors, Thebaud and the rest quickened their pace even though they might arrive too late to be of help to an attacked party. As if in proof of this a big gray farm horse, eyes white with terror, nostrils flaring, plunged along the track. A long, bleeding gash on its shoulder sprayed the snowy ground. The animal lumbered by, mane flying, but it looked too heavy to travel far. It could be tended to later on.

Aiming to jump enemies occupied with looting Jake signaled his men to increase speed so, loosening knives and war hatchets in their scabbards, the Rangers bounded forward savage and silent as wolves closing in on a crippled moose. Expertly they balanced firearms between boulders, tussocks and tangles of blackberry bushes and thickets, among white birch trunks and in hurdling wind-felled trees.

Possibly the insistent screaming of bluejays had alerted the ambushers, but in any case, while Rangers were bounding towards a wide, open space in the trace, a fellow wearing a wolfskin cape suddenly jumped out from behind a rock and, shouldering a brass-barreled carbine, shot Paul Thebaud through the heart. Not making a sound the half-breed flung wide his arms and sent his weapon flying into a snowbank before he collapsed into a clump of withered blackberry bushes. His limbs made just a few convulsive movements.

Only moments before a canvas-covered wagon, furiously aflame, was sighted. Ambushers must have cut the traces of a team of big-footed draft horses. Snorting their terror, they plunged off through the underbrush followed by a brown cow and her half-grown calf.

A quick glance about assured Jake, while whipping Jenny to his shoulder, that the enemy numbered about the same as his own party. Without stopping to sight he shot between the eyes a tall, black-bearded man who was shouting orders. One of Jake's party killed another ambusher, a full-blooded Indian and a Mohawk by his light skin and Greek warrior's crested scalp lock. Another died from a bullet tearing through his throat.

The remaining ambushers, true timber beasts by their shaggy hair and buckskins, fired back, but too hastily to be accurate. With no time to reload Jake snatched up his blood-brother's rifle and shot a fellow who, too late, had dropped the dripping scalp he'd just lifted from a scrawny yellow-haired man lying sprawled in the thin snow. The fight quickly resolved itself when a pair of ambushers unable to reload muskets drew long knives and, raising screeching war cries, tried to charge. They didn't get far, for the men from Ticonderoga deliberately shot them in the stomach so they might suffer brief but acute agonies before tomahawks split their skulls.

Flames crackled louder in the blazing wagon, spewed whirling billows of smoke and so drove terrified livestock deeper into the woods. After a brief silence the Rangers while cursing Thebaud's death understood what had chanced. A bald, thick-set farmer, his wife, the yellow-haired man who'd already been scalped and a lanky youth of about eighteen lay sprawled in ungainly positions. Their blood was sketching bright designs over trampled snow.

Jake noticed that the ambush had been so skillfully arranged that only the farmer and one other had been able to discharge their weapons.

The woman whose scalp had been lifted could never have been considered pretty but now she looked hideous. Nor had the ambusher who'd shot the youth been able to complete his job for the boy's long, soft-looking brown hair had been only partly ripped off.

The ambushers' leader, the lean, red-bearded fellow Jake had shot, still breathed, made small bubbling sounds such as men will when shot through the lungs. Of all things this burly character over a linen hunting shirt was wearing a pair of dingy white crossbelts secured in front by a tarnished square brass plate buckle bearing the number "54."

Jake shaking the fellow snarled, "Who in Hell are you?"

The dying man stared dazedly upwards, choked, "Fergus Jamison, late Serjeant, 54th Highlanders."

"Where you from?"

"I—we—"

He got no further because Jake stooped and with a single quick slash cut the murderer's hairy throat. After wiping clean his blade on the body, Jake beckoned a long-legged Ranger, reputedly a fast runner. "Pete, I want you should make tracks to

334

the Fort fastest you kin and tell 'em what's chanced. We'll finish this patrol."

From near the burning wagon's rear commenced a series of thin screams and wails. "My God! Must be a kid in there!" A Ranger holding his forearm for a shield from the heat leaped towards the tail gate, reached inside and dragged out a small squirming bundle wrapped in a dingy red-and-yellow quilt.

Memories commenced to take shape in Jake Razors' mind, reached backwards twenty or more years. Of course he'd been too young to recall much of that tragedy. From what he'd been told over the years he'd gone unnoticed by his parents' slayers only because when the savages had struck he'd strayed from camp along a creek in search of frogs. Frontier-trained even at three he'd had the sense to freeze like a hunted snowshoe rabbit till the raiders had departed. Present sights and sounds all at once seemed familiar.

Plunged into a black mood, Jake started off in search of straying stock but paused long enough to call over one shoulder, "You fellers want skelps I'll take no heed, but don't ever say so." Colonel Knox was adamant over the matter of taking hair.

Once Paul Thebaud and other bodies had been buried in a grave hastily dug under a tall pine where the ground hadn't frozen extra deep nobody wasted time. Jake ordered the team of farm horses, the brindled cow and her calf rounded up and haltered.

Very little of the murdered family's possessions could be saved except oddly enough a few books which must have been packed near the wagon bed's rear end and so had tumbled onto the melting snow. A Ranger named Lucas stooped, picked up a volume bound in badly chafed calfskin. "Hey! Damned if this here ain't a Bible." He passed it over to Jake. Still beset by poignant recollections, he riffled through its front pages and saw what looked like a column of names written by several hands in various degrees of faded ink. Unable to read or write, he passed the book back to Lucas, a literate Ranger, who explained these entries recorded births, marriages and deaths concerning an Armbruster family originally from Dartmouth in England.

"What's that last line say? Looks fresh," said Jake, keeping one eye on the squirming baby who, yowling, had pushed arms out

335

of its wrappings and had begun to threaten the smoky air with tiny pink fists.

Lucas frowned, stepped back a few paces from soaring flames. "'Tis writ here—'Baby male, born April 11th, 1775—'"

"What's the sprat's given name?"

"Don't see any. Guess there weren't no preacher handy to christen him, proper-like."

"Well," Jake drawled, again eying the wriggling blanket, "once we get back to the fort I'll see to it this sprat's taken care of." He hesitated, glancing at that low hummock of snowy dirt beneath which lay his blood-brother. "When they list this here babe's name I aim to have it read, 'Jacob Thebaud Armbruster.'" He reckoned wasn't much of a name for the child, but still 'twas better than being named for a barber's instrument.

CHAPTER 42 🙰

"A NOBLE TRAIN OF ARTILLERY"

FOR THE FIRST TIME in weeks Captain Andrew Orne Hunter in Albany was able to relax briefly. How fine to occupy a comfortable, clean room, to bask in front of a Dutch stove built of white-and-blue tiles. It was queer-looking all right but gave off plenty of heat. Best of all, he'd been able to soak his evil-smelling and grimy muscle-corded frame for a good while in a tin slipper-tub filled with steaming water from buckets lugged upstairs by a buxom, full-bosomed blonde serving-wench.

Apparently she enjoyed his company so much she even offered without charge to launder his filthy shirt and small clothes. Oddly enough, this pert young female put him in mind of Sarah but in a coarser pattern.

What could be happening in and around Boston these days? No dispatches from that direction had reached Headquarters for a long while. Had the British suddenly sallied to rout the ill-organized, half-starved and freezing Rebels besieging them along too great a perimeter?

Surely, out of sheer necessity, even sluggish Lord Howe would have been forced to reach some such a decision.

Nobody at home he mused while scrubbing his arms would be having an easy time. Still, what with the Hunter family being old Cambridge residents and Captain Timothy having been a man of considerable stature, Mamma and Ellen ought to be making out fairly comfortably; also Sarah Hilton should she still be living with them.

Pray God none of them had fallen victim to a communicable disease which, especially in winter, could spread alarmingly because in cold weather people tended to crowd together and effectively spread infection, a theory supported by increasing numbers of medical men. Therefore, whenever he thought of it, he prayed Sarah and his family might escape smallpox, ship fever, dysentery or any other of those dread diseases which daily were killing off civilians and the military by the dozens.

Today being a Sabbath many men had refused to labor, leaving Andrew free to revel in the simple comforts of this clean little bedroom. After donning a spare shift of clothing he delved into a bulging horsehide haversack till he located his pen case and the journal he'd neglected so disgracefully of late.

He stooped to pat Felix, a small, black-and-tan mongrel which appeared to have adopted him. The dog's ancestry was mixed, to say the least, yet it possessed limpid, soulful brown eyes which bespoke devotion more tellingly than many a human tongue.

After cutting a fresh point to his quill he sat back, pen poised but before writing, reviewed events of the past week. Finally he wrote:

DECEMBER THE 12TH, 1775

Today the Vanguard of a motley Flotilla now lies off Fort George after being greeted by a series of Cannon Salutes, a fine gesture but a waste of scarce Gunpowder. Our Armada present a ludicrous Specktacle in that it included everything from craft suggestive of Noah's Ark to a lumber Raft. Our transport includes bateaux, Durham Boats, Gundelows and Sailing Scows; all are flat-bottomed and therefore will prove poor Sailers into a Wind.

This morning my friend David Mason informed me that

338

when the last of what some jokesters term "our Noble Train of Artillery" arrives here, it will number 59 pieces of ordnance selected at Ticonderoga. Forty-three guns are cast of bronze, brass or iron and require various weights of shot for which a Suitable supply of Projectiles has been found. Also we bring 16 Mortars and a Brace of Iron Howitzers. The Total weights of this Artillery to be transported comes to not less than 300,000 Pounds!

Although no one voices Doubts few among us Honestly believes so vast a Weight can be transported overland to Cambridge in mid-winter.

Descending Lake George two Gundelows got Sunk through Misadventure or poor Seamanship. If only Tom Izard and others of his sort had been on hand! However, all the "drownded" (as they say around here) Pieces were recovered among them a huge Siege Gun our People have dubbed "Old Sow." It is of forged iron double-forted at the breech and weighs not less than 5,000 pounds! Being eleven feet in Length it has proved exceeding difficult to Maneuver and Transport.

Were it not for the great good-will of local Inhabitants and the help of some Civilized Indians, the latter being well paid, we would have met much Trouble in raising the Gundelows which fortunately Sank in only a few feet of Water.

At this time Everyone prayed the Lake would not Freeze over, just as now we pray, just as Earnestly, that the Hudson will Freeze sufficient solid to permit our hauling the Train over it to the Road to our next objective, Kinderhook on the far shore.

Majors Lamb and Wm. Knox and I, a lowly Capt., have accompanied the Col. in scouring the Countryside ahead to Colleckt Labor and all manner of Transport. Lord! How cold we get! Think when this War ends I will go settle in Jamaica or some other tropickal place.

Frowning, Andrew dipped his pen while attempting to recall essential details from the recent past.

Whilst the last of our Water-borne Guns were being unloaded at Fort George the Weather turned cruel Cold and the Lake quickly Froze over so then came the dire Necessity of finding Transport for other than the field guns which are mounted on wheeled carriages, together with Limbers and Caissons rebuilt under Major Mason's direcktion over a long and rough Road to Glen's Falls and thence on down to Albany where they now lie.

One cannot too much Admire the rare Industry, good sense and Foresight displayed by General Schuyler and our Colonel at this Time. Our light Field Pieces alone being Capable of immediate use were Guarded by Detachments Soldiers or Militia.

Everyone now prayed Snow would fall since the heavier Field Cannon, Mortars and Siege Guns such as "Old Sow" can only be transported aboard Sledges or Sleighs drawn by Oxen.

The Almighty has heeded our Prayers for, in as many days, two hard Blizzards struck, enabling our heavy Artillery to resume its slow progress towards Albany where I now write.

No pretense at formal Military Discipline is Maintained aside from Despatching Reconnoitering Parties as directed by our Chief Scout, Serjeant Razors, who is familiar with this Country and the ways of its Inhabitants, white, red and mixed.

When Snow ceased to Fall Weather turned so bitter Razors insists our Enemies will stay where they can keep warm and are not likely to Pester us. Let us hope he is right! We, poor Wights, were forced to endure such biting Winds not a few of our Number have suffered from Severe Frost-bite, and some Pickets have even frozen to Death.

24TH DECEMBER, 1775

Today our Train reached a little Town called Saratoga built at what expert Military Engineers deem a Strategically Important Point.

It is decided to Celebrate the Anniversary of our

Saviour's birth at this place, principally because our Men
and Beasts stand in dire need of Bait and Repose for a few
days, not to mention warm clothing, however, Col. Knox is
most Impatient as ever to move on.

Most members of this Expedition are being Generously
entertained by the Inhabitants with the best they can
provide. Meantime, repairs are made to Wheeled Vehicles.
Also, Thanks be to God, more and more determined Patriots
have appeared in Saratoga with sledges and draft animals
for our Convenience. But there remains a Possibility of
sudden attack by nearby Tories and Supporters of which
reportedly there are many in these parts.

Among other Necessities I was able to purchase two
pair of thick woollen Hose and a sett of ugly but Sturdy
cowhide Knee Boots. Those I was wearing were so cracked
and full of Holes they admitted Snow and Water—and a
consequent risk of Frost-bite.

Andrew paused, sat before the fireplace and grew so comfortably warm he unbuttoned a plain gray homespun jacket he'd brought as a substitute for his military tunic which, of course, must be reserved for formal occasions.

For no particular reason he found himself all at once wondering how Caleb and Amy Twisden might be celebrating this holy day. To his astonishment he found himself really hopeful that the *Franklin*'s cruise might have proved extra successful since every British supply ship captured offered a considerable contribution towards comforting General Washington's hungry, rag-clad troops besieging Boston. Most of these, he guessed, remained little better than armed mobs; desertions must be frequent.

Inexplicable how often memories of Amy came to mind unbidden: could this be because by rough calculation she must be well along towards giving birth to a child—his? The very thought of becoming, in part, the creator of a human being was sobering.

When absently he reached down to pat Felix's head the dog emitted a happy whine, looked up with adoring eyes. Good dog.

Good dog! Only the Lord knew how badly Andrew Hunter yearned for affection at this moment.

When a coal popped out of the fireplace he picked it up between calloused fingertips and threw it back before adding a fresh log to the blaze then, from a bottle on the mantelpiece, he moodily brimmed a tall glass with claret. Instead of returning to the table he'd been using for a desk Andrew settled into a wooden armchair comfortable with a seat of plaited straw and relaxed, stared into the flames. He let his mind review the past half-year. Lord! How difficult it was to realize Breed's Hill had been fought only last June and here it was December of the same year! How utterly impossible it seemed that six, no, seven months back he'd been an ambitious and generally well-regarded officer of the Royal Navy. Yes, a year ago tonight he'd been treading the decks of H.M.S. *Lively* searching his soul to decide what course to follow.

At the time, he remembered that he, like most everybody aboard, had felt confident this absurd uprising could and would be contained and stamped out without too much effort. Of course matters hadn't turned out that way following Lexington and Concord. Then Breed's Hill had solved his problem. Aye, that battle effectively had terminated security and an orderly career.

Adding to this confusion there'd been Sarah Hilton. Amazing, how from the start he'd taken a mounting interest in the girl and she in him, for all they'd only rarely been alone. Sarah had had a frivolous air about her but it was lively, often humorous.

Linking fingers behind head he pushed newly stockinged feet towards the fire, stared unseeingly past them. What might have been his fate had that precedent-shattering battle on Breed's Hill not been fought? Although at that time his mind had been badly confused, now he could recall, quite clearly, details of the night he, Tom Izard and a few others had managed to desert. How absurd that long years of study and devotion to duty should have gone for naught because of a few low-aimed cannon balls fired without his knowledge or consent.

Then there was that arrival in Marblehead to mixed reactions among inhabitants. Of course by the time he'd got the battery on Peach's Head near completion most 'Headers appeared ready to

342

accept him as one of their own—probably because his mother had been an Orne.

Then there had been Amy, tall above average, whose charm and easy smile had gone far towards rebuilding self-confidence. Although not at all well off Amy Orne designed and sewed simple gowns which set off to advantage a tawny complexion and naturally wavy reddish-brown hair. But what stood out most clearly in his memory were heart-shaped features, uneven but unusually white teeth and fascinating small dimples winking at either side of full, dark-red lips.

When Felix again nuzzled a cold nose into a palm dangling beside him he absently stroked the dog's pointed and rather fox-like head. Why was it, right from the start, Amy Orne had exuded an allure defying analysis?

The Marblehead girl's figure wasn't as full and shapely as Sarah Hilton's but Amy stood taller and slimmer perhaps because she wasn't too well endowed about the bosom. A large part of Amy's attraction lay in a voice; although low-pitched and musical it seemed to hint at powerful emotions and depths not expressed through her lips. Best of all, Amy possessed a keen sense of humor and, even better, a lively appreciation of the ridiculous.

During occasional barn dances few girls appeared more spirited or less concerned over the extent which they exposed shapely limbs whenever some spinning step caused skirts to flutter and rise well above the floor.

Listening to the wind, he recalled that warm evening they'd exchanged first kisses on the Izard Brothers' wharf To the best of his recollection, neither of them had said anything or had made any overt movement before, all at once, she was in his arms, lips avid. Clasping her, he'd become aware this young woman was by no means as wiry as he'd imagined. Her shoulders and back felt surprisingly soft.

Gaze fixed on wavering flames he attempted but failed to recall what had been said. All he remembered was that this iridescent moment had been inexpressibly tender.

Sighing, Andrew took a sip of claret. Why, at that uncertain stage in their relationship had he dared propose seeking the sail loft. Why had she gone without even a coy gesture of protest?

The storm increasingly rattled shutters and sent chill drafts scurrying across the floor. Surely it must have been the Devil's own devising that his seed should have taken root on the brief occasion he and Amy had coupled. Still, somehow, he rejoiced with realization that their get had been conceived through love rather than common passion. A good thing Amy's baby at the least would bear an honorable name.

How would Amy, with so much more at hazard, be feeling towards him these days? If he'd correctly estimated her character come what might she'd keep their secret inviolate. Some comfort was to be found in the notion Amy wasn't likely to suffer want. Although Caleb Twisden wasn't rich he was an up-and-coming young lawyer, well connected and so should be comfortably well off in his own right, provided his practice hadn't been assimilated by less devoted Patriots, of which there were a-plenty. Still, Caleb's pay as lieutenant aboard even a successful cruiser wouldn't take care of more than bare essentials. Again, he found himself sincerely hoping the *Franklin*'s cruise might have proved unusually successful.

A knock on the door abruptly diverted his train of thought. A pinch-faced and very young militiaman appeared wearing a long overcoat of coonskins and a dingy red woolen muffler.

"Fer you, sir." He presented a finger-marked envelope. On it Andrew at once recognized Ellen's scrawling, immature handwriting. Few females, even among well-to-do families, received instruction in writing beyond rudimentary calligraphy.

Ellen's note had been dated November 21st. Alas, public post never had proved either swift or dependable even in untroubled times; that this letter had reached him at all was something of a wonder.

Ellen wrote she and Sarah Hilton still were attending sick and disabled soldiers in various hospitals and homes scattered around Cambridge. Sarah, she wrote, had been occupying his old bedroom but hadn't disturbed any of his belongings. He paused. Imagine Sarah occupying the narrow but comfortable bed Papa had fetched back from Antigua, one of the Sugar Islands in the West Indies.

Ellen's letter also reported no news about the fate of Papa and his brig. Tom Izard, stopping by recently, had described how all shipyards in Gloucester, Marblehead and Beverly nowadays were building real ships-of-war even if only cutters, schooners or small sloops. A pity her Bro. couldn't be on hand to supervise installation of their armament.

Ellen also wanted to know how Colonel Knox's mission was progressing, if newly commissioned Captain Hunter capably was discharging responsibilities. How often she and Mamma had knelt and prayed for his well-being, Sarah Hilton usually joined them.

Squinting in light fading rapidly because another blizzard seemed about to strike he turned the single sheet, to learn the privateer *Franklin* had returned to Gloucester a week earlier.

During a cruise among islands off the mouth of the St. Lawrence she and her consorts had prized a goodly number of merchantmen. Unfortunately, many of these had turned out to be captured American-owned vessels. Following General Washington's express orders, such vessels could not be condemned as prizes, so the *Franklin*'s cruise had shown only a small profit.

Tom, she added, had mentioned something which might interest him: off Cape Breton Island the *Franklin* had prized a schooner laden with cargo so valuable Captain Selman had sent his lieutenant, Caleb Twisden, to board her. Twisden's small prize crew had been attempting to reduce sail when a sudden sleet storm had struck. Helplessly, Ellen wrote, the *Franklin*'s crew had watched their prize driven onto a half-submerged reef upon which she speedily had broken up. Only three survivors had been rescued. The prize captain had not been among them.

CHAPTER 43 ❧

"KNOX'S FOLLY"

PROGRESS FOR "KNOX'S FOLLY," as Tories and other disaffected persons were terming this painfully slow artillery train, was further delayed not far south of Albany by a sudden thaw. For a few days it created ice floes and rendered it nigh impossible to ferry ordnance across the Hudson onto a rugged post road leading southeast to Kinderhook and Claverack, still in New York.

Then to render progress even more difficult temperatures plunged to fifteen degrees and sometimes twenty degrees below freezing. When such frigid blasts roared down from Canada they brought no useful depth of snow, causing ox-drovers and teamsters no end of anxiety since siege guns and mortars had to be transported on sleds and sledges, also other fieldpieces too ponderous to be moved on ordinary gun carriages. Shot, powder and loading equipment, stowed in farm wagons, made especially slow progress.

Henry Knox, at long last commissioned brigadier-general on the twenty-seventh of November, kept on bellowing for faster progress, just as if the Devil was holding a red-hot pitchfork against his massive buttocks.

As a rule the two heaviest cannon "Old Sow" and "Albany"—the latter having been so named because of that town's generous hospitality—usually were hauled as close behind the column's vanguard as possible on the thesis that should such monsters negotiate especially dangerous stretches of the route guns of lesser weight could do the same with comparative safety. Next came guns of medium calibre firing 6- or 8-pound shot which, if they ever arrived at their destination, should wreak havoc with a massed infantry assault and also shatter General Howe's fortifications on Boston Neck.

By now pessimists became convinced, often for sound reasons that only light field artillery could hope to reach its destination. Only irregularly and occasionally did information come back from the new General and his staff, riding about two days in advance of the stumbling train in order to collect new men, animals, transportation and food supplies from a now very thinly settled countryside.

Captain Andrew Hunter among others expected Henry Knox's endless exertions might somewhat reduce his formidable proportions; they failed to do so. The ex-bookseller, always cheerful even when chilled to the bone, still tipped the beam at close on 300 pounds. Often, derisively cheering men suggested the General dismount and add his weight towards pulling or manhandling cannon. A few times he did so amid surprised cheers.

His brother, Major William Knox, and long-faced Major John Lamb, both experienced military engineers, usually accompanied the Commander to devise how some serious natural obstacle might best be circumvented.

Andrew estimated that on the average nearly a thousand men composed of volunteers of all descriptions and occupations, from hard-bitten timber beasts and frontier traders to idealistic scholars, merchants and soft-handed professional men, toiled in the tenuous, winding column heading east from Claverack. Most welcome of all were numbers of tough, hard-muscled and generally bearded local homesteaders.

Serjeant Razors and his company of far-ranging woodsmen undoubtedly were to be thanked for ensuring the safe arrival in the column of so many men, horses and oxen from remote farms, hamlets and little crossroad villages.

Jake's followers, Andrew decided, must have used powerful arguments to persuade men to quit the rude comforts of home, in mid-winter, to march, ride or drive stock capable of hauling ponderous vehicles over traces which until recently never had felt the weight of anything exceeding the feet of hunters or war parties.

Long before the column entered the glacier-smoothed but heavily timbered Tatoctin Hills the value of a well-tempered axe or a good saw came to equal that of a sound musket. Iron pinchbars, stout spades and pickaxes also gained values they never again would approximate.

For General Knox and his staff it proved prodigiously encouraging to notice how rapidly these volunteers, often aided by well-meaning but often inexperienced militia, could convert a narrow trail, often barred by extensive rockfalls and windfalls, into a passable road. From first daylight till darkness fell axes rang and two-man saws rasped and whined; picks and crowbars manipulated by sweating laborers levered snow-covered rocks out of the way or used them to fill low spots along the route.

In mid-January the weather for a few days turned really mild to the surprise of all save local inhabitants who averred such thaws weren't uncommon on these parts during the month of January. This warmth wasn't enjoyed by Knox's men, for when snow melted, ground softened into mud. Teamsters did some inspired cursing when wheels bit even deeper into patches of this country's virgin black soil.

Andrew wrote later on he'd no means of describing by how many ingenious means the train was kept crawling along. Sometimes it covered only two or maybe three miles in a day, other times it traveled much farther, provided the terrain grew less formidable.

Everyone felt increasingly discouraged until General Schuyler, sickly but courageous, volunteered to keep traveling till the Massachusetts border was reached.

Death in various guises continued to stalk the expedition. Sometimes a man would be lost through so simple an act as going off to catch fish through a hole in the ice unaware that a spring hole suddenly might give way under added weight. Sometimes amid a raging snowstorm lonely pickets could not be relieved and would lose their way back to the column and next day were located, frozen stiff.

Also it was inevitable that men should slip on icy surfaces and suffer broken bones. Others sustained wounds caused by falling trees or by axes inexpertly wielded. Others fell ill and soon died of exposure or of some undeterminable disease.

Nor did draft animals suffer less. More than a few beasts suffered broken legs and had to be shot—not an unwelcome accident since its flesh would provide a treat for ravenous troops and laborers. Due to Henry Knox's foresight nobody really went hungry. Besides, Rangers now and then sent for packhorses to bring in the carcass of an elk, a moose or a deer. But this happened infrequently; and, only senior officers and a selected number of civilians, valuable for local knowledge or influence, tasted such game.

Much of the time snowshoes became a prime requisite, especially of the bear-paw shape, oval and lacking the racquet type's long, trailing stem difficult to manage in heavy underbrush.

Frequent arguments broke out when certain drovers and teamsters positively refused to journey more than two or, at the utmost, three days' travel away from isolated homes, farms or hamlets left undefended.

Now and again oddly clothed militiamen might appear from somewhere and jaw a bit before pitching in to help the column along to the best of their ability. There was one thing the men liked about such part-time soldiers: some might fetch along a stone jug or two of hard cider which would go a long way towards raising flagging spirits.

Once the expedition struggled into the foothills of the Berkshire Hills as many as three yokes of oxen or six horses sometimes were required to haul a single gun carriage jolting across shale slopes, jagged rocks and past the lopped-off branches of some great fallen tree.

Fortunately, as the Berkshire Hills grew steeper, a series of heavy snowstorms struck carpeting the countryside, very helpful to sledges and other vehicles on runners.

What with ice and rocky going Andrew soon wore out a pair of crude bear-paw snowshoes presented by Jake Razors. Usually he explored the next day's line of march to determine the best route for those two huge stone sledges transporting "Old Sow" and "Albany." Both cannon were handled as if they'd been forged of metal far more precious than iron.

On occasion as many as eight yokes of wide-horned, slow-footed oxen were shifted from other vehicles to haul the great guns over an especially steep or difficult stretch of the track. Among the Berkshires matters took a grim turn when more than the usual number of draft animals began to fall sick or play out for want of grain and hay, or broke legs in the incredibly rough going. At the moment there seemed no possible way of replacing them for all Henry Knox ordered Jake's Rangers to scour the countryside ever farther out. Then, as if to compound the column's misery, the temperature plunged so low softwood branches cracked loud as rifle shots in the woods. If a man died during this period his outer clothing was yanked off before his cadaver had begun to stiffen.

One evening while huddled together under blankets arranged hood-like over them, Major Lamb, through chattering teeth, confided to Andrew, "No use denying—come a few more days like this the Virginia Gen'ral is going to have to whistle for heavy artillery."

Any professional soldier would have winced and looked aside at the present aspect of Henry Knox's expedition. Most were wearing anything to keep them warm: Dutch blankets, sheepskin and bearskin blouses and even women's mantles. Mittens or gloves became worth their weight in gold or silver—of which metals nobody had any worth mention.

On those now rare occasions when a party of militiamen appeared nobody could offer the newcomers a more cordial welcome than Captain Andrew Hunter and what were becoming known as his "Big Gun Boys." When militiamen got invited near the biggest fires they sometimes offered scarce tobacco, even a little applejack. Once tarpaulins were cast loose militiamen were encouraged to inspect "Old Sow" and "Albany" proclaimed to be the biggest cannons in all North America: an outrageous lie, but one which impressed credulous backwoodsmen.

His footgear was wearing out so fast Andrew wondered whether, come another day or so he, like many others, might have to resort to binding up broken boots in rawhide thongs or strips of rag cloth. He was spared such a necessity when Serjeant Jake Razors, restless-eyed as ever, but looking well fed, joined the train on one of his unpredictable appearances and from his pack produced a pair of soft but sturdy elkskin shoepacs Indian-stitched and lined with muskrat fur.

"Dunno how long these will hold out," drawled the Chief Ranger hunkering closer to the campfire, a thick yellow beard almost completely masking long and leathery features. "Mebbe I'll come acrost another pair ere long."

Andrew passed over a small flask of prime 4F gunpowder. "Wish I'd a better way of thanking you, Jake, but I guess we're down to hard-scrabble times nowadays. Not enough of anything except snow and ice. How're you and the rest of you timber beasts faring?"

Awkwardly, Jake bit off a chew of tobacco. Like so many others on the verge of scurvy he'd recently lost another front tooth. "Not bad, exceptin' three of the fellers ain't been seen in over a week. Reckon likely they broke a leg somewheres and froze to death or got run down by wolves or maybe got jumped by some stray Injuns, but that ain't extra-likely. Like I said back in Albany ain't many hostiles will venture abroad in such weather, so there's been no fighting. Hell! Us riflemen deem this is a pretty damn' thin excuse for a war; 'specially since we're forbidden to take skelps." Using the back of a grimy hand Jake wiped a pellucid drop from the tip of his hawk's beak of a nose then leaned forward and lowered his voice. "Now lemme tall you something in confidence. Once this outfit gets clear of these here mountains most of us fellers don't aim to take one step nearer to Boston."

"What will you do?"

"We plan on joinin' up with Dan'l Morgan's Rifle Brigade somewheres to the south'ard where we hear he's marchin'. Ain't none of us enjoyed a good scrap in a month of Sundays and you know damn' well our sort don't git along with spit-and-polish reg'lar troops. Ain't yet forgot the look of them crossed halberts and that serjeant standin' all ready with his whip."

Andrew glanced over the flames. "Guess I understand your thinking; among regulars you're like fish out of water. Oh, by the bye, what became of that baby you fetched into Fort Ti? I mean the tyke you named after Paul Thebaud and his kin?"

Jake licked greasy lips, tossed a stick onto the fire, "Wal, little Jacob Thebaud Armbruster is luckier than I when I was pretty much in the same fix; just before we quit Albany I come across a English-Dutch widow-woman who'd just lost a brat of near the same age."

"What was her name?"

"Something like 'Katrina van Dyke' or mebbe it was 'van Wyck.'" He pronounced the latter name 'van Wick.' "Before I go to join Morgan first chance I get I aim to drop by and learn how the little bugger's makin' out."

"How's this widow fixed?"

"All right, I guess. She's got plenty of close kin in the fur trade. The young one ain't likely to go hungry."

CHAPTER 44 ❧

HALF-MOON POND

ANYONE WHO PARTICIPATED in the ordnance column's advance even over a short distance never forgot the experience. For years old men would hold grandchildren enthralled by accounts of tribulations and trials suffered during the last days of December 1775 and the bitter months of January and February 1776.

Occasional thaws softened or melted creeks and ponds and caused waterfalls to roar once more till a hard freeze struck them silent again and permitted the strange oddment of vehicles to crawl onwards often leaving bloodstains on the snow in their wake. Men toiling to accomplish this at first glance suggested nothing better than a shaggy, lousy, malodorous and ill-disciplined band of ruffians. Only here and there could one sight among the miscellany of headgear the weathered black tricorn hat and cockade of some officer.

Because Rangers consistently reported no hostile forces Tory or Indian within striking distance, some teamsters, drovers and axemen rather than hamper their efforts unwisely took to leaving firearms in the nearest vehicle.

Frequently Captain Andrew Hunter scouted the proposed

route for heavy guns with General Henry Knox. Local guides and selected members of his staff still rode at least a day in advance of the column's van. Courteously, he would listen whenever locals suggested some means of overcoming or circumventing natural hazards peculiar to their region: sheer cliffs, raging rapids or maybe windfalls where timber felled by some tornado offered near impassable obstacles.

Acting-Adjutant Major Lamb could and did explain why Henry Knox kept shouting encouragement to urge onwards the mile-and-a-half-long column dark across the winding wintry landscape. Andrew, enjoying Lamb's confidence, learned why this urgency to keep moving. From Cambridge had arrived dispatches describing the rapidly deteriorating state of the Continental forces.

Desertions again were reported to be increasing, particularly among rifle units. No form of punishment, however brutal, was proving an effective deterrent. Again, a great number of volunteer enlistments had expired on the first of the year. Ranks, therefore, were growing thinner by the day while the spirits of those remaining in service drooped like frost-bitten plants. Worst of all was the accelerated spread of contagious diseases. Cold, improvised hospitals in which toiled dog-tired surgeons, doctors and volunteer male and female nurses were overflowing.

In his latest dispatches the Commander-in-Chief had confided: "God alone knows how much longer this travesty of an Army can remain in being. Its chief hope reposes in the belief that siege artillery soon will arrive together with a goodly supply of shot, gunpowder and fine Indian flints designed to bombard Boston and drive out the King's men and his men-of-war from their anchorages."

Time and again the artillery train, hampered by raging snowstorms and prolonged blizzards, would toil up still another steep rise by means of temporarily hitching draft animals—mostly oxen now—from one conveyance to the next. Then, once a big gun had been heaved up and over to some crest, its descent on the reverse slope had to be controlled by means of drag chains, pinch-bars, blocks and tackles and, more often than not, a succession of logs thrown under the runners to check speed.

354

Had it not been for the arrival from settlements, near and far, of footgear, stockings, mufflers and coats of all descriptions the advance would have ground to a frozen halt. As it was, all too often some farmer would drive his animals out of camp ostensibly in search of feed and would not return, despite bona fide offers of sizable tracts of public land.

Town-bred volunteers and even some backwoodsmen soon learned how warming it was to roll up in a blanket and lie alongside an ox lain down to rest.

Horses, more restless, were not popular as bedfellows but all the same they had plenty of company. David Mason and Andrew, like many others, paired up to share the same animal's body under all the blankets they could secure—not always with the owner's explicit knowledge or consent.

Always chilled and weary to the bone as they were, marchers paid small attention to glimpses of wild life: lynxes, bobcats and foxes or packs of wolves slinking among trees and underbrush. By day such animals kept pretty well out of sight but once darkness fell they sometimes came so close to campfires their luminescent green-gold eyes could be seen, two-by-two always two-by-two. Wolves howled like lost souls in torment and quickly converged to feast on the scanty remains of a dead draft animal. Sometimes such predators even pulled down men straying too far from the column.

Major David Mason better than anyone else could fully appreciate the skill of local wheelwrights and carpenters called in to rebuild gun carriages and caissons damaged on the tortuous route from the New York line. Whenever possible these artisans used only seasoned white oak, chestnut or hickory to replace damaged sleigh and sledge runners and splintered spokes and axles. As a rule rural blacksmiths proved no less adept in shrinking wrought-iron tires, heated red-hot, onto wheels. Nevertheless, breakdowns continued and often men had to risk frostbitten fingers to mend or replace broken pieces of equipment. As usual farriers and blacksmiths were kept busy doctoring sick animals and replacing worn-out ox- and horseshoes.

Not far short of the village of Otis, in Massachusetts, that section in the van conveying the heaviest siege guns reached the shore of a long and narrow lake known to locals as Half-Moon

Pond. This, they said, had been created by beavers which had dammed otherwise unimportant brooks or creeks into lakes or ponds. Natives swore its waters were frozen solid.

Following established procedure, Andrew sent across several 12-pounders—heaviest and most useful calibre of field cannon—to cross and test the soundness of Half-Moon Pond's surface before ordering forward the massive sledge transporting "Old Sow" weighing some 5,000 pounds—only a little more than "Albany." It seemed encouraging that draft animals, six yoke of oxen, lowering heads and giving off steaming clouds, advanced willingly over the pond's flat white surface to the "Gees!" and "Haws!" of their drovers.

The sledge was only a few yards out from shore when, causing a loud, crackling report, a great section of snow-covered ice broke, collapsed and split into dozens of jagged segments. "Old Sow's" sledge lurched forward then foundered out of sight under black water. Oxen pawed frantically, bawled, fought their yokes so hard all but the last pair succeeded in winning free flinging sheets of ice water high into the air. The doomed span soon quit thrusting and bellowing; the water was too paralyzingly frigid.

For a long instant everyone froze, then a few brave souls ran out on the snow to hurl ropes or hastily snapped-off saplings towards the yelling, struggling ox drivers.

Sledges on either side of Half-Moon Pond pulled up so short they bumped into one another. Fast as mirrored sun signals the bad news spread in both directions. Immediately, Andrew ordered roaring fires kindled and shelters improvised of canvas cannon covers to help revive the dazed and half-drowned drovers. Lord above! Why on top of everything else did *this* have to happen?

The train was left no choice of crossing the pond at any other point because towering cliffs of gray granite hemmed in this artificial little lake. Although many a man present had earned his living trapping beavers or trading in their pelts everyone joined in whole-heartedly cursing such overindustrious animals.

Runners on snowshoes were dispatched to Otis, the nearest village, even before General Knox came galloping back the instant he heard one of his precious great guns had been sunk. Roaring like the biblical Bull of Bashan he ordered axemen into the

356

woods and out onto the ice to build a corduroy log road at a point which natives claimed to be a shallow part of the pond.

Scarlet-faced, Henry Knox reined in a huge, steaming mount, roared at Andrew, "That gun is your responsibility! Don't give a thin goddam how you go about it, but fish that piece ashore before dark! Commandeer anyone and anything you need to cut free those drowned bullocks, raise the sledge and get that gun *moving!*"

Following a brief conference with the General and Andrew Hunter, David Mason ordered expert axemen from among the militia to fell tall, straight lodge-pole spruces cut just long enough to distribute weight evenly over ice to create a corduroy road and so avoid the possibility that other invisible spring holes like the one responsible for this present disaster might exist.

Following cautious reconaissances and soundings David Mason and other engineer officers reported the bottom at the spring hole to be muddy and around nine feet deep but the ice surrounding it thick and sound.

"So," Mason announced, "it should be practicable to rig a hoist frame sufficient strong to grout 'Old Sow' out of her wallow."

Once Mason had indicated blue spruces of suitable diameters a hoisting frame was contrived from its crossbar, a ponderous block, tackle and grappling hook were rigged over the hole through which the great cannon had disappeared. First hauled ashore was that ice-coated stone sledge which had surfaced unassisted, a fact which disturbed David Mason no little. Andrew queried the reason.

The engineer blew a streaming nose between calloused fingers. "It can only mean, you great dumblock, that when the ice broke, 'Old Sow' rolled clear of the sledge; she's lying on the bottom."

Young volunteers stripped and though screeching in pain scrambled out to cut free the drowned oxen and also managed to attach tow ropes to the sledge, then blue-lipped, stumbled ashore quickly to be swathed in warmed blankets.

Literally hundreds of onlookers congregated to see how the engineers might go about recovering "Old Sow." They saw a huge grappling hook of wrought iron lowered, but no matter how deftly forked sapling yokes maneuvered it back and forth they failed to connect the hook with "Old Sow's" twin dolphins—often ornately ornamented iron handles welded onto a gun barrel's top to permit its being raised or lowered.

Around noon thick clouds of hard, dry snow commenced to fall and whirl about veiling woods and pond. Major Mason, his broad face gone gray-pink with cold, growled to assistants, "Near as I can figure when that damn' cannon went down she settled so's her dolphins either are lying far down to one side, or else they're completely beneath her, which would explain why the grappling hook don't take hold."

Well aware of the value Knox placed on this piece and "Albany," now being hauled across the ice over the corduroy road, Andrew yelled, "I'll pay twenty pounds sterling to anyone willing to dive and slip that grapnel hook onto one of the dolphins. How about that, MacPherson? Heard you like baubees."

A long-bearded woodsman stopped urinating against a tree long enough to snort, "Cappen, I *might* look crazy and I do love money but I ain't no fool! Divin' in that there ice water would make gettin' patted on the head with a sledge hammer feel nice!"

Again the grappling iron was lowered and sapling poles were repeatedly manipulated in all directions but it never brought up anything other than weeds, beaver-gnawed sticks and water-logged branches. To further discourage operations the snowstorm continued to worsen.

Dancing to warm his feet and holding red-mittened hands under armpits, David Mason grunted, "Looks like the siege will have to be won or lost 'thout 'Old Sow' even should we manage to haul the rest of these crotch-blistered guns over these damned mountains. Hi! What in Hell are you about?"

Casting loose coat buttons, Andrew rasped, "When I was in the old Service"—he didn't say "Royal Navy"—"on most ships it was considered an officer's duty to attempt things nobody else would dare tackle. I'll have a try with that grappling iron."

"Holy God, no! You won't last three minutes in such water."

Once two fires were blazing as close as possible to the hole and a tent improvised out of a wagon's cover, Andrew, naked beneath a horse blanket, ran to the hole's edge, grabbed the dangling hoist hook then swung it out over the hole. To his astonishment the water felt boiling hot against his skin rather than the contrary, but all the hammers of Hell belabored his head, confused him.

Never would he forget the excruciating pain suffered once the initial shock had worn off, but, using a forked stick to steady himself, he explored mud and bottom debris till his toes encountered the drowned cannon's muzzle. The brown-black waters proved to be only about seven feet deep—maybe a trifle shallower, so, gritting teeth, he worked toes along the barrel till they encountered what must be a dolphin.

Grabbing the hoist block's hook he drew a huge, shuddering breath and sank out of sight. Only semi-conscious, he managed to work the great iron hook through the handle-like projection just before he surfaced, lungs crackling, and clutched a stick tied to a rope's end and shoved to the hole's edge.

Only dimly did he realize he was being hauled onto solid ice then swathed in heated blankets and, stiff as any day-old corpse, lugged into the tent where a bearded, red-nosed so-called doctor from Otis held to his lips a flask of powerful brandy.

Only vaguely did Andrew become aware of many hands chafing nearly paralyzed limbs; he nearly passed out before Knox's brandy took hold but the liquor somewhat cleared his mind. As from a great distance he heard yells and cheers and Major Mason's shouting, "B'God, you did it! We've got 'Old Sow' ashore!"

CHAPTER 45 🎝

OLIVIA

ONCE AMY ORNE TWISDEN had done nursing the baby she dabbed bluish-white and unattractive-looking milk from the baby's face and then her nipple. Next she draped the infant over one shoulder and patted Olivia Orne Twisden's back till she'd emitted a satisfactory number of tiny belches.

For a moment Amy lingered before the fireplace absently stroking the baby's cheek with a forefinger. Lordy! What if Olivia eventually grew embarrassingly to resemble Andrew? Of course right now, as Jonathan Izard wryly put it, her offspring, like most new babies, resembled nothing better or worse than a poorly poached egg with a couple of raisins poked into it.

Satisfied that as yet there was no need to change swaddling clothes, Amy placed the infant in a half-barrel cradle lent by the Jonathan Izards now that she'd come back from Gloucester to reoccupy her old bedroom in the Widow Milburn's home. At the moment still another freezing gale was rattling windows, pounding hard against the cottage's weathered gray shingles. Lord, how tired she was feeling, how much more weary and dispirited she ever would let on. How could a body have experienced such a variety of joys and so many sorrows in so brief a period? Certainly, she must have been born under some particularly unlucky star.

First, had come that dreadful afternoon in Gloucester when Captain Archibald Selman of the privateer schooner *Franklin* had driven a hired pung up the drifted lane leading to Caleb Twisden's modest yet comfortable dwelling near the edge of town. The sea captain's features, framed in gray whiskers, had looked mighty uneasy and he had attempted to be very tactful in presenting condolences especially after he'd noticed how far advanced was her pregnancy.

Said he, revolving a beaver turban hat between big, brown-splotched hands, "Yes, Ma'am, your husband was shapin' into a first-rate officer and born leader, uncommon fast to learn. From the start he was firm yet just with the hands, which they recognized and appreciated." He concluded by saying, "Reckon, sure as shootin', Caleb soon would have earned a ship of his own. Yes, yer husband would have riz high in the Regular Naval Service we're startin' to put together. I—all of us are plumb distressed over his loss."

Momentarily, he had clasped her hands between calloused fists while piercing, red-rimmed blue eyes expressed sympathy far more eloquently than words escaping lean, ruler-straight lips.

"I allow 'tis only Job's comfort, Mrs. Twisden, but I can tell you you're far from bein' alone in your sorrow; nowadays all too many new-made widows are livin' hereabouts."

Frozen inside but outwardly composed Amy had offered Captain Selman a tiny glass of the last of Caleb's finest French brandy. The *Franklin's* master had tossed off the precious liquid in a single gulp which would have horrified a connoisseur such as Caleb Twisden.

"Comes anythin' I can do to smooth yer way, Mrs. Twisden, send word through Jonathan or Tom Izard; they keep me in touch about doin's round Marblehead. For sure," he'd added quietly, "I'd be pleased and honored to help Caleb's widow any way possible." After he'd glanced about the handsomely furnished room he'd remarked, "Allow you don't want for as much as some others."

Obviously he couldn't know that before long she'd have spent the last penny of ready money Caleb had left before the *Franklin* had stood out to sea. Nor could Captain Selman suspect that Caleb's less patriotic competitors right now were busy dividing up his law practice. What really troubled the pregnant widow was that for some reason she hadn't been able to fathom why any of her several in-laws hadn't proved at all anxious to help. True, most of Caleb Twisden's immediate family had paid brief and formal visits of condolence. Some few had dropped in later on from time to time possibly to appraise her home's contents. This had made her so mad she'd had a hard task to remain civil.

The baby gurgled a few times, so, after poking up the fire, Amy sought the crib but found Olivia blissfully asleep with minute bubbles forming at the corners of her tiny pink mouth.

Even with the passage of time relations with the Twisden clan hadn't improved but a majority of folks in Gloucester gradually had become more friendly—in public at least. Still, none of the Twisdens had lifted a finger to make life easier. Could they somewhere have learned what had chanced on the night of the raid?

Amy sagged onto a rocking chair, relaxed, remained staring into the flames until, unbidden, the image of Andrew Hunter appeared. Where at this moment might he be? Was he well? Was he wounded? Or, God forbid, dead? No telling. All she knew for certain was that Andrew had accompanied Colonel, now General, Knox as a gunnery expert all the way out to a fort called by an outlandish name of "Ticonderoga." Only thing folks agreed about was that said fort lay a long way off, in the upper part of the New York Colony.

On occasion rumors had reached Cambridge and Cape Ann that General Knox's column had been encountering so many difficulties it became a standing bet around the town's taprooms and public houses his so-called "Train of Artillery" never could get through the steep and roadless Berkshire Hills at this time of year.

Whenever possible, Amy left Gloucester and sought Peach's Head to be comforted by the unwavering friendship of Elizabeth Milburn, Tom, Jonathan and Deborah Izard. All four lent cour-

362

age when she'd been so shaken and hopeless after learning of Caleb's death. When her term was nearing its end it was Deborah and Elizabeth she'd sent for in the early hours of a very cold day. It was they who, just in time, had located an experienced midwife.

Twelve days following Olivia's birth and after "Biddy" Scroggins the aged crone whose help was all Amy could afford as an "accommodator" had retired to her bedroom off the kitchen Amy roused to loud crackling, snapping noises and a bitter smell of wood smoke. At first she imagined that wind beating down the fireplace's chimney was the cause but so many choking, eye-stinging fumes invaded her bedroom she rushed to the door only to recoil at a leaping glare from below and hearing Biddy Scroggins' shrieks of, "Come down! Quick! *Quick!* Hull kitchen's afire!"

There'd been scant time to wrap Olivia in a thick quilt and fling a cloak over her shoulders before, coughing, she'd stumbled down the narrow front stairs against smothering, whirling blasts of smoke, heat and sparks roaring up from below. How she ever managed to locate the front door she never could tell; all she knew was that all at once she was standing wheezing, half-blinded and barefooted in the snow.

The baby continued to scream. Gradually, neighbors began to appear half-dressed and attempted to form a bucket line to the nearest well. Because of the high wind nothing much could be accomplished. Soon Caleb Twisden's home had dissolved into a flame-spouting mound of embers. All that remained standing were the stark outlines of two red-brick chimneys.

Frigid drafts scurrying across the floor recalled Amy to the present, prompted her to seek the softness of that same narrow bed she'd occupied long before the Izards and their tragic-faced passenger had appeared in Marblehead.

Because of the chill Amy didn't peel off thick woolen hose she'd knitted or either of two flannel petticoats. She only pulled a quilted bed-jacket over her undervest then tugged a seaman's long-tailed stocking cap over her head till it lay level with her brows.

Gradually her body's warmth spread beneath the counterpane but, for some inexplicable reason, sleep eluded her. For example, would Marblehead's selectmen decide to keep her on as a permanent schoolteacher? This job she'd secured only because her predecessor had perished of one of the strange and often loathsome diseases imported to town by seafarers. She guessed so far she'd been doing well enough; the School Board's head had seemed both surprised and pleased by the firm manner she managed even the most unruly youngsters. How lucky Pa had seen to it that, for a female, she'd been uncommonly well lettered. Her pay, ten shillings a week, was minimal, but better than nothing till Caleb's small estate could get probated. Every school day, in all kinds of weather, she had to tramp a long half-mile to the one-room schoolhouse then at midday hurry home in time to nurse always voracious Olivia.

Ten shillings weekly of course couldn't go far towards paying warm-hearted and witty Aunt Elizabeth Milburn for board and keep.

Deborah, Jonathan Izard's garrulous, plump but industrious wife once her housework was done and often lonely now that Jonathan was kept busy shipbuilding over in Beverly where half-a-dozen large new vessels were expected to form a weak but regular little Navy, would gather knitting needles and balls of yarn spun on that same spinning wheel her mother and grandmother had used and come to visit with Amy. Aunt Elizabeth declared woolen mufflers, socks and mittens, every day, were fetching higher prices. More often than not she would teach Amy new and useful stitches.

For Amy it wasn't surprising or unpleasant how often Andrew's name entered conversation. To exist in this sort of limbo was proving all but unbearable especially since quite a few men, generally too young or too old to go to war, were inventing excuses to visit the Widow Milburn's gray-shingled cottage. In Deborah's opinion more men would be taking an interest had not most eligible males been absent in one Service or another.

Whenever Amy's courage weakened she recalled a favorite dictum of her father's: "'Tis wiser to bear the ills we know about than fly to others we wot not of."

For the time being she and Olivia should continue to enjoy warm shelter and plenty of plain but filling food. Best of all, she'd retained dependable friends no matter what the Twisdens might have hinted. However, there was one encouraging aspect to the Twisdens' attitude. Whatever they might suspect concerning her baby's paternity they'd kept it among themselves so far.

Chapter 46 🍂

ILL TIDINGS FROM CAMBRIDGE

THOSE WHO PARTICIPATED in the journey from Otis to Springfield, Massachusetts, would never quite forget it. Spirits drooped to the vanishing point. Weak or sick men quit, deserted or just plain vanished. No replacements were to be had, no matter what the inducements offered. The countryside just wasn't sufficiently populated. Besides, few men in their right minds would leave a relatively comfortable home to endure blizzards and storms which everyone agreed were the coldest and most prolonged in the oldest inhabitant's memory.

On the way to his quarters, a frigid little room in some Tory's looted and abandoned house, Andrew decided to pause and thaw out at the Bull & Bear, the only tavern in the vicinity. Lord, how his feet ached! That last pair of boots he'd secured had been carelessly cobbled and soon had begun to split and cause raw patches on his feet. Nowadays, were a fellow to travel in the rear of this long, dark column, slipping, sliding and creaking over a seemingly endless succession of ridges he would have noted more and more blood-spots, animal and human, staining the snow.

Ages seemed to have elapsed since Ticonderoga had been left behind. For the rest of his life Andrew always could conjure up recollections of an irregular, black-brown train now thick, now thin, depending upon the terrain, winding slowly among trees over snowy plains and rugged slopes. He could recall oxen leaning into heavy yokes, plodding with heads held low through snow often reaching up to their bellies. The sledges laden with canvas-shrouded gun barrels yawed, dipped and lurched wildly now up, now down, like so many land-borne ships in a rough sea. When progress slowed, rear elements of the column bunched up behind leaders hauling the heaviest cannon.

Then red-nosed, sniffling, and often youthful drovers swaddled in a weird miscellany of garments used goads, but sparingly; usually, they obtained better results through petting their beasts and calling them by name. "Haw there, Buck! Keep even with Dan!" "Dammit, gee, Billy! and you, George, pull together. Thaat's it! Let's show them overgrowed goats and dairy cows behind how to pull!"

Officers from Brigadier-General Knox on down spurred gaunt and stark-coated mounts, ceaselessly ranged along the line.

Everyone cursed when trail markers, tied to leafless bushes or saplings, indicated another ridge ahead.

On entering the Bull & Bear's smoky, warm interior reeking of beer and whiskey, Andrew paused on recognizing eerie, ear-piercing screeches and yowls peculiar to well-liquored Rangers and other long hunters.

Although the tavern was jam-packed he only managed to squeeze inside by turning sidewise. A quick survey revealed the cause for the tumult. Apparently a party of Pennsylvania riflemen had paused here on their way south where, they claimed, real fighting was about to take place. These rangy, hairy and quick-eyed men were whooping and screeching loud as if they'd just sacked a hostile Indian village. Soon Andrew ascertained most of these rampaging fellows' enlistments had expired but plenty more, bored, had plain deserted the tenuous lines besieging Boston. To a man they cursed warfare, European-style. Most riflemen claimed to be on their way to join up with Colonel Daniel Morgan's command, supposedly camped somewhere near New York.

Through pungent clouds of wood and tobacco, Jake Razors came weaving over grinning like a friendly wolf. "Heyo, there, Andy! Try a swig of this panther piss." Fending off the crowd with an arm he offered a cow's-horn cup half-filled with a throat-searing liquid some optimist might have described as whiskey.

Downing a big mouthful of stuff so fiery Andrew claimed later he'd oozed smoke like a frame house afire. "Say, Jake, can't you talk some of these fellows into coming back, joining up with us? You know how desperate short-handed we are of everything, most of all men and draft animals."

Violently, Razors shook his narrow head. "Right now I claim them guns got no more chance of winnin' through than a snow-ball in Hell. By the bye, Andy," he lowered his voice, said seriously, "hate to remind you this here place is 'bout to close to Boston and a whippin' as I aim to travel. Done my duty, ain't I?" he demanded fiercely. "Ain't never been none of our forces got cut off or ambushed."

"Sure you've done your duty and then some. Do you really intend to desert?"

"Naw. Ain't desertin', can't be, 'cause I ain't never been proper 'listed since I got drummed out o' camp last summer. Nor am I leavin' on account of hardships, 'tain't in my natur' to quit when the goin' gets rough." He narrowed his ever-restless and slightly slanting jet eyes. "Look, Cap'n, you and me been through a lot together so tell me true; are us Rangers actin' coward-like if we double back on our tracks so we can go to killin' Lobsterbacks accordin' to our own style? Us fellows just don't see sense bein' stood up in thick ranks so's some lousy Britishers who can't hit a cow on the tail with a bull fiddle can mow us down by volley fire. You know them furrin soljers don't aim muskets, they just point and cut loose for general results."

His red-brown and wind-sharpened features relaxed a trifle. "Besides, I'm aimin' to head south by way of Albany. Want to make sure little Jake's fine and dandy. Knowin' what kin happen to a orphan, don't want the poor little brat should suffer like me."

Bursts of song and ringing war whoops drowned out the balance of what he was saying. Razors offered his hand. "Andy, promise you won't hold it 'gainst me if I travel south with the rest of these Rangers?"

"No. I can't blame you, but I don't know how the General's going to take such news—he's been depending on you for so long."

"Needn't find out I've gone, lest you tell him. Besides, ain't been no red hostiles roamin' these parts since long ago, he don't need timber beasts like us no longer." Jake's grip tightened and his voice softened. "Andy, I mean, Cap'n Hunter, 'tis seldom I take to a body like I have to you and poor Paul Thebaud. Was I a prayin' man whenever I thought on it I'd drop onto my hunkers and beg the Lord if He'd mind pertecktin' you special-like 'cause I figger 'fore this here war ends you'll need plenty pertecktion. Even if these damn' guns ever do reach our lines I don't see how we kin hope to win. Once ice breaks up in Boston Harbor there'll be so many damn' Redcoats reinforcin' the enemy our side is bound to git skelped and plowed under."

Andrew, through cupped hands, shouted over the din, "If we do lose this war what will you and like-minded fellows do then?"

Jake's hairy throat jerked hard several times before he drained his cow's-horn cup. "Well, me and the fellers have bin talkin' serious 'bout that. If our side gets licked we figger to make tracks acrost them Allegheny Mountains and raise us up a big new nation on their far side 'thout no Reg'lar Army drill masters or high-and-mighty Philadelphy lawyers tryin' to tell us how to go about it."

Some bush-bearded riflemen, howling like hungry wolves, started a fight. The last Andrew saw of Serjeant Jake Razors he was plunging into the brawl whooping as loud as if he'd just lifted a prime Mohawk scalp.

Fortune favored Andrew Hunter and David Mason that their duties rendered it possible for them to enjoy a couple of nights in another modestly comfortable house recently deserted by a Tory family under threat of violence.

For the first time in days the two were able to bathe after a fashion out of a steaming wooden laundry tub and then experience the luxury of donning fresh small-clothes contributed by the local Committee of Safety.

Bowls of hot beef stew provided by an ox which had broken a leg so restored Andrew that, after making sure "Old Sow," "Albany" and the fourteen long 18-pounders were properly guarded, he returned to his billet and, as usual, found the engineer Major sound asleep and snoring mellifluously.

Feeling guilty over having for long neglected that journal Sarah had given him so long ago Andrew moved two tallow drip candles closer together and by their sputtering and evil-smelling light commenced to write:

NEAR WORCESTER
FEBRUARY 1776
(*Can't remember the exact date.*)

Alas, I have not made Entry in many weeks but Weather has proved too Harsh; indeed Everywhere 'tis claimed this is the Cruellest Winter anyone can Recall.

News from Cambridge proved very Discouraging. Couriers report Numbers of our troops are Deserting our Siege Lines, fearful not only of a British sally in strength but even more of Diseases which reportedly are carrying off People of all ages Sorts and Conditions like unto a plague out of Egypt. 'Tis said only our Commander-in-Chief's Inflexible Will to continue the Contest keeps even a semblance of our Forces on Duty.

This has proved a most Discouraging Week in that a number of sleet Storms have caused the Breakdown of many Vehicles and deaths of many draft Animals which now are most difficult to Replace this Countryside having been scoured time and again.

Quite a large number of light Cannon, mostly 8- or 10- and 12-pounders, are to be left behind, temporarily, for want of sufficient beasts to draw them.

First to be left on the Line of March were Waggons laden with Shott, Powder and Artillery Equipment. Also, during ice storms, Animals to their Owners' Financial and often Personal grief, have slipped on ice-covered Stones and suffered broken limbs. Many Drovers acted as sorrowful as if they had lost a Human Member of their Family.

*None-the-less the big Siege Guns still are being
advanced yard by yard Despite this terribly broken
Countryside. Somehow we manage to cover a few Miles
between Dawn and Dusk. Especial attention always is
devoted to the Progress of "Old Sow," and "Albany" and other
heavy pieces. They serve as a sort of pledge of our
Determination but unless this terrible Weather soon abates
and Fresh Drovers and Animals appear I fear we shall be
quite Undone.*

*Should this happen, which God forbid! nothing it
would Appear can keep together our besieging Forces.*

*What most disturbs our men are reports of the spread
of Deathly Sicknesses—many of them heretofore not before
encountered. 'Tis stated that crowding together people to
escape the Cold may be the Cause, but the Doctors—as
usual—cannot tell with any certainty. God send, Mamma,
Ellen and Sarah have escaped such afflictions.*

Near to Framingham, Massachusetts, General Knox ordered
the column to halt for the night at crossroads and park artillery
near a favorable spot consisting of wide, stone-studded grain
fields and pastures encircled by dense growths of silver birches
and evergreens. When sleighs and sledges labored into sight they
were directed to park near a scattering of stone farmhouses and
barns.

It was a blessing in disguise, Andrew discovered. He'd been
kept so busy and hadn't found time to miss Jake as much as otherwise he might have. He wasn't particularly astonished when
inspecting the condition of vehicles transporting his favorite
fieldpieces, mostly iron 8- and 12-pounders, a runner tramped up
on bear-paw snowshoes with orders directing Captain Andrew
Hunter to report to General Knox at once. There was nothing for
it but to turn over responsibility for the great guns to Major
Mason now shaggy-haired, hollow of cheek and eye but keeping
his wry sense of humor intact.

The messenger turning aside awkwardly blew a juicy nose.
The day being so wickedly cold, near thirty degrees of frost, he
didn't dare remove homespun mittens. Said he, "Gen'ral wants
you should come to him and fetch along yer things."

Why so? The significance of this instruction wasn't lost.

"Gen'ral's 'bidin' in that big brick house down the road a piece towards Framin'ham."

Andrew found Knox and his staff occupying a large farmhouse belonging to a red-hot Patriot by the name of Herbert Harrington. The Harrington home indeed proved to be one of the most impressive structures seen since the Train had quitted Albany. As usual Knox could be heard long before he was sighted. His amazingly ebullient spirit appeared as unflagging as ever.

"Well, sir, and how are my guns?" was the first thing he demanded once Andrew had saluted and straightened to attention.

"Still coming in, sir, but only a few at a time on account of we now are forced to relay draft animals from one conveyance to another. Lost an 18-pounder this morning, sir, when a sledge runner broke. It fell into a deep ravine but," he added hastily, "it can be recovered without too much trouble, sir."

Soon it became evident he'd been summoned because the General wanted dispatches delivered to the Commander-in-Chief in person. "These," Knox announced after accepting a fat and heavily sealed envelope from an aide, "are urgent requisitions for supplies we must have without loss of time. I've told that so many of our animals have died or been driven off, we're main-hard put to keep moving. If my cannon are to reach Roxbury before spring more draft animals *must* be found somewhere and forwarded immediately."

"Sir, may I inquire why I've been selected to go in to Cambridge?"

"You, better than anyone else, can explain to His Excellency, General Washington, our urgent needs and the nature of the ordnance we have brought thus far. Pray, Captain, explain to him that all our guns are fine, sound pieces of brass, bronze or iron. Also, we are fetching along plenty of shot to fit them."

A major in the background wearing the conspicuous scarlet tunic of Connecticut's Wethersfield Regiment asked, "What is the situation in our lines?"

"Can't hardly say," a local militia officer replied. "All we know is that people around Boston have grown so fearful of plagues, town authorities won't allow anybody coming from Boston or the siege lines into their communities. Sometimes they even shoot to drive people off, no matter how pressing their business or what rank they hold, but, coming from this direction you ought to be all right."

Once more Henry Knox exhibited the extent of his liking for young Captain Hunter; as few others, Knox could appreciate the extent of this ex-Royal Navy officer's experience. Certainly, he'd demonstrated his knowledge at Ticonderoga during selection of guns for the Continental Army's first and thus far only Train of Artillery.

An aide on being beckoned offered a document. Knox took it concealing his mangled hand as usual. "Captain, I will dispatch tonight a duplicate by another hand in case you get waylaid or intercepted by the enemies, Tory or British."

He clapped the artillery officer's shoulder. "Go with my blessing—for what that's worth. 'Tis far too late for you to start this evening but there'll be a strong mount ready for you here first minute there's enough light to see by." Fixedly he considered Andrew. "I've selected you to transmit these requisitions chiefly because you know Cambridge and its environs intimately. As I recall you have a family domiciled there?"

"Yes, sir, but I have had no word from them in weeks." Abruptly, he felt contrite that he'd not even given a passing thought to the people in "Fair View," also that his journal remained so sadly neglected. All the same, he reckoned Sarah might understand.

Knox's big voice impinged on his thoughts. "Well, sir, have you any immediate practical suggestions?"

"Sir, I think for the time being we ought to leave 'Old Sow,' 'Albany' and the long 18's behind. In my opinion 'tis more important to get our 12-, 8- and 6-pound fieldpieces into our lines without delay; 'twould prove encouraging for our troops to touch or even see cannon captured from the enemy."

Knox inclined his large head. "You've made a telling point—higher spirits mean much at this moment. Now go enjoy a hot meal in my personal mess." He grinned. "It'll be good. Guess you know I enjoy my vittles more than most. Look like it, don't I?"

CHAPTER 47 ❦

LOW TIDE FOR REBELS

THANKS TO TWISTING, frozen ruts and icy patches covering half-hidden stones Andrew Hunter and his escort, Corporal Benny of the 7th Connecticut, the same dispatch rider who'd fetched the dispatches from Cambridge, made poor time so dusk was setting in when familiar steeples in Cambridge became etched against the sky.

To Andrew's relief Corporal Benny proved uncommunicative, only slumped and bumped in his saddle with all the grace of a sack of grain. While following the Boston–Framingham Post Road, Andrew noted increasing and ominous signs of unrest. For example, on several occasions, when he and Benny rode into sight disorderly little groups of armed men ran off the turnpike and made for the nearest woods.

"Who will those be?" Andrew queried.

"Them's sure 'nough deserters, sir. Time-expired soldiers wouldn't take cover."

In mounting concern Andrew noticed how many pickets, points and outposts stood empty and apparently recently deserted. Further depressing were huge flocks of crows winging by

374

towards some central winter roosting place. Their raucous cawings seemed to intensify an already lugubrious atmosphere. Here and there in bleak, snow-covered clearings were seen the roofless, charred remains of homes, barns and sheds. Corporal Benny allowed as how these likely had been set afire by careless smokers among departing troops.

While nearing town, Andrew's attention kept shifting till presently he sighted the familiar outlines of the Ruggleses', Joseph Lee's and then Judge Sewall's handsome residences ranged along "Tory Row." Because of intervening structures "Fair View," lying closest to the Charles, couldn't yet be seen.

To Captain Hunter's amazed dismay he and his companion weren't once challenged on their way into town, not even when close to Continental Army's Headquarters. Sentries who should have stood on the alert remained swathed in scarves hunched over little fires, they didn't even bother to turn heads at the sound of hoofbeats.

Presently Corporal Benny reined in, pointed. "This is as far as I go. A left turn will take you to the Virginia General's Headquarters at the Vassall House inside three shakes of a lamb's tail."

"I know where it is. Goodbye, Benny, mind you care for that horse, he's been stumbling a lot recently."

In Cambridge people, military and civilians alike, appeared downcast, miserable. Soldiers kept slouching along with heads bent, bundled in an outlandish assortment of garments. Cheering lights glowed in only a very few windows.

To conquer an impulse to head straight for home proved difficult. First, he must present Knox's requisitions to the Adjutant of the Commander-in-Chief.

He dismounted, turned his horse over to a soldierly-looking private then tramped into the Vassall House and through persistent questioning, located Colonel Glover and some field-grade officers of the 21st Regiment. Also present was Tom Izard who'd become a lieutenant, judging by that pale-blue cockade stitched to his flat-brimmed seaman's hat.

Following a bone-crunching handshake and an affectionate bearhug, the Marbleheader drawled, "B'God, Andy, you sure look like you've just been drug through a tight hawsehole. Tell me true; would you liefer go back to sea or go on handlin' cannons on land?"

Andrew managed a stiff grin. "I'm going back to sea the minute I'm able. After all, wasn't I trained to handle naval guns?"

"Sure. Come over to the fire and thaw out. Hope you've fetched along cheery news. Troops are growin' so discouraged their sperrits droop like a whipped puppy's tail."

"It's bad as all that?"

"Yep, and then some. What with shortages of food and fuel, disease and desertions this here Army's hair hung on the brink of comin' apart at the seams. 'Twould have broke up long ago savin' for our Commander-in-Chief's unwillingness to admit how bad things are goin' for us. Southerner or not, Mister Washington's a whole man."

Momentarily Andrew listened to the cheerful and fragrant crackling of white birch logs in the fireplace. "Well, Tom, you can spread word that all the guns we're bringing have been hauled past Worcester and some were being parked outside of Framingham just before I left for here."

"That God's truth? You ain't funnin' to raise my heart?"

"No, my word on it. Cannon, big siege ones, still were coming in when I left. But, Tom, lest a lot of fresh draft animals are found in a hurry, most of our siege artillery is likely to rust in Framingham till spring."

Colonel Glover, who'd sauntered up in time to overhear Andrew's last remark, observed grimly, "By which time the harbor's ice will have begun to break up and the British will get supplies and reinforcements and what's left of our troops will head for home." His steely eyes fixed Andrew. "Better than most, you know something encouraging needs to happen and in jig time. Captain Hunter, in your opinion, what must be done?"

"Well, sir, I think, first off, some companies of our most reliable troops should be sent out towards Framingham at once but they must be well disciplined and healthy-looking. General Knox believes 'tis the fear of catching disease more than anything else is responsible for many recent desertions from our Train."

Glover nodded. "Grant you that, I'll tend to the matter. Meantime, can you give me a complete list of the ordnance you've been transporting?"

"Yes, sir."

"Good. Tomorrow I'll get your list printed like a pamphlet and have it circulated where 'twill do the most good; may serve as a sweetening for souring spirits."

Tom Izard drew near and, for a miracle, stood to attention before the Colonel till the latter snapped, "Stand easy, Mister Izard." Glover then said, "Captain Hunter, is General Knox expecting you to return straightaway?"

"Not until some relief arrives, sir, and his requisitions honored."

Little crow's-feet deepened at the corners of Glover's eyes. "How'd you like to get reassigned to my—to the 'Marblehead' Navy?"

"As soon as possible, sir. Truly, my feet ache for the feel of a deck moving under 'em."

"Very well, Captain, I'll see what can be done. Should be easy when, as and if Knox's guns arrive." So saying Glover moved away to join a group of tired-looking senior officers.

Once the Colonel had moved away Tom drew near; something in his expression captured Andrew's attention when he asked, "Seen my family recently?"

Slowly, Izard inclined his head. "Yep. Last few days I been stoppin' by yer home whenever I'd the chance and I—I—well." All at once his huge calloused hands sought and tightened on Andrew's shoulders. "Andy, brace yerself for some mighty bad news. Your Ma died day only before yesterday; buried her this mornin'."

To steady himself Andrew drew a series of deep breaths, heard his voice saying, "What did she die of?"

"Last week she got took by some sort of strangury fever; none of the sawbones Glover sent could set a name to it. She just seemed to burn and shrivel up, but suffered no pain thank the Lord. Andy, there's such a lot of sickness about hardly a home hasn't been smitten."

John Glover, who'd been listening without seeming to, came back, placed an arm about Andrew's quivering shoulders. "Sorry, but that's the way 'tis. Now you head straight home. Your people should find a deal of comfort seeing you still in one piece."

"Thank you kindly, sir. You are most considerate."

"I aim to be, whenever possible. I'll see about your reassignment to the 21st soon as possible." He smiled. "Might even find a small cruiser for you to command soon's the ice goes out. Know you'll make good use of her, 'specially if and when Congress authorizes a Continental Navy, which those flannel-mouthed jackasses down in Philadelphia should have done long ago!"

Glover turned his back towards the fire. "Goes without saying I'd like to hear how Henry Knox and you overcame some of the troubles you encountered after leaving Ticonderoga, but that can wait. Your family comes first. Return here tomorrow, soonest possible. Mister Izard, go along with Captain Hunter. A true 'Header comes in handy when seas turn stormy."

Andrew felt dazed rather than overwhelmed with realization that Mother was dead. What a loyal, unselfish and capable wife she'd always been to the late Captain Timothy; tender and understanding towards their children but a strict disciplinarian when the occasion demanded. He'd never have such luck in marriage—or would he? How would Ellen be bearing up under such a loss? Probably she'd do well, having inherited much of Father's even, outwardly unemotional temperament.

Tom's voice interrupted. "Expect you're wonderin' about what's chanced with Sarah Hilton; that gal you kind of doted on."

"Yes. How is she?"

"Sarah's still with yer family. She and yer sister, Ellen, all along have been busy nursin' anywhere they're needed."

Sarah! Mention of her shook him out of his semi-dazed state. "Sarah? How—how is she?" he asked for the second time.

"Lost a mite of weight I'd hazard but reckon she could spare a little. She's still pretty as a speckled pup."

"She's well?"

"Was, day before yesterday. Oh, speakin' of females—recall that Amy Orne you met back home?"

A brief catch of breath delayed Andrew's query. "Of course. How is Amy faring?"

"Not too well. Shortly after she married Caleb Twisden and moved into his house in Gloucester, news came Caleb had been lost at sea while prize master of a captured coaster. Sure pity that young woman."

"Why? Thought Caleb was pretty well fixed."

Tom's gaze shifted. "For some reason no one can figger out, nary one of the Twisdens hev lifted a finger to help Amy; not even when her home burned to the ground only a few days after she birthed a girl baby."

"A girl baby?"

Somewhat like a weary boxer suffering a series of hard jabs from a powerful opponent Andrew attempted to marshal thoughts in order. Amy, poor Amy. Life seldom had proved kind to her. Losing both parents when young she'd been condemned to an orphan's fate. Nevertheless, she'd made her way without complaint. Yes, Amy always had evinced courage combined with charm and industry. What was Tom saying?

"When the Twisdens wouldn't do anythin' for Amy, Brother Jonathan and Deborah took in her and her baby. Poor thing had nothin' left 'cept the clothes she was wearin'. Elizabeth Milburn, her old aunt, offered shelter till Amy could find a place to 'bide."

Hesitantly, Andrew queried, "What does Amy do for a living nowadays?"

"Teaches school or so I've heard."

They turned off the King's Highway and headed down Spring Street towards the Charles. By now it was almost dark. Candles and lamps were burning, well away from windowpanes silver-rimmed by frost.

Fluttering in the icy wind was a large bow knot of black crêpe knotted to the brass door knocker shaped like a leaping dolphin—the same Pa had brought back from Jamaica long years ago.

A few people Andrew didn't recognize were departing as Andrew and Tom drew near. He noticed the picket fence separating the house from Spring Street was gone; probably used up for kindling. Dutifully, he kicked snow from his boots before entering "Fair View."

Just inside he encountered Ellen, eyes swollen and red. She uttered a strangled cry and surged into his arms. Whimpering, she clung to him, slight body shuddering to violent sobs which gradually slackened.

After lingering on the front stoop a long minute Tom Izard

379

said quietly, "Sincere sympathy, Miss Hunter. If there ain't anythin' I can do, reckon I'd best report back to Headquarters."

"Must you?" Andrew asked.

"Aye. Cunnel Glover fears some sort of serious trouble is about to break out."

"What sort of trouble?"

"Dunno, but sounds like it's mutiny or more wholesale desertions. There's been considerable talk about it 'mongst even the steadiest regiments. See you tomorrow, early."

Andrew nodded. "Thanks. Tell Glover I'll be on hand first thing tomorrow."

Once he'd closed and bolted the brass box-lock on the front door Andrew half-carried his sister into "Snug Harbor" as Captain Timothy always had termed the office *cum* library in which he worked on holidays or evenings to complete tasks unfinished in his counting house at the end of the dock below.

Apparently certain mourners must have tarried in here; an empty bowl of punch and wet glasses were creating rings on the late Captain's gleaming table desk. Pa usually had kept a bottle of extra-fine Jamaica rum in its lower left-hand drawer. Sure enough, one was there. Probably Mother had kept it there in hopes of Pa's sudden return. Andrew poured a pair of drinks, held one to his sister's lips.

"Take this, Ellie. Know you don't drink, but right now you need a touch of spirits if ever a mortal did." He felt the same way.

Footsteps sounded above. He guessed they might be Sarah's but Ellen, perched on his lap as if again she was a troubled small girl with a favorite elder brother, said, "Mamma was buried this morning. Undertaker claims ground was frozen so deep he had to burn nigh on a cord of wood to thaw the earth deep enough for her grave. Pretty expensive."

"Of course, Ellie, but let's take comfort knowing Mamma won't have to worry over this damned war any longer. If only I'd known about her sickness earlier."

"Don't blame yourself. Even you couldn't have helped matters." Ellen sniffed and her arms tightened convulsively about him. "When Colonel Glover heard about Mamma's condition he sent some of the best m-medical men he could find, but-but there

was no curing the con-congestion which c-carried her off. Just before she went away she became lucid enough to c-call your name and say she was passing peacefully in the confidence you'd always do your duty by our Country and will carry on the business when peace comes."

Again light footsteps sounded upstairs.

"Sarah?"

"No. Sarah's poorly. Poor thing took a terrible chill out at the cemetery. Some neighbors, Mrs. Freda Bott and Susan Outerbridge are tending her till I can take my turn."

Sarah ill? A whirling sensation gripped Andrew much as when he'd been delirious during that bout with ship fever; emotions overwhelmed him like waters rushing through a dike suddenly breached.

Said he abruptly setting his sister on her feet, "Ellie, I *must* see her. I'm going up. I'm dead beat. Is my room empty?"

"Yes. Had a Hampshire staff officer using it till last week when he disappeared without paying his bill—just like a Hampshire man or a Rhode Islander." She sniffled. "He may have left bugs."

"Deserted?"

"No. Just before he took off he let drop his time was about up."

When the door was opened the two young women at Sarah's bedside turned to face him. One said, "Evening, sir. Are you a physician?"

"No, Ma'am."

"Then why are you here?"

"I'm Andrew, Ellen's brother." His attention sought and remained fixed on the flushed damp face and small bright head nearly concealed among goose-down pillows.

"What ails her?"

Mrs. Bott, the sprightly younger of the two, said softly, "Just listen to her trying to draw breath." She placed her hand on Sarah's forehead, said over her shoulder, "She's feverish, been burning up since last night. Doctor Bainbridge was here, left just now saying in his opinion Sarah's suffering from a disease he called a severe congestion of the lungs. Gave it some fancy Latin name, but round here folks mostly call it 'galloping consumption' on account a body either gets well quickly or gets called to Our Lord's Mansion."

Breathing quickly, shallowly, Major Hilton's daughter commenced to mutter under her breath. Nerves taut and jangling, Andrew bent low but could make no sense whatever of Sarah's babblings.

Stated Mrs. Outerbridge, "Sometimes she opens her eyes and they roll about, but poor girl recognizes nothing."

Mrs. Bott said, "You must be the 'Captain Hunter' Sarah keeps asking for. You just have arrived in Cambridge?"

"Yes, Ma'am. Have just ridden in from Framingham and General Knox's Artillery Train." How utterly helpless he felt—he who'd solved so many knotty problems along the route from Ticonderoga. "Think she might need another eider-down over her?"

Mrs. Bott, standing straight and slim as an arrow for all her thirty-odd years, said, "Don't believe so. The poor thing is fairly burning up already. Doctor Bainbridge believes a 'crisis,' as he terms it, may come sometime tonight or tomorrow, in which case he'll come to bleed her."

Ellen appeared looking haggard and even paler. "How is she?"

Mrs. Bott told her crisply, "As good as her condition warrants, I guess. 'Twill do neither her nor you any good to linger here. 'Specially you, Captain, if you don't mind my saying so, look worn to a frazzle, near the edge of collapse. Ellen, hope you didn't also take a chill in that freezing churchyard."

Possibly thanks to the rum she'd been ordered to swallow Ellen, usually self-controlled, swayed a little before meekly allowing Mrs. Outerbridge to guide her to her bedroom.

"Well, young man," demanded Mrs. Bott, "I know you're grieving for your mother and are terrible worried over Sarah, but right now you must get some rest; you look like the wrath of God." With two days' stubble of beard and eyes grown cavernous, this was true enough.

Said he heavily, "You're right." Then authority re-entered his voice. "I'll go rest, but first I need to be alone with Sarah for a little space."

"It's as you wish, but I doubt anything will come of it. Sarah's taken leave of her wits."

The neighbor drew herself up and stalked to the staircase straight as a Grenadier on parade.

Andrew collapsed rather than seated himself on a chair by the bedside then took Sarah's hand squirming restlessly about the counterpane and was appalled by its shocking heat. He bent low. "Please, my darling, this is Andrew."

Sarah seemed to rally, turned a scarlet and sweat-sodden face. "When war's over—you—me—have many children. So—so proud— you—don't leave—" Sarah's voice faded then she relapsed into incoherence.

Andrew felt too weary even to seek his old room, found barely enough strength to rise and drop a couple of logs on the fire before collapsing in a wing chair set close by the fireplace, before lapsing into unconsciousness rather than sleep.

CHAPTER 48 🌿

MALCONTENTS

SHORTLY AFTER DAYBREAK Lieutenant Tom Izard appeared looking almighty concerned when Betsy, the old cook, unbolted the front door. During the preceding night Tom had seen and heard enough to sense critically serious events were about to take place unless some drastic measure were taken before sundown of this day. In the first place, spies had reported Lord Howe's forces about to make a sally in strength out of Boston designed to capture the Commander-in-Chief's Headquarters and at the same time to stampede cold, half-starved and ill-clad Continentals and militia into flight.

From the foot of the stairs Tom yelled fit to bring the roof down, "Andy! Andy! Come quick! Johnny Glover wants you straightaway!"

Andrew appeared, disheveled and half-awake, "Wha'—wha'—wha's the matter?"

"Right now our Army's on the verge of mutiny or large-scale desertion. Ringleaders claim there ain't no point stayin' in the siege lines till we freeze to death or die of plague. They say, too, minute the ice goes out the bloody British will get all the supplies and reinforcements they can use! Expect spies must have reported how low our spirits have dropped."

If only General Knox had been here instead of Framingham. That portly individual possessed such an astounding knack of resolving, swiftly and efficiently, what appeared to be insuperable difficulties.

Betsy appeared carrying mugs of steaming mutton broth—nowadays real tea or coffee couldn't be had for love or money. The two drank hurriedly, sopped crusts in the broth and were tying scarves when Mrs. Bott called down from upstairs, "Captain! Captain! Sarah isn't restless or delirious any more. Susan and I agree her fever's broken and she's now fallen asleep."

"Thank you. I'll come back first minute I can."

Hurrying towards Colonel Glover's quarters the two encountered increasing and ever more alarming evidences of disorder. Squads or even companies of troops were shambling along in sullen disorder, muffled heads drawn low between shoulders and footgear creaking on the frozen ground.

Never before had Andrew seen Colonel Glover appear so grim. His long brown features had turned gray-pink and wrinkles not ordinarily perceptible creased his visage.

Abruptly, he resumed his usual manner. "I want you and Major William Knox to come to the Common right away. Grumblers seem to be gathering there." While they strode along Cambridge's littered, manure-splashed streets Glover spoke rapidly. "I want you to speak about General Knox's Train of Artillery. Tell those chicken-hearted bastards how many guns he's bringing. Give 'em a full description of the ordnance and if necessary, lie a little about their weight and number. Main thing to impress on them is that right now guns lie close to Framingham—not two days' march from here. Go. Wait for me outside the Court House. I'll join you directly."

As if to encourage potential deserters the sky darkened and a raw, biting gale commenced to blow out of the northwest. Andrew noticed men in considerable numbers quitting a number of red-brick dormitories belonging to Harvard College and assembling in the Yard. What most disturbed him was that so many of the insurgents were lugging knapsacks or blanket rolls along with cooking kettles, firearms and other personal items, arguing they were leaving for good. Most of these displaying no spirit headed for the now treeless Common. Never a drum was beaten or a fife sounded to lend malcontents even a semblance of order.

Andrew noted the arrival before the Court House of Colonel Glover with his aides and a detail from the 21st Massachusetts. All were fully armed but looking ill-at-ease.

A squad of steady Marbleheaders escorted Major William Knox and Andrew to a group of field officers from the Commander-in-Chief's personal staff. They stood on the Court House's granite steps.

With them, Glover's party moved out along Menotomy Road till a dark mass of men were sighted milling about the Common.

Once the party from Headquarters became recognized the would-be mutineers' clamor swelled into an ugly roar. Surprisingly the malcontents parted, allowing the party from Headquarters to advance into a small, hollow square formed by Continentals and a few riflemen drawn up in tight double ranks. Someone had had sufficient foresight to bring a few drummers inside the square; these without pause commenced to beat the Long Roll.

Heartsick over events at "Fair View," Andrew followed Glover into the little square. The moment Glover and his entourage arrived drums beat and fifes shrilled the tune called "Yankee Doodle" devised by the British to ridicule bumpkin Rebels but these had adopted it, converting it into a song of defiance.

When at last a prolonged rolling of drums succeeded in quieting the crowd a brigadier-general nearly as portly as Henry Knox but with a face rather like that of a confused old sheep was boosted onto a big stump. From this point of vantage he waved hands shouting, "Friends and fellow-countrymen. We of the Staff are well aware of the miserable conditions you have been enduring so patiently, so patriotically. Fainthearts have departed, but *you,* gathered here, have proven yourselves faithful to the justice of our Cause, so listen to news which will warm your hearts better than strong spirits."

Prolonged jeers and catcalls caused the fat officer to jump off the stump whereupon Glover quickly leaped up to replace him then shouted for silence in a voice capable of carrying to the royals of a tall ship in a gale. Recognizing the redoubtable Marbleheader, many quieted.

"Huzza for Johnny Glover! Had us more officers the likes of him us wouldn't suffer the fix we're in!" The speaker was a tall individual wearing the brown uniform of some Rhode Island unit.

Like the skilled public speaker he was, John Glover raised hands and remained silent till the hubbub subsided save along the mob's outer perimeter. Finally he drew himself up bellowing, "Don't quit now, boys! Come a day or so more and we'll be granted means of driving the Redcoats out of Boston!"

There came shouts of, "Oh, stuff such twaddle!" "More empty promises and moonshine!" "We've been took in too often afore!"

Impassively Glover waited for the tumult to subside before resuming his stentorian, quarterdeck voice. "By this time tomorrow night I swear by the Almighty the first cannon General Knox has fetched from Ticonderoga will enter our lines!"

People yelled, "Don't nobody credit him!" "That's just another lie, 'cause in mid-winter real big cannons can't nowise get hauled above three hundred miles, across mountains and a wilderness."

"I'm speaking God's truth, you damn' blockheads!" Glover bellowed. "Now shut up and listen to a couple of fellers who've actually made the march!"

Willing hands heaved up Andrew and William Knox onto a stump barely wide enough to accommodate the both of them. When Glover introduced Major Knox shouts went up at the very sound of his name. Unfortunately, William was by no means as gifted a speaker as was his older brother; all he did was to describe the route the guns had followed and describe some of the difficulties encountered: shortages, steep hills, sunken gundelows and trackless wildernesses. His was an uninspired account which didn't go far towards satisfying malcontents.

"T'Hell with them troubles!" shouted a brawny corporal. "Bet this is just a lot of lying moonshine contrived to keep us poor starvelings here. Lest you talk more convincing-like, we're goin' home, ain't we, boys?"

A roar of approval made the Common resound.

Aware of William Knox's failure to reach the crowd, Glover

turned to Andrew while drums rolled to quiet the throng, "Shut up, you blackguards, listen to Captain Andrew Hunter, a native of this town. He has been along of General Knox all the way from Ticonderoga to Framingham! Be quiet so's you can hear what he's got to tell you!"

How he managed to find the right words to describe the Train's progress down upper New York and across southern Massachusetts Andrew could never explain yet, somehow, he made the mob see gundelows, Durham boats and scows bucking ice and guns transferred to land vehicles at Fort George. Also he vividly described scouting precautions General Knox had taken, the way he'd attracted civilians and their draft animals in sparsely inhabited regions. Briefly he then explained how a succession of steep mountains and hills, some almost as sheer as cliffs, had been conquered through the use of blocks and falls, by the use of improvised windlasses, of pinch-bars and the blood and sweat of men determined to bring the guns to their destination.

Aware he'd captured the crowd's interest, Hunter evoked a huge laugh on telling about "Old Sow," "Albany" and other great siege guns; he even described their ornamentations.

"Fine! But how far kin they shoot?" shouted the obstreperous corporal.

"Mortars and the larger siege guns, mounted on Dorchester and Roxbury Heights, can range not only Boston but also the Royal Navy's anchorages."

A faint cheer arose, swelled to an uproar.

A Rhode Island serjeant shouted, "You willin' to swear on the Bible you're telling us the plain whole truth?"

Andrew grinned. "Sure. Trot a Good Book over here and I will take oath on it. I've not lied in the least, as you'll learn as soon as sufficient draft animals can be found so, stand fast lest the British don't sally out to capture these cannon. Mind you, Tories and other spies are keeping Lord Howe well informed, so for all our sakes don't back out after we've all done and suffered so much!"

Somebody deep in the crowd bawled, "How many cannons you claim to be fetchin'?"

Without hesitation Andrew shouted back, "In all we've

brought 59 pieces of ordnance of which 43 are cannon and 16 mortars."

A tall, red-nosed serjeant shouted, "How much do 'Old Sow' weigh?"

"Around 5,000 pounds," came the instant reply.

"Sounds about right," shouted a New Hampshire captain. "Know enough about artillery to vow this feller ain't lyin'."

When, amid a gale of applause, Andrew jumped off the stump John Glover immediately took his place; significantly, there were visible scarcely any men wearing the distinctive 21st's pea jacket, tar hats and bell-bottomed pants.

Cupping hands, Glover yelled, "If some of those guns don't reach the Roxbury lines inside two days' time any yellow-bellied skunks among you can feel free to sneak home and live with your consciences the rest of your lives! Dammit! You've just heard Captain Hunter, an experienced artillery officer, who, though he's been too modest to praise himself, personally raised 'Old Sow' when she broke through ice and sank. Moreover, up in Ticonderoga, 'twas him who did more than his share in picking the right kind of guns for our purposes.

"Now," Glover's voice blared like a bugle, "you sniveling, rascals get back to duty! Dis-miss!"

CHAPTER 49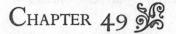

DORCHESTER HEIGHTS

ON THE NIGHT of March 2nd, 1776, the heaviest pieces mounted on hills commanding the sprawling hamlet of Roxbury opened fire on Boston Neck. Although the weight of their shot was insignificant and couldn't inflict serious damage the bombardment nevertheless caused British batteries to open in reply. Also to little effect.

Later, Andrew discovered the reason behind this seemingly purposeless bombardment from Roxbury. It had been designed to divert British attention from even higher Dorchester Heights where, in the dead of night, swarms of men used picks and shovels to throw up earthworks, much as they had on Breed's Hill and on a far grander scale.

Once dawn had broken on the 3rd, Sir William Howe was both astonished and aghast to realize that Gage's error of last June had been repeated but with much greater significance. Bitterly, his staff wondered why Billy Howe hadn't dispatched even a single battalion to occupy such manifestly strategic heights. Possibly luscious Mrs. Loring's favors had distracted him? No one knew or, if they did, maintained discreet silence.

Even the Commander-in-Chief, General George Washington, smiled as he seldom did nowadays when, following a small escort of cavalry, the first sledge swayed into sight along the deeply rutted and frozen road to Framingham. From a scattering of troops burst ringing cheers which, gathering volume, spread like a spring tide over a low marsh when, along the road to Roxbury, the double span of red-and-white wide-horned oxen hauled into view a pair of the biggest cannon most had ever seen.

Had the British elected to attack at this moment they might well have broken through the siege lines; almost everyone able to walk or hobble was making his way towards the Framingham —Roxbury turnpike.

Once the sturdy sledge conveying "Old Sow" drew near men threw into the air headgear not secured by a scarf or a length of woolen cloth and pounded one another on the back, cavorted and cheered until crows, foraging for gleanings on nearby fields, took alarmed flight.

One after another more sleighs, sledges and a few high-wheeled wagons drawn by locally impressed beasts at long last hauled the "Noble Train of Artillery," as many were beginning to call it, towards its destination.

General Knox's staff, amplified by members of the Commander-in-Chief's entourage, swelled with pride on witnessing the culmination of a march quite as incredible as that which the Carthaginian General Hannibal, had made across the Alps long centuries before.

Andrew, having directed replacement of draft animals the day before tramped over grimy snow alongside "Old Sow," that huge gun which had come so close to costing him his life.

For a wonder this day had dawned so exceptionally mild that here and there patches of snow had commenced to melt on hilltops and on top of great granite boulders. For above an hour the decorous Commander-in-Chief, his aides and principal lieutenants sat their mounts in a dark cluster atop a knoll watching more and more sleighs, sledges and wagons appear but at ever longer intervals. All were beaming as if some important victory just had been won which, perhaps, it had.

Long since, Generals Knox's and Washington's chief engineers had selected tactically important battery sites concentrated along

Dorchester Heights overlooking the whole of Boston and its surrounding waters. Indeed, these heights posed a far greater strategical menace to Boston than Breed's Hill ever had.

The weather continued too mild to admit rapid progress of the train, but during the next forty-eight hours all the pieces and ammunition carriers had arrived, were ready for positioning.

In the dead of night masses of Continentals, militia and civilians began to manhandle selected siege cannon into crude, half-finished embrasures. Most positions still were awaiting finishing touches when daylight came but an impressive number of guns stood ready for service. Noting this quite a few deserters returned to duty shamefaced but eager to atone.

Increasing detachments of militia commencing to appear from the surrounding countryside proved an inspiring sight. To behold Pine Tree Flags of different sizes; one displayed a bright red field instead of a white background, with a lone evergreen showing in its canton corner; flapping above Dorchester Heights they were heartwarming.

Roundly, albeit silently, General Howe was being cursed by his veteran officers who, all along, had warned of the strategic importance of Dorchester Heights now fairly bristling with cannon.

By now Andrew, David Mason and others who'd made the "Long Haul," as it was becoming termed, knew most of the men under their immediate command by name. Tackles, expertly handled, heaved "Old Sow" off her sledge and, under Andrew's supervision, carefully was lowered onto a stout field carriage especially designed to bear a siege gun's weight. All along the row of batteries much the same scene was being repeated.

Startled British batteries hastily opened fire but weren't able to achieve sufficient elevation to range the Heights; their round-shot fell harmlessly short on slopes sweeping up to the Continental gun positions still as ominously silent as they'd been on Breed's Hill.

Once "Old Sow" had been sited to Andrew's satisfaction its gun crew personally drilled by himself lugged forward a supply of 24-pound roundshot, but no lighter projectiles such as shells, fire carcases, grape, canister and other loads which could not hope to carry over Boston Neck into Boston or to naval anchorages.

To his astonishment Andrew noticed that, thus far, no men-of-war appeared to be making preparations to open fire. Undoubtedly the Royal Navy still was entertaining the illusion that no enemy cannon sufficiently powerful to range their anchored ships had been positioned.

Chapped and hairy recruits and veterans thronged to gaze in wonder upon those impressive monster guns "Old Sow" and "Albany." Onlookers soon became such a nuisance Andrew had to order guards to keep them at a distance.

Once heavy charges of powder had been rammed home Andrew himself selected the first roundshot and, shoulders hunching, drove it down "Old Sow's" gaping throat. Finally orders arrived to open fire. A linstock wound with the usual glowing slow match in hand, Andrew experienced a curious sense of uplifting, of exhilaration marred by a struggle between past and present loyalties.

"C'mon, Cap'n," shouted Number Two gunner, "let's hull one o' the Royal Tyrant's warships!"

Despite everything, Andrew somehow wasn't able deliberately to train his gun on a British man-of-war: this shot might kill or maim men he'd known, liked and had served with for years. Squinting, he made certain the priming charge of extra-fine triple-F gunpowder had been spread smoothly over the touchhole, then trained "Old Sow" on a pair of large merchantmen anchored off the charred ruins of Charles Town in observance of orders issued by Washington himself, that the City of Boston shouldn't intentionally be damaged. Through a spyglass Andrew watched swarms of red-coated infantry columns stream from their earthworks and start hurriedly retreating over Boston Neck.

A mounted orderly pulled up, breathless. "You Cap'n Hunter?"

"I am. What is it?"

"Gen'ral Knox allows he wants heavy pieces to get shooted first."

"Very well. Present my respects to the General."

Having shouted Knox's instructions to his own and nearby batteries, Andrew, suddenly calm, blew on his linstock's match till its fuse glowed yellow-red.

Not being overconfident about the strength of "Old Sow's" breeching tackles he ordered his sweating gun crew to stand well clear, drew a deep, deep breath—and reached another turning point in his career. Hand trembling, he pressed the slowly sparkling match into the touchhole's priming charge; a plume of fire spurted vertically. "Old Sow" emitted a mighty roar, a belch of flame, and, amid great clouds of rotten-smelling gray-white smoke, recoiled into its breechings like a skittish colt about to be saddled for the first time.

Along with his gun crew Andrew watched "Old Sow's" 24-pound roundshot arch high, high and higher until, attaining its zenith, it commenced to fall. Just where this particular roundshot landed Andrew couldn't be too sure but it must have hulled one of the merchantmen since its fore-topmast tottered and fell, splashing alongside. He aimed the next shot at the same Long Wharf on which less than a year earlier he'd landed, career in ruins, hunted, friendless, without direction or purpose.

Other siege guns commenced a thundering, deep-throated roar such as long ago had shattered forest stillnesses around Lake Champlain. To note how smartly his gun crews started to reload was encouraging. Mortars had not as yet been brought into position but, long before dark, they would start lobbing flaming carcases and heavy shells into enemy defenses on Boston Neck.

For a short while British batteries on the Neck continued to fire but fell silent once fieldpieces: 10-, 12-, 14-pounders, commenced to range them from the Heights.

Shortly afterwards, men-of-war one after another upped anchor, shook out topsails and moved off on the tide. Grimly, Andrew locked jaws while watching vessels of the Royal Navy commence scudding off to safety in the lee of Deer Island and Castle William, a sensible move since they'd no hope of bombarding the Heights.

Vaguely, Andrew wondered whether H.M.S. *Lively* might be among those sloops-of-war down yonder; even now he hoped she wasn't, too many pleasant associations couldn't be erased.

The effects of bombardment from Dorchester Heights and batteries in Roxbury soon became apparent. It turned out that a lieutenant captured on patrol duty recently had served with Lord Howe's headquarters and, during interrogation in Cambridge, rather readily stated, "You Rebels once more have caught Billy

Howe with his pants down or," he sniggered, "in bed with Mrs. Loring. To tell the truth, our troops have become utterly dispirited, so cold and hungry no promises or threats short of drumhead court-martials and prompt execution could persuade our rank-and-file to attack established earthworks like yours. What chanced at Breed's Hill ain't been forgotten, not by a damned sight! They want no more blood-baths of such a nature."

"What about the men-o'-war?" someone queried.

The prisoner shrugged. "Oh, those Navy fellows know their number's up. Warrant you'll view the last of their sterns afore long. 'Tis your Tories who are wildly imploring Lord Billy not to offer resistance: Patriots in Boston are fearful lest their homes and businesses be destroyed. Every thought in the High Command tends towards quick and complete evacuation of that damned, trouble-making port."

The Lieutenant's prediction proved well based. Although General Howe did go through the motions of mounting a massive night assault against the Heights but his heart wasn't in it so he and numberless others silently rejoiced when, on the eve of embarkation, a screaming gale arose out of the northeast and prevented the landing of reinforcing troops ordered from Castle William out in the harbor. Therefore, the prisoner stated, Lord Howe's probable next move would be to evacuate the port and set sail for Halifax while means and opportunity still offered.

Sure enough, next day a senior British staff officer, a portly lieutenant-colonel, put out aboard a cutter wearing a white flag at its single masthead. Once landed, glowering and haughty, he was conducted to the Commander-in-Chief's advance headquarters. Here he announced that at a council, held last night in Province House, Lord Percy strongly had advised Lord Howe against any attempt to hold Boston until spring came. The main purpose of his mission, the Briton declared, was to secure an undertaking that Rebels would not bombard the city itself. Boston's selectmen, he reported, had been especially earnest about forwarding this plea. If the Rebel Commander-in-Chief would agree His Majesty's Commanding General solemnly promised to offer no more than passive resistance to any American attack.

On this point General Washington refused to make any formal written commitment, only indicated, in his gravely courteous manner, that should the British evacuate the port and take along their Tory adherents he would order no attacks or bombardments by the Continental forces, but if His Majesty's forces attempted to assume the offensive no restraint would be exercised.

As a result on March 16th, 1776, approximately a hundred British vessels of all descriptions straggled out of Boston Harbor transporting some 10,000 troops together with around 1,100 miserable and often penniless Tories.

Escorted by ships of the Royal Navy, this unhappy armada nevertheless made an impressive sight with its multitude of sails catching the sunlight. Soon they shaped a course out into Massachusetts Bay then headed for the big British Naval Base in Halifax.

That strategically invaluable Boston had fallen seemed almost too good to be true. Even by European standards this was the American Rebels' first victory of real importance.

Not before the night of March 6th did Andrew Hunter feel free to leave his command even for a brief while. He was feeling extremely fatigued what with endless inspections of gun emplacements and instructing utterly inexperienced artillerymen in the principles of loading, aiming and firing. Seldom had he enjoyed more than a few hours' sleep which wasn't refreshing for, at the back of his mind, persisted mounting anxiety over Sarah's condition. And to think she lay, or was getting about again, less than an hour's easy riding distance! Being young and vigorous Sarah likely would overcome the dreaded lung fever. What shook his confidence and determined him to ride to Cambridge, no matter what, was the arrival of a lanky civilian bearing a brief note from Ellen stating he was required at home.

Cambridge, enveloped in thick fog, was quieter than it had been since thunder of artillery fire on Dorchester Heights had died out. Ellen met him at the door and in a rare display of emotion flung arms about him and clung, shaking like a colt sniffing the nearness of a bear. "Thank Heaven you're here, Andy! I—I've not sent word earlier because Sarah seemed to have mended so smartly she forbade me to bother you."

"Then why summon me now?"

Numbly Ellen bowed her narrow and sleek dark head.

"She's suffering a serious relapse. She was coming on so strongly Doctor Bainbridge was mighty encouraged, but this very morning her fever suddenly returned, worse than before. She's often out of her wits, burning with fever, and her breath's growing shallower—I, well, Andy, you'd best go upstairs straightaway."

That Sarah's sick bed should have been shifted into his old bedroom seemed ironic. How often he had savored a boy's poignant enthusiasms and disappointments in there. A single candle cast a light so dim he barely could make out a bunch of dead cattails he'd long ago stuffed into an earthenware pickle jar. An amateurishly stuffed raccoon still slumped on his chest of drawers. Then there was the beaded Indian powder pouch and greasy-handled tomahawk Grandpa Elijah had fetched from the Provincial Siege of Louisburg back in 1745.

He choked, knelt beside the bed. "Sarah, dearest one!"

Her eyes shifted, rolled, "Oh, Andrew! So—so happy—you nearby. Feel better already—" but her speech was faint and irregular, due to the shallowness of her ill-smelling breath. Her hands when he took them no longer were hot but so icy it was shocking.

Frantically he searched for something, anything, encouraging to say: "Good news, darling! I've just been assigned to duty at Headquarters! I can be with you more often now." He kissed her brow, felt it cold under a faint sheen of perspiration. This was too outrageous to be true. He'd often noticed a similar sheen and the same unnatural brilliance in the restless eyeballs of a gravely ill person.

Her voice now was so low he had to kneel to hear. "Don't leave—I—I—mortal weary."

"Sarah! Sarah! You'll grow stronger soon. We'll make up for all the happiness we've been denied."

Faintly she shook her head and, eyelids fluttering, whispered, "Come closer. Must confess something."

"You confess? What in God's name?"

"All along, dearest, despite your honest and tender love, I—I— been aware of—of a presence between us."

"A 'presence'?"

"Can't explain—too tired. For all you—tender and true I—al-

397

ways—aware since this sickness came—I—I've never possessed
—whole—your heart."

"Not so! Oh, Sarah, Sarah, before God, I've always been
devoted to you and to our love!"

She sighed, "You have. Yet I've learned about—girl in Marblehead. Right now I—aware of her—between us. May she make
you—as good a wife as I would have tried—to."

His fingers tightened over hers. "No! No! You will, you *must*
recover—we've so much to enjoy over the years."

"Oh yes, yes. Now so weary feel like sleeping. Please go—"
Closing her eyes she turned aside a rumpled head, usually so
neat, so well combed.

Ellen standing in the doorway emitted a muffled sob. "Come,
Andrew. Can't you realize she's fallen asleep? See how peaceful
she looks?"

So she had, but it was a sleep from which Sarah Hilton never
would rouse.

CHAPTER 50 🎎

TWILIGHT REUNION

UNCONSCIOUSLY GRACEFUL, Amy Orne Twisden stooped to ignite a paper spill at the fire then light a single smelly and sputtering beef-tallow drip candle, the only available source of artificial light till yet another British supply ship might be captured and her cargo auctioned off. Glancing towards the Izard home she noticed the silhouette of a tall, cloaked horseman in the act of dismounting before it. Although twilight was dimming fast she'd not the least doubt of yonder rider's identity. Vivid as heat lightning on a dark summer's night memories returned of that time she'd first encountered the hunted ex-British Naval officer, the first time they'd kissed so unexpectedly on the Izard Brothers' wharf. Also returned rapturous recollections of later that night when Andrew's incomplete battery had been assaulted.

Mechanically Amy attempted to select from a horn book a subject for tomorrow's school exercise. What a pity paper had grown so scarce pupils had nothing better than slates to chalk upon.

Strange, why, at this of all moments, should she think of Caleb? God alone knew where his bones might be resting. Like

399

all too many others for a long space she'd hoped and prayed that Caleb Twisden might reappear—an event which occurred just frequently enough among seafaring families to nurture a flicker of hope. Caleb—God bless his soul—must be at rest, unaware he'd left behind none of his seed. Dutifully, she'd prayed for the repose of his spirit every Sunday in that drafty little Congregational Church she attended along with the Izards.

Always she rejoiced, yet remained deeply disquieted, whenever Tom Izard came home on leave; only through him could she retain a tenuous link with Andrew Hunter. Through discreet listening and a very occasional query she'd learned about his promotion and some of his duties. How heartwarming to hear tales of Andrew's achievements, especially his raising of a great cannon from a frozen pond somewhere in southeastern Massachusetts.

And now. What possible errand could have brought Andrew back to Marblehead this blustery March evening? Blinking, Amy forced herself to concentrate on text barely readable because the tallow drip kept on spluttering as no sperm whale oil candle ever would. She reflected that news, often inaccurate concerning the Marblehead Regiment's doings and whereabouts arrived only now and again. Andrew! Why would he appear after so many months?

Whimperings attracted her attention, apprised her that Olivia was growing hungry. Dare she straightaway satisfy the baby's appetite? After hesitating an instant Amy crossed to the cradle, bared a breast and commenced to suckle the infant. From the corner of her eye she saw lights going on over at the Izards'.

Olivia just had satisfied her demands when a knock sent blood surging to Amy's face and throat. Characteristically, she didn't flinch. Still carrying the baby, she unbolted the door. Andrew entered amid a blast of cold air. He made no effort to kiss her—only fixed his gaze on the infant. By now he'd learned from the Izards sufficient to understand the situation beyond any question or doubt.

"Amy," said he steadily, "if you'll have me, we'll get married as soon as may be."

Still cradling the infant, Amy moved near, taller, handsomer and more self-possessed than ever.

Smiling, she said briskly, "Andrew, may I present our daughter?"